I0708794

ALSO BY JAMES L. PETERS

The Dancer and the Swan

Turntable

Shrugging

VISIT THE WEBSITE:

JamesLPeters.com

FOLLOW ON FACEBOOK:

facebook.com/James.L.Peters.Author/

FORTUNE FALLS

James L. Peters

Six by 9 Publishing

First Edition

LIBRARY OF CONGRESS
CATALOGING-IN-PUBLICATION DATA:

Peters, James L.

Fortune Falls / James L. Peters

ISBN 978-1-7366098-7-3

Set in Garamond Typeface

Excerpts of "Here in the Amiable Dark"
from *Into the Good World Again*, by Max Garland
Copyright 2023, Holy Cow! Press
Used by permission

Dedicated to the memories of
Lloyd Walter Peters
and
Barbara Sue Peters

above the lethal math of plague
and dearth of love, amid
the new ruins

and ransacked history

where the same familiar beast
with a different mask
is always slouching

above the daily count
of final breaths
we console ourselves

by pretending are not ours,
persuade ourselves are *other*
and *elsewhere*

here in the amiable dark
where we are walking tonight,

> ~ from "Here in the Amiable Dark"
> by Max Garland

Prologue

The detour sign came upon him abruptly, just over the rise of the hill, vibrant orange in the headlights and unapologetically square. Bold black blocks of letters sunk into the florescence, insistent arrow diverting him from the road home. Behind all that, strobes of yellow and silhouettes of lumbering behemoths gnawed at the road ahead of him.

He slowed the car, stopped it, and the sign filled his windshield. The radio played on, and he only realized his complacency within the nostalgia of the tune as it ended, stillness of the car adding volume to some advertiser's insistence. He pushed the volume knob and silence replaced the announcer's pitch, overtaken by the rumble of destruction.

He stared at the arrow, turned his head where it directed him, and studied the country road that went straight into the obliteration of evening. *I just want to go home,* he thought, and that seemed so pathetic he decided to say it out loud.

"I just want to go home—" Flaccid. "Damn it."

The car idled. Still, he did not move.

He had woken that morning to the tender strokes of his wife, made love to her before the sun had introduced itself to the day, wonderful musk of morning breath across his cheek as she whispered, "Happy birthday" just as he lost himself inside her. He had bathed in October sunrise hues with steaming coffee on the sun porch as his seven-year-old son bounded onto his lap and handed him a colored construction paper card— "Happy Birthday Dad" cut from yellow and orange dancing across the page.

Later that day at work, it was slaps on his back from boss and team members after the launch and fruition of a seven-month-long project. In his head rang the echo of his team's celebratory banter after work at the downtown bar while the golden glow of satisfaction spread down and through his insides.

A day like that shouldn't end this way—obstructed by a detour while construction churned his road home to rubble. Of this he was certain, no matter how petty the thought.

Maybe it was the alcohol, maybe it was the birthday, maybe it was the culmination of so many little things, but it seemed like the world had its arm around his shoulder.

The arrow on the detour sign seemed to stretch and flex as it pointed right.

Fine, he thought, *but don't think you're going to ruin this day. You can't. I'm untouchable.*

He looked in the direction where he spun the wheel and turned onto the detour, down and down the sloping side road.

Too long. He'd been driving too long. There should have been a sign directing him left, back east. There was none.

To either side of him, empty fields running to the horizon

under the star-speckled expanse of sky. The dash display read 8:07 p.m. He should have been home by now, thought about calling Jen to let her know he'd been rerouted. Irrational logic insisted he had no reason to—he would be home soon. He kept his eyes fixed to the achingly straight southbound road.

Cresting another hill, he saw nothing but more road undeterred. He pulled over to the narrow, gravel shoulder and spoke his address into the GPS. After suspenseful moments of calculation, the unsympathetic voice told him to make a U-turn when possible and take the very road the detour now forbade him to travel. Global positioning didn't even identify him as being on a road. To the all-knowing satellites above, he was exactly nowhere in the outskirts of Fortune Falls, Wisconsin.

Impulse pushed him out of the car. It seemed like the only way to confirm this nowhere place witnessed through the comfort and safety of the Lexus was actually real. The damp chill of the air tightened his face, widened his eyes and made him want to stretch out his arms and pump his legs. Suddenly, the location and the moment seemed significant, vital, in a way that observing through a windshield could never be. Beyond the ravine beside the road, far across the field, he caught a glimmer, like a fleck of daylight winking in the distance. It pulsed and captivated.

He scooted around the car and stepped down the steep ravine into the long brown grass, climbed up the other side to a barbed wire fence. Hunching down, he pushed the top wire up, lifted a leg over the bottom strand and went through.

His thoughts became independent of his actions. His consciousness was a passenger, perception a face pressed against the window of a dream. In some vague sense, he realized that, had his day been different, had he met adversity and struggle and disappointment, maybe he would have turned away from that glimmer, remained snug in his car and found the road home.

With a day like today, a glimmer only beckoned and promised. The alcohol tingling his blood encouraged, the tangy chill of autumn air enticed, and every step forward into the field thrilled.

Jen would have told him to come back, don't be an idiot, and she would have been right. But something made tonight different. Something insisted upon climbing through barbed wire into the unknown.

His shoes were clumped with mud and slick with dew. The glimmer was gone, nothing but fields fading to the fuzzy black horizon. He kept moving forward, a tall black shape giving him the only certainty that he headed toward anything other than more fields.

Behind him, the car could hardly be discerned—glossy black against nighttime dark. Ahead, the shape stood at his full height, a small obelisk in a muddy field. Far off, the moaning moos of cows unseen.

He hummed the song from the radio and remembered being seventeen with the summer night brushing back his hair and streetlights scrolling by as that music played. The hum stuck in his throat as he stopped before the object.

A slot machine. It was some kind of slot machine in the middle of a dirt field off some county road.

The chill air began to seep and burn like frost.

Antique. Old enough to be ageless. Dark wood braced and bracketed with cast iron corner pieces and cabriole legs at the base sinking into the mud. A blaze of inlaid veneers on the front forming a multi-pointed starburst, like a compass. A smaller, central burst of silver. Cast iron laced the corners. He looked downward where a front panel angled like a podium top, three slits side-by-side-by-side showing only white. On its side, a metal crank.

And all around, nothing but the four corners of night.

He was scared, but it was an exhilarating fear. He coughed

a chuckle of disbelief.

His hand reached for the crank arm. The handle wasn't cold. He had expected it to be cold.

Tension at first as he wound the handle clockwise, felt the drag against gears, whir of machinations in motion, then the crank went slack. He let it go, the machine clicking and tacking and whirring. The three window slits blurred with gray, the spin of cylinders beneath the framing of a silver faceplate.

The first one slowing, the blur more defined, black shapes coalescing. The clunk of a catch, the cylinder locked, the slit showing words—

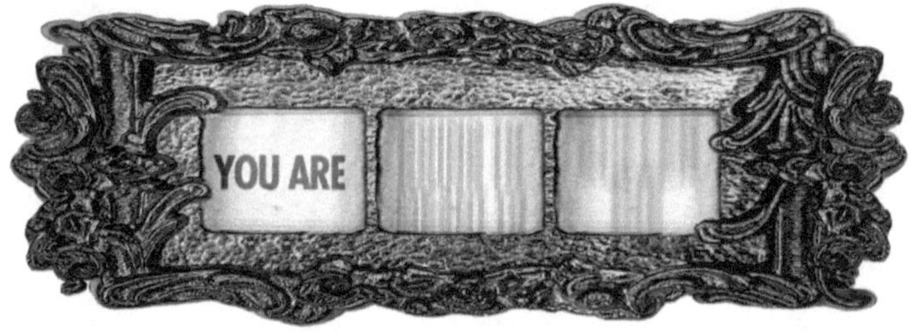
YOU ARE

The second slit, slowing, fragments of black shapes, letters, stopping with a chunk—

YOU ARE
GOING TO

Every part of him now existing within the spinning blur of the third slit, slowing, ticking clicking slowing, clack of the catch, and the last word glaring—

10

11

Breath like liquid, lungs needing to force each sloosh of air from him like a cough—much like forty years ago, to the very second of the clock, when Jason Lahey had been born into the world.

Part 1

Chapter One
Wednesday, October 30, 2019 – Morning

Slogging through the mire of dark morning sleep, Jason guided himself to the master bathroom. Jen had smacked the snooze button without missing one tick of dreamtime. A nine-minute reprieve for her.

Light switch flicked and his senses jarred to the flare of white walls and tile. He ran water for a shower and waited for the water heater to deliver a much-needed morning scalding to thaw his head.

He tensed to emotions orphaned from cause, head foggy from too much drink last night. The constriction of panic, a thunderbolt strike to his nerves, flash and fade before he could understand or react. Details recessed into the cracks and grooves of his consciousness—unreal fragments he recalled that mixed with vague recollections of his dreaming. His body thrummed in an idle of fight or flight, but he didn't know why.

He stumble-stepped into the stream of water and let his

perplexity run down him and trickle into the drain. Scoured his torso, arms, face with soap. The more brisk and aggressive his motions, the more images flashed in his head—flickering memories of last night like jumbled puzzle pieces.

A birthday cake with big wax numbers aflame, declaring his forty years lived. Jen singing happy birthday while Nicholas mumbled and giggled along. Before that, the detour, and him off-course. A farmer's field, and something in that field.

Jen asking him what's wrong, and him telling her nothing.

Spinning dials and a disturbing message from a bizarre antique machine.

How had he got home? When had he gone to bed? What had he dreamed?

He rinsed the soap from his arms and torso under hot spray of water, put his face right in front of the shower head and held his breath as his thoughts cleared. The dreamlike vagueness of last night slowly washed away, leaving behind the realities of the day. He turned, wiped at his face, took a deep breath and exhaled. Could it have just been a dream?

He squeezed a pink daub of shampoo into his palm. A smaller portion each year. He had hoped for the genes on his mother's side to maintain his hairline, but had received only her brown eyes and pinched nose, a touch of her wry humor and the body fat that proved ever more resilient to his three-mile jogs and low-fat diet.

His father had given him six feet worth of perspective on the world, girded by common sense and healthy skepticism. "Don't look down on people," he'd told Jason once. "Just look past them." The sturdy mentality of a self-made man.

He rinsed his hair until it squeaked, gave his face one more blast of wet, and shut the water off. Naked and dripping, the last of irrational worries cleared with the steam of the room. He slid the shower door open, grabbed a towel, and stepped out.

"I'm still angry with you." Jen, wrapped tight in her yellow terrycloth robe, the short, wavy bob of auburn hair pressed flat against her right side where she always rolled to after nuzzling into his shoulder before sleep.

"I wasn't that bad." He ran the towel over his upper body, through graying chest hairs.

"Bad enough."

"I'm sorry."

She took her toothbrush and clattered through a drawer for paste. "Don't be sorry. Just don't do it again."

He came behind her, brushed hair away to the crop of freckles on her neck and tasted them for the hundredth time. "Mmm. Strawberries." His hand stroked her back. "Won't happen again. Promise."

Toothpaste squeezed onto soft bristles. "What did you do to your shoes?"

That machine loomed before him for a moment, sitting in that barren field. He heard the clicking whir of its spinning cylinders.

So unreal. He couldn't parse reality from dream.

He shrugged, avoiding her quizzical look. "Stepped in some mud."

"Obviously. Are you feeling better?" The brush went to work, one tooth at a time.

He wrapped the towel around his waist and tucked it tight over his belly to hide the swell of hips. That fooled the mirror enough to make him happy. "I really wasn't drunk, you know."

A soft puff of exasperation escaped her lips. "Oh yes you were." Back at it with her circular scrubbing.

"Why do you say that? I had three drinks and a shot. Wait. Four?" He rubbed on deodorant and combed his hair into place.

"It was your birthday dinner. You were moody and quiet all night." Slurred by bristles and foamy paste. "Just like when you're drunk. You barely said two words to me."

"I was just tired."

Jen swooshed her mouth with a cup of water and tapped the toothbrush against the sink. "Alcohol makes you tired. That's why you shouldn't have driven home."

"Okay, Jen. I get it already. I won't do it again."

She turned and pushed her short, round curves against him. "Just love you, that's all."

"Love you, too." His hands found her sides, the solid curve of hips he loved so much, that perfect place, the center of gravity in the rolling slope of woman. "Hey. It's hump day."

"Halfway to weekend."

"And tomorrow, Halloween. We doing our thing?"

"Been looking forward to it. Trot the kiddle out for some trick or treating, put him to bed, then our time. Scary movies. Roasted pumpkin seeds—Oh! Don't forget the pumpkin or Nicky will have to carve you up instead."

"Right."

She moved out of his light grasp and to the shower, ran water, untied her robe and slipped it off. All skin now, ripe peach peel blush of cream. Her curve of tummy the softest place he's ever known, pucker of belly button throwing a kiss. He forced himself to the medicine cabinet and popped a multivitamin. The usual detachment from morning bathroom nakedness wasn't functioning in him. His eyes touched every part of her soft, swelling flesh. Jen stepped into the shower and he lathered his face, picked up his razor and scraped at cheeks and chin while hot water ran from the sink. Thoughts of work, of Halloween and the upcoming weekend, scooped up like shaving cream on the razor's edge.

Slim pickings on pumpkins. Jason walked the produce aisles of Shop N' Save, appraising the orange heads laid out in dwindling rows below vegetables being misted under a fine spray. The few remaining gourds were pockmarked by brown rot age, webbed by green varicose veins, rinds bubbled with leprous lesions. Misshapen, deformed. Jen had wanted to pick up a pumpkin over a week ago, but Jason kept making excuses and put it off.

He remembered his father coming home with the pumpkin to be carved. That usually happened a couple days before Halloween. His parents didn't decorate much for holidays, didn't drag out the ceremony and circumstance, but that didn't mean they didn't celebrate holidays. In his father's hands would be the biggest, roundest, tallest Halloween pumpkin from the patch. It would sit on their stoop that night, a sleeper gourd waiting to awaken, to terrify and ignite with candlelight. His father would cut the face of a grotesque into that pumpkin rind, make it grimace and groan while it looked over the neighborhood. His mother always had a bowlful of candy ready for the kids and dressed in her glamourous witch's outfit—a stylish witch with the hat and flowing black dress, perfect make-up, fair skin and never a wart to be seen.

Walking through the door with a Halloween pumpkin ready for carving felt like authentic fatherhood. He wasn't coming home as Jason, but as Dad.

A poor excuse for a patriarch if he had one of these sad pumpkins tucked under his arm when he came home. He shouldn't have procrastinated.

He hunkered down, eyed up one that seemed a decent shape, turned it and watched the pumpkin tumble to its flattened side from its crooked base.

Getting late. Time to adjust his thinking. It was Halloween, season of the grotesque and macabre. If he couldn't find a plump, healthy pumpkin, then he would do the next best thing and find a really ugly one. Carve up the scariest pumpkin on the block. Yeah. As his old man used to say, "That's making lemonade."

A little attitude adjustment and suddenly he had options everywhere. He still needed one that was essentially healthy, solid and full of plump seeds. Some rind-knocking and physical examinations found him the perfect candidate. A good, deep hollow sound and no soft spots. But this thing was a true Elephant Man—the John Merrick of gourds. Horribly disfigured, but sitting tall with relentless dignity. Cauliflowered greenish pustules down its side. Cankerous white boxer's nose in the middle. Neanderthal forehead. Disgustingly beautiful.

"Johnny-boy, you're coming home with me."

CHAPTER TWO
Wednesday, October 30, 2019 - Evening

Fairview Lane lounged against a smoldering persimmon skyline. A thick growth of trees surrounded the strip of neighborhood in the distance, the oaks and birch dropping the last of their crisp colors while pine trees stood tall and green. Farm fields spread out beyond the trees and up to the interstate that ran beyond the eye but not quite the ear.

The windows of Ollie and Lynn's blue one-level ranch were splattered with Halloween clings like bugs on a windshield. Spiders hung from their cobwebbed birch tree. Mrs. Polnzy's place was dark as usual, her gravel driveway strewn with leaves from the big oak in her front yard that seemed to be wrenching itself from the ground by its thick roots surfacing from her struggling lawn. A five-foot disco-boogie Frankenstein's monster haunted the Peterson's two-story as it bopped to "Monster Mash" whenever anything within one hundred feet passed by. Near the cul-de-sac, Glen Overby's bi-polar duplex displayed a neatly trimmed and thick lawn bordered by brick landscaping and a freshly seal-coated driveway on his side; scraggly overgrown grass and scattered toys on his tenant's half.

Jason drove straight to the end of the road, up his driveway and hit the garage door remote. He sat for a moment in front of his four-gabled Colonial as the carriage-style door opened. Jen had set up tasteful arrays of corn stalks and hay bales on their porch. Solar pumpkin lights ran along their sidewalk from the driveway to the porch, and a "Happy Halloween" sign stuck into the ground beside their mailbox.

Everything before him, from the house to the riding mower parked in the third garage bay, was validation. When Jason was seventeen, his father had been the age Jason was now. Impossible to really accept that other than by the numbers. How could Jason be that old now, yet still feel like his father's son? Could the authority of the father have been filtered through the same amount of uncertainty as Jason still experienced?

But the half-acre of land, the twenty-six hundred square feet of home, and the lack of want or need for anything, were all things he could touch and feel to remind him that he had exceeded his father's success. He had prospered in ways his dad with his hardware store had never been able to. He could provide for his family as his father had only dreamed.

If his father had lived long enough to see Jason's success, maybe he would have appreciated it. Perhaps he would be proud of Jason, even if he'd never show it. Edward Lahey, of course, had other hopes and plans for his son that Jason had no interest in, but if his father could have seen the fruition of Jason's success, he might have understood.

His father never had the chance to achieve true success. He fought and struggled to build a moderately-successful life, worked long hours and took big risks. In the end, fate had devised other plans for Edward Lahey.

Still seated in his idling car in front of his home, Jason heard the clicking and whirring again, those spinning words coming to rest on that ominous message. He dismissed those fragments of a dream-like night as he would wave away a bothersome fly.

Jason pulled into his garage, entered his domain, and took in everything he had achieved. He thought, *too easy. Too damn easy.*

He lingered on the creamy comfort of leather in the Lexus, breathing in the new-car smell that followed a month-long wait for the custom order, his hands gripping the wheel that still had the sexy stiffness of steering. In the passenger seat, Johnny Merrick roosted like an alien pod ready to unleash some horror.

Time to finalize Halloween.

In the mudroom, he slipped out of his jacket and hung it on the hook, sat on the bench with the pumpkin beside him and peeled off his shoes. He scooped up the sad, lumpy gourd and abandoned his briefcase for the kitchen.

Jen, at the sink, rinsing vegetables, wearing her black sweater with wispy ghosts and sparkly letters spelling *BOO!*

"Hey, you," she said. The TV clamored from the living room. One of Nicholas's YouTube shows. Lots of *boings* and *bangs* and loud, elastic voices.

"Hi, beautiful."

She dried her hands, stepped up and kissed him. "How was your day?"

"Fine. Glad to be home."

A pause. Jen's eyes lodged into the pumpkin under his arm. "*What* is that?"

"Our pumpkin."

"You're joking."

He hefted the gourd to his chest and cradled it under his hands. "It's perfect."

"Jason—" Her taut voice twisted his name.

"Just as da Vinci said the art is waiting in the stone, our

Jack-O'lantern is in here, crying to come out."

"That was Michelangelo."

"Whoever."

"I told you we should have picked one up sooner."

"Glad we didn't. I might not have found Johnny-boy here."

"You named it—"

"It was written on his underwear."

She turned away, back to her sink, done with him. "Nicky's not going to like it."

"You're right." He walked behind her, leaned in close to her ear. "He's going to *love* it."

Around the island and into the living room, he found his straw-headed boy kneeling before the flickering color of the big screen TV, face studious, even subservient. Blank seven-year-old mind waiting for instruction, topaz eyes receiving the signal.

"Hey. Kid."

No response. Nicky was fully immersed in what he watched, just as he tended to hyper-focus on his video games, puzzles, coloring books or Legos.

"Nicholas."

Wave of hand tossed up, attention still entrenched in the box. "Hey, Dad."

"Look what I got."

Magic words to a kid. So much promise, so many possibilities. Nicky's head snapped around with full moon eyes.

For about a second. Then his face scrunched up with seven-year-old plasticity. "Gross."

"Right. Gross. Halloween is all about gross."

"It's cruddy."

"Nix, this'll be the coolest pumpkin on the block. Look at the nose, and the eyes right here. He'll be all scary and nasty, like a zombie."

Nicky's face slid into the mortification of childhood tragedy. No eye contact from him at all. "It's not Halloween. Not how they're s'posed to *look*." Just a slurring monotone now.

"Come on, kiddo. Trust me, huh? Give this a shot?"

Nicholas stood and dangled like a scarecrow. He mumbled and shuffled his feet, hands twitching at his side.

"You're really letting me down, Nix. I'm telling you, we'll have a blast with this one."

Nicky sulked past him toward the hallway. "Don't want to." Thump thump thump of sock-covered feet down the hall to his room.

Jen leaned over the counter. "Bravo, Jase. He loved it, all right."

Jason held the pumpkin up to his face and tried to find all that promise of the perfect Jack-o-Lantern. *Jesus, Johnny. You are a sad, ugly pumpkin.*

"Goddamn it."

Nicky came down to dinner insisting to eat with his Batman mask on. Jason suggested that he eat dinner as Bruce Wayne and leave the Dark Knight to fighting crime.

A cozy dinner, sprinkled with conversation mostly about Jen's half-day at the office designing mail order catalogs for classy frivolities like scented candles, engraved stepping stones for gardens, and other gifty items bought by people who already have everything. A quarter of the magazine's SKUs were scattered about their house and yard.

Stomach satisfied and solid, Jason helped clear the table with Jen. Nicky slipped his mask back on, declared his half-eaten pork chop a villain and began smiting it with his fork.

"Hey!" Jen snatched his arm in mid-thrust. "I think it's had enough, Batman. You done eating?"

Nod of mask.

"You have any homework?"

"Kinda."

"Well then, get to it. No fun time until that's done."

The Batman cowl looked up with molded, perpetual intensity. "But—what—"

"Now."

Nicholas bolted.

Jen carried the plate of food back into the kitchen. "That kid never eats."

"It's a phase."

"What does that mean, exactly—'phase?'"

"Well, it's—it describes the psychological—the mental stages of— It's what you say whenever your kid is acting stupid."

"Right." She stomped on the garbage can pedal and the lid flew open. She scraped the food off the plate. "*Your* kid."

"Hey, I just added some sauce to your omelet, honey."

Jen barked a gritty laugh. "Whatever."

In the pantry, Jason dug for a paper sack, laid it out on the kitchen table, grabbed the pumpkin and set it center of the bag. He examined his cutlery options and drew a fillet knife, paring knife and serrated blade from the block on the counter. "Time for surgery."

Jen slipped the last plate into the dishwasher. "Good luck, Dr. Frankenstein."

A masterpiece. It was brilliant. Jason sat and admired it, then turned it toward Jen.

"That's twisted." Jen stared at it across from Jason, her hands slimy with orange pumpkin innards as she squeezed off seeds from a mushy lump of pulp into a bowl.

"My finest work to date." He spun it back round to face him and wiped off the grimacing visage with a paper towel, cleaned around one squinted eye, then the other wide eye dripping into the pumpkin cheek. Two uneven slits for nostrils dug into the existing knot of nose. A snarling mouth snaggled with infrequent teeth.

"It should be put out of its misery."

He stood and took the gourd in hand as if it were a Grecian bust. "No eye for art."

The fast, hard raps on the patio door made him almost drop the pumpkin. A shape behind the glass held up a six pack of New Glarus Fat Squirrel.

"Jesus. Glen."

Jen waved at Jason. "So long, then."

Jason held a finger up to the patio door and squinted apology at Jen. "Just a couple, huh?"

"Go, go, go. Take Gourdy Grotesque with you."

"Sam just put his winterizer down on his lawn. 'Bout time, I say." Glen's feet were up on the porch railing, arms in his lap, hand around the beer he sipped. He never made eye contact on the porch. Evening beer-sipping, porch-sitting etiquette precluded that. When he said anything, the statements seemed offered to the breeze, to carry out across the neighborhood for the circumstantial ear to catch. Glen was, to Jason, the Narrator of Fairview Lane.

"Lawndoctors are coming for ours tomorrow."

"Oh, that's right. You use those fellows, don't you?" Glen took two quick nips of brew. "I'm for the hands-on approach, myself. Keeps me active. I'm mixing my own brew now, you know."

"Are you?"

"One part beer to two parts dish detergent and molasses. Top it off with some turf food, then piss in it."

Jason choked. "What?"

"Sure. Human urine is the perfect non-chemical fertilizer. Has all the nitrogen you need to keep a lawn nice and green. I used to use ammonia, but my pee has the grass looking better than ever. Downright perky."

"That's just wrong."

Double-nip of beer and Glen's underplayed grin. "Nobody can say I don't put myself into my lawn."

"Sure, and the added bonus that you've just kept me off it for life."

Glen raised his bottle to the night. "There's the payoff."

They fell into familiar silence, a silence slowly honed by the years. The sized-to-fit lack of talking that Jason used as a gauge to measure friendship. Acquaintances, when put alone together, felt the threat of silence, the imperative to fill it. Given time and the total comfort of the right person's company, that silence arrived like the floating buzz of a nursed brandy high.

Glen turned to Jason. "I'll piss on your lawn if you want. I'm cheap."

Jason laughed. "Glen, I happen to know for a fact you've pissed on my lawn."

Glen shrugged. "Perhaps I have. Possible. Just look for the thick patches of healthy grass."

"Whatever. Pass me another pee-maker."

Glen leaned over to Jason with the bottle, his combed-back pompadour of black and gray hair, predominant forehead, boxed face and narrow gaze always reminding Jason of James Garner from the later years of *The Rockford Files*. Glen, the tough old bugger, ex-truck driver, widower with soft-spoken intensity, opinions gently applied and easily rescinded when apt to do so.

Holding to his leaning stretch, Glen studied the winking light of the pumpkin beyond Jason that perched on the porch railing. "You know, I've been all across this country in my rig, seen all kinds of things, but never, ever have I seen such a God-awful-looking pumpkin in my life."

Jason turned to it and raised his bottle in a toast. "So ugly it's beautiful."

"Nope. Just ugly."

Jason aimed a fertilized grin at him. "Ugly recognizes its own, you old bugger."

"No cause for that, now. No cause at all."

The block was so dark, so quiet. The earlier breeze had seized up into a thick, time-sinking calm. Few streetlights on the lane, but the night was transparent and Jason marveled at how clear and motionless the neighborhood looked.

Glen looked over at the new house to the immediate west of Jason's property. "Any sighting of your new neighbors?"

"If the Johnsons ever make an appearance, I'll let you know."

Back in early spring, Jason and Jen met them briefly during the Johnsons' house construction. They were onsite going over details with the contractor and looking over the progress. Since moving in, there were barely any sightings of them, only coming and going. They were obviously a busy young couple.

"Their lawn could use some help," Glen said.

"Why don't you go pee on it?"

"Hrmph." Glen sipped his beer. "Did I tell you that Polnzy was on my case again last week?" Glen stared three houses down the street at the old woman's dark house that sat across from his duplex.

"About Travis and Dawn's lawn?"

"She hates the idea that my rental got in this division before any covenants were established. Tough. That little extra each month is my retirement fund."

"I suppose she has nothing better to do than complain about the neighborhood, and you're right out her window."

"Old bat. She just wants to make everyone else as miserable as she is."

From what Glen has shared, she certainly made her neighbors miserable. Sam and Delilah Peterson were constantly being told by Mrs. Polnzy to shut up their old bloodhound Liver. The dog did bark sometimes, with a persistence that made you believe old Liver the hound dog had a story to tell, but it never bothered Jason.

Ollie and Lynn Mickelssen had been around for as long as the Polnzys have been in the neighborhood. They knew Mrs. Polnzy better than anyone, and they took great effort to have nothing to do with her.

Jason's eyes drifted windward to Polnzy's darkened ranch house—sparse, yellow lawn, weathered shingles starting to curl on a tired roof over peeling siding. "Yeah. A sad life she lives, though."

"A sad life she makes for herself."

Maybe true, and Jason had little defense held in reserve for her. That summer, Jason had coaxed Nicholas to come with him to ask her if she would like her lawn mowed. He wanted Nix to have exposure to older people, as the boy had none. No grandparents, not really. Both of Jason's parents died before Nicholas had a chance to know them, and Jen was still mortaring new bricks on the wall between her and her parents. He had met them once, sixteen years ago, when he and Jen became engaged. His idea, and not his last bad one on that subject.

In retrospect, the stroll down the street to Mrs. Polnzy's had been incredibly naive, holding to some black and white television sitcom scene of the old woman serving up a plate of chocolate chip cookies and a glass of milk for Nix while she ruminated about long ago days and Jason clipped her lawn in neat, even rows.

"I can take care of my own grass." Her hair, fine like metallic filaments, mashed to one side of her head, wilting eyelids peeled to pink. Slippers over gnarly toes, nails yellowed and fungal. A bad time for Jason to realize it was he who was so uncomfortable around old people.

"I didn't mean to imply—" His hand had reflectively, protectively, fallen to Nicholas' chest.

"No thank you." The door slammed shut. Looking down at Nix, his fair hair and smooth, trouble-free brow, bright eyes looking back to their house, Jason realized the last thing he wanted to do was expose Nicholas' youth to the curmudgeonly distain of withered wisdom. What had he been thinking?

He wondered if he unintentionally incited Polnzy to lash out at Glen about his tenants and their lawn. An old woman's reflective retribution, pickled with pettiness. She had probably taken his neighborly offer as a complaint and affront to her lawn care, so she went after Jason's neighbor and friend about the lawn he is responsible for.

"You should just mow Travis's lawn and add it to their rent. Either they get the picture or you make some extra money. A win either way. You know you can use my mower if you want."

Glen ground a hand against his nose, pinched and flicked. "Eh. Travis. He's a git-round-to-it kind of guy. Grass. Snow. That P.O.S. Lincoln he had on blocks in the driveway for two months. The guy works twelve-hour shifts six and seven days a week. Dawn doesn't do crap to help out. Their three little trolls for kids scamper about. But he gets the rent in on time—mostly. These days, I just don't care about much else long as they keep their bitch poodle off my lawn. Pretty soon, I'll be doing more dying than living, and some things ain't worth the trouble."

Jason wanted to step on Glen's comment—Glen was sixty-seven, spirit still fully charged—but no good words came to mind. Only spite. Dying's no way to live. He heard that somewhere, probably in a movie. It had the chiseled edge and polished luster of an action/adventure quip snarled through cigar smoke after drawing back the bolt of an Uzi. It resonated with undeniable truth. He could use it to answer Glen, speak with Schwarzenegger Austrian mush-mouthed manliness.

No. No talk of death tonight. Wasn't good for Glen, and even less so for him. There was, after all, a reason for burying the dead deep, for rolling out plush sod over churned earth, and keeping cemeteries like city parks with trees and flower beds and benches behind wrought-iron fencing.

"How's that Lexus of yours?" Glen asked.

"It's a damn sweet ride." Jason tipped the bottle to his mouth and swallowed, hops and barley leaving a crisp, bitter aftertaste as he tried to ignore the faint recollection of whirring and clicking running in his head.

Chapter Three
Thursday, October 31, 2019 - Halloween

Nighttime trick or treating was quickly becoming a memory of the old, like milk delivered to your stoop in the splash of dawn, unlocked doors at night, and a gallon of gas for under a buck. Only the smallest towns dared do it now, and even in Fortune Falls, the city council kept threatening to switch it over to daytime. But sheriffs and politicians in small town America always buckled quickly to the fever of nostalgia. Any official who wanted to be voted back next term learned to succumb, and even embrace, the locals' tendency to see things how they should be, not how they are. And "should be" was strictly translated to how things were back in their day. Anything else might be considered progress in "those big cities," but here, progress was just another way of saying the world was going to hell.

Jason had done the big city. Shortly after he married Jen, he had taken a programming position at 3M in Saint Paul. Jen found a graphic design job at a web design company in Minneapolis. They had left their hometown of Fortune Falls during their Hamburger Helper days, the Allen-wrench-assembled, pressboard furniture life, wearing ratty underwear and washing clothes as little as possible to make them last longer. They arrived at their six-hundred-square-foot apartment in a nineteen-foot Ryder truck stuffed tight with nothing and waited for that first paycheck that promised everything. Four months later, they vowed to never eat anything that came from cardboard or tin again.

The Twin Cities, last bastion of northern metropolitan culture until the west coast. Frozen urban metropolises: Saint Paul the older, Victorian brother of labyrinthine streets; Minneapolis, the hip younger sister of sleek lines, steel and glass—smiling to each other from across the trickling twist of Mississippi River headwaters, but thumbing a nose or flicking a finger when one of their skyline backs were turned. Both strutted all the pride of an east coast hauteur stepping into the slush puddle of the west for the first time. He and Jen had mocked the pretensions at first, then dove in with all the gluttony starvation could afford at a banquet.

They ate at four-star restaurants and bought premium tickets at the Guthrie for shows starring once-famous actors, though they couldn't stomach the burnt sludge of espresso or in clear conscience spend fifteen dollars each for sandwiches in the lobby. They attended the symphony at the Ordway Center, telling themselves they enjoyed the performances, but maybe more as a way to condition them to a culture they were shifting into. All the pomp and regalia of the orchestra and the marbled hall were utterly contrary to canned beef chow mein in front of the television. Jason wore the red scarf Jen had bought him for Christmas tied under his chin and tucked into his broad-shouldered trench coat, presenting himself like an east coast mayor or CEO. They walked, bought and lived the extra zero that had nuzzled up to their income.

Five years there, sixty months of heads turned up in thrall of skyscrapers and aimed down from the glamour of the Minneapolis Skyway, of wintry Christmas strolls down the fantasies of St. Paul's Summit Avenue mansions. But, in all that time, never any friends and not a word spoken to neighbors. No deep-rooted feeling of permanence. They couldn't shake the feeling of being on a long stint. When Jen missed her period and got a pink plus on her pregnancy test, they sat all night in the sunken living room of their Highland Park apartment in a stupor of joy and panic. The one thing neither of them ever considered was the possibility of raising a child in the Twin Cities.

After six months of job hunting across the eastern border, Jason secured a job as an IT manager at Boswell Software back in Fortune Falls, Wisconsin, and Jen locked down a part-time position doing catalog layout for a company that manufactured automotive towing equipment and sold OEM parts. They headed back east to their birthplace, a Pan Am semi-trailer full to the ceiling following them, and headed for their freshly built new program home on Fairview Lane. When they crossed the St. Croix River and saw the *Wisconsin Welcomes You* sign, Jen turned to him and said, "That was the longest damn vacation of my entire life."

A hundred fifty miles to the west, the doors were always locked, security systems engaged, a stranger's gaze safely avoided, and trick or treating always, always took place at two o'clock on or before the Saturday of Halloween.

Jason never had cared much for the symphony, and besides, the buildings still scratched at the sky only two and a half hours away, waiting for them to visit.

His little Batman charged up the steps of the next house, plastic cape flapping and cowled mask bobbing and spinning on his head. A half-size superhero in black pajamas, swinging his orange jack-o-lantern bucket half-full of fun-size candy bars, gum-centered lollipops, black and orange-wrapped peanut butter kisses, and hard candies.

"Hold up there, buddy." He'd said it so many times tonight it had become a meaningless catchphrase. He squeezed Jen's hand.

"What do you think?" she asked. "One more block?"

"Yeah. Loop around and make back for the car." It had been a five-minute drive from Fairview Lane and the outskirts of town to get to the nearest neighborhood cornucopia of candy-givers. Felt a little like sneaking into someone else's backyard barbeque, but they only had eight houses on their block and just a spattering of homes in the rest of their still-growing division amid farms, fields and forest.

Nicky's finger jabbed at the doorbell three times.

"Hey. One time does the trick, Nix."

A middle-aged woman opened the door, one arm cradling a big mixing bowl full of fun-sized treats. "Why, if it isn't Batman. Are you keeping the streets safe?"

"Trick or treat."

"Here you go." A Snickers bar and a Kit Kat plopped into his outstretched pail.

"Thank you." Nicky cleared the three steps with a bound and landed in front of Jason and Jen.

Jason waved a hand to the woman. "Happy Halloween."

"You, too."

Behind them, the choral cries of children, thin as the breeze, singing "trick or treat," vowels stretched like taffy. The scamper of feet against pavement past them, an occasional giggle and a little girl's ecstatic squeal of terror. The glow of pumpkins on porch rails and stoops gave off the sweet rot smell of hot wax and musty rind. Bats and witches and bestial silhouettes peeked out from windows. Quarter moon crescent hung from the dense shadows of clouds.

There was a precarious balance required to set the perfect atmosphere. Rain, cold and snow ruined so many Halloweens, but tonight was it. The titter of bare branches and the rustle of dry leaves blowing by. Jason could almost hear the long, drawn note of ominous music. He slipped Nicholas' youth over him like a costume.

They strolled up a long walkway to the next house, Nicholas motoring a good dozen paces ahead of them, stepping on his cape, stumbling, righting himself.

Just before the porch steps of the home, from the bushes, a dog-headed boy with snarling teeth and lolling tongue leapt out at Nicholas and roared.

Jen jumped and clamped Jason's hand. Nicholas screamed and pumped feet for Jason and Jen. Stopping just ahead of them, Nicholas looked back at the wolf man, his little man's stance rigid. Jason laughed and his heart knocked.

The werewolf mask slipped off and a teenager, maybe fifteen or sixteen with short, stiff hair spiked like cleats, smiled wide. "Ha. Sorry about that. Did I scare you, kid?"

"That's not funny." Jen's voice deep in her throat, a thrum of steel chords. Jason turned and saw her cougar-pounce glare.

The smile on the boy faltered. "Sorry. I was just fooling. Didn't mean anything by it."

"No harm done. It's Halloween." Jason put a hand on Nicholas' shoulder. "You're okay, right, Nix?"

Nicholas sniffled under his mask.

The boy reached around the porch and his hand came back with a fistful of treats. "Here you go, kid. Happy Halloween. You okay?" He held his candy-filled hand out to Nicholas who didn't move.

Jason nudged him. "Go on, Nix. It's okay."

Nicholas crept forward and put out his bucket.

"No hard feelings, huh? Here you go." The teenager dropped the candy in the bucket and Nicholas ran back to Jason and Jen.

Away from the house, Jen's arm clamped around Nicholas and drew him close to her. "Little shit," she muttered. "Should talk to his parents."

"Oh, he didn't do anything bad. Just getting into the spirit of things."

"Not when you're scaring a seven-year-old to death. That's crossing the line."

A skeleton and a ghoul passed them on the sidewalk, between a skip and a jog, the compression of excitement released in bursts of yells and laughter. "You're too sensitive, hon."

"Whatever."

Jason crouched down before Nicky, hands on his son's arms. "Give it to me straight, buddy. Did that guy back there scare you?"

Nicky's head bobbed.

"But it was kind of fun though, too, wasn't it?"

"I don't know—"

"Maybe just a little? Kind of like a tickle in the tummy?" Jason's hands crawled like scampering spiders around Nicky's sides to his stomach and his boy giggled and squirmed.

"Yeah. Mom was more scared than me."

"What?" Jen's fists dug into her hips.

"Oh, *way* more scared, Mom."

Jason grinned and gave his boy a wink. "I think you're right, Nix."

Jen moved ahead at a brusque pace. "This, from the little screamer."

Such a strange holiday, really. One which the meaning has

been largely lost within mainstream tradition. A couple thousand years ago, the Celts celebrated it as the new year. They called it Samhain—the end of life-giving harvest and the emerging death brought by winter. Still celebrated by some pagan religions today, the eve of October thirty-first was, to them, the thinnest border between the living and the dead.

There were a couple of overtly Christian people at work, the kind who met once a week for bible-readings the way others met for Tupperware parties, whose piety rested upon their noses and flared their nostrils. They sneered at Halloween, at the carnal, hedonistic and cultish aspects of the holiday.

Catholics had no such problems. The Mexicans rejoiced and celebrated the passing of loved ones during Hallowmas with skulls and flowers and candies; they visited their dead in the cemeteries. Even Glen went to mass on All Saints' Day and All Souls' Day to light candles for Maude. It was her last wish to him. "Gotta make sure I keep dragging you to church," she told him, "even after I'm gone."

Jason never thought about death or the dead on Halloween. He never honored past lives or the ending of the season. No masses or respecting the martyrdom of saints.

He honored the fear. It was the essence of Halloween. The same kind of fear that put others prostate before the altars of their gods, that withered ego to penitent awe before the magic and mystery of mortality. All the years of experiencing the nature of the holiday, but until now, Jason had never put it to clear thought. Tonight, it goosefleshed him.

Jason guided Nicholas along behind Jen. "Come on, buddy. Mom probably needs to get home and change her shorts."

"No," Jen called back, "Mom needs to toss some sheets on the couch for Dad tonight."

"Hey, Nix?"

"Yeah?"

"Now I'm scared."

The family room was dark other than the television showing the quick-cut, dim-lit scenes of horror. Jason crunched pumpkin seeds from the bowl between him and Jen. Both of them were stretched out, legs up on the reclining leather sectional. Nicky had been tucked into bed an hour ago after Jason peeled his sleeping arm from his candy bucket, Nicholas's head lolling on his shoulders in the recliner while Linus camped out in the pumpkin patch waiting for the Great Pumpkin to come.

The corpse-white mask of Michael Myers replaced Charlie Brown and friends. Such a tame movie by today's standards, but watching it tonight, that death mask figure lurking in the daylight from the periphery of normal life, watching from behind the hedge of a quiet neighborhood, between the billowing sheets of hanging laundry, and Jason felt himself watched, haunted. Not hunted like Jamie Lee Curtis flaying arms and stumbling down the street—"*Oh God somebody pleeeeaase, help me!*"—but rather as if calm, dispassionate eyes looked on, patient, awaiting the inevitable. That bizarre dichotomy of finding pleasure in the discomfort.

When he was immortal and seventeen, he and his friends had taken First Street along the river at over eighty miles an hour, hit the ramped incline where the old railroad tracks sat, and broke free of the Earth. They sailed for three long seconds upon the exhilaration of air. Earth came back upon them hard with a wallop that destroyed the transmission and exhaust system of the old Ford Fairlane. The four of them had laughed and cried and screamed, recharged with whatever life energy had been drained by the vacuum of high school and peers and authority bearing down on them. At that age, Jason was merely a reactive organism, a gauge of stimuli, primate survival confused by the perplexities of questions and emotions sweltering like a fever in him.

The immortality of youth was simply ignorance—the lack of an essential concept to life. Yet, he had been aware that something was missing, something was out there waiting to be discovered. Was that why he had stepped into that field the other night? Was that what had compelled him to turn that ancient machine's crank?

His stupidity at seventeen could only be understood at the precipice of forty, half-way through the forest, when for a moment—standing somewhere between walking in and walking out—the compulsion hits to look up, look beyond, because the woods encroach and obstruct, and the only broad view will come at the terminus. He certainly had no perception of this at that time.

Whether real or dream, he had no idea what sent his forty-year-old self into that field two nights ago. He did know that, at seventeen, he and his friends were looking for the figure in the death mask, the one watching them from the bushes. The one who would meet them at the end, when the trees cleared to field.

CHAPTER FOUR
Sunday, November 3, 2019 - Early Afternoon

The world had turned. Colder. Grayer. Older. Liver, the Petersons' aging dirt-brown hound dog, barked from their back yard—a measured, methodical declaration thinned by the chill wind. Not an excitable bark; it was merely pertinent, like a report. A statement waiting for acknowledgement. The distant, stale echo shared a somber message.

Jen cleaned counters, dusted furniture and vacuumed carpeting like she always did before the Monday maid service came by. Jason had long ago given up pointing out the irony of that. Better to stay out of her way. He headed for the garage.

Cleaning and organizing the garage was a late autumn ritual—the resolution of fall and the coming of winter. He stowed away the rakes and trimmers of spring and summer and hung up the bicycles. Climbing the ladder, he pulled down those winter implements that were tucked away in overhead storage—the shovels and long-handled snow scooper for the roof. From the shelving, he carried bags of salt that soon would be sifted onto the driveway and sidewalk. He brought down the boxes of Christmas lights and garland they'd put up on Thanksgiving weekend. The Briggs & Stratton 27-inch dual-stage snow blower was uncovered, filled with gas and oil checked. He set the choke and engine timing and started it up with the push of a button. It grumbled and growled to life. He let it run for a few moments before shutting it down, almost eager to plow through that first heavy snowfall.

He backed the Lexus and Jen's Subaru Crosstrek into the driveway, wiped down shelves, and started sweeping the garage floor to a clean, buffed and glossy cement.

His workbench sat along the wall by the door to the mudroom, impeccably clean. Shiny twelve-inch laser-guided miter saw, cordless drill, router and bits, vise, and a peg board with chisels, hammers, screwdrivers, ratchets, planes, levels, straight edges, and seven years' worth of other tools hung within their designated outlines. As he pushed the broom past, noticing nothing but dust and dirt and not one shaving of sawdust collected ahead of it, he caved to an obligatory thought. *I should build something.*

But he hadn't for years. Repair? Modify? Jury-rig? Sure. His work area had become a corner workshop of quick fixes, not creation. Apparently, the only thing it helped to create was a lackluster regret for not making anything significant to warrant the array of tools.

He swept past the workbench and thought instead about the leftover pork chop in the fridge that would become a lunchtime sandwich once he put it between two pieces of bread.

The side door opened and Nicky charged down the steps in his winter jacket, hood up over his head, mittens dangling from his sleeves. He moved with absolute purpose to the back of the garage, to a big bag of salt where once his bike sat. Little hands fluttered at his sides as furrowed brow kept eyes locked on the spot. "Dad. My bike."

"I hung it up for the winter. I didn't think you'd be riding it anymore. It's gotten so cold."

"No. I wanna ride." His voice thinned with the threat of a whine, arms swinging like an engine revving up.

"Fine, fine. Hold on. I'll get your flipping bike."

Jason hoisted the step ladder off its hooks, got under the bike and brought it down. The bike looked like some silly space-age scooter out of a Japanese cartoon. Big, bulky pieces of plastic between the handlebars and on the body frame, stickered with green and blue faux buttons and lights. A rocket bike with wobbly, hard rubber training wheels.

Jason grabbed Nicky's helmet from the shelf and held it out to him.

Nicholas grimaced. "Do I hafta?"

Jason looked at the helmet, then at his son. He put the helmet back on the shelf. "I never did as a kid. Just don't tell your mom, okay?"

Nicky nodded.

"Hey, Nix. Should we get those training wheels off?" Nicky had been fighting him all summer long, always muttering, "Not yet," as he pedaled away, rocking left to right on those clattering training wheels. The neighborhood presented no kids his age to show him that it was past the time for such childish things.

"I just wanna ride it."

"You will, Buddy. You'll ride it like a pro. Come on, give it a shot, huh? You're a big guy, now. Almost eight. You don't need training wheels anymore."

Nicholas showed no eagerness to take on the challenge. Were Nicky's grandfather still alive, that man would have blamed it on a mother's apron made too available to hide under, of Jason trying too hard to be a friend instead of a father. Jason would have avoided any argument with the oversized man, but until this moment, he thought he could have stood righteous before his father's old, dry eyes.

"Come on, Nix. Time for these things to come off. Time to ride on your own."

His childhood had dried up, baked by the heat of age into a crust of maturity. In becoming a father, it staggered him to realize how much of his life had dissipated from memory like a breaking mist. Not even the residue of events to wonder about. How much of his forty years still lived in his memory? When Jason focused and tried to travel back down his lifeline trail, he realized what a dismal fraction remained, as well as how much more he refused to recall. So many pieces of him had winked out, gone without trace. The profundity of Glen's comment, of doing more dying than living, became so much more than a comment about advancing age—more a verity of existence.

But raising a child, watching him grow and develop, offered some small dose of miracle, of resurrection. When Nicky was fifteen months and taking his first fumbling steps, little hands clamped around Jason's index fingers, Jason almost recaptured his own first steps, heard his father's voice over him, prideful and encouraging, the secure clutch of two thick fingers that slipped slowly from his grasp as the world teetered below his feet. It was often like that as a father—catching the faint, familiar scent of the past, just enough to remember that it had been forgotten.

It was the wrong time of year to teach Nicky how to ride a bike. Shivery, nose-runny gray day, abrupt gusts shoving past them. This should have been a sunny summer father and son moment, but he had allowed the clouds and cold to move in. Nicholas tensed and huddled in his bulky jacket, Jason short and impatient, thinking more about the cold cut of pork in the fridge than making a fond memory strong enough to survive the years.

Nicky wrestled with the handlebars, kicked at the pedals, and Jason jogged beside him holding the handle bar and seat.

"I can't do it."

"Don't fight it. Just trust me and feel for balance."

"Don't let go."

Tentative, reluctant Nicholas. He was growing fast, a spindled sapling that, around fifteen, would fill in that lank height with girth, just like Jason. All that potential pulled at Nicholas, stretching him, and he bowed and bent to his awkwardness.

Jason took his one hand off the handlebars, put it with his other on the back of the seat and moved behind the bike.

"No don't—"

"I'm not letting go. Not yet. You're doing great."

"I'm gonna fall."

"You might. That's okay."

They kept rounding the cul-de-sac in a jittery circle, Jason at a trot, his breath thinning, and Nicholas all knees and elbows, the bike already too small for him.

"Don't forget—step back on the pedals to stop, then get your feet down so you don't tip over."

"I'm not ready—"

"You bet you are."

"Dad—"

He let go but kept behind the bike as Nicky twitched and jerked the handlebars and stomped at the pedals. Instinct made him want to reach out and steady the bike, keep Nicky up, but he fought it, knew that falling was maybe the most important lesson for his boy to learn.

Nicky stabilized a bit and broke his circular path, pedaling straighter down the street.

"That's it, Nix. You're doing it!" Jason slowed and watched his boy make his way on two-wheeled determination. Not such a bad day after all. No need of the sun to warm a moment to fair weather memory.

Nicky pedaled more than halfway down the street and headed toward the main road. "Nicky, turn it around. Come back this way."

Nicky veered left, not nearly enough to swing around, the space scooter bike angling, heading for the curb. The handle bars wobbled and fluttered, a foot went down on the pedal to brake, but the pedal was too low and the bike wouldn't slow enough. The front tire hit the concrete curb, turned ninety degrees, and Nicky went down in a twist and tumble of gangly limbs. Jason sprinted to him.

"Nix? You okay?" He reached Nicky, the boy's legs tangled under the bike frame, body pinned by bike and curb and draped over the edge of Mrs. Polnzy's lawn. Jason reached for the bike. "You hurt yourself, Buddy?"

Eyebrows squirmed and butted together, face wound up for the burst of a cry, but Nicky held it back. Jason slipped the bike out from between Nicky's legs and laid it beside them.

"Anything broken? Bleeding?" He hunkered down and looked Nicky over.

Nicky sat up gingerly, wiped at his nose and sniffed with a bubbly snort.

"Got all your limbs?"

"Yeah."

Jason lifted the hood over Nicky's matted hair. "All your brains still in there?"

The slightest giggle and Jason's hand batted away. He was fine. Rubbermaid.

"You did good, kid. Learned to ride, and learned to fall." Jason pushed off his knees, stood and put out a hand. "And now you'll learn to get back up." Nicky took his hand and Jason pulled his son upright.

"Is my bike okay?"

"Should be fine. But when you tell your mom, the story is, you were wearing your helmet. Kapische?"

Nicholas nodded.

Jason took a few steps toward the bike that lay at the lip of Mrs. Polnzy's driveway. Her mailbox door sat open, mouth of the box stuffed to overflowing with junk mail circulars and letters. He looked up to the house, always dark and drawn and no different now. By her door, a pile of newspapers rolled and rubber banded and stacked like birch logs for a fire.

The lifeless house, put to sleep by drawn blinds and the empty driveway, gave every indication of her being somewhere else. Except it always looked that way, other than for the box puking out mail and the door blocked by a week or more of newspapers. She could be on a trip, but she would have stopped delivery on her paper and had someone check her mail. Maybe she had been rushed to the hospital and didn't have time to make arrangements.

Jason looked around the empty block. Every house was sealed tight against the mercurial temperament of late autumn, everyone practicing Sunday hibernation under fleece blankets, cursing or cooing their NFL teams or binging on web-streamed entertainment. And before today? How many times had Ollie and Lynn driven past Polnzy's crammed mailbox and just kept going up their driveway, perhaps wondering but doing nothing? What about the Petersons? They walked Liver up and down the street almost every night. Did they question it like him, then traipse by and close the door of their world behind them?

Is that what he would do? By the time he got home, warmed up that pork chop and got his mouth around the sandwich, he would forget about Polnzy's mail and all the supposed guilt he should feel for not checking in on a neighbor. All the better for him, because if he walked up those steps, knocked on her door and she answered it, he'd be accosted by a wrinkle-lipped sneer plus seven-and-a-half decades of resentment spat at him with her creaking voice. He knew it, and so did everyone else on the block. Just leave the old bag alone like she wanted.

He stuffed his hands into his pockets and scraped heels against the gravel of her driveway. "Stay here, Nicky. I'll be right back."

The cement of her sidewalk tented up from the encroaching roots of that colossus oak that stole all the water and sunlight from her scraggly lawn. On her stoop, he glared at her door and told himself to knock and get it over with.

He knuckled the wood door hard and quick and his hands went right back to the sanctuary of his pockets. Even from outside, against the brisk breeze, he caught a sour scent of old, coarse soap and soiled linen, bland broth and stale air. The kind of odor that can't be identified, but is the amalgamation of the withering lifestyle of the aged. The smell of nursing homes and hospitals, of a sedentary life amid very old things under the sediment of time. Would this smell surround him in forty more years? Not if he kept his health and prosperity. At all costs, he would remain active, healthy, and smelling good.

He knocked again, louder and longer, then turned to look back at Nicholas and held out a hand to him. *Stay put.* He faced the old door and counted to thirty. Silence from inside, even when he put his ear close to the door. He grabbed the doorknob—waited and deliberated and became certain he was making a huge mistake—and turned it.

The door opened. Unlocked. That seemed very wrong.

"Mrs. Polnzy?" Not quite a shout, but loud and projected through the crack of the door. If he intended to proceed, and if she was inside, he absolutely did not want her thinking he was breaking in. "Mrs. Polnzy?"

A point of no return had been reached. He was too convinced that things were not as they should be for him to turn around now, despite his strong sense of overreacting. "Nicky! Grab the mail from the box and run it up here for me."

Nicky stood and floundered a moment, much like Jason convincing himself to go to the door moments before, then trotted to the mailbox. He grabbed all the mail in two fumbling, mittened hands and hustled up to the door.

Jason took all of it from him. "I want you to head on home, okay? I'll be there shortly."

Nicky stared with stern concentration in Jason's direction, either confused by the situation and sensing something serious, or horrified by the idea of his father going inside alone. Whatever the cause of his intensity, it kept him there, like a stone, eyes locked on Jason's chest.

"Nicky. *Go*. Now."

Nicky went. Fast.

He opened the door wide, toed the newspapers aside, and took two steps in. The smell dowsed him, humid and thick. It weighed him down like gravity. He covered his nose from the rank slap of air like rancid meat and fecal waste with a sweet note of fermentation.

"Mrs. Polnzy? It's Jason Lahey. Your neighbor." He would not shout yet, but he expelled the words from deep in his chest, the sound of his voice low and unfamiliar, the unease in his tone making his stomach tingle. "Are you here? Are you all right?"

It was an old ranch-style home, one of the first built in this area when most of the land spread out in fields of corn and wheat. The house was, to the best of his knowledge, an actual farmhouse back then. Agnes and Morton Polnzy had moved in sometime in the fifties or sixties. He had died young, just after Ollie and Lynn had built their house. A coarse drunk, Moe Polnzy was coarse and terse when sober. He had never acquainted himself to Ollie and Lynn Mickelssen, and with the little that Ollie and Lynn saw Agnes Polnzy, they quickly discerned the Polnzys were the type best left to themselves.

Agnes and Moe had two kids, a boy and a girl. Squealing tires and occasional swearing were supposedly the only ways they had made their presence known. The daughter left home at sixteen, the boy shortly after at eighteen. Apparently, Ollie and Lynn Mickelssen crossed paths with the daughter infrequently before she left, but that was all.

Linoleum under Jason's feet in the small foyer, gold Victorian floral pattern, scuffed and scraped and curled up at corners. A hallway led straight to the kitchenette with a door to the left. A few muted pastoral paintings in fat old frames hung on the wall to break up the yellowed, cracked plaster. To the right, an archway, plain and squared off, led to the living room and its brown and umber carpeting.

"Mrs. Polnzy? I'm coming in. This is Jason. Jason Lahey. I have your mail."

He left the door open. He had to. If he closed it, he was positive the pressure of the home would build up, press against him from all sides and grind him into the floor. The place needed to be aired out, and as long as that door stayed open, a queer sensibility told him he could keep a phantom leg outside, like he was only leaning in, but not actually committing to entry.

The front living room was dark, the heavy drapes of the picture window shut tight. In front of those drab taupe drapes, an old white and gold floral-patterned couch with end tables to either side. Two uncomfortable-looking orange chairs sat against the opposite wall, their upholstery worn bare to threads at the seat middles. The sparse decor seemed so unlike an old woman's place. The room was hollow, chilled, unlived. The living room continued ahead to the left, around the wall. Jason stepped carefully, as if the floor were about to give way. The big stack of mail in his hands crinkled as he tightened his grip.

"Mrs. Polnzy? Are you here?"

He stepped around the corner and saw her sitting in a plain, spindled wooden chair in the center of the room. His breath hitched, his body caught and jerked to a stop.

A suspended arm, ghastly-white hand dangling through the hole of a duct tape roll, the metallic gray ribbon running up, round and round her neck, cinching the red and white Shop N' Save bag over her slumped head. One leg kicked out, slipper hanging askew from her toe. The other leg drawn under the chair, cocked and splayed. Nightgown hitched up to her blue-veined, waxen thighs that hung over the chair seat in a slouch. A swell of distended belly, anemic, almost translucent.

The smell, the violence of posture, the humility of her nakedness, filled his throat. He retched and coughed, covered his mouth and nose with his hands. The mail spilled to the floor. Jason read "occupant" and "current resident" in laser-printed sans-serif font as he regained some of his composure.

He stepped closer. Dead. Had to be dead. Obviously dead. Otherwise the bag over her head would be moving. But he needed more confirmation than just what seemed to be, because Jason couldn't process what sat before him, and he was shocked stupid.

He kept a hand to his mouth and pinched his nose shut, took hot, shallow breaths through his fingers. He stood over her. The shadowy gape of mouth and dead stare were barely visible through the plastic. His hand trembled as he reached for the ashen, tissue-paper skin of Agnes Polnzy's arm. Grazing her forearm, he yanked his hand back after feeling the cold, clammy skin.

He walked around the chair, saw her other arm dangle at the side. Her curled fingers, purple at the tips, hovered centimeters above the old, gritty carpeting, hand curved as if in memory of the pill bottle that laid open and empty against the leg of that old, rickety kitchen chair.

A sad life she makes for herself. Glen's voice, from the porch just a few nights ago.

"Jesus." He meant to swear, but the husky breath sounded so much more like a prayer that he was disappointed by his original intention. "Sweet Jesus." His head shook as tremulous hands found his pockets. Time to go.

He turned. Nicholas stood there in the living room, frozen, staring. Jason yelled out and raced for his ghost-faced boy, his sweet boy with those eyes too wide, too hard, cold and gray as November.

CHAPTER FIVE
Sunday, November 3, 2019 - Dusk

The medical examiner and coroner rolled the gurney down Agnes Polnzy's gravel driveway, white sheet rippling, a spectral flapping over a vaguely female form. They collapsed the gurney legs and slid it into the back of the black Marathon County coroner's van. Rear doors shut with dry thumps and the Petersons' Frankenstein Monster danced and sang as the van drove away.

Jason spoke with the police officers, told them everything he knew, and repeated it when they asked again. The two officers were politely disinterested. The female officer, petite but severe like a paring knife, maintained a stony expression throughout her direct questioning, occasionally offering a grimacing smile of encouragement as she listened to Jason's responses. The male officer, young and clean-pressed with fleshy cheeks, kept mainly to stoic nods. To these two, there was nothing suspect, no mystery or crime to solve. Cut and dry, and worst of all to

Jason by their demeanors, apparently familiar. One officer kept inside after getting the perimeter secured by the gravity of yellow police tape. Another kept by the two patrol cars parked in a 'V' before the driveway.

Jason kept glancing at his neighbors who had stepped out of their doors to stand at the ends of their driveways. Each of them looked out on the scene from the secure reassurance of their property lines until, in a slow, silken glide like mercury, they pooled together into one puddling mass across the street. The Petersons stood at the front, Sam in his Dockers and leather Green Bay Packers jacket, Liver's leash in his hand, the Basset Hound between him and Delilah. When the dog lunged forward, Sam snapped him back with the tug of his tether. Delilah, in sheepskin and high-heeled brown boots, tried to calm Liver with absent rubs of his head. They were the perfect spectators at some local event. All that was missing were the red and white popcorn boxes the neighborhood curiosity club could munch on while they watched.

Glen stood rigid at the back of the block party crowd, behind Ollie and Lynn. He nodded once to Jason and appeared tense and suspended. He didn't seem to say much to anyone other than the occasional faint movement of lips responding to the flapping of Lynn's, then his head would angle to the ground, hands in his pockets. Ollie, his silver tufts of hair on the sides of his bald head sticking out like antennae, flung his attention about the scene, squeezing his eyes with a desperation to learn the what's and how's and when's he couldn't immediately know. Back at the end of the cul-de-sac next to their house, Fred Greely, his other adjacent neighbor he shared the cul-de-sac with but not much else, peered at the commotion with arms crossed as he leaned against the post of his porch. His wife, Vivian, stared out from their large living room window.

Jen kept away from the crowd, hunched down in the middle

of the cul-de-sac, arms enveloping Nicholas. She whispered a steady stream of soothing words as she clung to him and rocked him. He wished Nicky had stayed in the house, but when the police arrived, he had become agitated and restless. Jen could only calm him by bringing him back out. Jason told her to bring him back inside, and Nicky had squirmed out of her grasp, said "No," and stood there, eyes directed to the scene, but not seeming to see anything. They had no idea what to do and didn't feel they could or should force him into anything. Nicky no longer felt like he belonged in their custody, but was instead supervised by this incident, of Agnes Polnzy's death.

The female officer looked over to Jen and Nicky. "How's your boy?"

"I don't really know."

"You should probably get him inside, away from all of this."

"That's exactly what I plan to do, as soon as you're done with me."

The officer closed her notepad and stuffed it in her pocket. "We're finished here. Not likely to be much of an investigation. We have your information if we need to ask you anything else. Go take care of your son."

The two officers headed for the crowd. Jason stood, ready to move away from all of this, but found his first step heavy, a perceived chasm between where he was and where he wanted to be. It felt like days ago, not hours, that he had taught Nicky to ride a bike. He forced his foot from the ground and placed it ahead of him. The other followed suit.

Jen stood when he reached her and Nicholas. He kissed her lightly and lowered himself to Nicky's eye level. "Let's go home, buddy."

Nicky's attention still strayed to the orderly commotion of police vehicles and uniformed officers and assembled neighbors, but allowed Jason's hand to guide him down the street and to their house.

"Was there a break-in? Everything alright?"

Jason turned to the right where Fred leaned over his front porch railing sporting a North Face pullover and tan Chino pants, eye squinting with concern that closely resembled scrutiny.

"Hey, Fred. No. No break-in. Mrs. Polnzy passed away."

Fred's eyes widened. "No kidding?" He drew back to stand straight, hand putting whisps of hair blown by the chill wind back over his bald scalp. "Heart attack?"

Jason shook his head and kept him and Jen moving to their garage. "No. Sorry, Fred, but it's been a rough day. Promise to catch up and fill you in."

"Yeah, yeah. Sure." Fred scratched at his thin salt-and-pepper-stubbled cheek.

Jason kept close behind Jen and Nicky as they stepped through the garage. He brushed the back of Jen's coat and Nicky's jacket in what felt like a failed attempt to reassure. When he pressed the orange ember of the button by the door to the mudroom, the garage door rumbled and slowly closed its eye to the emergency vehicles, the crowd, and the entire aftermath of the brutal day. The grind and grate of moving parts as the fading gray light of day squeezed to a slit was like a boulder rolling before the entrance of a tomb.

Inside, Jason felt sluggish, limbs wading through wet silence. Jen's motions were abrupt, too fast for Jason. She set Nicky on the bench, flung his boots off and peeled his coat from his body. She was in some kind of race, as if she thought something could be bested. Overcome.

"I'm going to try and get Nicky into bed for a nap," she said.

"Good. That's good."

His son sat with his arms dripping down his sides, legs leaking off the bench. Liquid lethargy, no more than a body adrift below the current. That's how Jason saw him, undulating like seaweed on a lake floor, eyes drooping like overstretched elastic, an echo of vague concern about something now passed. Even his hat hair swirled to the swell of eddies.

Jen grabbed Nicky's hand and he trailed behind with a rubber arm's length between them. Jason pushed through the mudroom into the kitchen.

He passed the desk built into the corner of the kitchen just before the counter and the stove. Papers, mail and booklets overwhelmed it. So many things piled high on the desktop and stuffed into pigeonholes with the best of intentions to be done, and none of it being done. It would be, though. Jen would make sure of it. Give her a week or two and she would take issue with that clutter.

There would always be more things to accumulate on it, though. Life kept happening. What if, one day, it just stayed clean, the wooden desktop always clear, and each cubby hole empty? Did Mrs. Polnzy get tired of looking at a desk that refused to collect anything but dust? Nothing that waited for her to do something about it? Did she finally realize that she herself was the last thing to be done in life?

A restless urge to twitch and shake out his muscles drove him forward, past the desk and to the cupboard where they kept the liquor. He pulled down a bottle of rum, found a glass and pressed it against the tongue of the refrigerator's ice dispenser. On the rare occasion he had liquor, he'd drizzle rum to the level of ice and fill the glass with cola. Now, he poured the rum. He didn't bother with the cola.

Some people died, and some people just stopped living. Jason had been made keenly aware of that with his mother. Not that he would think about his mother now. She kept threatening, but he was used to dodging that impulse, of avoiding many things related to his parents. He learned that well during their time in the Cities, when their relocation had become a convenient way to evade all the complications that had arisen with his parents.

But why did Polnzy choose such a terrible way to stop living? She had the pills. She could have laid down and gone to sleep peacefully. She didn't do that. As if she wanted the struggle and violence in the act. Like she had settled a score with herself.

None of that mattered, though. He had no idea why Polnzy had killed herself, nor the reasons for her method. He never would know, and even if he could, would that knowledge serve him in any possible way?

"Are you stuck?"

Jason looked at Jen standing at the end of the kitchen, his drink halfway to his mouth and making no forward progress. "Huh? Oh, I'm— I don't know. Just thinking."

She walked up to him, took the glass from his hand and set it on the counter, then slipped her arms around his waist. Her head pressed against his chest and he had the sudden awareness of his heart pumping, like Jen was transmitting the sound of each beat to him. "He's in bed. I don't know if he'll sleep, but he's in bed."

He stroked her hair. "Good."

"He's barely said a word since it happened."

"Hon, he's not a big talker to begin with. Listen, it'll take time. He'll be fine, don't worry. Kids are pretty durable with this kind of stuff."

"We need to talk to him about this. Get him to talk to us about it."

Of course Jen would say that. Something wasn't the way it should be and she'd be determined to put everything right as soon as she possibly could. She wouldn't be right until it was.

"Sure," he said. "Let's not rush things, though. Give him some time to let this all fade a bit to memory."

"I'm going to keep him home from school tomorrow. I'll

take the day off and stay with him."

"I don't know if that's such a good idea. I mean, we should try and get him back into a normal routine as soon as possible, don't you think?"

She lifted her head and pulled away slightly so she could look up at him. "No, Jason. I think that's about the worst thing we could do."

"Why" came to his lips—the wrong kind of "why" that would challenge her opinion. Jason made sure to disagree judiciously and sparingly in their marriage, and this definitely didn't seem like the right time to question her. Not with so much confidence and assurance in her tone.

The ringing of his cell phone saved him from making any response. He slipped away from Jen, pulled the phone from his pocket, and answered it without any attention to what displayed on the screen.

"Hello?"

"Jason, it's Zeke. Look, I'm sorry to be calling, but—"

Adrenaline and heat rushed through him. Jason was hyper conscious of himself not looking at Jen.

"This isn't a good time." His voice went instinctively low and obviously suspicious. He berated himself for not screening the call.

"I'm sorry, I just—Dee's found out she's got breast cancer. I thought you—she—ought to know."

That shut Jason's eyes. Are you kidding? What else could possibly pile onto this day?

He stayed quiet a moment, tried to figure out how to feel, decided it was way too complicated amid everything else that has happened, and put it aside for later.

"I'll call you back," Jason said and hung up. His eyes opened to a corner of floor tile his gaze had stuck to the moment he heard Zeke's voice. He didn't need to look up to sense Jen lasing him with her stare.

"Was that—?"

He looked up and saw the dread stillness of mouth and weight of eyes.

"Don't worry about it."

"I don't like that, you know. I don't like it at all." She inflicted her words onto him, jabbed him with each syllable.

He shifted in place. "I'm sorry. Listen, it's not the time to argue about this."

Jen did not move. She did that when she became irate. A fury of paralysis. Jason's own stubbornness bore the scars of too many times speaking when she was like that, of toying with the trap when its spring was tight and its trigger sensitive to a hasty breath. Jason knew the next words spoken needed to be from her.

"What was Nicky doing there, Jason? Why was he in that house?"

He tasted the pepper of accusation in her voice, the burn of recrimination. He forced a quiet calm to his answer. "I have no idea. I told him to go home. I can't imagine what would have made him turn around and come back."

Her nod gave him no impression of satisfaction, but only of the subject being closed. He hated Zeke in this moment because of that one phone call. With it, Zeke gave Jen all the power. Because of that one phone call, Jason was forced to concede to her completely, regardless of how he felt.

"Keep Nicky home tomorrow. I'll call the school and see if they have any suggestions about this."

"Good." She turned and began walking out of the kitchen.

He reached for his glass on the counter. He wanted to say something average, something every-day that would set them back upon the groove of normalcy, but it was all so out of reach. Normal somehow seemed taboo within the context of the day. Maybe that's why he blurted out his next words without any thought.

"Just so you know, your mother has cancer."

She paused her step, started to look back, but didn't. She resumed her pace, out of Jason's sight.

Jason took a drink.

CHAPTER SIX
Monday, November 4, 2019

Someone from the office who had a habit of listening to Fortune Fall's police scanner caught the police dispatch that sent officers to Fairview Lane yesterday. By the time Jason passed through the door at 8:00 a.m., everyone had heard about it from someone else. The consequence was wasting half a day thanks to people asking him to reprise the morbid events for their entertainment and curiosity, followed by them sharing their closest similar experience.

Matt Shay in marketing had a great aunt Rosa who his cousin discovered expired on her toilet she had first roosted on almost two weeks prior. Julie Wittenberg in accounting lived next to someone who owned an apartment building downtown and had found a tenant in the middle of the living room floor—"lying naked in his own pee and poop," Julie said with more grin than grimace—dead of an overdose. Brenda Fleischman, as every-one eventually found out if they lingered too long at the receptionist's desk, had been eight months pregnant as she watched her fiancé pull the trigger of his sawed-off twelve-gauge shoved under his chin after he threatened to do it to her first.

Jason couldn't figure out what shocked him more—that so many people apparently had such macabre moments darkening their pasts, or that so many people were eager and willing to share those stories with others. Other than Brenda, which wasn't a shock at all considering she told the story as many times as she could, always with the same hasty titter of speech as she tugged at her red tangle of hair and stared unblinking with wide open eyes.

It should have been an obvious realization that most have a tale of death to tell. Everyone died, had to die somewhere, and eventually someone else found them. Not everyone died in the sanitized, controlled environment of a hospital where some overworked and underpaid nurse pulled the sheet over the body and wheeled it away. But somehow Jason had never bothered to think about how so many people squeezed melons in the produce aisle and plucked dandelions from their lawn in the summer and drank highballs with friends and coworkers, all while the spark of a death throe or the empty gaze of a familiar corpse lingered as a haunted memory in their mind.

Psychologists and philosophers probably argued that death tinged every action and motivation of an individual. Eating to stave off death. Bonding with others to avoid being alone at death. Pleasure as a means to distract from the reality of death. Sex to procreate and thus supplant death. Creation to outlast death.

All which did nothing to explain the fascination alongside the fear of death. It did, however, explain why, by lunchtime, Jason locked his office door and told his assistant Marissa he didn't wish to be disturbed for the rest of the day.

The workstations and hallways of Boswell Software were rarely noisy. Tempers could crest in the squall of a deadline, voices rising over the storm, but normally only a light chatter carried above the constant clatter of keyboard keys. When lunchtime came, Jason noticed the pressure of a humming silence against his door.

It wasn't unusual to put in extra time at Boswell. So many times, the offices were occupied until six or seven. Sometimes the programmers churned out lines of code until nine. But lunch hours were sacred and all but a scant few took it down the street at Clancy's Sports Bar. Jason usually joined them, except when he worked through lunch to get caught up. Or like now, when he called Jen's parents.

"Hey, Zeke. It's Jason."

"Hi, guy." Zeke's voice, curled as if strained through an apologetic grin, maybe a dash of dimpled irony. "Sorry about the call yesterday. I really caught hell for that from Dee."

"It's okay."

"I was just sitting there alone while Dee's in Medford with her sister before the surgery, feeling sorry for myself, and picked up the phone without thinking."

He had probably been drinking. It was always hard to tell with Zeke. Jason could usually tune in to the wistful obstinacy of an inebriated Zeke. But even if his blood coursed one-third alcohol, Zeke never sounded drunk. Not that he drank like that anymore. At least, that's what he told Jason.

"Surgery? So, she's—?"

"Yup. They chopped it off. 'Cut it off,' she said, just as soon as the results came back. I tried to get her to take some time to think about it, but she wouldn't give in for a second."

Zeke's typical coarse bluntness. "Wow. I'm sorry to hear

that, Zeke. A mastectomy is the best way to make sure the cancer doesn't come back. She probably made the right decision."

A sucking inhale, likely of a Pall Mall. "For a time, she was talking about getting them both cut off. She didn't want to be a lopsided freak. Jesus. I talked her out of that. Told her to think about reconstructive surgery. Not sure if my insurance covers that, though. Still have to find out."

Jason shook his head and tried to restrain his response. "That's rough, Zeke. How's Dee doing?"

"Fine. I'm still with her at the hospital until she's released in a few hours. I took the last couple days off."

"Give Dee my best, huh?"

"I will." Another deep drag of cigarette. The suspension of a slow exhale. "I sure would like to give her Jenny's best, too."

Jason had called Jen's parents seven years ago. It had probably been a mistake, a rash moment. Maybe he had called because he was so thrilled to be a father and had recently lost his parents and it was the kind of news best shared with parents. Maybe it was because he thought that, no matter what Zeke and Dee had done to irreparably sever their relationship with their daughter, they should know they were grandparents. Maybe all he had done was give them the false hope of an eventual reconciliation.

When they started to contact him, he couldn't tell them to stop calling. He didn't have Jen's history with them to make those kind of words come easy from his mouth. It seemed harmless enough to merely keep them informed of Nicholas's first words and first steps. When they got together with Jen's brother Seth and his wife Rachel, Jason would hear Seth talk about his two boys growing up with doting grandparents. That made his contact with them seem all that much more appropriate. Surely, over time, Jen's resentment would diminish like the ache of a wound.

When Jen finally found out, it had been a long night of talking with her. "Who the hell do you think you are to be calling them behind my back," she demanded. "What kind of game are you playing?" He let her throw one condemnation after another at him and tallied each one with a weak, submissive "sorry" as he kept his attention locked on her. She wasn't able to maintain that level of hostility, and then they were actually able to talk. He had felt bad, but at the time, he wasn't sorry about it. Like so many things he had done back then, he felt vindicated by dispassionate rationality and logic. He had been certain he could coax that same reasoning into her.

And he had, after a fashion. Or he simply exhausted her to a conceded impasse. "Do whatever the hell you want," she had said, "but I don't want to know anything about it." So he kept in communication with her parents and his contact with them was not discussed—just reluctantly accepted.

Too late he realized that Zeke's last comment had opened up the hole of a thought that Jason fell into. His silence only aggravated Zeke.

"Just how long will she keep this up? I mean, Christ Almighty, we made mistakes. We know that. We weren't great parents. Too young, too stupid. I get it. Dee gets it. Why the hell won't she let us make up for it? That's all we want."

"I'm not getting into this, Zeke. I've told you from the start, I won't play sides in this. That's not my position, and you can't expect it of me. I won't defend her to you, and I won't defend you to her. Everything that's between you and Jen is and always will be exactly that."

A few old pictures and one short, long-ago visit were all Jason had to go by to envision the reaction on Zeke's face. Blonde hair, buzz-cut in a faded and yellowed picture of him at nineteen, cigarette pack rolled up in the short sleeve of his white tee shirt, beer bottle dangling from a long arm hung from narrow shoulders, flat eyes turned down to the small patch of fenced-in back yard. His seventeen-year-old wife beside him, black hair short and frazzled, square-framed with skinny legs and no hips, lean like a farmer and holding one-year-old Jen like a sack of potatoes under one arm.

Twenty-two years later and the first and only time he met Zeke and Dee. It was at Jason's insistence, four months before he and Jen were married. Jen sat next to him on her parents' rock-hard mint green couch while dusty sunlight sifted through the rusty screens and silted windows of their living room. Zeke like dried-out wood on his duct-taped leather recliner, hair a little longer, eyes thinned and squinting, but with a universal smile that could be both good-natured and condescending, humorous and bitter, sincere and cajoling. Dee, fleshier on top than in that picture at seventeen, but still the lean legs and the slight bow that gave her walk a swagger. Her dark hair too dark and slicked back, her leer like she was looking at Jason through gun sights. Her every sentence began with the sandpaper scratch of a laugh, like clearing her throat. She sat at the end of the dining table— border patrol between the living room and dining room. Her boisterous voice sounded like she was having a better time than her severe face implied. That weekend visit lasted four hours.

"We'd like to see our grandson, Jason. Time's running out for us, you know?"

"Zeke, I wish things weren't the way they are, but some-times it just doesn't matter how sorry you are. You can be sorry as hell. You can be choking on all the goddamn sorry you're swallowing, but it doesn't guarantee any forgiveness." Without meaning to, he noticed his tone harden, his words squeezed by some agitation not rooted in this moment. With the pause of a breath and focused effort, he loosened his words. "Sometimes, you just have to face the fact that there may be no forgiveness to give. Maybe not even any comfort if there was." He had digressed, scratched too hard at a nagging itch and tore off the scab of an old wound.

Jason clearly heard Zeke's restrained inhale on the other side of the line and an the abrupt exhale. "Yeah, well. She's got no understanding. No sympathy. You two have had it good. You got everything we never did. Maybe she should think about how it would be for her if she had had nothing like we had. Maybe she'd be having some regrets and looking for some forgiveness herself."

"Gotta go, Zeke." Spoken hastily, but Jason didn't care if it sounded abrupt. If Zeke hadn't figured out by now that Jason wouldn't put up with that self-pitying garbage, there was no point in saying it again. "Keep me updated about Dee, would you? Give me a ring here at work."

"Sure. Right." The contempt returned, words gnashed between teeth and spit out. Exactly what had led Jen out the door sixteen years ago dragging Jason with her by the arm. The flame of it would go out quickly, but the ember would glow for some time. Jason doubted he'd hear from Zeke again for a few months.

And that was usually for the best.

Jason poked at the baked chicken thigh on his plate while listening to Jen narrate her day with Nicholas. She had driven him to the little neighborhood park on the corner of Lexington Avenue a few miles away on the south side of town. A little less than an acre lot partly shaded in the summer by a couple tall maples, it offered a swing set, merry-go-round, and a crayon-colored plastic slide with mini obstacle course of wobbly bridge and child-sized hamster tunnel at top. Nicky slid down the slide, swung on the swing, and merry-go-rounded, then did it all three more times. When he tired of that, she took him to the Culver's drive thru and treated Nicky to a hot fudge sundae.

Now, at the dinner table, Nicholas was more quiet than usual while he poked at his peas, licked a spoonful of mashed potatoes and gnawed a few pieces of dark meat. He left the table and his half-full plate to meander into the living room and turn on his video game, where he played with distracted interest

"He seemed okay," Jen mentioned after dinner, handing a plate to Jason to towel dry as they looked through the open space over the sink into the living room. "Quiet, but he's always quiet."

Jason watched Nicholas kneeling before the TV screen as he tried to steer his cartoon buggy around a crazy stretch of video game raceway, turning and twisting the game remote in the air and smashing at buttons.

He understood Jen's concern for Nicholas, but the fact was, Nicky had always been a child of few words and in his own world. That had been hard for Jason early on. When he found out he was going to have a son, he thrilled with excitement for the opportunity to be an eager, engaged father, to play games with his son and laugh and goof around with him, throw the ball and wrestle and be all the things Jason's father never quite was. What happened instead? He got a son who took much more after Jason's father than after Jason—distant and withdrawn.

But as a father, Jason adjusted. He figured out ways to interact with Nicky that his son responded to. It could simply be sitting with him while he colored and asking him questions about the pictures. It could be building a Lego ship together, or building something next to Nicky while his son built something else.

Jen, meanwhile, took on the role of nurse, caregiver, and nurturer. She spread her wings of protection over him, a motherly guardian angel. Every tantrum coddled, every frustration fixed, and every obstacle removed. He suspected it was difficult for her now because there was no skinned knee to bandage or physical problem to resolve. Whatever was going on in his head she couldn't immediately hug or kiss or make better.

"The school referred me to a child therapist," Jason said. "I gave her a call. She, of course, strongly suggested making a round of appointments. No surprise there when she's charging $150 an hour."

"Make the appointment." No hesitation. "I'll bring him in."

Words stuck in his gullet and he swallowed them down. He methodically wiped the plate in his hand and gave a tight nod.

It wasn't the money. It was about dragging his little boy into a room with some clinician who would make sure Nicholas realized he had seen a very bad thing. Something disturbing and wrong. Sure, the clinically chosen words suggested the opposite, but changing his routine, putting him in front of a stranger asking him questions and dragging out one bad moment over weeks or months that would have otherwise receded into obscurity? Jason couldn't see how that would help Nicky move beyond that singular event.

He put the last plate in the cupboard and tossed the damp towel on the counter. "I'm going to head over and check on Glen."

"Now?" As close to a "No" as she would dare say.

"Just for a little bit. I got the impression this whole thing bothered him."

Jen huffed. "You mean like how it's bothered your *son?*"

He looked at her, silent, maybe a bit too long. Finally, he turned and went to the refrigerator. Opening the door, he grabbed the empty plastic ring dangling from half a six pack.

"I won't be long."

Everything felt off. Wrong. He was off-course. Misplaced.

There was an indefinable, cumbersome obstruction between him and Jen, as if they were both wearing bulky protective coverings—interaction through emotional hazmat suits. He should be home, talking things through with her and holding her for comfort. He should be on the living room floor playing video games with his son, or helping his boy snap Lego blocks together into one of his spaceships.

But here he was, alone on the darkened street, the hollow echo of his feet scrapes against the blacktop an intrusion upon a night silent as a breath as he headed to Glen's place.

Movement to his left turned his head. Spiderwebbing rippled from the bony branches of the Mickelssens' young, naked oak, undulating like a tattered silken gown clinging to an emancipated body.

The Halloween decorations still up at the Mickelssens' took on a different air. Styrofoam tombstones in the yard suddenly suggested a stone-cold heaviness. Skeletal window clings mocked more than amused with empty eye sockets and slack jaws. Farther down the street, behind the Petersons' arborvitae that grew beside their porch, he could just make out Frankenstein's monster. No singing. No dancing. It simply lurked in the shadows, waiting.

Jason stepped up to Glen's door and rapped lightly. It had been a while since Jason had been to Glen's place. He used to come there quite a bit—sometimes with Jen, many times by himself—either to help Glen with a project or task, or stop by for a neighborly chat. Maude would be in her rocker, usually working on a quilt or some embroidery, or she'd be in the kitchen canning or baking. She was always present in a big way. Her personality had filled a room.

Maude had worn her German and Welsh heritage with pride. She didn't know how to not be occupied by a task, and her ruddy, big-knuckled hands and broad shoulders made it clear she could heft any load or swing a hammer and axe with the best. Most of those muscles had developed during her thirty-plus years of rolling over, hoisting up or lending support to rehab patients on the ninth floor of Mother of Mercy Hospital. She had retired early, her excuse being, "Well, I got so much to do and no time to do it!"

Those hands were happiest in the dirt. May through September, her bony butt would be in the air and thick-skulled head down in her tomato bushes, potatoes, cucumbers, radishes, and peppers, tending to the raised garden Glen had boxed in for her in the backyard.

When she worked outside, she never let a neighbor pass without a, "Hi-ya," or "How's life treatin ya?" She barked laughter, growled disdain, and her humor had teeth. She was a favorite of the neighborhood and the pride of Glen. "Maude's a tough ol' broad," Glen would say, "and she's all mine."

When she started complaining about back pain, there was no worry, no alarm. *Of course* a 64-year-old woman would have back pain, especially a retired nurse constantly leaning over to stitch fabric or boil and seal jars of raspberry jam. "Hells bells, been married to a pain in the neck for 40 years. No back pain's gonna slow this old girl down!"

But the back pain spread to her stomach and took the place of her appetite. Jason watched worry tug on Glen's long face. "Maude, I swear to God almighty, I'll toss you over my shoulder and carry you in to the doctor myself if you don't go."

"Don't nag at me, you ol' goat. I'll get there. Just need to get my cukes pickled before they go soft. And I'm behind on getting that memorial quilt done for Betty 'fore her birthday."

Twenty pounds lighter from her already lean frame, stomach distended like an old man's beer belly, breath failing to catch, and Glen did all but shove her in the car and drive her to urgent care. It took ten minutes with the nurse practitioner and they were sent to the emergency room and on to imaging and lab work—and learned the ugly truth that Glen had feared all along and Maude had refused to face.

Stage four ovarian cancer.

She went through surgery, endured chemo, but the cancer was aggressive and spread like an invasive weed to her stomach, intestines, liver and lungs. More surgery and more chemo was called for. Maude told them forget about it. "Leave me be. Let me have peace. I've got no regrets. No need to start now by making my final days miserable."

Glen sold his rig in order to stay home and take care of her. A hospice nurse came by regularly, and Glen's sole obsession became doing whatever he could to keep Maude comfortable and savor the time she had left.

Jason and Jen stopped by at first. Jen made a casserole or soup and they'd sit in the living room to chat away the hours while the Maude they knew slowly faded away in her chair. After a couple visits, it seemed more appropriate, more considerate, to let them be. To suffer was bad enough. To be a spectacle while you suffered was not something Jason could imagine going through.

It was almost two years ago that she passed. Glen and Maude had just managed a Thanksgiving with their children and grandkids. Glen later said it seemed as if she had drawn up the last little bit of life she had in her to be mother and wife one last time. Something squirmed and pushed against Jason's chest as he thought about Glen alone in that room as the calendar turned its page to December, watching the first flakes of snow fall outside the window, his wife's body lying beneath it, as he wiped old, salty tears from his eyes.

Maude Overby, age 67, wife of Glen, mother of Michael, Betty, and Christian, died at 2:07pm from complications due to ovarian cancer.

How easy it had been at the time to justify his and Jen's avoidance.

Jason rapped harder on Glen's door.

"Have a seat. Sorry for the mess."

Jason slid a folded-back newspaper from the corner of the couch and sat down next to where Glen dropped into his over-stuffed recliner with a grunt, sighed and cracked open a beer.

There were pictures everywhere—of Glen's two sons and their families, of his daughter and her husband. And, looking over her family, eyeing Glen with cocked-head whimsy or raised brow scrutiny, cradling a grandchild proudly, ready to break into a big laugh or glance up while nuzzling their daughter's poodle in her arms, was Maude.

Two lamps sat on old cherry end tables and provided the only break from darkness other than a floor lamp in the far corner. The melancholy lighting was subdued but not murky in a room packed with memories and artifacts of the past. Jason's eyes fell briefly to the rocking chair in the far corner of the small living room.

"How's your boy doing?"

The neighborhood buzzed over the event, sharing bits of information with each other, even though Jason hadn't talked to any of them. Jason doubted anyone on Fairview Lane knew everything, but they seemed to know enough.

"Good. I mean, he will be. He's young. I doubt he fully understood what he was seeing, you know?"

Glen leaned forward with elbows on his knees, right hand holding his beer. "And what exactly *did* he see, Jase?"

Jason put a beer in his hand and popped the top. "You don't want to know, Glen."

"Not sure if I do." He took a sip of beer. "Still. Curiosity, you know?"

Jason did know, and he regretted allowing his curiosity to lead him to such a horrible discovery. Jason took several gulps, closed his eyes as he swallowed and clung tight to the can. "I've never seen anything like it, Glen. Never want to again."

Glen drew back with some concern pushing up his bushy black eyebrows. "Now, there wasn't foul play, was there?"

Jason shook his head with a sour chuckle. "Foul's a good enough word, though. That's what I found. Foul."

"It was suicide, right? That's what everyone's saying."

That word sat heavy on his chest, too hard to acknowledge.

"Listen, if you ain't comfortable talking about this, I understand."

"Yeah, she killed herself, Glen. But, she did it—I don't know—violently. Spitefully." He shook his head, trying to shake the words and image out.

"Was there blood? Did she use a blade? Good God, is *that* what Nicky saw?"

Jason drank down a quarter more of the can. "No. But almost as bad. I—Christ, it's hard to—I just can't—" The vision pounced upon him, of her sitting alone on that uncomfortable wooden chair, wearing nothing but her night gown, taking the pills, pulling the bag over her head and winding duct tape round and round and round her neck.

"Hey, Jase. It's fine. I shouldn't have asked. Not my place. Not important."

"It was just—it was—" The words, the memory, were lodged inside of him, stuck sideways in his windpipe like a chicken bone.

Glen's eyes locked on Jason. He reached out and put a big hand on Jason's shoulder. "Hey. How are *you* doing?"

"What? No, I'm fine. Really. Just not, not the easiest thing to talk about right now, I guess." Jason tipped back the rest of his beer, set the empty on the end table. His eyes fell to the third and last beer locked in the plastic six-pack ring. "You mind?"

"Hell no. Have at it."

Jason grabbed the beer, yanked it out of the plastic yoke and popped it open. He took a deep gulp.

They sat quiet for a moment, Jason wresting himself free from a yesterday that had seeped into his today. Glen's eyes strayed to Maude's chair, her Afghan still draped over the back and spilling onto the seat in knitted greens and blues and browns.

"I guess tonight is the night for asking—how about you?" Jason asked. "Seems like something's weighing you down."

Glen sipped at his beer, leaned forward again and spun the can slowly between his hands. His eyes seemed to droop more, his mouth parted slightly either in reflection or simply in preparation to speak. Jason stayed quiet, passive and reflective.

"Coming on two years since Maude passed. Don't know, but since yesterday, I haven't been able to stop thinking about those last couple months. The pain got bad. Real bad. Not even the morphine could cut into it. It got hard, you know? Hard. Seeing her suffer like that." He sucked in air and exhaled hard and slow. "She asked me, you know. She asked me if I would."

Jason knew immediately what Glen referred to, but the shock of hearing it struck him stupid. "What? You mean—?"

Glen gave a somber nod and eyes turned to steel. "Do you know she never cried once during her cancer? Never made a sound. She took everything in silence. Stoic." His eyes glistened. "She was a tough ol' broad." Dry chuckle as his gaze fell beyond the moment. "She said she wanted to be done with it. 'Grab that pillow, Glen.' That's what she told me. 'Grab it and get it over with. Please.' Only time during that whole goddamn disease I ever saw her come close to tears."

"Jesus Christ, Glen. Jesus God. I—I'm so sorry."

Glen put out a hand and took a breath and a moment. Drilled his eyes into Jason. "I grabbed that pillow, God damn me to hell. I grabbed it, Jase. I was gonna do it. I was. But I was too weak, too selfish. I cried like a baby. Told her I was sorry.

I'm so sorry."

Jason tried to imagine the horrific scene, but he couldn't picture Glen carrying out such a fatalistic action.

"She forgave me, right then and there. Apologized for asking. Never complained again. And you know what, Jason? You know what happened next?"

Jason shook his head.

"Two weeks later we had that Thanksgiving dinner and Maude came back. She came back and she lived and loved and laughed for one last time."

Jason had heard Glen talk about that Thanksgiving Day so often it had almost become his own memory. "It sure sounded like a perfect day."

Glen's face twisted and turned ugly. "And I almost took it away from her."

Jason set his beer can down so fast he almost spilled it. He hopped his butt forward to the edge of the couch, his head only a couple inches away from being over Glen's lap. "Glen. Holy God. I—Don't do that to yourself, man. You can't guilt yourself over something you didn't do."

Glen slouched back into the seat, head turned to the side, eyes still looking to some other moment in time. "Sure. I know it ain't rational, but ever since yesterday I can't stop thinking about it."

"Why?"

"She died alone, Jason. Polnzy. Killed herself and no one was there to stop her. No perfect day for her. I don't know. It doesn't make sense, but it just makes me think of Maude and what I almost did, and what a horrible, miserable way that would have been for her to end. I just feel goddamn awful that Agnes did what she did right across the street from me."

Jason drank down the last of his beer and held on to the empty can, head down, as thoughts bounced about—his worry over Nicholas, his concern about Jen, the complicated mess with her parents and her mother's diagnosis, his deepening regret for what he now realized was his abandonment of Glen during his time of need.

Mixed in with all of that, a darkening realization that, until this moment, he had felt no sympathy for Agnes Polnzy and her suicide, only an absolute revulsion.

Home again, and with him, the heavy pall of the evening. He shed his shoes in the foyer, stood there for a moment and listened to the television coming from the living room. He kept pushing aside images of Agnes and memories of Maude. Every time he did, there was Dee, Jen's mother, in a hospital bed. A mother without a daughter by her side.

Too many parallels. More than he wanted to admit. His thoughts were short-circuiting on crossed wires of dismay, regret, and guilt. They were driving him to something he didn't want to do, but knew he must. The realization added a tangle of dread to his sparking emotions. Jen was not going to want to hear what he had to say.

First to the kitchen. He grabbed a tumbler, dispensed a few ice cubes, snatched the bottle of rum, splashed the liquor a third the way up the glass, popped open a Coke and filled the glass the rest of the way. The liquor was kept more for guests and special occasions since Jen was partial to her merlots and he usually kept to a beer or two.

Well, at least until the last two nights.

He mixed his drink with an index finger, took a slug, and braced himself before stepping into the living room.

"Hey."

"Hey." Jen sat on the couch watching some reality baking

show. She did not look at him. "How's Glen?" Her tone fell somewhere between sincerity and bitterness.

Jason sat in the recliner kitty-corner to the couch. Nicholas curled up on the far end of the couch, poking distractedly at his iPad screen while his eyes drooped. "He's okay. This whole thing with Agnes stirred up memories of Maude and has him in a bit of a dark place."

Jen looked to him then, eyes softening. "It's still got to be tough for him—Oh, God. And coming up on the anniversary of her death. That just hit me. Wow."

"Yeah. Rough." Jason took a swig of his drink.

Jen's eyes widened to the glass. She raised an eyebrow at him. "Really?"

He ignored the comment.

"Listen. Jen. We need to talk." He tried his damnedest to keep his eyes locked on hers. They wanted to dart all over the room and be anywhere but fixed in her gaze. "About your parents."

Her expression congealed and set. A rigid apathy edged with resentment and blaring silence.

"Your mom's in the hospital. She had a mastectomy. Breast cancer."

He caught something—a crack in her hostility, just around the corner of her eyes. It made him hope she might be receptive to reevaluating her embargo against her parents.

She paused the TV. "Is that what the call was about?"

"Yes."

"How's she doing?"

He shrugged and took another drink. "Fine, I think. I haven't talked to your dad since this morning. She had the surgery yesterday."

Silence again, though it looked like her demeanor had lightened.

"Zeke was hoping you might reach out. Maybe wish your mom well."

Jen set down the remote, looked at Nicky, then looked back at Jason and pointed to the kitchen. She got up and stepped past him. With the clink of ice, he finished his drink and followed.

She was leaning against the island with arms crossed as he made a slow approach.

"You know, cancer doesn't get rid of all the shit they did." Each word hissed and spit like steam.

"I know."

"And it sure as hell doesn't make up for all the things they *didn't* do."

"I agree."

Jen squinted an eye and leaned into him. "Do you? Do you, Jason? Then why are we talking about this right now? Obviously you think I'm in the wrong."

Just like that, he lost her. She's pushed him into Zeke and Dee's corner and now he had to play defense to her offense. Exactly what he had feared. "For chrissake, of course I don't. Did you not want me to tell you about your mom? Should I have kept quiet?"

Hands to hips. "You could not take his goddamn calls, that's for sure."

He put up his hands. "Listen, I know things were rough—"

"*No.* You don't. What you have is the vaguest notion based on the little I've shared with you. You aren't the first person to think I've overreacted. I get shit all the time from Uncle Will and Aunt Sal. Even from Seth. Jesus, I swear to God, people seem to think as long as you aren't sexually assaulted or beaten bloody, you grew up with Mike and Carol Brady. Do you want to know what it was like, Jason? To be locked away by two drunks? Not trusted for anything, barely allowed to go anywhere or do anything while your own brother got to do whatever he wanted?

Meanwhile, you hope to be ignored because otherwise you'd be screamed at, put down, or pushed away."

He hated seeing her this agitated. He loathed being the cause of it. She was right, he couldn't understand. All he knew was that two terribly flawed people who were full of regret and shadowed by their twilight years wanted a chance to make amends. And they were hefting all their rueful desperation on him.

Jen really had long ago given them a chance to make amends. Against almost every fiber of her being, she conceded to Jason's pleas when they first got engaged to give it a chance. He hadn't understood how deep and wide the rift spanned between Jen and her parents. He thought he and their marriage could be what drew daughter and parents back together.

But Zeke was still Zeke and Dee was still Dee. As much as they poured affection on Jason and Jen and lavished them with the meager gifts her parents could afford and treated him and his soon-to-be wife to whatever small indulgences they could manage, Zeke was still a bitter, bigoted man and Dee was still a detached woman.

Neither had given Jen the apology she came there expecting to receive.

To Jen, her parents were two people who had taken away her childhood, her young girl dreams, and her right to cherished memories. More than that—to Jason's mind—they had taken away her willingness to rely on and trust others.

As the oldest and the daughter, Jen took the brunt of their paranoia and neglect. Her younger brother Seth faired a small amount better, though he was just as happy and quick to leave as soon as he could. Seth's reconnection with their parents, however infrequent it might be, continually aggravated Jen, and often became a triggering topic in their conversations. Seth learned to keep their parents out of any casual discussions as much as possible.

Initially, Jason was more than happy to support Jen's wish to cut off her parents. He certainly hadn't been comfortable around them. He had done his part—tried to mend the family tree—and it didn't work. He contacted them to let them know they were grandparents. Obligation over.

But the arrival of Nicky into their world, and having Jason's parents, the only grandparents his son might have known, dying so close together before Nicky could know them, drew Jason back to Zeke and Dee. Their continual messages to him asking about Nicholas, sending gifts every birthday and Christmas, while respecting the distance Jen wanted to keep, began to wear on Jason—

—and, over time, it was what put him in this kitchen now to torment his wife with a past she wanted to erase.

She stood straight, shoulders back. "I do not want to see those people. I do not want to hear about them."

He nodded to her.

"And it hurts me deeply when you try to make me."

Jason put out his arms. He hoped, he prayed, she would accept them.

Slowly, hesitantly, she did, stepping into his arms so he could wrap her in a tight apology.

"I'm so sorry. I'm so sorry," he said, and tears welled up in his eyes.

That was one more thing he knew her parents had taken away from her—her tears.

CHAPTER SEVEN
Saturday, November 16, 2019

Mid-morning and there was activity down the street at the Polnzy residence. That would have been unusual even when Agnes had been around, but it was even more curious after two weeks of the house being darkly silent and sealed tight as a mausoleum.

Jason and Jen were bundled in winter jackets and thick wool stocking caps while the Witch of November blew her dirge to coming winter. Jen trimmed down the wilted day lilies to two inches of nub in the landscaping that hugged the front of the house. Nicholas stood beside her in flapped cap, bulky coat and Spider-Man mittens, holding out a garbage bag for his mother to stuff the dead leaves into. Jason tossed frequent quick glances at him from the driveway to make sure all remained calm and well and normal.

That first night after "the incident"—how Jen referred to that fateful Sunday after Halloween—Nicholas was more quiet than his usual quiet self, but otherwise appeared fine. That, however, did not last.

Monday night after the argument with Jen over her parents, they put Nicky to bed. Twenty minutes later, while they watched a Netflix show they snuck in during their few moments of evening adulting, Jason turned his head. There in the hallway stood his boy, statue-still, his stare cast in their direction yet falling somewhere else.

"Everything okay there, pal?" He grabbed the remote and paused the show.

Nicholas, staring, arms limp at his sides.

"Honey? Are you all right?" Concern wound Jen's voice tight.

"Nix?" Jason rose from the couch as worry backed up into his throat.

They approached him, knelt down close to eye level. Jen folded a hand over Nicky's shoulder and around his midriff. "Honey? Do you need something?"

A slow shake of Nicholas's head had been his only response. His son's gaze passed through them. Jason had been desperate to crack that concrete stare and disrupt that vacancy before it swallowed his son completely.

Jason sprung up and lifted Nicky to his chest, snuggled him against his shoulder and held him tight. "Come on, Nix. Let's get you back to bed." He headed toward Nicholas's bedroom.

When they reached the threshold of his son's room, Nicholas became a sudden torment of raw energy in Jason's arms, screaming and writhing and wailing. Jason had barely been able to set the boy down. Jen swooped in to hug and stroke him as she kept asking, "Baby, baby, what's wrong, what's wrong, baby? Mommy's here."

They stayed like that in the hallway for long minutes, Jen consoling and mothering and Jason standing to the side in befuddled helplessness. That moment had ended with Jen's narrow, damp eyes piercing his wide ones as she hissed, *"You make that call tomorrow."*

Tuesday morning, 8:01 a.m., Jason on the phone with the therapist scheduling an appointment for her next availability. Nicholas spent the rest of the week out of school while Jen worked from home. Each night, he nestled between them in their bed. The following Monday, Jen brought Nicholas in for his first day of therapy.

Nicholas had become like sweating dynamite. Quiet and passive until a jostle of his routine or a bump in his play, and then—boom. Each eruption from that small and volatile body blew Jason and Jen a little farther apart.

Now, on a cold Saturday almost two weeks past "the incident," Jason ran the garden hoses down the sloping driveway. They bled out H2O into the gutter. He gave each hose a hardy blow, his wind-burned cheeks flaring as the last of the water spat out their ends like an old man's phlegmy hacking coughs.

When his attention wasn't tugged in the direction of Nicky, it was pulled in the opposite direction, his eyes drawn to a beat-up black F-150 in Agnes's driveway. A dull dirty-white and gold-flowered couch—Agnes's couch—was stuffed into the truck bed and hung over a crimped and dented tailgate. Piled on and around the couch were a table, chairs, boxes and miscellaneous items.

Two men had carried the sofa and table out earlier. Since then, they made frequent trips back and forth between house and truck. The two men's dour intensity as they hustled to clear out what they could from the house gave off a suspicious air, but the flattened nose, heavy brow and slicked-back dark hair of the one in the leather jacket made Jason wonder if he was watching Greg Polnzy, the estranged son of Agnes and Moe.

Before he knew exactly what he was doing or why, he dropped the end of the garden hose he had started to carefully coil and began a slow stroll down the street toward the Polnzy house.

As he walked past Glen's place, he caught a glimpse of Glen looking out his picture window at the commotion at Agnes's place. Glen's eyes shifted to Jason and he gave a minimal wave. Jason raised a hand back and kept his steady pace.

He reached the end of Agnes's driveway just as the older leather-bound guy he thought might be Greg—followed by his younger partner in the hunter's hat and navy blue peacoat—pushed out of the front door. They each had one end of a curio cabinet in hand. They fast-stepped down the front stairs to the sidewalk that led to the driveway as Jason looked on with hands in pockets. They wore the stern gazes and brisk motions of wanting to be in and out quick. Neither shared more than single-word commands with each other to "lift," "turn," "swing," or "drop."

The two men hoisted the curio into the truck bed and tried to position it across the couch while spitting out a few expletives. The one in the navy coat hopped up on the back bumper and swung a leg over the tailgate. Jason's attention drifted to the front of the house where he could see the wooden screen door swinging open in the breeze.

"Help you?"

Jason startled to the words, jerking his attention away from the door. The question came from the one he thought was Greg, standing beside the truck with bated hands hovering near the curio.

"Oh, ah, sorry." He took a step back while he nodded and smiled too big and wide.

Peacoat Guy, still in the back of the truck, stared at Jason. He no longer had hands around the curio and instead kept to a kind of pounce, watching and appraising.

"Sorry about that," Jason said again. "Uh, you—you're, um, Agnes's son, right? Greg?"

The man started a slow walk toward Jason, arms gradually finding rest at his side. "Who are you?" Cautious. Apprehensive. A bit of underlying threat behind those small dark eyes set into a weathered, deeply-lined face.

"Oh, yeah, um," Jason pointed toward his house. "Jason Lahey. Live right down the block." He put out his hand as Greg came almost within arm's length.

Greg stared at Jason's hand. "Okay."

Jason held his hand out a few seconds more, then withdrew it. "I'm the one that found her. Found your mother. Agnes."

"Huh." He drew the back of his hand across his nose, slow, and wiped it on his thigh.

"Just wanted to give my condolences. Very sorry for your loss."

"Yeah, huh."

"Yes."

Greg stared at Jason. Jason held his ground, eyes locked while his stomach turned over and his chest coursed with the electricity of fight or flight.

Greg finally released his grappling gaze. "Appreciate it, mister—"

"Jason—"

The crack of a smile crimped a corner of Greg's mouth. He leaned in slightly. "Jason." Said with slow exaggeration. "Now, if you'll excuse me. I'm just trying to take care of the shithole my dear mother left for us to clean out. And I need to be fast about it before my bitch of a sister comes in and tries to clean me out of any of this junk that might be worth something."

Jason stared.

Greg gestured back to the truck and the house. "So, if you don't mind?"

Jason nodded slow and waved a hand in the direction of the house. He was beyond processing this moment—overcome with revulsion and rage and fear and intimidation. He took cautious steps backwards as Greg returned to the truck and to the business at hand. Jason turned and started a brisk walk back to the sanctuary of his home.

From the living room window, he watched the Polnzy residence while sipping a beer. Greg and his cohort finished before noon after tossing two end tables and a coffee table on top of the other furniture. The pickup truck drove off, leaving a plume of black smoke that lingered over Agnes Polnzy's driveway.

The old house sat silent, the slow swing of the screen door the only movement—a stunned victim after an assault.

Not right. Nothing about that felt right.

And it definitely didn't feel right to leave that house naked and bleeding. Watching that door swing free in the breeze like a wounded arm reaching out, he finished his beer, went back outside and headed for the Polnzy home.

As he neared Agnes's house, that swinging door and its motion became more like an ominous provocation. He was transported back to that Sunday afternoon after Halloween and what had waited for him—and Nicholas—inside.

His breathing tight and his steps slow, he moved up the driveway, onto the sidewalk and up the steps to the porch. The neighborhood rested quiet and still in the cold, gray day. The only sound was the whine of the screen door against rusty hinges, its broken spring hanging like a cut and retracted tendon on the lower half of the frame.

The sturdy wooden entry door hung wide open. Where the door jamb once existed, a large piece of wood hung, split and torn away from the deadbolt notch.

So there it was. Greg had forced entry—kicked the door

in, which split the old wood framing. Jason took a cautious step inside.

His mouth opened and larynx clamped shut before the impulse to call out to Mrs. Polnzy. All this was far too familiar. He choked on this reenactment of that day. The difference, however, was the amount of debris and ruin scattered about the floor.

Dead leaves rustled in the entryway and crunched underfoot as Jason stepped into the living room. All around him was the scattered junk from emptied-out drawers and cabinets and items flung from the countertops to clutter the floor. Pages of file papers and emptied drawers of pens and rubber bands, scissors and penlights and staplers, and little pads of pink and yellow Post-It notes. Dishes, utensils and more covered areas of the kitchen. Greg and his buddy had rampaged the place, dumping out anything they didn't want, anything not of value or in the way. The disarray felt as dispassionate as it was destructive.

Jason moved into the living room, his stomach flip-flopping as he recalled his last time here. A pictoral gardening book lay open on the ground next to Elvis and Johnny Cash CDs along with a few *Home and Garden* and *Amac* magazines. Broken ceramic birds lay in the far corner of the room where the carpeting remembered the weight of that curio cabinet.

As he came around the corner, his heart beat hard and fast and his breathing came in short, hard gasps. That old wooden kitchen chair sat right in the middle of the space, amid the ruin. It all rushed back. The leg extended, the hand suspended. Her naked, purpling thighs spread. The loll of her bagged and taped head.

He closed his eyes, felt his throat spasm, but he swallowed and concentrated on his breathing. He forced those images out of his mind.

He could feel Agnes's bitter presence in this room. Scorn

for Greg's violent entry, offense at Jason's intrusion, and shame for how her life had ended up. The residue of Agnes laid like a thick coat of dust upon every inch of what remained.

All about the chair and throughout the room, letters and postcards, notes and statements littered the floor. Fighting the resistance of Agnes's spirit, Jason reached down and grabbed a lone photo album that sat splayed open on the floor.

Old pictures, yellowed and crisp and held to the thick paper pages by glued photo corners. A young Moe and Agnes, standing straight and emotionless as they stared into the camera, a field behind them that spanned several acres, ending at a distant border of trees. He hastily turned pages. Agnes holding a baby with pink bow clipped to wispy blonde hair while a three-year-old boy with dark, sunken eyes stared morosely at Agnes. There were scenes of Greg about Nicholas's age, sitting and smiling a big and devilish smile as he locked his arm around his younger sister whose eyes looked puffy and near tears.

Each page, Jason looked for the suggestion of good memories, but the thin photo album presented few possibilities. He turned toward the end, to one of the last pictures in the book. Greg, around fifteen or sixteen, holding a crappie the length of his forearm by a fishing line. His eyes were as cold and flat as the fish and his impatient sideways lean suggested he had been told to pose, but wanted to be anywhere else. He held up the fresh catch like a middle finger.

After that, blank page after blank page.

Until he turned to find some scribbled words scratched out in pencil that ran down an otherwise blank page. A wave of fear clogged his windpipe, a paralyzing panic as if he walked straight into the path of a snarling wolf.

With stomach almost filling his mouth and muscles vibrating with anxious energy, he quickly ran out of the house, closing both doors as best he could behind him. The photo album and bleak memories of the Polnzy family squeezed tightly against his pounding chest.

He slipped quickly and quietly into his study and closed the door. He opened the album to the back and stared at the words he was certain Agnes had written, over and over again, on the page. They were written in such a way—in three pieces, in specific fashion—that forced the recollection of what he had, over time, relegated to the confusion of an alcohol-clouded evening before Halloween. He mouthed the words that repeated over and over down the page, afraid to speak them:

Everything was gray and still in the quiet neighborhood. Even time did not tick, but clung to him like soot.

He was on the street, in his neighborhood, but it didn't feel like home, like any place he could orient himself to. In fact, he didn't even know where his home was—where Jen was. But he saw Nicky down the street, wobbling on his bike, so he headed toward his son.

You're doing good, Nix, he called out. Now turn around and come on back.

Nicholas kept going, down the road and out of the neighborhood, front wheel jerked back and forth by the twitching of his death grip on the handlebars.

Nicky! He tried to shout but the space around him sucked the volume out of his voice. Nicholas! A hoarse gasp of sound lost to the thick, stagnant air.

He tried to run, but it felt like trudging through sludge, wading through water. Nicky rode farther and farther away, toward the main road. Jason began to panic.

And then he was facing Agnes Polnzy's house from curb-side, beyond her driveway at the edge of the Petersons' property. A darkness surrounded her home, a shadow cast from above as if from some unseen foreboding mass.

Agnes stood on her stoop in her nightgown. She was looking at him. No, looking beside him and pointing, bony finger aimed just beyond him, in the direction of Sam and Delilah Petersons' house. He turned to see their Frankenstein's monster lurching toward him, its green, rubbery face expressionless, lifeless. Pure terror swelled his chest. He slogged away from the looming figure, trying to run and instead barely keeping ahead of the encroaching menace that stepped stiffly in its big black boots.

He couldn't find his home, couldn't see it. His vision wouldn't focus and make sense of anything around him. Where was Nicholas? Where was Jen? Where was his home?

The monster gained on him. He could feel its mass behind him, so close, as if it could reach out and grab him by the shoulder. He turned his head and looked over his shoulder.

The creature was gone. The street was empty. Nothing moved behind him. He turned and looked ahead again.

Agnes stood before him, plastic shopping bag over her head, Shop n' Save logo sucking in and out with corpse breath, duct tape tight around her neck—

Jason jerked awake, gasping breath with gaping mouth. Had he yelled out? His guts pushed up into his chest with primal fear.

Jen faced away from him on her side, still asleep. He must not have made a sound.

With heavy breaths, he laid there and stared up at the ceiling. He tried to close his eyes but saw Polnzy, faceless, in front of him. He looked at the clock. 11:58 p.m. He'd only been in bed for two hours.

Absolutely no way he could stay in that bed. He felt watched.

Hunted. He had to move.

Covers tossed back, he swung his legs over the side. Naked except for his briefs, he went to the bathroom and slipped on his robe. Out into the hallway, he headed for Nicholas's room.

Nicky had just started sleeping alone again. Two weeks had passed. Three sessions with the therapist seemed to calm the nightmares and terror of being alone in the dark of his room. Jen said the therapist was using what she called "play therapy" with him. As long as it could get his emotions under control, Jason fully supported it. He had tried talking to Nicky about how he's feeling, but at best Nicky replied with a vacant stare, or at worst with aggressive avoidance.

His son slept soundly in his bed, his tiny nasal snore barely audible, but always a reassurance to listen for. Nicholas looked so vulnerable, little fist curled under his chin—a fist that less than six years ago would have had its thumb jammed into his mouth.

Jason's eyes darted to the window, almost expecting Polnzy, head covered by her recycled plastic death mask as her vacant eyes leered at Nicholas through semi-transparent plastic.

Jason moved quietly into the room and sat down on the small wooden chair in the corner. He watched over his son, watched as a guardian against what, Jason realized, was haunting them both.

CHAPTER EIGHT
Sunday, November 17, 2019

He had his morning coffee in the sunroom overlooking the "back forty," which actually comprised less than a half-acre of backyard until the pines, oak and birch took over on the yet unsullied land beyond their little crop of Fairview Lane neighborhood. In his wicker rocker, the thick atmosphere of last night's dream still hung about him. He had been quiet since he first woke up. That seemed to suit Jen's mood fine, as she made little attempt to start any conversation. This, to Jason, wasn't a red flag. It was years of being together and both of them recognizing they were laden with thoughts and lacking in words.

He often looked with pride out at the back landscaping around the stamped and stained concrete patio, the fire pit inset and ringed by large river stones. The gazebo sat farther back against the line of pines that bordered the property and offered shade until early afternoon. Between patio and gazebo, their tiered fountain had, until a month ago, babbled and chattered its faux stream across a wide stretch of their property. The design and layout were all his and Jen's. They hired crews to lay the patio and build the gazebo, but he and Jen did all the grunt work of reseeding the lawn where the heavy equipment had torn it all up and installed all the landscaping between house and patio and on the outer edges of deep-patterned concrete. It was hard damn work, but so worth it to see it finished and be able to enjoy it.

It took extra effort to not take it for granted this morning Or maybe more to the point, to find any joy from basking in the fruits of their labor.

He had to get out of this funk. It didn't make sense. This was his favorite time of the year, and he was overcome by a morose cloud. There was no reason for it. He had a great job, he and his family were healthy, they had a wonderful home in a great neighborhood. Whatever issues Nicky faced were being dealt with. All was well. He should count his blessings.

And yet, the writing in the photo album bothered him. He was probably jumping to conclusions, but it reminded him so much of that surreal memory he still—disturbingly—could not completely convince himself had actually happened.

Face it, Jase. You really were drunk. There's so much you don't remember about that night. No way to know what did or didn't happen.

Actually, there was.

And he was going to put an end to the guessing.

He took a last gulp of coffee and got up to shower and get ready.

"Jase." Glen looked pressed and spiffy in a stiff-collared button-up plaid shirt and blue slacks creased to a razor's edge. "I was just heading off to church." He had a meaty hand against the edge of the front door held partly open—that polite way of saying, "I don't have much time" without any words.

"Oh, damn. Sorry, Glen. Wasn't thinking. Don't let me hold you up. I can catch you another time." Jason turned to go. He felt a little relief. It had been a silly idea to pull Glen into this. Better to walk away and not risk losing any of his favorite neighbor's respect.

"Hold up, now." Glen opened the door wider. "You need help with something?"

Jason waved Glen off. Now he truly regretted his impetuous idea to come here at all and craved a quick exit. "Nah. Nothing important. Don't worry about it."

The mid-morning air had a nip to it, but the sun was breaking though gray clouds and made glory rays that cast down upon the distant horizon. A shiver rippled through his shoulder muscles as Jason stared into that backdrop of divine radiance so far from where he stood upon Glen's stoop.

Scrutiny narrowed one eye and raised the other brow as Glen leaned his weight against the open door frame. "Why are you not convincing me?"

"No, no. Go. Go to church. On top of everything else, I don't need God on my bad side because I kept you from service." Jason watched Glen stand there, rigid, eyes steady on Jason.

Glen scratched at a rough cheek, shook his head, and stood straight. "Nothing's been feeling exactly right lately, and you being here—I can see it on your face, Jason. Something ain't right with you, and that means it ain't right with me. What do you need?"

Jason sighed. "I'm sorry."

"Don't be sorry, just tell me what you need."

He looked Glen up and down, winced a little, and looked back at his neighbor with an apologetic grin. "Actually, I think I need you to change your clothes."

Farmland and the clutter of old trees scrolled past as Jason drove with Glen down the rural route toward that out-of-the way country road he had been detoured on almost three weeks ago. His first sinking feeling was when he realized he didn't exactly remember how he got from there to his house. It had started with him taking a different way home since he came from the downtown bar instead of work.

But the construction had shot him down some obscure farm road. Somehow, after whatever happened or didn't happen, he next remembered being on Fairview and approaching his house, squinting to stop the double-vision that had given him two garages at the end of two driveways.

Jen was absolutely right. He shouldn't have been driving.

Glen cleared his throat. "So. You gonna share any more about what this is about? Or are you trying to build suspense?"

"Glen, I know it sounds like the stupidest response in the world, but I just need you to see something. To verify something for me."

"So you said."

"I'm not trying to be melodramatic."

He cracked a dry laugh. "Doing a lousy job there, Jase."

"I know."

Glen looked forward, exhaled and slapped his hands on his now denim-covered knees. "Well, how far are we going? You're not driving me to Kansas are you?"

Embarrassed, Jason shrugged. "I'm not totally sure. I mean, I'm almost positive I was spit off onto this road."

"Because of the detour—"

"Right. I was on Old Mill Road, hit a bunch of construction and was thrown onto a little southbound farm road. I was on it a long time."

"You got a map?"

"GPS?"

"No, for Chrissake, a map. Paper. You know? With all the lines on it that tells you where everything is?"

"Sorry. I happen to be from the twenty-first century."

Glen muttered under his breath. "Trying to think here. If you were thrown off Old Mill Road—"

"To the south—"

"Right. To the south. And then, at some point—"

"I'd say eight or ten miles—"

Glen looked skeptical. "That's a long stretch."

"There were no cross roads."

"Alright. So, I'm thinking that road you got detoured onto was double-Q. It runs arrow-straight due south off Old Mill Road. That means you probably got off it on 93rd Street."

"And where is that?"

Glen hooked a thumb behind him. "You just passed it."

"Shit." Jason gave a darting glance in the rearview, slowed the car and swung over to the shoulder. A quick look both ways, then a stomp on the gas to make a hard turn around, digging deep into the opposite shoulder as tires spun on gravel before grabbing onto blacktop. At 93rd, he turned right.

Glen asked, "This look familiar?"

Jason looked ahead and to each side. "No."

"Hmm."

"But it was dark."

"Ayuh."

Jason kept on 93rd Street where open fields spread out, a few old two-story farm houses set way back and against dilapidated barns with sagging roofs.

"Here comes double-Q," Glen said, motioning ahead.

Jason slowed the Lexus, turned on his blinker and made a right turn onto the road. Occasional driveways led to aging ranch-style and colonial homes. Ancient oak and walnut trees stretched gnarly bare branches wide and to the sky. No farmland here. Just fields of cows and horses and the occasional copse of trees.

"This isn't it." Jason shook his head and looked around.

"You sure?"

"Yeah. Not it."

Glen thought for a moment. "Well, keep going. You'll connect with Old Mill Road in a few miles. We can find that construction and the detour and retrace your route."

Jason nodded.

"Sure am curious about what's got your knickers knackered."

Jason scoffed. "What?"

"One of Maude's sayings," Glen said as he gave a weak grin and looked out the side window.

"Sorry about this, Glen. I feel I'm wasting your time."

"Bah. Don't worry yourself. I've been wanting a chance to get in this Lexus." He looked back with a little grin. "Besides, don't tell God, but I wasn't exactly in the right mood to pay him a visit today anyway."

That was new. Glen didn't miss church too often, especially to head out blindly on some fool's errand. Jason had never heard him speak about his faith, had never had a conversation with Glen about it, but his neighbor had certainly been regular in demonstrating it.

"You don't miss often, do you?"

"Rarely. Don't want Maude coming back to haunt me."

"I can believe that." Jason smiled. "But, um, you believe, right?"

"Eh." Glen shrugged. "Maude did, that's for sure. Every ounce of her a Catholic. Me? I suppose I'm more like—a subscriber. I buy into the sentiment of it, the ritual and the community. And the music. I really like that contemporary church music. But believe? Can't honestly say one way or the other."

He had certainly never thought of Glen as some kind of bible-thumper. Still, hearing Glen talk about his beliefs made him wonder if he had misunderstood Glen up to this point. "More an agnostic, then?"

"Maybe. Don't really know the definition of that. I suppose I care about God about as much as He seems to about me." He rolled his shoulders again, more conclusively. "I don't muck about too much in the words of that book. There's good sentiment about it. Humility. Mercy. Duty. Honor. Dig too deep in those pages, though, it seems to start messing with people's sensibilities. Maybe even their decency. I'll keep to the Cliff's Notes. I suppose that's kind of what Mass is for me."

Jason never put much thought into his beliefs, but now he felt more in the dark about things he never thought needed further evaluation. He had no wish to put a name to those things, and now wasn't the time to pick them apart with philosophical, theoretical or spiritual utensils.

"Here comes Old Mill," Glen said.

Jason stopped the car at the four-way intersection and looked left and right. "I think the road construction has to be back west. We should hit it from the other side of where I came from."

"May be." Glen nodded.

Jason turned left and headed west up Old Mill Road which should run them into the other side of the road construction that had put him off course all those nights ago.

Another five minutes driving at a steady fifty miles an hour down the two-lane road. After crossing a bridge over railroad tracks, the landscape turned residential. A few more blocks and he came upon the streetlights at First Avenue on the outskirts of downtown. Nothing felt right about this.

"What the hell?"

"That construction. You're sure it was back there?"

"The whole road was torn up."

Glen turned his head back to where they had come. "No part of that road looked like it has been touched."

"I don't get it." He backed up, swung around, and took the Lexus back east down Old Mill Road. His foot sat heavy on the gas pedal as he reenacted his drive that night and headed down the same road in the same direction.

"Maybe they weren't working on the road. Maybe they were laying sewer or cable along the shoulder. It was dark."

"Maybe. I don't know."

Glen pointed ahead to his side of the road. "Hold 'er up. What about County P?"

Jason leaned into the steering wheel, looked ahead and to the right with strained intensity. "That's not what I turned on."

"You're sure about that. It was dark, and you said—"

"I am. And I did. But that wasn't it. I'm certain." Jason's eyes were transfixed ahead. He was close. It was right around here somewhere. He was as certain as he could be about such an uncertain night.

Ahead, he could suddenly picture it. A vision of the orange and white barricades across the road, the heavy machinery, the big detour sign pointing to—what? As he drove closer, nothing appeared to the right.

Wrong. Barely visible amid the scrub brush and trees lining the shoulder, an opening he swore had not been there when coming from the other direction. "That's it!"

He braked hard and turned the wheel sharp to the right.

"Ho!" Glen's hand slapped against the car roof.

The tires gave a small squawk and turned up some gravel as he swung into what became a narrow road with little shoulder, sitting high amid deep ravines on either side. It ran as far as Jason could see, due south.

"Sorry, but this is it. This was the detour."

Glen looked confused and swung his head around him. "I didn't even see this. Thought you were taking us off the road. What road is this?"

Jason kept his eyes straight ahead. "No idea." He pressed a button on the dash and pointed to the screen displaying the GPS. The arrow moved away from Old Mill Road and across a blank screen.

"I'm getting this real off-the-map feel right now," Glen said.

Jason nodded slow as he panned his gaze across acre after acre of barren fields. No farms, no structures, no signs of life. Just a road that kept going, rising and falling in hills and valleys, that cut right through the center of nothing.

Daytime should have set Jason at ease, somehow disarmed the ominous emanation of this area, but his vision darkened with memory. He caught the whiff of that night, a scent on the air. A mingling of manure and moist soil. Tempered fears returned, a knifepoint to the back, and he was forced to focus on the task to find something he did not want to find. An aberration that had intruded upon a calm, peaceful, perfect life.

Glen slipped a cigar out of the breast pocket of his flannel shirt, rolled it between his crinkled, thin lips. "Here, there be monsters."

The rise of the hill looked all too familiar, the embankment a marked memory. He pulled the car over as far on the narrow shoulder as he could. A heaviness in his lungs told him it was there in the distance. Looming. He looked but saw nothing other than a sky where the sun drew the cover of clouds over its face. A shadow seeped across the field, spreading toward them.

"This the place, huh?" Glen looked at him from the passenger seat.

"Definitely." Push of starter button and the car went quiet and still. "Up for a stroll?"

"Boy howdy."

Clunk of car doors hit the far-off hillsides and the sound came back dead and cold. Jason stepped down the steep slope and looked up to Glen. "You got this okay?"

Glen started to sidestep his way down. "Don't you worry about me."

Jason put his hand out against Glen's shoulder anyway to brace his neighbor for his final steps down. Together, they climbed the steep embankment toward the field. Jason gave Glen his hand and hoisted him up the last wide step.

Glen looked about him briefly. He put his hands before his face and clicked a lighter, cupped an amber flame and puffed until his cigar tip glowed.

Jason looked ahead, beyond the barbed wire fence, and tried to spot anything other than field and sky. Far from them, he saw a smudge of dark standing upright against the churn of cloudy gray day.

"Do you see that?" He pointed.

Glen strained as he peered ahead. "Maybe?" He used a hand to visor his eyes from the hazy glare of cloud-filtered light. "I think I—" Took his hand away and shook his head. "Nope."

"Dead ahead?"

"Naw. Thought I might have, but no. Eyes aren't too good, though."

Jason ducked and snuck through the barbed fence, then put his foot down on the lower wire and pulled up on the top wire. "You okay with taking a hike?"

Glen looked at the barbed hole, grunted and bent down to work his way through.

Jason headed for where he had seen that obscure shadow— where now just a gray horizon loomed across the barren, muddy expanse of earth-churned field. They walked for a minute. Whatever he thought he saw, there was nothing now.

Glen stopped and turned to Jason. "I've been pretty neighborly up to this point. Patient as a saint, yeah? But now I think it's time you tell me what's got your ghost." He sucked on his cigar and blew out a cloud as he looked across the field. "What're we doing here, Jase?"

He wondered the same thing. He desperately wanted to find an answer to a question he didn't fully understand. The murky memory of that late October night followed him like the stench of something he stepped in.

Looking all around him gave no answers. "I'm not sure if it was a dream, Glen, but real or not, it took place right *here*." He sloshed ahead a few steps further down the field. "And right out *there*, I found something. Something—old. Something—unnatural. And I think Agnes found it, too. I think she found it right before she killed herself."

Glen yanked the cigar out of his mouth. "Christ almighty, would you just tell me? What the hell was it?"

A swallow and a breath. "It was some kind of, I don't know— like a slot machine, okay? Old. Antique. Had a crank handle."

"What? Out here?"

Jason nodded, anxious but relieved to have finally shared that bizarre moment, real or dream, with someone.

"Like a casino slot machine?"

"No no no. Not at all. This was—It gave a message. It told me something."

"It spoke?"

"No. Printed words. In three little windows. When I turned the crank."

"What did it say?"

Jason opened his mouth to answer, but the words wouldn't come out. He couldn't say them. They were like an obscenity. A perversion. His revulsion kept those five words locked inside of him.

"Forget it. This is ridiculous. I was ridiculous. I just need to get home." Jason had enough. His foolishness had reached the point of brimming over. He shook his head.

"Jase, I—"

Jason put up a hand and cut Glen off.

They trudged silently back to the fence. Jason slipped through the barbed wire and made a wide clearance for Glen. Stumble-stepping down the embankment and up the other side to the shoulder, Glen took Jason's hand and help. Jason tried to look Glen in the eye, but his gaze slipped and fell toward the ground.

"Hey. Jase. Look at me." Glen puffed on his cigar. "I get it. You're shook up over this. Real or not, I get it. But let's face it. There's nothing out there now. As far as you know, some farmer was just moving it to a shed or to the garbage and only made it halfway there that night. I don't know why you think it means anything, but don't obsess over it, huh? Don't let it overwhelm you. You're just messed up over Agnes and your son."

Jason nodded passively, but not with any agreement.

"Let's get back, have a beer, and be sensible about this, huh? We'll talk it out."

"Sure. You're right." Jason opened the door and started to get in, but stopped and met Glen's eyes over the hood of the car. "But I'm telling you. I can feel it. Something is coming. Or has already come. Glen, I swear to God, I feel it like a chill up my back."

CHAPTER NINE
Monday, November 18, 2019

The clock on the wall displayed 3:20 p.m. and Jason sat in silence next to Jen in the waiting room of the Marathon County Child and Adolescent Therapy Clinic. Although warmly subdued, there were elements of lively color in the pictures on the wall and in the small play center that had activity tables, a chalkboard against the wall, and colorful puzzle-shaped rubber playmats.

On the TV screen, a slideshow ran of children from two- to twelve-years-old—some happy and smiling, others ponderous. Between those images, slides called out various modalities of treatment: play therapy, cognitive behavioral therapy, dialectical behavior therapy, psychodynamic psychotherapy, trauma-focused behavioral therapy, art therapy, and more. To Jason, they sounded at one extreme frivolous, and at the other, intrusive and menacing. More than anything, it was all foreign to him.

It had been a text from Jen he received around quarter to

three that put him in this waiting room. He was just wrapping up a meeting at work and his phone buzzed with her words: CALL ME. With Jen's texts, all-caps didn't indicate excitement or shouting, it blared an intense imperative.

"The therapist wants to meet with us."

"When?" His computer screens tried to win his attention with bold, unread emails in his inbox and flashing Teams meeting discussions. On his desk, a notepad scribbled with a list of to-dos waiting to be crossed out.

"*Now*, Jason." Jen came off as aggressive, but Jason recognized the undercurrent that carried her emotions. She was worried, and that made him anxious.

"Uh—okay. Okay. Just let me stomp out a couple fires and I'll be there."

"Hurry."

"Wait!" He had no idea where this place was or what it was called. "Could you text me the address?"

He ended up throwing way too much responsibility on Troy, one of his direct reports he trusted to be smart and sensible when confronting a problem, if not always the best at reporting back on progress. As he headed out the door, he gave Brenda an FYI about putting Troy in charge and to text Jason should any emergency arise. He did it without stopping so he could dodge a narrative from Brenda on her latest crisis or tragedy.

And so he sat, as he had for the last ten minutes, waiting to see Nicholas's therapist, who had finished her fourth session with his son earlier today. Nicholas was back in school and Jen was going to pick him up in about an hour.

Jen was too on-edge to talk, other than the initial speculation on what the meeting could be about. She worried that Nicholas had additional issues and Jason countered that the therapist probably just wanted to fill them in on Nicky's progress so far.

He watched the screen filled with wide-eyed children

responding to the thoughtful gaze of a caring professional, and his thoughts drifted back to the road trip to nowhere yesterday with Glen. He couldn't not think about it, even though he wasn't able to come to any conclusion about what he should think about it, no matter how many times he ran the end of that journey through his head.

After they had come back from the field yesterday, Jason started to turn the car around when Glen told him to hold up. "Just for shits and giggles, keep going. I'm curious where this goes. I wanna see where you got off this road and back on track."

Jason shrugged and obliged him.

So he drove.

And he drove.

And paved road turned to gravel.

And gravel turned to ruts.

And ruts filled to grassy field.

They sat in silence for some time in the idling Lexus until finally, Glen murmured, "Take us home, Jase."

On the way back, he and Glen sat in a similar silence that he and Jen now experienced in the waiting room. Pensive and at a loss of words. When Jason and Glen returned to Fairview Lane, the neighborhood seemed smaller to Jason, more encroached upon by the trees and wild scrub that surrounded the edges of their tiny peninsula of civilization.

He passed on the offer of beer from Glen. Instead, he asked Glen if he had Thanksgiving plans. Glen's oldest son and daughter were going to be at their in-laws, and his youngest son and family were vacationing in Europe, so Jason invited Glen to their table for the holiday. Once home, Jason poured himself a rum and Coke, made something up to Jen about where he had been, and told her that Glen was coming to Thanksgiving. Fortunately, Jen didn't mind, even though they were hosting her brother Seth, his wife Rachel and their two kids.

"Mr. and Mrs. Lahey?"

A larger woman professionally but cordially dressed in skirt, blouse and blazer leaned in from the door beside the receptionist desk. She peered at them over her glasses that sat low on her round nose. Jason and Jen stood and approached.

"Mr. Lahey? I'm Leslie Walrick." She put out her hand and Jason shook it briefly. "It's good to finally meet you." She smiled at Jen. "Good to see you again, Jen." She extended a hand down the hall as she held the door open. "This way. Second door on the right."

The hallway continued the theme from the lobby—bright and lively pictures of children playing, smiling and laughing. Bubbly graphics of encouraging messages amid the subdued interior of a clinic. Ahead, through the glass of swinging double doors, Jason saw a larger room and could just make out colorful bins filled with blocks and toys, a white board with children's drawings, a tree painted on the far wall with every color of construction paper leaf stuck on the limbs, and words scrawled on them that he couldn't make out. Before he could see any more, they entered the office.

The therapist came in behind them and closed the door. It was a standard office with tall filing cabinets, bookshelves with row after row of books, a computer desk in the far corner, and a small round table with two chairs around it to their immediate right.

"Please. Have a seat." She motioned to the table.

Jason and Jen sat down as the therapist rolled her chair around her desk and up to the table. She locked eyes with both of them, a reassuring yet pressing stare as she smiled warmly.

"Thank you both for making time to see me."

"Of course," Jen said. "We're just glad to have someone helping Nicholas through this. We want to do whatever we can to support his therapy and be there for him the way he needs us to be."

"It's been wonderful to get to know Nicholas. He's a smart and special boy."

Jason caught on that word—*special*—and squirmed in his seat. He opened his mouth to say something but felt Jen's hand over his. She gave him a quick look. Apparently, he was already off to a poor start.

"Thank you, doctor," he said instead of his intended reply.

"You're very welcome. And for the record, I'm not a doctor. I'm Leslie." She winked at him, possibly catching his brow raising in surprise. "Don't worry, I'm a licensed therapist and fully certified as both a cognitive behavioral specialist and adolescent trauma-informed professional, among other qualifications."

Jen removed her hand from his and leaned forward, elbows to knees. She asked the very question Jason wanted to ask directly but felt too uneasy and defensive to utter. "Is everything okay with Nicholas?"

"That's what I wish to talk to you both about. Nothing that should worry you, but I would like to ask you some questions."

Jason looked at Jen as she looked back at him.

"Of course," Jen said as Jason nodded.

Leslie leaned in ever so slightly. "Would you say Nicholas is a talkative or communicative boy?"

"No," Jen said. "Not really. He's actually kind of quiet. He's very good at keeping himself occupied."

"Does he often bring things to you, to show you?" Leslie asked. "Has he shown curiosity about things you are doing?"

"Well sure," Jason spoke before he had really given the question any thought.

"Maybe?" Jen hesitated. "But—No. I suppose not really, when I think about it." Jen gave Jason a questioning look.

"I guess I actually can't think of any times off the top of my head," he said, "but I'm sure he must."

"What about routine?" she asked. "Does he tend to have a set routine day after day?"

Jason thought about Nicky, always home from school and in front of the TV to play the same couple of games. Then, done with that and over to his blocks, stacking them into the same buildings and rocket ships over and over. The puzzle of Buzz Lightyear zooming across the starry sky he's taken apart and put together too many times to count.

"You could say that," Jason said. He grew more concerned with each question. He could tell by her careful, calm expression that she was getting exactly the answers she expected.

Jen nodded. "Yes. I agree. He definitely sticks to his same activities."

Leslie the Therapist nodded in a very therapeutic way. "During those times, is it easy to get his attention?"

"Oh, no," Jen said. "You have to call out to him several times before he even acknowledges you. 'Nicholas Alexander, I'm talking to you!'" Her laugh fizzled to a sigh. "He gets lost in his own world sometimes."

Jason looked at the therapist, then to Jen. She wasn't picking up on what was happening here, how Leslie the Therapist was herding them to some conclusion.

"What are these questions about?" he asked.

"Just things I need to ask in order to properly assess your son. So, what about when his routine is disrupted?"

Jen blew out a big breath. "Oh, sometimes he can get downright angry. He'll have some whopper tantrums." She turned to Jason. "You remember that time when we couldn't find a sitter and had to take him with us to Sal and Rudy's place? He threw a fit and wouldn't settle down. We ended up having to cancel the evening."

The therapist looked intently at Jen, then at Jason. "Does Nicky make eye contact?"

"Yes? No? I don't—" Jason's arms were crossed now, and he knew exactly how that must appear. "Where are you going with this?"

Therapist Leslie uprighted herself and stiffened slightly. "I apologize, but these are important questions. The fact is, after spending several sessions with Nicholas, and now hearing your answers, I believe your son may be on the spectrum."

Jason watched Jen turn rigid, her mouth slack. She was processing this new information. Jason had nothing to process because he had no damn idea what that meant. "Spectrum? I don't understand."

Leslie hesitated just a moment. "I think we should test Nicholas to see if he is autistic."

Jen sucked in her breath.

The therapist continued quickly. "I know that may sound terrible, but please just take a moment for me to explain more. First of all, Nicholas is a smart, capable child who has every opportunity available to him. This is not a disease, and shouldn't be viewed as a disability. Those with autism simply have different ways of responding to stimuli. Not a bad or wrong way, but different. It can make it more challenging for them to learn, communicate, express emotion, or socialize. But with some help and guidance, Nicholas can truly thrive and be exceptional."

A tempest of conflicting thoughts brewed in his head and he looked for shelter from them. His son was defective. *This was bullshit psychobabble.* His son needed special care. *Pandering would only weaken him.* This changed everything. *This didn't mean anything.*

But mostly, his mind started to make connections. Nicky's often terse, short words of avoidance or frustration. His fluttering hands whenever he was excited or agitated. His obsession with playing the same games and doing the same puzzles. What else had he missed? Not known? In what ways had he possibly wrongly judged Nicholas as being too sensitive, too slow?

"Is there—treatment?" Jen's hesitant question sounded far more rational and grounded than anything storming in Jason's head.

Leslie the Therapist gave a pandering smile as if to say, you poor thing. "There is effective counseling that can offer Nicholas successful strategies to navigate the pathways of his individual emotions and unique cognitive abilities."

Jason had an urge to apply a successful strategy for navigating his fist into a wall and telling this woman where to stick her unique cognitive abilities. This was his son, not some clinical guinea pig.

"There is, however," she continued, "the added complication of addressing his trauma, which is likely being magnified by his emotional sensitivity due to being autistic. This is a challenge, as it is important to discover the most effective way to make a psychological and emotional connection with him. Once I can make that connection, I can begin to help him disarm the triggers to the trauma he is experiencing."

What a pile of fancy words adding up to exactly nothing. He looked at Jen and saw her rounded eyes and parted lips taking in the words like oxygen from a mask passed to a diver whose tank had emptied.

"How long?" Jason asked, and he realized the question came out course and jagged.

Therapist Leslie leaned back in her chair. "There's no precise timetable here, Mr. Lahey. Unfortunately, this isn't a cut to bandage or a bone to mend. But, Nicky is bright and responsive, and I would expect him to respond well during our sessions. Please keep in mind, however, that you both will be a key component to his success and his ability to overcome the traumatic experience. I have some material for you to read with links to online parental toolkits and resources. I think it will help you…"

She droned on and he lost focus on her words. He was sitting in a room with some professional telling him his son was broken and needed fixing with a wife willing to believe anything in order to put straight whatever had gone askew in her world. Meanwhile, Jason never felt so protective of his son and so compelled to keep everyone and everything the hell away from his boy.

This therapist wanted to open up Nicky's head and rewire his brain. Jen seemed to want Nicky rebooted like some glitchy computer.

All Jason could think to do, all he wanted to do, was go home, hold his son, squeeze him tight and shield him until this nightmare passed them by.

CHAPTER TEN
Thursday, November 21, 2019

Jen sat in her study in front of her computer, typing away in her Parents of Autistic Children Facebook group. Over the last three days, she dove headfirst into learning everything she could about raising an autistic child. She already scoured the pamphlets Leslie gave them and underlined key points. She surfed the online parental toolkits. She now kept a notebook to record Nicholas's outbursts and identifying triggers.

"Make sure you give him positive feedback when he's being good," she told him multiple times.

"Watch for things he's particularly sensitive to—sound, touch, light."

She was role-playing with Nicky, doing arts and crafts, storytelling, and something she called, "creative visualization."

Poor Nicky was being therapied to death.

Jason fixed another drink and sat down in his recliner in the living room. Nicky roosted on his knees, playing his video game.

Just like a normal kid.

But he's not normal. Jason had to keep reminding himself of that. And why would he want a normal son, anyway? Like Leslie said, his autism was not a disease, and Nix had every opportunity to be exceptional.

He watched his son body-steer his sports car around the inner city tracks of his racing game, sharp ridge of furrowed brow fixated on the screen. Long, skinny limbs on lean torso so similar to Jason at that age.

Nicky's sports car rocketed into a hairpin turn on an overpass and crashed through the concrete sidewall to sail through the air to a fiery doom.

"You were flying, Nix!" he said with a chuckle.

Nicky tossed the remote and shut off the game console with deliberate motion, as if he were clocking out after a ten-hour shift at the factory.

"Hey, how about a game of checkers?" Jason finished his drink and stood.

Nicky grabbed the new Iron Man puzzle they had recently picked up for him and dumped the pieces out.

Jason knelt down closer to Nicky. "Come on. One game with the old man?"

Nicky shrugged, eyes locked on the pieces as he flipped them over and moved them around.

Jason stood, went over to the bookcase and grabbed the checkers box. He brought it back to Nicky, crouched down and unfolded the red- and black-checkered board. He dumped out the plastic checkers and set them up on the board. "You want to be red, pal?"

Nicky fit puzzle pieces together to make Iron Man's metallic face mask and gave a slight nod.

Jason slid a black checker forward. "Coming to get ya, Nix."

Nicky glanced at the board and pushed a red checker forward, then added another piece to Iron Man's armor while he bobbed up and down, piston to an engine of thoughts revving at idle.

"Bold move, my boy. Bold. But watch out, the old man is coming for you."

Each move Jason made, Nicholas distractedly followed suit, hand flittering with anxious motion. After four rounds, Jason saw his opportunity.

"Boom, boom, boom and boom! How's that? You see that? King me, baby!"

Nicky swiveled his head to the game, followed the path of his lost pieces, and with one sweep of his hand he wiped all the checkers from the board.

"Hey! Nicholas!"

Nicky went back to his puzzle, where he had Iron Man's torso filled in, muscled metal arms straight back, armored hands thrusting energy as he soared through the white clouds of a blue sky.

Jason looked at the cleared board and the black and red checkers off to the side. "What the hell, kid? Trying to have fun with you. What's your problem?"

Nicky rocked as he studied red and gold puzzle pieces and moved them around, looking for matches to puzzle edges.

Nicky had often exhibited little moments like this, but ever since the incident after Halloween, they came more often and with less predictability. In the past, they dismissed it as irritability from being tired or hungry. They usually responded by putting him to bed or occasionally in a time out. Now, apparently, they were just supposed to take notes and apply the latest proven methods of behavioral therapy.

Jason sighed and started picking up the checkers game. "Fine. Game over, I guess." He folded up the board, dropped it in the box and scooped up the checkers. "I guess I win."

Nicky focused on his puzzle and tried to get a piece to fit below Iron Man's glowing chest. The rounded nub of the male end was a bit too fat and slightly askew of the female end of the piece he was trying to fit, but he wouldn't give up. He tried to push it into place with a stubborn thumb.

"Hey, buddy. That one won't go," Jason said and reached for the piece.

Nicky slapped repeatedly at Jason's hand and shouted, "No!" He began to rock intensely and hum in a low, wavering tone.

Jason put a hand over Nicky's shoulder. "Nix. Pal. Hey—" but Nicky pulled away from him.

"Damn it, settle down for Chrissake. What's wrong with you?"

"Jason."

Jen's voice from behind him. He turned to see her scowling from the hallway. He regretted the words out of his mouth the moment he said them. He was about to get an earful. All he had tried to do was get the kid out of his funk. Now he would be declared the bad guy. More and more that seemed to be happening.

He mussed Nicky's hair affectionately, but Nicky yanked his head away as if Jason were a pariah. Anger popped and flared like flame to gas. What was happening? Nicky could be temperamental, overly emotional, but he had started to show an active repulsion to Jason. As if he was afraid or bothered by his own father's presence. Over the last three weeks, he had slowly been losing his son, and it was killing him.

Jen walked into the kitchen. Jason grabbed his empty glass and followed.

"What are you doing?" Jen's volume kept low while her words pressed thin.

"I'm getting a drink." Jason mixed himself one on the rocks.

"I thought we were clear about Nicky."

He sat down at the kitchen table and sipped his drink. "We

are." He wasn't going to get drawn into a fight. He would be calm but direct. Not confrontational.

"Then why were you agitating him?"

He rolled his eyes, too late remembering he was trying to be calm and nonconfrontational.

"Jason, please—"

He put up a hand. "Sorry. Sorry. It's just— Christ, we can't walk on eggshells around him. He isn't fragile. But if we treat him like he is, sooner or later he will be."

Jen moved to the table and sat down, never breaking intense eye contact with him. "No no no. Hold on. You are walking back on what we had agreed upon: to follow Leslie's recommendations and support Nicky's therapy."

He took a swig and dropped his eyes, finding it hard, as usual, to confront Jen when she was taking control. "No agreement. I was told."

Jen moved in close to him, her icy blue eyes warming as she placed her hands over his. "Jason." Drawn out in a kind of pandering sympathy. "I realize this is hard, but you know as well as I do that the diagnosis fits with so many things we've identified from the start with Nicky. We just didn't know any better. On top of that, he experienced something unthinkable, something his autism is making him even more sensitive to."

"I know, I know." Jen feeding him all this made him feel like more of an idiot. He realized that he had forced himself on Nicky, dominated play in a game his son probably didn't want to play, and then tried to tell him how to do his puzzle. Exactly the opposite of what his therapist said he should be doing. Apparently, he was just a fuck-up.

"I'm not trying to be a bitch, Jason. But listen. I need your support on this. I'm running on empty here. I'm working twenty-five-plus hours a week, taking care of our house, getting Nicky to school, getting him to therapy, learning as much as I can about what the hell this autism is and spending every remaining moment doing the activities Leslie wants us doing with him."

Really. She wants to play that card?

"I'm sorry," he said. "I'd help more if I could, Jen, but I'm working sixty-plus hours a week to keep our house and pay the bills." Jason finished his drink and stood. Ice clinked in his glass as he started to make himself another.

"Jason." His name delivered like a jab across the face. "I'm not saying you need to do more. Just, please. Don't undo everything I'm working so hard to do to help our son. Okay? And, the fact is, this drinking of yours—"

"Christ—"

"Hey! Don't. I mean it. You know what it was like with my parents. I've been so damn tolerant up until now, but you are drinking a lot every night. What's going on? Where did that come from?"

He worked his ass off, he provided for his family in ways so many others could only dream of, and she was going to pounce on him for a few cocktails in the evening?

"Jen. Work has been particularly stressful, and if you haven't noticed, we're going through some shit at home. Please don't make me feel guilty for a having a couple cocktails."

She drew back, quiet for a moment. "Okay. But please, can you just pull back a bit? A couple drinks are fine. But Jason, you're having more than just a few."

"I'm fine."

"Great. Then, just try to be sensitive to Nicky's needs right now. Give him some latitude."

For almost eight years they seemed to do just fine raising their son. He had grown up a healthy, happy, smart kid in a good home. A great home. A home better than a lot of kids ever get. So he was quiet, a little withdrawn, a little obsessive. So was Jason as a kid. You want to call that being "on the spectrum?"

Fine. He didn't see why this had to turn their life upside down.

His son saw something shitty—something Jason wished to hell Nicky had never seen. He'll get over it. Just like Jason had gotten over it.

Maybe Jason was a jerk for thinking this way. He just wanted his family back. His life back.

"Jen, I'm here however you need me. Tell me what to do and I'll do it. Let's just get this family back on track, okay?"

"Okay." She stood, kissed him on the top of his head and walked into the living room. She sat next to Nicky, to coddle and comfort him.

He watched her fawn over their son as he finished his drink, then he went for one more. Just one more. The way things were going, he needed a little night cap.

Chapter Eleven
Thursday, November 28, 2019 - Thanksgiving

A thin residue of joy and magic still clung to Jason on Thanksgiving, perhaps for no other reason than it wedged itself between his two favorite holidays. But no, it did have its own flavor and smell, its own texture. Thanksgiving was, in some strange way, a mac and cheese holiday to him. A comfort food. Not a dish you had regularly, and not even one you usually preferred. But there was a time and place where it was the perfect food—eaten right from the very pot where the noodles had been boiled and stirred with cheese sauce. Likely, the powdery cheddar and rubbery noodles triggered more sense memory than any particular taste bud, just not one he could put his finger on. But it made him feel nostalgic and safe. Thanksgiving was a big heaping serving of mac and cheese right when he needed it.

He awoke slowly, blissfully in and out of consciousness on a morning undisturbed by an alarm clock. He moved up against the headboard, grabbed the remote from the night stand and switched on the TV. He kept the volume low and indexed through channels until he found the Macy's Thanksgiving Day Parade. By the forkful, he ate up the balloons and floats and savored the cheesy Broadway performances and the commentary right out of the pot of that television screen.

Jen rolled over on her side away from him. He stroked her hair a few times and rested his hand on her shoulder as he tried to regain the wonder and special emotions of the holiday. Jen slipped an arm out from under the covers, folded her hand over his and gave it a squeeze and a pat.

Thanksgiving was one of the few times his parents seemed to celebrate being a family. Most of his life, he remembered being more part of a group or club than being a member of a family. There was certainly support and encouragement, but not much outward affection. At Thanksgiving, though, his parents spent all day preparing the turkey, the stuffing and the side dishes. The table presence and their good spirits were an expression of love they otherwise rarely displayed. They shared the warmth of the holiday with Grandpa Joe and Grandma Beth when they were over, or with Uncle Mark and Aunt Theresa and cousins Ted and Tabitha when they visited.

By the time Jason was eleven years old, he realized his father—born and raised in Fortune Falls—was a foreigner. As a child, his thoughts weren't as efficient as they were now as an adult, but his thoughts and feelings over his father equated to the same thing. His father lived in their home, spoke their language, ate the food and shared the experiences of Jason and his mother, but there was always an odd sense that this man belonged somewhere else. The language of father and husband was a clumsy second tongue, and the dinner he came home late to was eaten with little regard to taste—simply jaw motion and distant eyes. It was something he noticed and was unable put to words about his father, but what, as an adult, he now believed was the emanation of some other life that clung to Edward Lahey like an unfamiliar smell.

The cool light inside Lahey's Hardware never seemed to fully penetrate the canopy of overhanging equipment, tools and materials in the tall, narrow aisles. There was none of the color or brightness or sound of an inviting store, little order to the arrangement of products and even less effort to presentation. Nothing to tantalize a patron's eyes. Just iron, steel and wood that hung with blunt weight or glinted with honed edges. His father acclimated to that world. He had that block of forehead, pickaxe nose and two-penny teeth. He spoke of metal and lumber, gauges and weights, business and trade—occasionally a perfunctory comment about family and home.

His father was almost always Ed in the store, sometimes Mr. Lahey, and Jason had started to think of him by that designation when he saw his father talking to his regular customers and laughing or swearing in a way Jason otherwise never heard him do. There's Ed, he thought when he walked in the hardware store to do chores during the summer. Ed's a good guy. I'd like to know him.

At sixteen, Jason became a part-time employee at Lahey's Hardware, and Ed became the boss, telling him what to do and who to help and what to stock. Then, how to handle the unsatisfied customers and speed up the slow, talkative customers, how to serve up custom chain lengths and sharpen mower blades. By seventeen, his father showed Jason how to make entries into the ledger, how to reconcile the till at night, and gave Jason the combination to the safe. Somewhere around that time, he almost got to like his father in the way he had only respected him from a distance before. Almost, because eventually, they returned home and reclaimed the roles neither of them seemed completely comfortable playing—the father and husband, and the son.

Through all of that, his mother was pleasantly oblivious, or complacently accepting, of what to Jason felt like a household of acquaintances. But then, his mother was wholly superficial. She spoke well and intelligently about everything insignificant— the chin hair on the checkout woman at the grocery store and the funny little man down the street who mowed his lawn in his bare feet. His father half-listened and rarely returned a word or a look, though always—at least within Jason's memory—wearing a half-smile on his face. His mother's topics swirled like the curl of black hair lacquered in place on each side of her face in cursive flourishes—the same curls found in her high school senior yearbook picture.

Jason remembered being older than he thought he should be when he learned his mother's name, but his father never called her by name. He never addressed her by any designation other than, occasionally, "Bean," a Gaelic word Jason much later learned means "woman." He doubted his memory, but he remembered being around ten when he answered the phone and a voice asked for Florence Lahey. His reply had been, "Who?"

She responded to any affection with humor or sarcasm, but otherwise avoided any direct contact unless out of utility—wiping snot from Jason's nose with a reluctant swipe of tissue or placing the manicured fingers of her hand on his shoulder or around the back of his neck when out in public. A seven-year-old Jason once tried to hold her hand at the grocery store and his mother pulled her hand away and laughed. "What are you after?" she had asked and pushed him forward.

Jason had no real memory of Ed Junior. Had he lived, Jason figured he would have called him Alex, or maybe Al, since he was christened Edward Alexander Lahey, Jr. He couldn't have imagined calling his brother, "Junior."

Alex was two years older than Jason. At age four, Alex caught pneumonia, lapsed into a coma and never recovered.

Jason had only a residual memory of the funeral, of his father's face twisted and wet as he hugged young Jason tightly against him. It was a rare memory of his father's embrace.

For several years after his death, Alex became an imaginary friend to Jason. He talked to Alex, played secret agent with him, shared his toys, showed him his drawings, and read his Little Golden Books to him. That became Jason's only surviving memory of Alex—as a ghostly brother.

Whenever his parents caught him talking to "Alex," they made it clear there was no Alex and he shouldn't make up things like that.

But on Christmas, there was a Santa, and at Halloween, there were vampires and werewolves, and at Easter there was an Easter Bunny.

And on Thanksgiving, there was family.

"Hey, handsome." Jen kissed him on the cheek and he leaned into it, turned and brushed her lips with his while he shoved his hand up the backside of a twenty-pound turkey.

"Morning, beautiful." He grabbed another handful of stuffing from the extra-large Tupperware bowl he inherited from his mother and shoved it inside the bird.

On the radio, some chef being interviewed told him all the things he should and shouldn't do for a perfect, safe Thanksgiving. She all but declared how he would murder his family if he stuffed the turkey. Forty years old and he has never experienced Thanksgiving without in-the-bird stuffing. Still breathing, still kicking. He grabbed more fistfuls of bread mixed with herbs and spices, sauteed onion, celery and garlic cloves, blended turkey heart, liver, neck meat and gizzards—moistened with the watery broth from the boiled giblets, some milk and a stick of butter. The fact was, not only was stuffing inside the bird twice as good as any stuffing baked in a bread pan or thrown in a crock pot, it was tradition, and, as such, a necessity.

Stitching up the turkey, he felt the power of Thanksgiving. Some of that resonated from the mythology of the first Thanksgiving dinner—the fictional narrative of Pilgrims and Native Americans celebrating the harvest as they prepared for the harshness of winter. But those tropes, though iconic, didn't have the magic and excitement generated by a jack-o-lantern or a Christmas tree or colorful eggs or fireworks. Outside of some fall decorations, in truth, Thanksgiving had no flash or grandeur. Instead, the nexus of the holiday resided at the dinner table with serving after serving of roasted, candied and mashed tradition.

Ritual was the framework of tradition—even the sloppy, messy task of grabbing handfuls of stuffing and cramming it up the rear end of a large fowl's cold carcass. His father had done the same, and Jason used the very stuffing recipe his father had written on the back of Lahey Hardware letterhead in that perfect, block print of his. One day, Nicholas would take over with that same recipe.

Jen would make her thick-crusted apple pie filled with tart green apples diced up with peels still on just like her grandma did, glazed cinnamon and sugar to coat the top and every piece served with a slice of aged cheddar. There would be cranberry relish, and there would be green bean casserole, and there would be mashed potatoes and gravy, and candied yams, and corn. The feast would be served on his mother's China that only came out on Thanksgiving because that was tradition.

Jason looked over the counter into the living room where Jen had sat down with Nicholas still clad in his Toy Story pajamas. She snuggled close to him as they watched the parade on TV and Jason understood the importance of tradition in a way he never had before.

Tradition was the means by which one can endure. In good times, you went through the motions of tradition, to keep it at the ready. When trouble came, when adversity struck or tragedy befell, tradition became the sturdy support you reached out for and leaned on when you otherwise couldn't stand on your own.

Still feeling the squeeze of Jen's hand from earlier in the bedroom, her kiss on his cheek, and now watching her embrace Nicholas, all while Jason went through the required rituals of the Lahey Thanksgiving, he sensed a peace and comfort in their home he had not felt for almost a month. More than ever, his family needed something to lean against, and he appreciated that this holiday seemed to be supporting their weight.

The turkey was stitched up, glazed with garlic curry butter, and turning a golden brown in the oven. Jen took over the island chopping up her apples. She mixed in the butter, sugar, cinnamon, a dash of vanilla, and rolled out her crust. Jason stayed out of her way, well aware that Jen became tense when she baked.

The bird had another hour before he had to flip it over— so the dark meat juices could flow into the breast meat—then another two-and-a-half hours, which he would confirm by thermometer. Now, time to relax and enjoy the remaining quiet moments of the holiday before guests arrived. He fixed himself a drink.

"Already?" Jen said, glancing briefly at the tumbler in his hand as she ran the cutter in a wide circle around the dough.

The clock on the wall said 12:30. Not like it was morning.

"Five o'clock somewhere." He raised his glass to her in a toast, then walked around to the living room and eased back in the recliner.

"Uh-huh." That, he noticed, was a particularly disagreeable

affirmation.

"It's a holiday for Chrissake. Give me a break." He had intended that to come out light and playful, but it returned to his ears sounding defensive. "Say, you need any help, hon?"

"I'm good," she called back. "Just as long as this dough comes off the counter without tearing."

"God help us all if it doesn't," Jason said.

"Asshole," Jen replied.

He sipped his rum and Coke. Nicholas had moved to his bedroom, probably building his Lego rockets and having space battles. It had been ten days since Nicky's therapist told them he was autistic. Jason still hadn't acclimated completely to this new facet of his son. In so many ways, Nicholas appeared perfectly normal. Jason had to remind himself that autism was part of Nicky's normal.

Over the last week, Leslie reassured them that Nicholas tested very low on the autism spectrum. Although early in the evaluation, she felt that Nicky had every opportunity to thrive like any other child, or more so. "Nicky may be resistant to change, a little more frustrated by things he can't understand right away. He's a sensitive guy. He'll be more emotional at times, but he has so much to offer. Be patient with him. Be calm with him, and be clear with him."

Had that been told to his father about Jason, he had no doubt his old man would have taken a very different course of action. A coddled child becomes a weak man. A parent's job was to toughen a child, steel them in preparation for an unforgiving world. Jason still had a hard time not feeling that was his obligation to Nicky, but he also felt compelled to be a protective parent and shelter him from adversity and harm. This confliction—to gird or nurture—cast him to the side of Nicky's childhood. Meanwhile, Jen had swooped in as if rescuing a wounded animal.

He suspected this feeling of distance or removal from his son's development was an overreaction, and at least partly his fault, but he wasn't sure how to deal with that. One thing was certain. This Thanksgiving was more important than ever to strengthen the bonds of his family.

He got up to refill his drink.

Jason lured Nicholas from the solitude of his room with cheese and soda. The kid was picky about almost any food, but he loved anything orange: cheese, orange soda, carrots, Cheetos.

Jason sat with him at the kitchen table, finishing his drink and watching Nicky take mousy bites of cheese. "You ready for all these people coming over, pal?"

Nicky shrugged and nibbled.

"How about Tommy and Kevin? You looking forward to seeing them?" Nicky's cousins could be a little wild sometimes. They were boisterous kids, not at all like Nicholas. With them being two and four years older, they could sometimes get pushy with Nicky.

"They're okay," he said and slurped the last of his soda.

"Well, if they start bothering you, just ignore them and come over by us, okay?"

He nodded as he looked at the table, chewing this last bite of cheese.

"You looking forward to dinner? Huh? That turkey's looking perfect. And your mom's pie is going to be dee-lish."

"All I want is yammies. A whole plate of 'em." He smiled and, ever so briefly, those big brown eyes connected with Jason and made his heart beat faster. He missed his son. How absurd to think that when he was right here living in the house with them.

"Nix, you are going to turn orange the way you eat, you weirdo." Jason ruffled his hair and Nicky laughed. "You will try a little bit of everything, okay? But you'll get your candied yams. So many they'll be coming out of your ears."

Nicholas got up and trotted to the living room as he sang, "I. Love. Yammies!"

Jason sat there and watched his son as he grabbed his Batman coloring book and crayons. He thought about those leading questions Leslie had asked when she first met with them. Since then, he'd been hyper-focused on Nicky's mannerisms, his speech and how he interacted with them. He never realized how rarely his son made eye contact, and now that was all he noticed. Those few seconds ago, when Nicky had looked up at him, when he and his son connected for that one moment, he remembered holding his baby boy for the first time, when Jason had completely and willingly surrendered himself to another living being.

His emotional flood gates were wide open today.

Nicholas plopped himself down on the living room floor, flat on his stomach with legs up in the air and orange crayon in a death grip as he scribbled in half the visage of Harvey Dent, aka Two-Face, the one-time lawyer, now half-man, half-monster and foe of Batman, whose victims' fates were left to the toss of a coin.

Glen arrived first, a bottle of five-year-old Pinot Noir in one hand and a six pack of Oscar's Chocolate Oatmeal Stout in the other. They stood around the kitchen as Jen poured a glass of wine and Jason grabbed pint glasses for the Black River Falls brew.

Seth and Rachel came soon after with Tommy and Kevin

storming past to join Nicky in the living room. Seth and Jen hugged, Seth's big frame enveloping Jen's slender one. Rachel set a store-bought cherry pie on the counter. No doubt Jen silently seethed to see that, thinking about her home-baked apple pie in the wall oven, but she smiled and gave Rachel a delicate embrace.

Tall, broad Seth introduced himself to Glen and offered a firm handshake and a wide smile through his bushy beard that nested under sandy waves of hair. They all made small talk that competed against the increasing volume of Tommy and Kevin who had pulled out Uno and were trying to get Nicholas to play. Jen and Rachel took the wine and migrated to the sun room. Jason grabbed his instant-read thermometer and jabbed the turkey in three different places, then invited the men to join him downstairs. They gathered around the bar while he mixed three Old Fashioneds in crystal tumblers. Seth complimented Jason on the basement layout and décor as he often did, then conversation shifted to property taxes, the upcoming 2020 election and the soaring stock market. All talk remained politely neutral and politically neutered. No one stepped on another's opinions or beliefs, but each shared in the general concerns and trepidation of what they suspected to be a tumultuous time for both country and society while they sipped highballs in the cozy bunker of finished basement.

"How's your mom doing?" Jason asked.

"Good. Prognosis is really good. The chemo's a drag. She's getting through it, though."

"Glad to hear it."

Seth fingered his drink and looked like he was struggling for words. "Mom and Dad really want to hear from Jen."

Jason nodded but not with any sympathy. "Yeah, well, that's not going to happen, Seth. You know that. They know that. I don't pretend to understand what all happened, but Jen wants nothing to do with them, and I'm tired of causing her more grief by talking with them."

Seth grimaced, shook his head as he took a drink. "No offense, Jason, but she's over-dramatizing the whole thing."

"So you say. Let's just let it go there, Seth." Jason raised his glass to his brother-in-law. "I'm happy you were able to reconcile, but that's your prerogative, just as it's Jen's to keep her distance."

"I know."

"And we have a lot of shit going on right now, if you haven't noticed—"

"I get it."

"—so it's about the worst time for them to be looking for reconciliation."

Glen looked at them and slowly, carefully raised his glass. "Jen is a good woman, and I for one would support whatever she feels is right and appropriate. But, I can't help but acknowledge your parents, Seth, who regardless of how good or bad they were as parents, ended up bringing two terrific people into this world." He raised his glass. "Salut."

Jason winked at Glen and smiled. Just what they needed to put that conversation comfortably and decently to rest.

After cocktails and chitchat, Jason headed up to get the dinner finalized and served. Jen and Rachel made their way back into the kitchen and Jen checked on her yams and pie while she listened to Rachel chat about her hot yoga class. The sisters-in-law seemed to be in good spirits. Jason and Jen only got together with Seth and Rachel a couple times a year at most, despite living less than three hours apart. Jen and Rachel typically got along fine, while sister and brother tended to avoid each other. Jen and Seth were only as close as two siblings could be when both had totally opposite responses to their traumatized childhoods.

Which is exactly why Jason hung in suspense waiting for those two to come together and see which one would light the other's short fuse.

Nicholas had joined Tommy and Kevin at Uno. He seemed to be having a good time, though Jason did not miss how his son sat with his knees drawn in, head down in his hand of cards, body packed tight like paper wadded into a ball. He rocked back and forth as he scrutinized his cards, but showed exuberance when he slapped a card down, and even laughed occasionally.

Jason opened the main oven, checked temperatures again, and pulled the bird out. He set it on the island and admired it for a moment.

The turkey was glorious—a Better Homes and Gardens cookbook cover. Jason cut into the breast meat and the juices pooled along the blade edge and dripped from the cut line. The leg pulled away from the joint easily, torn meat flowering open with a juicy, purplish-brown glean.

A waft of sage, thyme and garlic filled the room as he scooped the stuffing out of the bird. Turkey drippings scraped and mixed into the savory mushroom gravy, potatoes mashed with sour cream and garlic. Jen pulled out the sweet yams, green bean casserole and apple pie from the wall oven and readied the cranberry relish and steamed corn.

Jason called out for everyone to take a seat and they filled in around the table, Jason at the head and Jen across from him. Looking across the spread of food, of the family and friend at his table, he took a moment to appreciate both the blessings bestowed upon them, and the hard work that made this moment happen.

He raised a fresh pour of oatmeal stout as he looked at everyone. "A moment. Before we dive in. I just want to say how thankful I am for the food we are about to eat, and how grateful I am to have you all here to share it with us."

"Hear, hear." Glen raised his glass.

"Thanks for having us, you two," Rachel said. "Everything

looks amazing."

Seth nodded. "You both outdid yourselves,"

"Happy Thanksgiving." Jason took a drink. "Now, dig in!"

Everyone passed plates and bowls of food and called out how good everything looked and tasted. Nicholas was his usual picky-eating self, but Jen tried to get him to take at least a bite of everything. He chewed some white meat, took a few bites of potato, a forkful of stuffing, but whined loudly when told to try the green bean casserole. He heartily munched two yams and a pile of corn, then asked if he could be excused. Jason and Jen looked at each other with humored frustration.

"Go on, get out of here," Jen said and Nicholas slid off his chair and shuffled off to the living room. Nine-year-old Tommy followed at full speed right after and left his older brother Kevin, who dug in to second helpings of turkey and potatoes.

"Tommy!" Rachel called out. "No running inside."

Tommy held his Superman action figure high and flew him across the living room to his next mission, which was apparently on the couch. He leapt onto it and joined Nicky who had grabbed his tablet and poked a finger at one of his video games.

"And no jumping on the furniture, okay, buddy?" Seth's voice carried loud, matching his imposing size. "If only we had that much energy, huh?" He grabbed a turkey leg from the plate of meat and took an impressive bite.

If only Seth and Rachel's kids had more respect for other people's property, Jason thought, but smiled and took a swig of beer.

"Are you still working, Glen?" Rachel asked as she finished chewing.

"I am," Glen said. "Over at Wexel Manufacturing. In shipping and receiving. Hoping to retire next year."

"Glen used to drive semi," Jason said. "Owned his own rig and everything."

"Really? Wow. Did you travel all over the country?"

"Ayuh. Had its ups and downs. Sometimes gone for several weeks, but other times home for a couple weeks. Most of the time, though, I was able to grab shorter runs and could be home most nights. Which Maude appreciated."

Rachel dabbed at her mouth with a napkin. "But you don't drive truck anymore?"

Glen shook his head as his fork ran through the green bean casserole. "Sold the truck so I could be home for Maude. Had to take the factory job to pay off the medical bills.."

"Glen's wife had cancer," Jen said, looking first at Rachel, then gazing softly at Glen and giving him a wan smile. "Maude's been gone almost two years now. We really miss her. She was quite a woman."

"Tough ol' broad," Glen murmured and smiled back at Jen.

"I'm sorry, Glen," Rachel said. "That's hard."

Glen nodded, then blew out a breath. "Still paying off the last of the bills, but hoping to be in the clear by summer next. Social Security and my 401k on top of the rent I collect on the duplex should keep me going for the time I have left."

"Our mom just had surgery a few weeks back for her cancer," Seth said, eyes skimming off Jen and over to Glen.

Jason tensed, his vision narrowing on his brother-in-law.

"Yeah, you mentioned her cancer downstairs. Sorry to hear that," Glen gave a nod to Seth and then an uncomfortable glance at Jen, who kept her attention fixed cooly on her plate. "I hope she does good through her recovery."

"It's going as good as you could hope. She had a mastectomy. Breast cancer. She's in chemo right now. Not feeling great, but hanging in there." He kept diverting his eyes to Jen, who would not acknowledge her brother's attention. Jen slowly, methodically, moved her forkful of mashed potatoes to her mouth and chewed.

"I've visited a couple of times," Seth said. "She's in decent spirits, all things considered."

Jen's attention remained on her plate of food that she was no longer eating.

Seth lowered his head, poked his fork at a remaining dollop of green bean casserole and leaned into Jen. "It would mean a lot to her if you dropped her a line." He was quiet, but his words came to a saber point.

Jen's fork froze in the air. She still wouldn't look at her brother. "*Don't.*"

Seth scraped up a forkful of stuffing and put it into his mouth. "Just saying."

Jen turned to face Seth and bored eyes into him. She held that penetrating gaze until Seth finally looked up and at her.

"The food is so amazing," Rachel said, spooning a small helping of more stuffing onto her plate. She fidgeted in her chair and stole a look and headshake at Seth.

"I don't think I've ever had turkey this juicy," Glen said.

Jason kept his attention on brother and sister, could almost hear that fuse sizzling as it burned down between them.

Rachel reached out across the table and placed a delicate hand over Seth's meaty paw, but he pulled his hand away. He grabbed the back of Tommy's empty chair and leaned in closer to Jen, his voice low, conciliatory yet abrasive. "Hey, sorry. You know? But all they want is to spoil your kid and try to make up for things. Why don't you just stop with the drama and—"

Jen's fork dropped to her plate with a clatter. She pushed her plate ahead, her chair back, and stood abruptly. Heavy steps drove her to the kitchen.

Jason polished off his beer and tried to give Glen an apologetic yet humorous look, as if to say, "Family, huh?" Glen simply returned sad, drooping eyes.

Seth looked at Jason with too much bemusement to be sincere apology. "Hey. I was trying to be reasonable."

Jason nodded, smiled painfully, and slowly stood. "Yeah. But you need to learn some better timing—" He headed toward the kitchen. "—and some fucking tact. Excuse me."

He walked to the kitchen where Jen was aggressively cleaning up the mess of Thanksgiving prep. She ran water into a foaming sink while she slammed smaller pots and pans and jammed plates into the dishwasher.

He put a hand on her back. "Hey, you okay?"

She stiffened and said nothing. He feared she would buck him off, but she finally reached behind her to put a wet and soapy hand over his. "Pissed off. Not at you."

Seth stepped into the kitchen and approached Jen. Jason turned around.

"Seth, swear to God, don't ruin our Thanksgiving."

"Let him say what he needs to," Jen said and dropped the sopping sponge to dry her hands as she turned to face her brother. "He obviously knows everything."

Seth leaned against the edge of the counter and crossed his fists tight into folded arms. "Listen. I get it. You had it worse than me, okay? And I had it so damn easy."

Jen reared back and threw the towel down. "You know exactly why I don't want to see them. Forget whatever you want about our childhood, but I won't. I will never forget."

Seth's voice rose. "Jesus. They weren't monsters for God sake. They were just crappy parents. It's not doing you any good holding on to all this resentment."

"Whatever resentment I hold has everything to do with *them*, not *me*."

Seth looked at Jason, but Jason wasn't going to give his brother-in-law any support. It would be foolish to get involved.

Seth backed up, his voice and his glare softening. "They've got nothing. And their health is crap. They just want to be a part of our lives and spoil their grandkids. What about your kid? Don't you want to give Nicky a chance to have grandparents who would do anything for him?"

Jen bent down and picked up the towel. She turned back to the sink and grabbed the sponge and a pot.

Jason tossed his head at Seth to back off and leave the kitchen.

Seth hesitated. "Come on, Sis—" His mouth opened to say more, but instead he shook his head and walked heavily out of the room.

Jason put his arms around Jen from behind as she scrubbed at the pot with building ferocity. "Your brother will never understand what you went through because he lived a different life."

Jen focused on the dishes with intensity. "He was *there*, Jason. He should know. But he makes up his own reality and tries to push it on me. I'm so fucking sick of that. I'm sick of being made to feel like I'm the problem."

He kissed her neck. "I know."

Jen turned back around, her expression settling like cement. "If you did, you'd stop taking their calls."

And, just like that, he became the bad guy again. Thrown in the dog house. Goddamn it, Seth. And to hell with Jen.

"Great. Fine. Thanks for that. Jesus Christ."

He grabbed the bottle of rum from the cupboard, a can of Coke, and retreated to the dining room. Glen gave him a weak smile as he sat down and poured himself a drink.

Seth said, "Sorry, man. Just trying to—"

"You're an asshole," Jason said and knocked back a heavy swig.

Rachel stiffened. "Jesus, Jason. All Seth was trying to do was—"

"Shut up."

Jason watched her jaw hang open, eyes wide. Seth looked ready to say something. Jason didn't care. He poured his rum. "Let's get back to being thankful, huh?" He topped off his glass with more rum. "And if we can't be that, then I guess we can just get drunk."

"Jason—" Glen spoke cautiously.

Jason raised a hand to his friend and gave him a reassuring look.

The table fell to uncomfortable silence. Jason took deep swigs of his drink while Rachel nibbled at the few scraps of food remaining in front of her. Seth's red face stared at his plate, and Glen looked directly at Jason.

From the other room, he heard one of the cousins say, "Draw four, Picky Nicky!"

Jason craned his neck to look over at them. The cousins were laughing as the three of them played Uno again. Kevin and Tommy were pointing at Nicky, whose knees were up, arms wrapped tight around his legs, head buried between his thighs as he rocked.

"But you have to. Draw four!"

The other cousin chimed in. "Yeah, that's the rules. You gotta draw four."

"What are you doing? What's your problem? Don't be such a retard."

Jason stumbled up, knocked over his chair and jarred the table hard enough to slosh drinks. He dashed over to the two cousins just as Nicholas sprang up and ran crying down the hall-way. Those two little bastards snickered like imps.

Jason grabbed the older Kevin by the back of the neck. "What the hell did you call him?"

"Ow!" Kevin's shoulders went up and his head went down and back, but Jason kept his grip.

"Huh? What did you say?"

Tommy went pale and his grin slid down his face in growing horror. "We were just playin'—" he stammered.

Fast steps approached behind Jason and he felt the sharp wrap of a small fist against his back. "Hey, goddamn it? Goddamn it!" It was Rachel. "Get your damn hand off my kid!"

Jason let go and Kevin scrambled to his feet to move behind his mother while he rubbed his neck.

"He called my kid a retard, the little bastard."

Seth approached, tall and broad-shouldered and cautious. "Back off and sit down, Jason."

Jason shoved Seth. "You back off. This is my house, damn it. You're fucking guests. You just had to ruin our Thanksgiving, didn't you? You and your bratty kids and your goddamn parents. Your fucking family—"

Jason watched Seth ball his fist and Jason stumbled backward.

Jen stood at the edge of the room, looking at him with slack-jawed shock. "Jason! What the hell is wrong with you?"

Did she not see what those monsters were doing? Did she not hear what they called their son? Is she ignoring everything Seth had just done?

"Jason," she pled, "sit down, for the love of God. Please?"

"Oh, really? Sit down? Sure. Fine. My kid's in his room crying but, yup, I need to settle down. Got it. Right. Sitting down."

Seth and Rachel stood at one end of the room, hands laid protectively on their kids. Jen stood on the other side of the dining room and looked at him as if he were a stranger. Glen still sat at the table. He wore the most piercing glare of all—one of absolute pity.

Jason stumbled back to the table, righted his chair and fell into it. He looked at all of them and raised his glass, sloshing rum and Coke on his hand and down his arm. "To family!" He took a deep drink and gave the roomful of gawking eyes one big smile.

Jason sat and enjoyed his drink as he watched Seth and Rachel scamper about in seething silence as they prepared to leave. Seth looked ready to exchange more words with Jason, but instead he put his arm around Rachel and they walked out of the room. Jason smiled and toasted their imminent departure.

Rachel shouted for Kev and Tommy to hurry up. She herded them out the door and snatched her unopened cherry pie from the counter on the way out. Jason stood and followed them to the door. He grabbed the door frame and tried to keep from swaying as he watched them desert the holiday battleground and escape to the driveway.

"Thanks for the pie!" he shouted as Seth and Rachel loaded the kids in the car. He laughed and slammed the door shut.

Jen had, to his annoyance, given a brief, terse apology to Seth and Rachel, then went down the hall to check on Nicky—and maybe to avoid him. That was fine. He didn't much want to see her anymore tonight.

Glen, who still sat quietly at the table, stood up with a grunt and a sigh. "Whelp. Suppose that does it for me."

Jason swaggered toward his friend. "I'm sorry, Glen. Not how I thought this day would be."

Glen put a hand on Jason's shoulder. "You, my boy, prepared an amazing feast. Thank you."

"Thank you, my favorite neighbor. Glad you enjoyed it."

Glen peered sternly at Jason. "Now, get to bed, sleep it off, and in the morning, apologize to your beautiful wife."

Jason shook a finger at him. "She's got some 'splaining to do too, you know."

"I don't doubt that. Be the brave one to make amends first. You hear me?"

Jason wasn't so keen on that.

"You hear me, now?"

Jason gave a reluctant nod.

"You're a good man, Jase, but I'm sensing your grip is slipping on that edge you've found yourself hanging over. Time to grab on to something sturdy and pull yourself back up."

It sounded like good advice, yet so much was twisted and tangled and garbled among all the things he felt he had no control over. Everything was blurry and fuzzy around him, but he locked his focus hard on Glen. "Glen. Glen, I'm sorry."

Glen waved his hand and pshawed. "It was a nice night, mostly. Don't worry about it."

Jason shook his head adamantly. "No. No. You don't understand. I'm sorry I wasn't there for you when Maude was sick. When she was— Sorry I couldn't be the friend you needed. I should have been. I don't know why I wasn't."

"Oh, God, Jason, don't."

"I'm so sorry," Jason said through heaving sobs. "I'm so Goddamn sorry."

Glen's expression broke and he grabbed Jason by the shoulders. "Jase, come on now."

But he had no control. He wept openly, sucked deep breaths, snot rolling down his face. The emotions came from out of nowhere. He didn't know if he cried for Maude, for Glen, maybe even for Agnes Polnzy. He just suddenly felt so Goddamn full of regret.

Glen pulled Jason into a gruff embrace and slapped his back in consolation. "It's all right. Never was any expectation. Don't do this to yourself, hey?"

A few more heaving sobs into Glen's shoulder and Jason pulled himself away, tried to get control of himself. He couldn't look at Glen. "You're the best friend I've got."

Glen smiled. "Well, then that is the best I can ever hope to be. Get to bed, my friend. Sleep this off and we'll talk soon."

Glen stepped around him and went into the kitchen. Jason could hear him talking to Jen, but not what he was saying or if

Jen was responding. After a few moments, Glen headed for the door, stopped to ruffle Nicky's hair and told him to be good and watch over his mom and pop. Then, he walked out the door.

Jason fell into the recliner as the world spun about him and he slipped into darkness.

CHAPTER TWELVE
Saturday, November 30, 2019

Twenty feet off the ground on his roof in eighteen-degree weather and fifteen-mile-an-hour winds, attaching strings of lights to his roof line. One more year of reminding himself he should do this at the start of November, not the end of it. If he didn't kill himself quickly by tumbling over the edge to the concrete driveway, he'd do it slowly by catching his death of cold.

Tradition. Christmas decorations go up Thanksgiving weekend. That's why he was scampering around on his rooftop to hang lights on their gutters and eaves while Jen worked below him on the ground stringing lights and hanging garland across the ledge of brick veneer on the house façade. Nicholas followed in tow to feed her lights and garland.

Tradition wasn't sitting so well with him during this holiday. It certainly hadn't saved Thanksgiving. The day after hadn't been a Hallmark moment either.

His hangover yesterday had been significant and arguably a proper and deserved penance for his behavior over Thanksgiving. Against all odds—and spirits—he managed to retain Glen's wise suggestion. As soon as his stomach and head allowed, he apologized profusely to Jen. She had stood before him and listened, but she hadn't exactly accepted his apology. Instead, she lectured him on his drinking. Apparently, by her account, he had been slurring his words and wobbling about before dinner had even been served. Not how he remembered it, but whatever. He was being the brave one to initiate reconciliation, so he stood there and took it.

He tried spending time with Nicky later that day, but his son had been in a particularly testy mood. Nicholas hardly spoke, and he had a fit and yelled and cried every time Jason tried to help with a puzzle piece or place a Lego block.

He and Jen had decorated inside for much of Friday. They put up and trimmed the upstairs and downstairs Christmas trees, even encouraging Nicky to hang a couple of ornaments, but he largely kept to himself. Rum-spiked eggnog loosened his and Jen's moods slightly, but so far, "merry" was not finding itself in front of their Christmas.

Over fifteen years of memories hung on the branches of two Christmas trees. The plastic Hallmark living-room-scene ornament with flickering hearth and cozy couple on the couch that commemorated their first Christmas together. The blue booty ornament that celebrated Nicky's first Christmas. Ornamental mementos of every trip they've taken together. Gifted ornaments from friends and family. These had always been hung with the warmth of nostalgia and sentimental recollections. This year, it was as if they had discovered each ornament broken.

Normally, the Friday night after Thanksgiving was reserved for watching *Miracle on 34th Street*, but no one's mood seemed particularly amenable to old movie holiday sentimentality.

Instead, after Nicky went to bed, Jason flicked channels until he settled on John McClane being a fly in the ointment of Hans Gruber. Their holiday weekend had become flat and lifeless. They were going through the motions.

He leaned over the roof edge to clip the next stretch of lights to the gutter. The pitch of the roof, in addition to his lean, made it feel like he was falling forward and his stomach lurched. He became more nervous every year being up on that roof.

With the coil of lights in hand, he stood up to move to the next stretch of gutter and his foot slipped on loose shingle granules. His left leg flew forward, his right leg went straight up, and he fell back on his butt, bouncing forward and sliding a half foot to the roof edge. His legs dangled over the gutter as both hands slammed down and clawed at the roof tiles to stop him.

"Jason?!" Jen cried out from below.

His forward progress stopped and all that seemed to hold him in place were his clenched butt cheeks against the lip of the gutter as his legs dangled in thin air.

YOU ARE GOING TO DIE

The memory of that message screamed at him in his head and he wondered why the hell he climbed up there to tempt fate in the first place.

With all the strength he could muster, he pushed up and back with his hands to gain a few precious inches of roof surface. He scooted hands and butt back, and back, and back, until he could get his legs up and feet under him to shove himself to relative safety.

"Are you okay?" Jen called up to him.

"Yeah. Fine. Just slipped."

"Well, don't kill yourself."

No shit.

His heart pounded and his breath was quick. He needed to

calm down. He took a moment and sat there, taking in the view of the neighborhood laid out before him. The Mickelssens had all their inflatables up—Santa and reindeer, elves, and Frosty. Glen had his modest lights around his picture window and cedar bush, plus a wreath hanging on his front door. The Petersons went all in on the multi-colored LEDs that phased in and out of flashing and chasing hues along their eaves and draped over and around their naked birch tree limbs.

Fred and Vivian Greeley, his immediate neighbors to the right, only had a cone of chasing lights flashing in their front yard and a small porch pot tree next to their front door. Their main decorations this season were political signs that lined the front of their yard just off the cul-de-sac. Those had gone up in just the last few days. For Jason, he didn't care so much about where in the spectrum of political extreme any of his neighbors fell. It had more to do with the boldness of the act. After all, it wasn't going to convince someone to vote for a candidate or side. The signs were just names against bold red backgrounds. They weren't going to convince anyone to vote any which way. Displaying those signs on their lawn was simply a way for the Greeleys to label and call attention to themselves, to blast their affiliation and beliefs. Each sign drew a line in the sand—a polarized demarcation that they dared anyone to cross.

Jason's father had never worn his politics on his sleeve. He certainly had opinions, but they were usually presented in a fairly nonpartisan way. Of course, as a businessman and store owner during the eighties, nineties and early two-thousands, his father didn't want to ostracize half his patrons.

The beating of Jason's heart settled and he felt ready to continue. As he lobster-crawled carefully over to where he needed to hang the next length of lights, he caught sight of a car in the distance coming down Fairview Lane. It turned into Agnes's driveway and came to a stop. Not a Ford F-150 this time, but an older gold sedan—a Saturn, maybe. He kept his attention on the car as its door squeaked open and a person stepped out—a woman. She wore a long, puffy maroon jacket, blondish brown ponytail spilling over the collar and past her neck. Too far away to see any other details. She walked up to the front door and stepped inside.

Daughter?

"Looks like more activity at Agnes's place," he said.

Jen looked up from below him as she unlooped a length of fake evergreen garland draped over Nicky's arm. "What's that?"

"Polnzy's house," he said more loudly. "Someone's there."

Her eyes narrowed and she looked up and sideways at him. "Why are you so interested? I still don't know what led you over there last time."

He scooted over and started attaching the last few feet of lights with plastic gutter clips. "I'm just curious."

"Yeah, and look where that got you." Jen went back to hanging the garland in even swoops along the stone ledge.

He sidled back along the roof and made his way to the extension ladder. Gingerly, he worked his way around and onto the top rung, then made his way down the ladder. Safely on the ground, he stepped forward to watch Agnes's house. Who would be over there? Maybe a realtor? Or, if the daughter, did she know about her brother breaking in?

"Hey." Jen walked over to him. "You're not going over there—after what that jerk was like to you?"

"It's not him. It's a woman. I think it's the daughter."

"So?"

"So—" But he really didn't have a 'so.' It was hard for him to understand, let alone explain, but he felt involved, a part of some narrative that hasn't been resolved yet. Whether he was a main character or just a walk-on role, he didn't know.

"I'm just a concerned neighbor," he said.

Jen handed him a length of garland. "Well, concern yourself with finishing the decorating. The other side needs garland."

"Yes, ma'am." He gave a salute. She returned a middle finger with the hint of a smirk.

That obscene gesture was the closest she had come to extending any forgiveness to him about Thanksgiving. He smiled wide and hummed "Jingle Bells" as he hung garland across the other half of the house front.

But he kept one eye on Agnes's place.

Nicholas wanted to hang the garland himself so Jason let Nicky give it a try. Instead, Nicky managed to pull part of it down. Jason tried to help him but Nicky started to get agitated. Jen stepped in to apply her usual calming magic with him, but this time Nicky went ballistic, so Jen led him back in the house. Jason was losing his patience. Jen's placid acceptance encouraged Nicky's outbursts. And his tantrums more and more seemed to be against Jason.

After Jason rehung the section of garland, he worked on getting the lights connected to extension cords. He tucked the cords into crevasses and cracks of siding and concrete to conceal them. He set the timers to alight the home in a festive glow at dusk and prepared to head back inside.

Down the street, he saw Ollie on the edge of Agnes's driveway with the woman who had arrived at the Polnzy house. He decided to take a stroll.

As he approached, he heard Ollie's buoyant, relaxed Norwegian drawl. "Sure, sure. Wish I could help you, but I didn't see a thing." Ollie looked over at Jason as he approached. "Now, here's a fella that just might be able to help you. Heya, Jason."

"Hey, Ollie. How's it going?" Seeing the woman up close,

he felt certain she was the daughter. A slight pinch of eyes, the bottom-lip curl of small mouth and fleshy cheeks reminded him of Agnes. Gray strands ran through her tied-back brown hair. She looked late-fifties, but Jason guessed mid- to late-forties.

"Oh, not too shabby," Ollie said. "See you're getting in the holiday spirit."

"Trying to keep up with your festive presentation, neighbor." Jason nodded to the mob of colorful Christmas characters inflated in his yard.

"Oh, yeah. Can't stand them myself, but Lynn just loves 'em. So, what's a fella to do?" Ollie turned to the woman beside him. "Suzie, this is Jason Lahey, the one I was mentioning to you." He looked back to Jason. "This is Agnes and Moe's daughter, Suzie."

Suzie gave a tight, thin-lipped smile. Despite the crinkle of time under her eyes and in the corners of her mouth, she had a plain but pleasant countenance, hardened perhaps by critical eyes, but made less severe by her round face and full cheeks. "Nice to meet you," she said.

With some hesitation, Jason extended his hand, remembering the last time he offered it to a Polnzy. She took it firmly.

"You as well," he said. "I'm sorry about your mother."

"Thank you. You're the one that found her?"

He nodded.

"I'm sorry for that. From what I understand—" She trailed off.

"Yeah." He wasn't willing or able to discuss that further, and it seemed she wasn't, either.

Ollie gave a nod to Jason. "Poor Nicky, his son, saw it all, too. Hey, how is Nicky? He doing okay?"

"Fine," Jason said with little conviction. "He's doing good."

"That's good. Lynn and I were worried about him. That was a rough day." He looked with sympathy at Suzie, then his expression widened. "Speaking of, Lynn is waiting for me. We're heading to the Kriskindlmarkt downtown at the Civic Center. I figure we'll be coming back with enough blasted snowmen to fill every remaining nook and cranny of our house!" He reached out and offered Suzie a hug, which she embraced fully. "Good to see you, darlin'. You take care."

"I'll try. Same here, Ollie."

"Sorry for all that's happening. Hang in there and let us know if you need anything."

"Will do."

Ollie stuffed his hands into the pockets of his jacket, gave Suzie a long, lingering look, and strolled off back to his house.

Jason turned to Suzie Polnzy, who watched Ollie walk away. He said, "I, um, met your brother here. A couple weeks back."

She looked up at him and her short, sturdy frame stiffened. "That's what Ollie mentioned."

He studied her expression and chose his next words cautiously.

"He, um, made quite an impression."

Suzie's laugh was more like a choking cough. "I bet."

Jason nodded. Paused. "He's kind of an asshole."

"That's *kind of* an understatement."

He looked over at the house, a dour façade made even more ominous by past events and accentuated by the haunt of dreams. "I got the impression he wasn't exactly supposed to be here."

She flushed red and her lips twisted. "The bastard broke in and stole everything he could. He has no right to the place."

Exactly what Jason realized when discovering the forced entry. That's why Greg and his partner arrived early to unload the place in a no-nonsense hustle. No wonder Greg had all but threatened him and pushed him away.

"That's horrible," he said.

Her fists clenched at her sides. "*He* is horrible. I'd call him a son of a bitch, but that would be an insult to my mother."

"Sorry if I'm prying but, I don't understand. Why doesn't he have rights to the place? Was he kept out of the will?"

She nodded. "You bet your ass he was. The estate was left to me. The house is in probate right now. That's why I'm here. I just came back from court. I was named executor. Now I'm just waiting to get final rights to the estate."

"Is he trying to contest it?"

"Hell no. He didn't even bother to show up. He wouldn't have a leg to stand on, even if he did want to contest, because of his criminal record. Wisconsin law. If you commit a crime against the deceased, you relinquish all rights to the estate."

That piqued Jason's curiosity. "He committed a crime against your mom?"

She nodded slowly. "Battery. He beat the shit out of her when he was nineteen. He had already left by then. He came back late one night and my mom caught him stealing the cash, checks and credit cards out of her purse. She threatened to call the cops and he broke her jaw and fractured her skull."

"Holy shit." Shocking, but it didn't surprise him. Thinking back to when he faced off with Greg, he recognized that violence in his look. Not ferocity. Not rage. It was a coldness that sat behind his eyes, that had leered at Jason with total apathy.

"Somehow, she was still able to call 911 and he was thrown in jail for three years."

He stammered for words.

"Mr. Lahey. My brother is a monster. He spent six months in juvie for kicking a sixth-grade classmate in the head until unconscious. He constantly threatened and abused my parents. He tortured me throughout my childhood. When I was fifteen, he—" Her words caught and her eyes dropped.

Jason jumped to a horrible assumption about what she couldn't say, and it made him sick.

"He's a violent, hateful, angry piece of shit," she said.

Jason realized the threat he sensed during his standoff with Greg was far greater than he had imagined. He was speechless. What she described was an unfathomable horror show, and it happened right here on Fairview Lane. How much did the Mickelssens know? Had they gotten involved? He saw how Ollie had said goodbye. Just what part had they played in all of this? And how could this piece of shit still be free instead of being locked away for the rest of his life? Why hadn't Moe and Agnes kicked him out, or sent him to a juvenile home, or something?

"I—I can't even begin to tell you how sorry I am. I can't imagine—"

Suzie kicked at the ground with a black boot as she swayed back and forth with hands shoved into her coat pockets. "I ran away at sixteen. Not from my parents. From him. This is my first time back in that house in thirty years."

"And you hadn't seen her since?"

Suzie wouldn't look up. "Not since I was seventeen. When she was in the hospital. I called her occasionally."

"Poor Agnes. I—Listen. She, well, she wasn't the most pleasant person. But, now I—I just—to be alone for all those—" He couldn't fathom it all. So many new details had stacked on top of what he thought he knew and what he was now learning. He tried to fight it, push the image back, but he couldn't help but recall that chair, her lifeless body in it. The weight of that absolute act Agnes had taken, amid all this history, stole his breath.

He could tell she saw it all on his face—his shock and pity—and he could only imagine how much his revulsion looked like an accusation to her. His disgust was like a mirror that reflected all the mess and horror of her life back on her.

Her hands came out of her pockets and defensively went to her sides. "Listen. I was a child and traumatized. The only two people who could have protected me didn't. Instead, they denied. They avoided. They hid. Fifteen years of fucking therapy and I'm still dealing with this shit."

He put up his hands. "Hey. I'm sorry. I couldn't possibly understand what you've been through."

He could see she was overwhelmed with emotion—anger, grief, fear, guilt. He also noticed her dry eyes and laser-intense stare. It immediately reminded him of Jen.

"I just need to get this place ready for sale and move on. I only came here to see what condition the place was in and find some memories of Mom and Dad that weren't covered in shit." She turned to the house, shoulders slumped. "He ransacked the place, just like he did our lives. I can't even find any family photos. The house is a disaster."

He could keep saying how sorry he felt, but that word seemed so ineffective as to be insulting. "I wish there was something I could do. Or say."

Her intensity returned. "There is, actually. I want to report this to the police. He can't do this. I was hoping you might consider making a statement? With a witness willing to testify, maybe—"

"Yes, absolutely. Just tell me what to do."

"If I could get your phone number, I can pass your info on to the police."

He reached for his phone from his back pocket. "Let's exchange numbers."

She told him her number and he put it in his contacts, then called her. She took her phone from her coat pocket, answered, and added his name.

"L-a-h-e-y," he said as she typed. She nodded and stuffed the phone back into her coat with the grit and severity of holstering a gun.

"I've been running away from him for most of my life." She looked back at the dark, dismal home, sapped of its yellow color by the cold, gray day as leaves from the oak tree rustled and blew across the yard. "No more."

He realized what he needed to do and held up two fingers. "Give me just a couple minutes? I need to grab something. Swear I'll be right back."

She gave a hesitant, confused nod.

He ran back to his house and through the service door of the garage. Inside, he passed Jen who was fixing a grilled cheese sandwich, one of the few sandwiches Nicholas would eat. "What's going on?" she asked as he zipped by her and into the den at the start of the hallway. In the closet, he snatched the photo album rescued from the ruins of the Polnzy house. He started to trot back but stopped, tossed the album on his desk, and turned to that ponderous page of words written over and over in Agnes's penciled scrawl.

All are meant to suffer

Suzie didn't need to see that. She'd obviously been through enough. She wanted to heal and resolve, and these words would only bring painful questions.

He carefully tore out the page from the album and slipped it into his desktop file organizer, upside down on top of a pile of papers.

Trotting through the kitchen again, he said, "Be right back!" and he dashed out the door and down the street.

Out of breath reaching Suzie, he panted as he held out the photo album.

She looked confused. "What's that?"

"Photo album," he said through heavy breaths. "I found it."

She continued to stare at it with perplexity. "You stole it from the house?"

Jason shook his head, face flushing. "No, no. Listen, when I saw the door wide open, I just went over to close it. But I saw the mess your brother made and, well, I went in to investigate. I found this on the floor and I took it."

"Why?" She eyed him with confused suspicion.

He didn't know how to answer that, other than realizing he had to lie. "It didn't seem right. This was on the floor, like garbage, with no way to secure the home. It was like he had thrown Agnes aside. I don't know. I had to rescue it from that mess, to save some part of her." He pushed it against her chest. "And now I know it will be safe. With you. Where it belongs."

He hadn't exactly lied. What he said was not insincere, it just hadn't been his original motivation. He was surprised, however, how genuine his words felt and sounded.

Suzie wrapped arms around the album and hugged it close to her chest. "Well, thank you," she said. Whether the wisp of wind or the sting of emotion, her eyes reddened and watered.

"I'll keep in touch," he told her.

She nodded and got into her car.

Eleven years ago. They had only been in the Cities for a year when he got the call from his mother.

"Jason, we thought you should know. They found some cancer in Ed's lung."

Over the phone, she sounded so nonchalant about it, like she had told him they needed to get the car's transmission fixed.

"God. Is it serious?"

"Well, it's cancer, Jason."

"Mom, I know. But is it—"

"It's treatable. He'll need radiation therapy, maybe surgery. We'll know more in a few weeks."

"How's he doing?"

"Ah. You know your father. You wouldn't even know anything was wrong."

"Listen. We'll try to get over to you in a couple weeks. I just need to look at the calendar."

"Oh, don't trouble yourself. You're busy." Florence could be very aggressive with her passive-aggressiveness. It drove him crazy, but he knew exactly what she was really saying.

"Mother, we will get to you. I'll email you some dates."

"Sure, sure."

"In the meantime, give him my best and tell him we're thinking about him."

"Of course, Jason. Goodbye, then."

He remembered holding on to the receiver for several seconds as he tried to decode that conversation. Was it serious? Terminal? Or was it something easily treatable? His mother could make a mountain out of a mole hill, but she could also treat a storm like a spring rain. She sounded as if she wasn't worried, yet she had laid a hefty guilt trip on him.

He and Jen made the three-hour trip back to Fortune Falls to see his parents the following month. They were, as always, pleasant and accommodating. They asked how things were going in Minneapolis, if they had any plans to start a family, what were taxes like over there? Perfectly normal. Had Jason not asked about the cancer, the topic wouldn't have been broached. What had been discussed was dismissed as quickly as possible. Considering how healthy and virile Ed looked, the cancer was easy to ignore and forget.

As Jason's career took off, life changed dramatically over the next year for them and they had less contact with his parents. His mother left regular voicemail messages.

"How's it going? Ed started his treatment. Doing good. Tired, though. A little sick some mornings. How's the big city life? See any good shows? Give us a call when you find some time."

BEEP.

"Hi, there. Well, doctors aren't satisfied with the results of the radiation therapy. They're putting him on a regimen of chemotherapy to see if that has better results. How are you both? Jobs going okay?"

BEEP.

"Hello. Hope you're both doing well. Ed is hanging in there. He's lost his hair. I'm still getting used to that. He's sleeping a lot. They have him on pain pills. I think that's partly why he's so tired. Hope to see you both before the snow falls."

BEEP.

He called when he could, but less than he probably should have. He was so exhausted by the end of the day, though. The job had been grinding him down. They eventually got over there before the Northwoods winter blew in. When they arrived, he was not prepared for what he saw.

Ed, so tall and broad-shouldered with lustrous head of black and gray hair, had become a bald, pale, emaciated shell of a man. His voice, once sharp with matter-of-fact Irish assurance, dulled to a weak, hoarse whisper. Having already been a man of few words, on that visit, Jason hardly heard him speak at all.

"Mother, he looks horrible. How bad is it?"

"They're talking hospice," she shared. "The cancer spread much faster than expected, and they say his heart just couldn't take surgery at this point."

"But, I thought this wasn't serious?"

She looked at him with sad but incredulous eyes. "Who told you that? It's cancer. It was always serious."

He had been so angry, so frustrated. He wanted to argue with her about how she had underplayed his father's condition.

He had one conversation with his father during that trip. It had not gone well.

"I'd like you to take over the hardware store," Ed rasped, his chest constantly heaving to catch a breath.

Jason was shocked his father would even suggest this. He

had had no part in that store for almost ten years. He already earned more than his father ever made. How could he ask this of him?

"I—I have a career, already. Things are going really well."

"You're my only hope keeping the Lahey name on the building." His yellowed eyes seared him with his hot, pleading glare and a bony hand grabbed on to Jason's lapel.

Jason didn't know what to say, what he could say. The request came out of nowhere. His father was being completely unreasonable—perhaps delusional.

"I'm sorry. That was never the plan, and you know that. I'm already building my future. I've done so well, I—"

His father's hand fell, his stare wandered. "I know. I just hoped—" He drifted then, eyelids fell, and his breath slowed to a steady, wheezing snore.

He and Jen returned home at the end of that weekend and started making plans for an extended stay to help out. He just needed to wrap up a pressing project at work. Next month, they'd get down there for a week.

Two weeks later, his mother called to tell him that Ed had passed. "It was peaceful. He was barely conscious. He had suffered so. It's for the best."

Edward Alexander Lahey, dead at 59. Survived by wife, Florence and son, Jason. Preceded in death by son, Edward Alexander Lahey, Jr.

Now, as he sat in the sunroom after his talk with Suzie, he sipped his third rum and Coke and he doubted. He doubted as he had been doubting for years about how he handled the entire situation with his mother and father. The weight of that doubt oppressed him more today than it had for a long time.

Had his mother really played the whole situation lightly? Or had he actually dismissed it because his father's cancer had been inconvenient to his life and career? Looking back, he can no longer rationalize how he could have interpreted his father's situation as anything other than gravely serious. He barely even remembered talking to Jen about it with any appropriate level of severity.

Not only had he ignored the gravity of his father's condition, he had left his mother—a woman so emotionally and physically ill-equipped to handle a situation like that—completely on her own, with no emotional support, let alone offering to help her care for his father.

Suzie had called Greg a monster. And sure, if half of what she said was true, he was a monster. But at least he wasn't pretending to be anything else. As Jason sat and thought about all those years ago, how he ignored his father's terminal cancer, how he dismissed his father's dying wish, Jason began to suffocate behind the mask of innocence he wore to conceal a monster hiding beneath.

His bladder was full to bursting. He finished his drink and walked to the bathroom at the head of the hallway. At the toilet, he relieved himself, intently focused on his aim as he swayed a bit. Through the wall, he could hear Nicholas singing. It sounded like a lullaby.

"…sleep in heavenly peace…" A Christmas carol: "Silent Night."

Nicky didn't sing often. When he did, it was more like humming or the repetition of a simple chorus over and over again. But there he was, singing most of the words. Jason stood there for a long time, hearing his son go through the complete first stanza a second time. Such a sweet song when voiced through the innocence of youth.

Jason zipped himself up, washed his hands, and went around the corner to Nicholas's room.

"…sleep in heavenly peace…"

Jason cried out. He froze in horror. He couldn't process.

"Jesus, God! No! Nicky, God no! What are you doing? Stop!"

He ran to his son, grabbed him, picked him up and shook him. He had to stop this, shake it out of him. This was so, so terribly wrong. "Nicky, stop! No! What are you doing?"

Nicky was crying, screaming, but Jason couldn't stop. He was repulsed. Sickened.

Jen rushed up behind him, screaming at him. "Jason! JASON! Stop that! For God sake, put Nicky down! What's wrong with you?"

She grabbed Nicky from him and glared with terror and fury.

"Look!" Jason screamed. "Look at what he's done! Jesus Christ, what's wrong with him?!"

Nicholas screamed and bawled. Jen had him so tight against her breast.

"What the fuck is wrong with you? You bastard! You're fucking drunk! You're always fucking drunk! Get out! Get the hell out of this house and pull yourself together, goddamn it. I don't want to look at you! Leave. GET OUT!"

He was paralyzed. The world was crashing down upon him. Everything was madness. It was a nightmare he couldn't wake up from. "But—Look! Jesus Christ, Jen. Look!"

"GET OUT!"

He didn't know what to do. He started to move toward Nicholas, toward her, but she recoiled from him to the corner of the room, cringing as if from some stalking killer. He shook his head, looked around, and knew of nothing he could do but leave.

He walked out of the room, turned and took a last look at Jen, at Nicky, and at all the stuffed animals on his son's bed, the bears and puppies and bunnies on the shelf of his wall—every one of them with their heads covered by plastic shopping bags.

Chapter Thirteen
Monday, December 2, 2019

Day number two waking to strange surroundings in a downtown Best Western. The second half of Saturday was a blur to him. He began his exile driving around the city aimlessly, unsure of what to do or where to go. He had become an expatriate of his home, and the once-familiar surroundings of Fortune Falls became a foreign land to him. Glen, other friends, family—they felt out of reach. He wasn't ready or able to face them and explain actions and behaviors he didn't completely understand himself.

When he finally checked into the downtown hotel, he headed straight to the cocktail lounge and spent the better part of late afternoon and early evening there, talking bullshit to bartender and patrons. After that, he stumbled to his room and crashed onto the overly-firm queen-sized bed. On the television, a petty husband and wife droned on from some ninety's sitcom, neither having any idea what real problems were.

Sunday had been surreal. After a complimentary hotel breakfast of cold powdered scrambled eggs, greasy sausage and freeze-dried potato chunks, he called Jen.

"I don't think we're ready to have you back yet," she had said.

We're? Did she seriously mean she had discussed this with Nicky and they both decided the two of them were better off if he stayed away?

"Listen," he said. "I'm sorry. It won't happen again."

Jen continued as if she hadn't heard his apology. "Nicky is seeing Leslie for his appointment on Monday. Be at the clinic at four o'clock." She hung up.

So, he walked down to the front desk to register for an extended stay, was told he needed to check out first, and checked back in for another night.

Realizing he had no clothes or toiletries, he headed to the south side of town to hit Target for appropriate work clothes and some basic personal care items.

The day was chilly but calm with light, big flakes of snow falling like blossoms from a Hawthorne tree in spring. Inside the store, he was overcome by decorations in red, green and white. Cardboard elves pointed out every deal, festive penguins in Santa caps punctuated sale prices and reindeer flew overhead on fish line, all while Perry Como mellifluously informed him that, "It's Beginning to Look a Lot Like Christmas."

He found toothpaste, toothbrush, razor, shaving cream and deodorant. As he looked for the men's clothing section, he walked past Christmas trees, ornaments, lights and wreaths, and aisle after aisle of toys. It's where he and Jen would be before too long, shopping for Nicky's Christmas presents and browsing the decorations. At least, that's what they would do in his normal universe. He wasn't sure what would happen in this parallel dimension of separation.

One month ago, his life had been perfect. Now, he found

himself trapped in the tragedy of another person's life, one who, piece by piece, was losing everything, and didn't know how or why.

A store length of women's tops, pants, pajamas and underwear later, he found the men's clothing section crammed into a corner of the store. He grabbed pants and polo and fled the bombardment of holiday as fast as he could. Brenda Lee serenaded his exit with "Rockin' Around the Christmas Tree" as he made swift steps out the door and across the parking lot amid the soft flurry of snowfall.

For dinner, he walked a chilly block of the small downtown to a steakhouse. When the young waiter arrived, he asked for an Old Fashioned. After he looked over the menu, he ordered a New York Strip medium rare and a refill. When the waiter returned and asked how everything was, Jason pushed his empty glass out to him.

Back at the hotel, it felt rude to not to say, 'Hi' to the bartender, so he stopped by the bar and ordered a rum and Coke. As the night wore on, he was certain they had become best friends and only reluctantly parted ways after some encouragement. He retired to his room around ten thirty.

Early in the morning, he got ready for work after a holiday weekend alone in a hotel. He showered using tiny bottles of soap, shampoo and conditioner. He tore open the toothpaste box and toothbrush packaging. He cracked open the plastic seal to get to the deodorant and spent a good couple of minutes trying to muscle open the clamshell packaging for the razor and blade cartridges. All that unsealing, cracking open, unboxing and de-tagging only emphasized his emergence into this brand-new reality of being alone.

He couldn't shake his dream last night that woke him up in a cold sweat. He had been back in Polnzy's living room, a living room that wound and twisted and turned like a maze. Photo albums lay open on end tables and coffee tables, each with yellowed photos of Greg leering at him, eyes following Jason as he walked through the dark, dank house. Turning one final corner, he saw the old woman in the chair, bag over her head and taped around her neck. Behind her, the old slot machine stood like an ominous monolith looming over her.

He walked up to the body in the shadow of the ancient machine as its three prophetic cylinders whirled and spun. With both hands, he grabbed the plastic and tore open the Shop n' Save bag.

His mother's dead eyes stared back at him.

Work was a slog. The minute hand dragged across the clock's face. Time ticked at a crawl on his computer. Stubborn minutes advanced laboriously on his office phone display.

He was in no mood for post-holiday banter and kept his office door closed. Other than a couple minor crises, no one bothered knocking on it.

At 3:45 p.m. he headed out without speaking to anyone and drove to the clinic. Inside, Jen sat alone in the waiting room. He hesitated a moment, just inside of the hallway, as if approaching a doe at the edge of a tree line.

She looked up and he flushed as he connected with her sad and intense azure eyes and delicate freckled cheeks under a blast of auburn hair. He was overcome by the desperate want of something he could no longer have. Not just her—his wife and mother of his child—but everything that came with her. Their life, their love, their passion, and the intensity they shared.

He saw her tense to his presence and felt he would buckle from the pain of that fear and rejection in her expression, but she relaxed and softened to a welcoming acknowledgement. He walked over to her.

"Hi," he said.

"Hi," she said.

"Where's Nicky?"

"In his three-thirty play therapy session."

"Oh." So she made sure his son was elsewhere and well-protected by the time he arrived.

Leslie's head popped out from behind the door beside the front counter. "Jen? Jason?"

Jen's head sprang up. "Yes." She launched herself off the chair. Jason lagged several steps behind.

They followed Leslie into her office area and sat at opposite ends of the round table in the corner. Leslie joined them in her office chair, her demeanor serious and direct.

"Good to see you both." Leslie's expression was oddly more apologetic, or maybe sympathetic. Either way, Jason had a bad feeling.

"Thank you for being so accommodating," Jen said, and it seemed apparent that much had taken place between them without his knowledge.

"Of course," Leslie continued. "Now, let's not beat around the bush. We're here to talk about Nicholas's most recent response to seeing your neighbor's suicide."

Jason shifted in his seat to such direct words. It was the first time he had heard someone use that specific term to describe Agnes's death. He knew exactly what she had done, but his brain kept swapping truth for emotional convenience and turned Agnes's act into a violent murder committed by some unknown entity.

"So, just like any child, each new stimulus he experiences, he needs to process it. For children, that often means experimentation and roleplaying. This is why children play house, have imaginary friends, play make-believe. Children are little scientists running experiments every moment of their waking lives. In this particular case, he witnessed something that was new information he needed to process. He's experimenting with it now using his stuffed animals."

Leslie removed her glasses and set them on the table. "I want to be clear. Without proper intervention, this could become an unhealthy obsession. Fortunately, I will be able to use this as an access point to his trauma and help him face what he is obviously trying to confront."

Jen took a relieved breath. "So we don't need to be worried?"

"I really don't think so. However," and she turned to look directly at Jason, "your response to him was a potentially damaging reaction to his otherwise relatively healthy one."

Jason squirmed.

"But, because of what an amazing little individual Nicholas is, he is responding very well to our interactions with him, and I feel really good about using this as a stepping stone to move beyond the autism assessment and start to address his trauma directly."

Jen's entire body relaxed and she smiled. "I am so glad, and so relieved."

"I want to emphasize, however, that at this juncture, it can only help if his home life is stable, predictable and supportive." She locked onto him again. He was definitely being singled out. This had been the point of the meeting all along. It was an ambush.

"We will make absolutely sure of that," Jen said and grabbed Jason's limp hand to squeeze it. Jason didn't say anything. It appeared fairly obvious he wasn't supposed to.

Leslie stood. "Excellent. Nicholas should be finishing his play therapy shortly and we'll have him brought out to you. Jen, do you mind if I have a private word with Jason?"

He looked at Jen, who seemed too obviously taken aback

and knowingly surprised to be either. "Oh, sure. No problem." She gave him a look he was certain she believed was reassuring, then she left the room.

He stood and looked straight at Leslie the Therapist with cold eyes.

"Jason. Do you mind if—"

"Mr. Lahey. Please."

She hesitated, drew back slightly. "Mr. Lahey. I know I'm not telling you anything you don't already know when I say that finding your neighbor, Mrs. Po—"

"Agnes."

Another wary pause. "Yes, Agnes. When Nicholas found her that way, he was terribly traumatized."

"Obviously," he said. "That's why we brought Nix to you."

"Yes, and you brought him to me because I specialize in child and adolescent trauma. But, that doesn't mean I can't recognize the effects of trauma generally in people."

He nodded generally.

"Respectfully, I think you should seek therapeutic support, Mr. Lahey."

He stared at her. "What?"

"I can suggest a person or two if you'd like."

For Chrissake, what was this? Was she getting some kind of kickback on referrals?

"I'm fine," he said, both with assurance and undercut with a threat to contradict.

She paused and gave him an appraising look. "It's up to you, Mr. Lahey. I just want to be very clear with you. If I hear of a single additional incident like you had with Nicholas the other day, I'm calling child protective services. Do you understand?"

It was as if she had slapped him across the face. He hadn't expected this level of directness. Boldness. He had an urge to leap up, grab her by the collar and show her what real violence was. How dare she threaten him? He could respect the care and concern she had for his son, but not her baseless accusation against him.

He had few options. Reluctantly, he gave a slow nod.

"I want to believe you are a good and caring father, Mr. Lahey. Please don't prove me wrong."

His first night home in two days. Nicky kept his distance. Jason respected that distance, even though it felt like his heart was being pulled out through his mouth. The fact was, tonight, he was a guest—the estranged uncle on a rare visit and desperate to win affection.

While Nicky occupied himself in the living room playing his Mario Cart video game, Jason sat with Jen in the kitchen. Her expression had flattened, her emotions discarded and draped over her countenance.

"How are you doing?" She asked it as if he were dying of cancer.

"I'm fine. Really."

"Where are you staying?"

"Best Western, downtown."

She paused and pursed her lips in strained thought. Finally, with a deep intake of breath, she went rigid and upright. "Listen. I'm not going to fuck around here. I love you too much for that. You hear me? I love you. But, Jason. Jesus. This last month, you've been so—unpredictable. It's not just your drinking. You've withdrawn from me. You seem preoccupied. On edge. And how you were at Thanksgiving—?"

He nodded, because he did know, even if she made more of it than she should.

She laid her hands flat on the table and pushed herself back.

"And, when I saw what you were doing to Nicky—"

"Jesus, Jen. I was just—"

"NO." She hissed her intensity at him. "You were shaking the shit of out him."

"Oh, come on—"

"Yes!" Her volume was low but her ferocity was at full. "And you were SCREAMING into his face!"

"Jen—"

She put up a hand. "I know what I saw, and I will know you're headed in the right direction when you admit to it."

So, it was clear now. He had already been charged and convicted of a crime, and he had no opportunity to state his case. "You know what? Fine. Do you feel good about your son suffocating his stuffed animals and murdering them? Great. Have at it. Not me. No damn way."

Jen calmed and took a breath. She seemed to think about her next words carefully.

"We need to be on the same page about our son, Jason. I don't think we are."

"Damn right we aren't. You're apparently okay with raising some kind of serial killer."

"For fuck sake—"

"I'm Goddamn serious! Look what he did! You don't pat him on the back and tell him he's a good boy!"

"And you don't fucking shake the shit out of him and scream at him! You want a sociopath? Keep doing that to him and see what happens!"

Jason threw up his hands. "Well, you obviously know how to be raised right."

She went limp, like her strings had been cut, her switch flicked. "You fucking bastard."

They sat and stared at each other in tense silence.

He immediately regretted the comment, yet still felt justified in saying it. She was so sure of herself and so certain he was wrong.

Jen stood and walked to the sink where she looked out into the living room. Her hands seemed to look for something to do, to hold. Not finding anything, they wrung together.

He got up and walked over to the sink, joining her as she watched Nicky play his video game in the living room. His boy rocked back and forth aggressively, eyes locked onto the screen. Jason's gut twisted. Had he been listening to them fight? How could he not have heard them? Leslie was right. Nicholas needed a stable home, and right now, this wasn't it. Jason wasn't it.

"Listen. There's an IT seminar happening next week in Springfield. I'm going to sign up for it."

She turned and faced him, her expression unreadable.

"I've been meaning to go the last couple years. I'll be gone for a week. I figure it'll be good for us."

She stared at him for a long time and said nothing. Her eyes narrowed in a way that could be questioning, frustrated, or disagreeing.

"Sounds great," Her marbled eyes looked beyond him.

"Fine," he said. "I'll just go pack my things."

CHAPTER FOURTEEN
Thursday, December 5, 2019

Troy stepped into Jason's office before Jason had a chance to grab a cup of coffee. His head was pounding. He stayed up too late last night having a few drinks. The Best Western lounge had become depressing, so he trekked halfway across downtown's main drag to the Pour House.

Troy stood in his jeans and rumpled polo and gave an update on their server migration, which was not going well. "We're getting dependency errors across multiple applications." A perplexed glance at his handful of papers. "I don't get it."

This was the last thing Jason wanted to hear. This was IT-101. He had laid out a clear plan to avoid these exact issues. "That can't be. Not if your team ran all the scripts."

"We did."

"Bullshit."

"Jason—"

"Bullshit. Bullshit. You ran them, but you didn't rerun from the start after a safety net error triggered."

Troy shook his head. "No, we—"

"A safety net triggered, you reestablished the path, and you forgot to run from the beginning."

Troy's jaw hung open, ready to deny, and Jason didn't want to hear any of it.

"You've set us back days. Fuck. A week."

Troy pointed at a stack of pages with line after line of code he held in his hand. "Listen, Jason, that's not the problem—"

"Troy. Listen to me. You need to go back, go line by line through the script to make sure you didn't miss something, and then you need to run it all again."

Troy looked at him as if Jason told him to grow wings and fly. "That—that's going to take days."

Jason turned his chair back to his computer screen and started typing an email to the CIO explaining the delay. "Then don't waste time here."

From his periphery, he saw Troy stand there for another five seconds before he walked out.

Jason couldn't tolerate any incompetence from his team. Not with all the shit he was going through. Was there no one he could depend on? He just wanted to survive the last couple days of this week and get the hell out of Dodge.

His cell phone rang. He grabbed it and looked at the screen. A local number, but not one he recognized. "Jason Lahey."

"This is Officer Harris with the Fortune Falls Police Department."

Jason's heart raced. For God sake, she's called the police on him. Or the therapist did. He tried to respond, but he couldn't let go of his last breath.

"Do you mind if I ask you a couple questions, Mr. Lahey?"

Slow exhale. "Not at all," he said with caution.

"Saturday, November sixteen. Do you recall that day?"

Jason had no clue the reason for the question, and he frantically paged through his memory. "I'm sorry. Saturday. Sixteenth of November?"

The officer continued with a direct and unwavering tone. "You may have encountered a Mr. Gregory Polnzy that morning."

Oh. Of course. Now Jason understood. This was about Suzie trying to get charges against Greg.

"Oh, that. Yes, I certainly did."

"Could you provide any details to that encounter?"

He flashed back to his engagement with Greg and shared what he could. Morning, the black truck with the dented tailgate. Greg and one other man clearing out the house in a hurry.

"He was very hostile when I approached him. Threatening."

"You're saying he threatened you?" The officer asked quickly.

"No, no. But he was—threatening. You know? He just had a very hostile attitude. He didn't shake my hand, he tried to get rid of me quickly, and he spoke very rudely of his mother and his sister."

A pause. A murmur. "But he didn't actually threaten you."

"I felt threatened."

"But he did not specifically, with words or action, threaten to do you harm?"

"No."

Another longer pause. "Did you happen to get a license plate number of the truck?"

"No, I'm sorry."

"Not even the state?"

"I think it was a Wisconsin plate."

More time lapsed. "Any indication made where he was going?"

"No."

"Could you describe what items you saw in the truck?"

"I think so." Jason rattled off what he remembered.

A long suspension of silence before the officer finally spoke again. "Thank you, Mr. Lahey. Should we need any clarification or additional information, we'll let you know."

The officer hung up.

Just before five o'clock, his phone rang again. He saw who it was displayed on his mobile screen.

"Hey, Glen."

"Hi, Jase. Sorry to bother you." Hard to tell from his cell phone, but Glen's tone sounded hesitant.

"No bother at all."

"Any chance you'd let me buy you a beer? Was hoping we could talk."

Jason could imagine what this was about. Had Jen talked to him, turned Glen against him? It would be good to sit and have a drink with his friend, but not to be lectured by him.

"That sounds great. Tell you what. You okay with joining me downtown? You could meet me in the Best Western lounge on First Street."

"Sure, sounds good. See you in twenty minutes?"

"Looking forward to it."

Jason stuffed his laptop in his briefcase, slipped on his jacket and headed out of his office.

Normally, this time of year, he'd dial in 91.7 on the car radio and play their twenty-four-hour Christmas songs as he drove, but he had been avoiding whatever seasonal reminders he could. It only made him dwell on this reality of being extracted from his wife and son, his house, and his neighborhood. It was impossible to imagine being alone over the Christmas season, but he had become more and more aware of the possibility. The potency of the holidays was strong—moments that could overwhelm with happiness and goodwill, or fester on the skin of loss and regret.

Back at the hotel, he parked in the attached ramp and headed for the lounge. Looking around the bar, he didn't see Glen. He sat, flagged his favorite bartender Barry, and ordered a rum and Coke.

Five minutes later, Glen entered the mostly empty cocktail lounge. Jason waved him over to the bar.

"Hey, Jase." Glen lowered himself to a stool.

"Good to see you, Glen." Jason waved to Barry. "Let me get you something."

"No, no, let me buy."

"Oh no, I'm buying. What can I get you? They have Ale Asylum on tap."

"Fine. That sounds good. Thanks."

Barry came over to them, his twenty-something face flat.

"Barry, an Ambergeddon for my friend here?"

Barry nodded and headed for the taps.

"Barry and I have become old friends," Jason said and chuckled.

Glen's expression was drawn as he looked at Jason. "How are you doing, Jason?"

Jason rolled the question off his shoulders. What was he supposed to say? "Hanging in there, Glen." He raised his glass to his reflected self in the mirror on the other side of the bar and took a drink.

Glen looked at the bar top and ahead at the bar mirror. Like their times on the porch, communication did not include eye contact, but what usually was a result of comfortable and casual observation had now become plain and simple avoidance.

"I had a chance to talk with Jen," Glen said, his words stiff.

Jason's head bobbed in reaction. He had no words to contribute. He was certain Jen had given Glen plenty of words.

Glen turned to him, eyes pushing, pleading. It was hard to return his look. It cut right through. "What can I do, Jason? How can I help? Talk to me. I'm here however you need me."

The easiest thing to do would be to ignore Glen's questions, just talk a bunch of shit and have a good time and enjoy his company. He certainly had no clear answers to offer Glen. He had a lot of raw emotion and instinctive reactions squirming around inside of him.

He thought back to his wrestling days in high school. He had never been good on his feet against an opponent. His height and his lank frame put his center of gravity too high and he became an easy takedown. Once down, however, he turned into a different animal—all long arms and long legs that found ways to tangle and knot around his opponent. He felt like he had just experienced a hard takedown standing up against his foe, and now he struggled to find a way to slip his arms and legs into weak spots, to try and put a submission hold on a life that was trying to pin him down for a three-count.

"I need you to watch over my family. Until I can dig my way out of this hole."

Glen reached out to Jason. "Grab my hand. I'll pull you out."

Jason finished his drink. "Careful. You might get pulled down with me."

Barry the bartender came with the Ambergeddon. Glen thanked him, drew the pint glass of amber ale close to him and kept his eyes on it. "Damn it, Jason. I don't understand what is going on. Neither does Jen. Is all this about Polnzy? Is that what's got your head so messed up?"

That tended to be how people approached an issue. They looked for a single cause. An obstacle to be removed or some missing piece to slip into place. Polnzy's death? Her—come on, call it what it was—suicide was perhaps the spark, but it was the dead and dry kindling of his past and present that had caught fire and turned into a blaze he couldn't stomp out.

"Jen is slipping away from me. She's against me and I don't know how to win her back. She's taking Nicky with her."

Glen laid a big hand on his shoulder. "Jase, do you think it might be you that's pushing her away? Maybe not intentionally, but with your drinking?"

"Why the hell can't the drinking be because of how Jen has turned against me? Huh?" Jason raised his empty glass in the air and waved it around until the bartender acknowledged him.

Glen winced. "Jason. She has not turned against you."

"She has. I know she has. And I don't know, maybe I don't blame her so much." He looked at Glen. "I don't know what's going on, Glen. But I know I don't like what's happening all around me and I don't know how to deal with it. I have just enough sense in me to realize that I'm no good being around them right now."

The bartender came back with his rum and Coke and Jason took a big swig.

"You're no good around them doing that," Glen said, pointing at the tumbler of rum and cola.

Jason gave Glen a hard stare. "Would you think less of me if I said it was the only thing getting me through this right now?"

"Damn it, Jason. Do you really think it's getting you through this? You gotta realize it's just digging you a deeper hole. You've fallen hard and fast. You can come back just as hard and fast." Glen spun his chair a quarter-turn to face Jason directly. "I have an idea what's going on, and I've watched lesser men than you destroy their lives over it. But you? No, Jason. Not you. I won't believe you're going to let it suck you in. You're no drunk. I know drunks. You ain't it."

Jason gave his friend a wan smile. "I wish I could put it all into words. I really wish I could. But things just aren't right. And there's other things that I thought were right, but they've come back on me. The past is circling back in ways I can't process." He swigged his drink and exhaled loudly. "Fuck. I'm talking a bunch of bullshit. Not sure what I'm saying. Just—be there for them when you can, huh? Tell them I love them and that I wish I could be there with them. Tell them I'm working on it. Working through it."

Glen shook his head. "Sounds like the kind of thing you should be telling them."

Elbows to the bar, hunched over his drink, he spun the glass round and round as he glanced up at the mirror. "Don't think they want to hear anything from me right now."

They sat in silence. Glen sipped at his beer and Jason drank down his rum and Coke. He thought back to the detour on that long-ago night in a different world. He wished like hell he had driven right through it. Part of him felt like he never made it home that night, that he was still lost on that long, lonely dark road.

CHAPTER FIFTEEN
Sunday, December 8, 2019

He drove into Springfield, Illinois, after about six hours on the road. He thought about flying, but whether out of Minneapolis or Milwaukee, it would have been two-and-a-half or three hours to get to the airport, then processing, baggage claim, and flight. It would have saved no time and been more of a hassle.

He pulled up to the entrance of the Crown Plaza Convention Center, put on his flashers and checked in, then parked his car and grabbed his luggage.

His home for the next seven days was five floors up. He had splurged and got an executive suite since company dollars were paying for it. In his room, he unpacked, set up his computer, hit the bathroom, and then headed to the Long 9 Lounge on the second floor.

The bar and restaurant looked cozy with high back, leather-padded chairs at the bar, comfortable lounge chairs around drink tables, and leather sofas around glass coffee tables. Chocolate-colored wood framed the chairs, the bar, and partitioned the walls with decorative molding. A large, fat Christmas tree stood against the far wall with frosty white lights glimmering amid deep red ornaments. The dining area was a segregated room next to the bar, brighter with padded, upholstered seats and mosaic-tiled walls. Garland boughs with large red bows draped the wainscoting. A light jazz rendition of "Away in the Manger" played through overhead speakers.

At three o'clock, the place was empty other than the bartender, a tall middle-aged woman reading a book as she sat on a stool behind the bar off in the corner. She looked up as he took a seat at the end of the bar, her chestnut eyes flaring under dark mahogany hair streaked with bold grey.

"Welcome, traveler," she said as she hopped off her seat and walked over to him. She crossed arms against her black vest over starched and collared white shirt. A red rose adorned her left breast. "Might I interest you in a libation?"

"Rum and Coke," he said as he surveyed the room.

"Single or double?"

"Double."

"Coming right up." She went off, scooped up ice in a large glass, poured rum and squirted in cola. She came back and placed it before him. "As ordered."

"Thank you." He took a drink and tried to ease the tension out of a day's travel through Madison, Bloomington and Rockford interstate traffic.

"You are very welcome." She moved back to her corner stool and picked up her book, but didn't look at it. "Are you here for the IT conference?"

He nodded.

She returned the nod with an eye-squeeze of either confirmation or smugness. "I suspected as much."

"Did you."

"Oh, yes. I see two primary types of people come through here, depending on the conference. Those of the right brain, and those of the left. You, sir, reside on the right side of your gray matter."

That amused him. "And why do you say that?"

She hopped off her stool again, her frame tall and big-boned, but shapely. "Oh, a few indications. Number one, you wasted no time ordering your drink. You knew exactly what you wanted."

"Okay."

"And what you ordered isn't a drinker's drink, so you aren't executive level, or you'd have ordered top-shelf scotch or bourbon straight."

He begrudgingly gave her that.

"But you didn't look over the signature cocktail menu and order some hipster drink with seven different obscure ingredients, so you aren't marketing or graphic design."

He laughed at that.

She came up to him, leaned over on the counter, her face drawing close to his. "Rum and Coke? Seriously? Most definitely IT. I suspect management."

He raised his glass to her. "Director. Close enough. You win, although I find your deductive reasoning to be dubious at best."

She smiled, her dark-lined eyes under her mop of silver-streaked ebony hair intense with self-satisfaction and perhaps some mischief. "I am a dubious soul, to be sure."

He winked, enjoying the banter. "Thanks for the warning. I'll tread with caution."

She sauntered back to her stool and picked up her book.

"What are you reading?"

She lowered the book and squinted with a red-lipped smirk.

"Not much at the moment. I'm trying to read *The Blind Assassin*." She held the bloated, dog-eared and worn paperback out to him. On the cover, a woman sat, glancing over her shoulder, looking like she was out of the 1920s.

He took a long drink. "Never heard of it. Any good?"

"Either that, or I enjoy suffering. This is my third time basking in its literary glow."

He tried to think if he had ever read anything more than once. He couldn't readily recall the last time he had read anything other than technical white pages and journals.

"I don't get it. You already know what's going to happen. What's the point?"

Her stare was hard and appraising through a splash of hair curling over her forehead. "You, my friend, appear to be all about the destination, not the journey."

He clicked tongue against cheek and jabbed a finger her way. "You got it." He drank the double down to a single.

She abandoned the stool and surrendered the book onto the seat. "I know your kind. I've had one too many guys like you in my life. In fact, I guess you could say I'm here because of a guy like that."

"You don't say."

She gave him a sideways glance. "No, I did say. But I find it curious that anyone can ever be that confident knowing what the destination actually is."

Apparently, she was one of those philosophical types. He had worked with a few of those back in the day. Nothing but trouble. Their favorite question tended to be, "Why," even when it was a clear and commonsensical answer. He found it exhausting.

He finished his drink and pushed his glass to the edge of the bar in front of her. "I think your destination is the rum."

He thought that would end the discussion—even cringed

inwardly that he may have come off too abrupt or harsh—but she let out a loud, quick, barking laugh, took the glass and placed it in a bus tub.

She grabbed a fresh glass, scooped ice, poured the rum, and shot in the cola. "So, you could indeed say that my destination is here, obeying your command." She speared a liquor-soaked cherry from a jar and garnished his glass. She walked over and he received the drink from her. "Or you could say my destination is here, serving your order."

He looked at the glass. "A cherry?"

She grinned. "Luxardo cherry. Only for my special customers." She turned and looked toward her stool. "Of course, my current destination is back to that stool so I can submerge myself in Ms. Atwood's lyrical prose."

Jason waved a hand, feeling the jab of a point. "Please. Don't let me stop you."

She leaned against the back of the bar and crossed her arms again, a tall and commanding presence. She took complete ownership of the space she occupied. "But, even this job is simply a wayside to the journey, just as everything that happened before has brought me here so I could serve you that drink."

He swallowed a mouthful and set the glass down. "Yeah, yeah. Life's a journey. I saw that commercial. I get it."

She moved forward, hands grabbing the edge of the bar, and she leaned into him, close. "Life is *the* journey. All of us are trying to *avoid* the destination as long as possible." She held her deep brown eyes on him and he felt a sinking vulnerability that made his gaze fall.

After some extra moments, she pulled away from him, grabbed a bar rag and wiped at the counter. "Well, like I said. I've known a guy or two who were fixated on the end of the journey." The swirl of the rag slowed and her gaze meandered. She fell to silence for long seconds, then her wiping became intense and her eyes focused. "I wouldn't suggest it."

"I'll keep that in mind." Strange woman, but intriguing in an odd way. Somehow she had turned his mood dark and thrown him off the taste of booze for the moment. Besides, he was tired and could use a nap before finding some dinner. He finished his drink, slapped thirty dollars on the counter and stood.

"See you around—?" he tossed her a questioning gesture.

"Pauline."

"Jason." He tipped an invisible hat. "Happy trails."

He rested for a half hour and, although he drifted away, he never left the ponderous shoreline of his waking mind. His brain wouldn't shut off, and little good came of that, lately. His thoughts these last few weeks tended to regret and recriminate, to lead him down dark currents churned by eddies of questions and waves of doubts. Those thoughts crashed over him and drew him under.

What happened to his happy family? Where did his perfect life go? How could everything have gone so wrong in so little time? He tried to escape these questions because they led to an easy and obvious answer that was far too self-reflecting.

He thought more about his childhood. About his mother. His memories thrummed like a hollow drum. Hammering his wooden work bench toy in the living room while his mother watched her soap operas. "Jason, honey, go play outside. You're giving your mother a headache." As a toddler, he had been a chore for her to cross off her daily list—bathe, clothe, feed, repeat. She had acclimated much better to his older years. She seemed to enjoy raising her little man, dressing him in snazzy clothing and showing him off in public. He couldn't impress her with good grades or athletic achievements, but the right shirt and pant combination, a good pair of shoes had her fawning over him. She reeled with delight when he brought a high school date home. As a teenager, he found his mother's superficiality to be oddly endearing.

But he realized how little happiness he recalled being his parents' son, and he had few memories of offering his mother any more affection than she gave him. He had been content as a child, but that wasn't the same as being happy, and this undercurrent of thought threatened to carry him away.

Had his family ever been happy? Had there been joy and love between him, Jen and Nicky? Were things ever truly okay?

He wanted to hold on to that belief, to know he had made the right choices and done all the right things to build an ideal life for his wife and child. He was desperate to hold on to a reality where he was successful, content, loved. That he was a good man and deserved what he had.

He began to realize he wasn't that man. He had just been extremely good at pretending.

He failed to recognize his son's special needs. He deliberately and continually went behind his wife's back with her parents. He abandoned close friends and neighbors as one of them slowly succumbed to cancer while the other helplessly watched. He ignored his father's condition until it was too late. And his mother's death was—

He got up. He was getting lost inside the darkest recesses of himself, and he wanted to be as far away from there as possible.

He grabbed his phone and dialed Jen. It rang. She didn't answer. It went to voicemail.

"Hey, it's me. Just wanted to let you know I'm here. No issues. I hope all is well at home."

Words caught in his throat and he coughed and took a breath. "I—I need to know. We were happy once, right? I made you happy? That happened, didn't it?"

He took another shaky breath. "Miss you. Tell Nix I love him."

He hung up, dropped the phone on the bed and his head into his hands. Fingers clenched and rubbed and pulled at skin, as if he could peel away his face.

He had dinner in the hotel restaurant. There was a decent crowd for a Sunday night, but still little more than a half-full room. He ordered a salmon filet over risotto and asparagus spears drizzled with a dill cream sauce, but had only a few bites while sipping an Old Fashioned. His plate looked little different than Nicky's would be when finished. He missed his skinny, sandy-haired son.

He settled the bill and walked over to the bar where he saw the lounge chairs and sofas full with what he assumed to be chatting team members from the IT departments of companies attending the technology conference, or human resource managers here for the other convention being held at the conference center. He could have bet on which were HR and which were IT. Human resource staff were loud and animated, dressed smartly to make a good impression. Many women and a few younger men. Their boisterous laughter and appropriate gestures were obvious. IT folks were mostly male with lots of facial hair, mostly jeans and t-shirts that blared various 80s and 90s geek culture references or post-millennium hard rock bands.

At the bar, there were several open chairs and he took the one at the far end. An older gentleman behind the bar, smartly outfitted in black slacks and bow tie around a crisp white collar, shook a cocktail over his head and poured out a rosy concoction into two martini glasses. He shaved off two orange peels, ran them over the glass rims, grazed the rinds with the lick of a blue flame from the flick of a lighter and dropped them into the drinks. They were served to a pair of younger women, cleanly but casually dressed and laughing quietly at one of their phone screens.

Pauline, the tall bartender with the cascade of dark hair, stood at the other end of the bar tending to a man and woman.

The older bartender approached Jason. "Good evening, sir. What's your preference tonight?"

He needed a change, a wrench to toss into the machine of his routine. He decided to be adventurous. "Any specialty cocktails tonight?"

The bartender tossed a drink menu in front of him. "Indeed. Are you leaning more toward whisky, brandy, gin, rum?"

"How about rum."

"Oh. We have a delightful item we just added. Change of Seasons. Rum, shaken with muddled baby peas, lime juice, simple syrup and tarragon, served with pomegranate, beet juice and allspice dram ice cubes."

Jason shook his head and laughed. "Wow. Okay. Well, why the hell not? Serve it up."

"Right away." The bartender stepped away to start juggling bottles and pouring dashes of this and splashes of that, intensity and deftness a cross between mad alchemist and competent chemist. Jason had no idea what that mess of ingredients would taste like, but he welcomed the complete diversion.

"Why, my Journeyman has returned." Pauline smiled as she grabbed a bottle of vodka and scooped ice in a tall, skinny glass. "Rum and Coke?"

"Change of Seasons, actually. Your partner is fixing it for me."

She froze in place. "You're joking."

"Didn't I tell you? Just changed careers. I'm a web designer now."

She laughed loud and it felt good to receive a positive reaction from someone, especially her.

"Well, congratulations on the new profession and your hipster transformation. If you start sporting a man bun, however, I'm calling for help."

She dumped orange juice and vodka into the glass and made heavy steps to a fifty-something woman with a neck scarf and floral blouse.

The two bartenders stayed busy for the next two hours. Both mixologists moved to-and-fro along the bar length, pouring and shaking creations and serving the customers sitting at the bar and lounging in chairs and sofas. The din of conversations was steady, but despite the enthusiasm of topics, the room absorbed enough of the sound to keep the volume comfortable.

He had been taken aback by the Change of Seasons when first served. Although the deep red body invited, the seafoam green head challenged and dared. He took a sip. Sweet and fruity up front, but it took a bit to adjust to the earthy finish. By the end, he was ordering another.

Walt, the bartender serving him, headed out a little after nine along with two-thirds of the customers. After Jason's third Change of Season, he felt like he had enough of the earthy sweetness and he switched to rum and Coke. He finished his third when Pauline stepped up to him. He was one of four people left up against the bar.

"Need a water?" she asked.

He winced. "Can't really hold my water. Better just go with another rum and Coke."

She locked on him for a moment, as if she wanted to say something, but instead nodded and mixed it up for him.

"Make it a double," he said and watched her oblige.

"Early start for you tomorrow?" she asked as she put the rum and Coke in front of him.

He shook his head. "Nah. Keynote speaker at nine. Never any useful information in a keynote. Just an opportunity for some successful asshole to ego trip across the stage. I think I'll pass."

"Ah." She stepped back to rinse out a cocktail shaker. "Not one to be inspired by another's journey, I see." She gave him a quick, sharp grin.

He smiled as he drew back from the bar counter. "I'm catching a bit of a theme here. You seem kind of focused on this whole journey idea. Care to share the backstory to this?"

She shook her head.

"Oh, come on, Pauline. Spill the beans. Sounds like there was a guy involved? Maybe a past love interest? Hmm?"

She grabbed a bar towel and started wiping down the countertop. "How's that rum and Coke?"

"Oh, she has a weak spot. I get it. No worries." He threw up both hands in surrender. "I relinquish and offer mercy."

She tossed the towel to the back shelf, put hands to hips and looked down at him. "A true gentleman. And what about you? Where are you coming from to be educated in the technical wizardry of modern informational technologies?"

"Wisconsin. Fortune Falls."

"Nice area."

He nodded and drank.

"Wife? Kids?"

"Yes and yes. A son."

"That's nice. Sounds like a nice life."

He finished his drink and pushed the glass forward. "No rush."

She didn't move immediately, and it seemed like she might say or do something, but she finally took the glass and mixed him another double. Setting it in front of him, she asked, "So, you come to this conference every year?"

He shook his head and drank. "First time."

"Travel a lot for your job?" She walked over to the soda gun and shot herself a glass of water.

He shook his head again. He had no interest talking about himself tonight. "What about you? Married? Family?"

"I don't think I was cut out for it." She ran her finger around the rim of her glass. "I had thought that was where my life was headed, but it took a very different turn."

He caught the regret that flattened her tone. "I can certainly relate to that." He tipped back his glass.

She sipped water. "Is that so."

"Let's just say I'm better off here for now. Or my family's better off with me here. Who the hell knows?" He drank again.

"You?" she answered, though she didn't make immediate eye contact with him. "You certainly should know." Once she did connect, her eyes didn't break from his.

He held on to that stare as long as he could—felt the burning recrimination of it. He shook off her statement and her judgement with a bitter and apathetic shrug. He was so tired of condemning himself while allowing everyone else to do the same.

Pauline nodded and left to tend to her remaining customers. He sat in silence and tended to his drink, mulling over the last few fragments of their conversation. That led to the conclusion that there needed to be more drinking and less talking.

When she finally came back, he set the glass in front of her. "Let's go with one more. Little heavier on the rum, huh?"

He gave her a wink, but she didn't seem to receive it well. To be honest, he wasn't exactly sure if he meant it in a friendly way or more to suggest he had enough with getting to know each other.

The evening had turned. He felt surly and wasn't sure why. His head was thick and heavy and the conversation with Pauline had become tedious.

She looked at the empty glass, at him, then turned and grabbed a new glass. She scooped ice into it and shot it full of water.

"Tell you what," she said and put the glass in front of him. "Drink that up first and then I'll get you another."

He looked at the water and then at her. Was this a joke? If so, he wasn't getting it. And if it wasn't a joke, he was about to get upset. "What are you talking about?"

"I'll make a deal with you. You wanted to hear my backstory. Well, let me close out the last few people and I'll come back. If you indulge me with that water, I'll tell you a little of that story and then the last round is on me. Okay?"

He glared at the water and at her. He didn't need this shit. Not today. He didn't know who she thought she was, but now she was judging him, and that was bullshit. He tried to maintain some amount of humor, but started to seethe with resentment. "Hey, what's going on here? You aren't refusing me service, are you?"

She halved the distance between them as she moved closer to his face with her bold, dark-lined eyes and piercing gaze. "Jason—It's Jason, right? Jason, I'm offering to buy your next round and bare a bit of my soul that you seemed very interested in a few moments ago. All you need to do is drink one glass of water. But, hey. If that's too rough for you to handle, I can get you another rum and Coke right now, and you can just sit there alone, never knowing what captivating past this intriguing woman was about to share with you."

It was tempting to tell her to bring that rum and Coke and put her in her place. Fuck her for playing games with him. But then she would have the higher ground. She would feel like she won something and that he was weak. He would unwittingly prove something to her about himself that he didn't want this woman to believe about him.

Not taking his eyes off her, he took the water glass in hand and sipped. "Mmmm. Smooth."

She flashed a bright red-lipped smile. "Be right back."

He watched her move with a determined, almost lumbering motion to the few other customers. She served a bourbon and ginger to one of them, poured a soda for another, and closed out all their tabs. She had a natural rapport with each. Despite the offense he had taken by the glass of water that sat in front of him like an accusation, he found himself again intrigued by her, drawn to her. It wasn't an attraction exactly, though there was a brute sensuality about her. This Pauline was compelling, even if to a somewhat unsettling degree. For just a moment, while she had looked so deeply at him, he had weirdly, inexplicably, almost felt like confessing to her.

She returned with her stool and dropped it down in front of him. "Mr. Jason. I must first make clear to you that I do not know you. My story is my story, not yours. If you decide to relate it to your story, that is your problem, not mine. Do you understand?"

He absolutely did not understand, but he wanted to move this uncomfortable situation forward. "Sure. Whatever."

She gave a half-smile, apparently content with this acknowledgement of her verbal waiver.

"So, some twenty-seven or twenty-eight years ago, during my college years, I was a drunk."

For Chrissake, he knew it. She was pulling this shit on him.

She smiled and held up a hand. "Settle down. My story, remember? You asked. I'm telling. Drink your water."

He took a sip of water.

"I would have been around twenty at the time. I was hiding from things I couldn't face. My parents were loving but stern, and I knew I was disappointing them. I was a devout Christian, and I knew I was disappointing my Creator. I was pursuing literature and liberal arts at college but conflicted by the lifestyle surrounding that world. And I was constantly disappointing myself, because I was failing at being either of the two people my conflicting worlds were telling me to be. So I drank. A lot. And I did a lot of things to try and kill the parts of me that cared about either of those worlds.

"I led myself into some terrible trouble and made a decision that, had I been clear-headed, I would not have made. But, like so many other parts of myself I was trying to kill off, in my clouded and distorted rationality, I believed killing off one more part of me was the right decision.

"Overcome with regret, I realized I had to make a change. Drinking had become my way of removing myself from the responsibilities of my life and the decisions I needed to make."

"Listen, don't try to compare your drinking with—"

Pauline put up a hand. "My story, remember? Not yours."

Against all his urges, Jason stayed quiet.

"I joined AA and cleaned myself up. I was dry for a year. I was doing better. I was fragile, estranged from both my parents, but on a path to better days. Got a good job as a librarian, made a couple of friends, was writing poetry. Then, I met this guy. Believe it or not, someone in a darker place than even I was. It did not go well. He felt he was on a predetermined path and was fixated on the destination. In the end, his journey did not include me, and as I result, I fell off the wagon. So, I ran away again—from a good job, from this guy I think I might have loved, and from everything that I had started to build up again.

"I cleaned up over the next few years as I wandered, thinking I was on some kind of journey to find myself. It took me the better part of a decade to realize that the me I was searching for wasn't at the end of some enlightened journey. She was *on* the journey.

"So, now I'm back with AA, living the twelve-step life."

After moments of silence, Jason drank the last of his water and pushed his glass forward. "This one's on you."

Pauline gave a slow nod, got up, fixed him a rum and Coke and stood silent in front of him.

"And you're telling me all of this why?"

She grinned weakly. "Don't flatter yourself thinking you are the first person I've shared this story with. I find it—therapeutic. To the right ears, of course."

"Okay."

"But also. Jason. You have to realize that we recognize our own."

He smoldered from the insult of insinuation that heated his face. "You're calling me a drunk."

"No. I can tell you're not a drunk. You don't drink like a drunk. You drink like a college kid just turning twenty-one. But you seem to be someone who is running away. I could be wrong, but I sense a fear in you that I recognize. I've seen it before. In me. In that guy I was talking about."

This conversation had become very uncomfortable. Inappropriate. Who the hell did she think she was that she could analyze him after just a few hours at a bar? He didn't need to put up with this.

He took a deep, long drink. Ice jumped and clattered when he set the glass heavily on the counter. He slid off the chair and steadied himself against the bar. "I'm sorry you've had trouble in your life. I'm sorry you've made bad decisions. That has nothing to do with me." He pulled out his wallet and slapped his credit card down. "Now, how about closing me out?"

Her smile seemed a bit too big and too tightly stretched. "I'll be right back with the check."

CHAPTER SIXTEEN
Monday, December 9, 2019

He slept late. The digital display on the hotel clock told him it was 8:34 a.m. That pretty much ruled out any chance of him making the keynote address, even if he had reconsidered, which he hadn't.

His head and neck throbbed and his stomach churned. He sifted through memories of last night. There definitely were some gaps, but he may not have been the most warm and receptive person to that woman bartender last night. Of course, he seemed to remember her doing a respectable job of making him feel like crap as well.

Moving a bit slow, with caution, he got himself out of bed and into the bathroom, beelining for the toilet with a fierce urge to urinate. He passed a long, strong stream of dark yellow piss that foamed in the toilet. The relief was mildly orgasmic.

He looked at himself in the mirror. Sunken, red eyes buried in deep, dark bags. Sallow cheeks. Protruding paunch threatening to fold over the elastic band of his briefs.

Jesus.

Three months ago, he still felt relatively good about his physical condition. Not exactly trim and toned, but healthy. Even youthful, to a decent extent, other than the start of a widow's peak and a touch of gray, which made him look distinguished. Or so Jen claimed. Now, a sad man reflected back at him and he didn't know what depressed him more—that his condition had deteriorated this far, or that he simply didn't care.

Sluggish movements got him ready for the day. He spent a long time in a hot shower, which took the edge off the hangover. Grooming and dressing, he at least felt better of himself, enough to face the public with an amount of confidence.

Out of the bathroom, he checked his phone and saw that Jen called last night. He had missed it. Truth be told, that was a blessing. It would have likely turned ugly if he had answered the phone last night.

He tapped the voicemail icon and listened to the message.

"Glad you arrived safely. Everything is fine here. Nicky's doing better. He'll be in to see Leslie tomorrow." Pause. "Jason, why would you even ask such a thing? Of course we were happy. You made me happy. I don't know what to tell you now. I just know you are making yourself terribly unhappy, and that's making us unhappy. Please. Figure out what's going on and be the father and husband we love and who makes us happy, okay? Call me if you want to talk. I'm here." Pause. "I love you."

He wiped his eyes, took two heaving breaths, erased the voicemail, and left the room.

The hotel swarmed with people whose dangling lanyards and badges tagged and labeled them. Dressed in varying degrees of casual business vogue, they lugged tote bags and briefcases at their sides and notebooks in their hands. He dodged, weaved and sidestepped the flock of conventioneers, stepped through the lobby and out the sliding doors to the parking lot. The weather was brisk but mild for what he was used to by this time of year. He zipped up his jacket, grabbed his phone, and hunted down an Uber. No destination came to mind, he just wanted to get downtown. He typed in "Lincoln Museum." Three minutes later, he climbed into a Toyota Prius.

"First time seeing the Lincoln Presidential Museum?" the driver asked.

"Yeah."

"Let me tell you, every American should be required to go to that museum."

"Yeah?"

"Oh, yeah. It's pretty amazing."

Jason didn't feel particularly talkative this morning. If this guy wanted to talk, let him. He was just going to enjoy the ride.

"It's shocking how relevant the past is to our present, you know?"

The driver's words felt like they had snuck up from behind. "You don't say," Jason said.

"The past fucking haunts us, man. All of us. Excuse my French."

Jason could only nod slowly and continue trying not to think about such things.

In less than fifteen minutes, the driver pulled up to the large, marble building that took up the entire city block between East Madison and East Jefferson. He thanked the driver, gave a tip and rating via his phone, and walked toward the round glass and columned rotunda of the institution's main entrance. He had not intended to actually go to the museum, it just seemed like a good central location to get him downtown. It was only 9:45—

too early to hit a bar, even for him. He honestly didn't have anything better to do. What the hell. He could spare an hour or two for the sake of history.

He went inside.

At half past three, he finally walked out of the museum. He was still overwhelmed by the scale of it all—of the building itself and the exhibits, sure, but much more so the scale of events displayed behind red velvet rope and under glass. The country rent in two, its leaders and its people vehemently divided, taking up arms and killing each other in the fields of their very own lands. One man of humble beginnings, self-educated, flailing arms to maintain balance as he teetered on a political and moral tightrope, trying to hold the union together as millions of his citizens massacred each other for the sake of what they thought was best for their country. Meanwhile, an entire race of people caught in the middle between enslavement and freedom, with little opportunity to take action or raise a voice for themselves.

While he walked the hallways of wallpapered political cartoons and listened to the talking heads of past politicians spout sesquicentennial rhetoric on video screens, Jason recognized how that messaging still echoed across the country today from the mouths of pundits, the teleprompters of television and radio, and the sounding boards of social media. How there were, even now, citizens who appeared eager to take up weapons, not to defend their land or their lives, but instead attack what didn't fit into a mythical ideal sold to them by pithy talking points and shallow memes.

He had shown little interest in current politics—only annoyance and disappointment. Suddenly, next year's election and the modern politics it reflected seemed to be at a more critical juncture than he realized.

The past still haunted the zeitgeist of modern day. Just as Jason's past was a poltergeist to his present.

But no museum or memorial would draw him into confronting his ghosts head on. Not with so many other forces working against him.

He walked south for five or six blocks down the modest metropolitan thoroughfare of 6th Street in downtown Springfield. It being a Monday, quite a few places were closed, but he came upon a little tavern called Obed & Isaac's Microbrewery, walked in and sat at the corner of the bar. A quaint, inviting location, he found the brews to be tasty and had several while he chatted off and on with the bartender, a friendly woman with a welcoming demeanor.

After three darker beers, he strolled northeast and found a well-rated Italian restaurant called Saputo's that was open. It was a small brick building on the corner of East Monroe and 8th Street South with a vintage incandescent sign that stuck out and over its single door entrance.

Inside, the dank atmosphere harkened back to the seventies. A long bar ran along the room with basic tables and chairs along the wall and more dining in back. Dismal lighting, brooding colors and bland décor. The bartender was a gruff woman with shaggy blonde hair serving mixers in pint glasses. A man who looked to be in his late seventies got up from his bar stool to seat Jason.

Once he ordered, though, he found the food to be authentically and deliciously Italian. The chicken cacciatore was tender and savory, and his several rum and Pepsi's were generously poured. The waitress was all business, but the bartender was a spitfire and he enjoyed bantering with her about the town, the food and the forties and fifties crooner music playing.

Feeling good after his third double at Saputo's, he hailed a ride to get him back to the hotel.

When he returned to the Crown Royal lobby doors, he thought about heading straight up to his room. It was getting close to eight o'clock and there were sessions tomorrow he should attend that started at eight. But he wanted to make a quick stop in the Long 9 Lounge.

A decent-sized crowd filled the lounge. Two bartenders raced back and forth. As he drew closer and took a seat at the bar, he saw that neither of them were Pauline.

A younger bartender with full beard and hair tied back to a small brunet bouquet at the point of his head approached him in the establishment's uniform of black slacks, white starched shirt and bow tie. "Hey, man. What do you need?"

"Pauline working tonight?"

"No, sorry. Off on Mondays and Tuesdays. Can I pour you something?"

"How about a Change of Seasons?"

"You got it." He went to work.

Jason wasn't completely sure why he hoped to see her. The story she shared had slowly started to trickle back into his recollection as the day wore on, and he vaguely remembered being dismissive of it. And honestly, why not? It was a major dump of personal information on a virtual stranger. Add to that the obvious fact she correlated his drinking with her drinking problem. Even if he did have a drinking problem, it was out of line for a bartender to point the finger at a new customer and single him out as an alcoholic. Tact and professionalism didn't even begin to enter into that.

And yet, he felt the desire to apologize. He had been an asshole when there was no reason to be an asshole. He could have blown her off, ordered the drink and not taken everything so personally.

Why the hell had she felt compelled to share such a personal story with him, anyway?

Pauline triggered a compulsive curiosity in him. He was alone in a hotel, estranged from his wife and kid, and he felt an inexplicable draw toward the enigmatic bartender. Not necessarily sexual, though intellectual intrigue and physical attraction could charge emotion in a similar fashion.

The hipster bartender served him his Change of Seasons and he sipped at it while he tried not to think about Pauline. Instead, he wondered how Jen and Nicholas were doing, and how he would spend his day tomorrow.

Three Change of Seasons certainly shifted his weather. The next morning, his head pounded and it felt like his stomach was pushing chicken cacciatore back up into his throat. The clock beside the bed said 9:03 a.m.

Did he have any intention of hitting some sessions at the conference today? The thought of sitting through hours of Powerpoint presentations on internet protocols, firewalls, virtual server partitioning and security made his stomach turn over.

He took care of his usual morning maintenance, then high stepped it out of the hotel and into a rideshare. Destination: downtown. This time, to the State Capitol building.

On a Tuesday at ten in the morning, he was the only person there for a tour. The capitol was magnificent. It displayed a managed riot of color and pattern—combinations of pinks, reds, browns, blues and teals that shouldn't have worked together but did. The paint, structure and artwork inspired awe. The influence of the French and Italian renaissances was overt. There was obviously a reason it was listed as a top-five state capitol building.

The tour guide shared how the building was the tallest of all state capitols built in the classical style. It was the sixth and final Illinois state capitol building, erected in 1867 after the old state capitol was deemed insufficient. In the previous capitol building, Lincoln had argued supreme court cases, debated Stephen Douglas, and gave his famous House Divided speech. The guide also mentioned that Illinois was the first state to ratify the 13th amendment to abolish slavery.

Jason marveled at the beauty and spectacle presented by a government building of a free republic. He looked up and up and up at the stunning dome interior rounded by copper reliefs, columns, ornate woodwork and stained glass that had all the pomp and grandeur of an autocratic palace or religious cathedral. Yet, it ironically stood as a beacon for secular rule by a representative government of the people and for the people.

It was no wonder how the public, rallying to either political side, could become confused about how to view and respond to their leaders—either as saviors or devils.

At one point during the tour, Jason's phone buzzed. He looked at who was calling, thinking (hoping) it might be Jen, but it was only Troy at work. He declined the call.

After the capitol, he walked eight blocks against a brisk, cold wind through the gray of the day and stopped into the Anvil and Forge Brewery to warm up and check out their taps. He ordered a flight and received four five-ounce glasses nestled into a metal anvil-shaped serving tray. Their stout was particularly good and he ordered two more pint glasses.

He left the microbrewery, meandered through downtown and came upon a pub called JP Kelly's. It had just opened for the day and presented itself as a quiet and inviting neighborhood bar. He lounged about for a couple hours and ordered an Old Fashioned and a couple rum and Cokes. He also tried a Jameson and ginger, realized he may have discovered a new favorite drink, and ordered another.

The bar started to fill up by five. He was hungry, hadn't eaten anything yet that day and the alcohol sat heavy in his gut and light in his head. He wandered outside and tried to summon an Uber, but the app caused too much frustration so he hailed a cab.

The driver didn't seem to understand him at first when he told her to take him back to the hotel, but he spoke more slowly and she got it. Walking outside must have taken a bit out of him because, before he knew it, she called out to tell him they had arrived. He got out, paid the driver and headed inside for the restaurant.

There was a short wait for a table. He needed to sit, so he said he'd eat at the bar and found an open chair to plop down on. Walt, the older bartender, worked alongside the hipster bartender. He flagged Walt down and asked for a Change of Seasons and a menu.

He went with a third-pound ground round burger with bleu cheese, caramelized onions and bacon. When his food came, he ordered a whisky and ginger and tore into the burger.

About halfway through the sloppy third-pounder and some potato wedge fries, he started to feel off. He finished his drink, hoping that would help, but his head swam and his stomach churned. He stumbled off his stool and looked around the bar area that rocked like a ship at sea.

"Bathroom." It was more a thought he spoke out loud, a verbalized imperative to his legs. The woman next to him apparently took it as a question and pointed him in a direction.

Around the bar, down a short hallway, he pushed open the men's bathroom door and all at once, instinct—some command from his limbic system that wasn't going to waste time explaining itself—drove him like a rocket to the first of two toilet stalls. Half a hamburger, a handful of fries, and at least six of the approximately eleven drinks he had imbibed that day shot out of him and into the toilet bowl, over the toilet plumbing and handle, and against the tiled wall. He collapsed to his knees and heaved out the remaining drinks along with the chunky dark pink bile of what was likely yesterday's chicken cacciatore. He heaved and wretched twice more, with little more coming out of him other than a string of saliva.

Gasping for air, he leaned over the toilet bowl that, for the moment, became the only reality of his world. With deep, hitching breaths, he fell against the side partition. Where he was and what he had just done started to sink in, along with the stench of his own vomit dripping down the wall and off the chrome pipes.

He heard the squeak of the bathroom door open and steps enter. He quickly reached up and over to slide the lock in case they were going to use the toilet. Instead, he heard a stream of urination. He listened for the zip of the fly, flush of the urinal, run of water, yank of paper towel, and swing of door open and shut.

Jason got up slowly, weak-kneed with a pounding, sloshing head, and made a half-assed attempt at cleaning up his mess with toilet paper. He only succeeded in sliding his slimy filth around and getting it on his hands, which made him retch and almost throw up again.

He left the stall and washed his hands at the sink. His body wouldn't stop swaying. As he dried his hands with paper towels, a gray-haired man in a suit stepped in. The gentleman grimaced as Jason, avoiding eye contact, passed him and exited the bathroom.

At the bar, he pushed his credit card across the surface and called out, "Settle!" The older bartender gave him a look, grabbed the card, ran it through, and returned with two credit card receipts while Jason tried to steady himself against the bar rail. At least he knew what those brass railings were for now. Genius.

He added a thirty-dollar tip to the fifty-dollar bill, slid it ahead, apologized to the bartender who was no longer in front of him, and stumbled away.

This was no way to spend a vacation.

Especially since this wasn't a vacation to begin with.

He laughed out loud and ignored the people who looked at him with disgust.

Chapter Seventeen
Wednesday, December 11, 2019

Waking up was similar to coming out of anesthesia. He came to slowly, with little cognizance of self, of location, or of past. It was, quite possibly, the closest thing one could come to experiencing the awareness of a newborn with a blank slate mind.

But, with dribs and drabs of fragmented moments, he began to regain awareness and identity—a past and a position in this reality.

Doubtful, however, that shame would be one of the first emotions felt by a newborn, but it certainly came upon him early enough, even before he had any clear idea what he should feel shameful about.

His head throbbed, stomach roiled, and embarrassment rose. It was a simple and obvious assumption that if he woke up feeling like this, while having little memory of how or what brought him to this state, chances are he should be deeply ashamed.

But those memories were filling in like sand sifting through an hourglass. He started to retrace his steps downtown, which made him take a fairly accurate tally of his alcoholic intake. He couldn't remember how he got to the hotel, but recalled having dinner at the bar, and then—

He jumped out of bed and ran to the bathroom. Whatever sludge remained in his stomach spewed into the toilet, along with a good amount of relatively clear liquid. He dry-heaved for half a minute before he collapsed to the cool tiled floor.

He remembered now. Remembered getting sick in the bathroom. Remembered what he must have left for staff to clean up.

He was mortified.

He wiped off his face and brushed his teeth to try and get the foul taste out of his mouth. His throat burned and his stomach muscles were sharply sore. Out of the bathroom, he looked at the clock. 10:03 a.m. Christ. His third day into a conference he hadn't even checked into yet.

He felt absolutely horrible, but he had to regain some element of responsibility. He checked his phone, saw a message and remembered that Troy had called yesterday morning. He went into voicemail.

"Jason. Check your email. We're having serious issues. It's a shitstorm here. Need you to call me."

His gut sank and he went to his laptop, opened it and logged in.

So many emails and Teams chats. From Troy. From customer service. From Wayne, the CIO. He didn't know where to begin. As he scanned through them, the depth of the problem and degree of his responsibility began to take shape.

Was he looking at the end of his career at Boswell? Data loss. Website down. Potential data breach.

He looked at Wayne's last email:

What the fuck were you thinking leaving town during a critical

server migration?

He couldn't even begin to reply to that. Of course he shouldn't have left. No director of information technologies in his right mind would have.

And clearly he was not in his right mind. He hadn't been for a while.

Last week, Leslie suggested he seek out professional help. He had been so offended by that. Now look at him.

Take a shower. Try to regain your senses. Call Troy. Get control of this shit. Get control of *your* shit.

In the bathroom, he cranked the hot water in the shower and slipped off his underwear. In the mirror, a naked, pale and trembling man slowly faded into the obscurity of steam.

He spent most of the day trying to mitigate the disaster he had at least been partially responsible for. Troy had been right all along. The problem hadn't been running the scripts that checked for file dependencies. Instead, Jason neglected to account for personal settings on local drives when he put together the master outline. He also never followed up with Boswell's CRM software vendor to confirm certain protocols and ensure data integrity.

Fortunately, by the end of the day, he was able to mend the situation enough that their CRM was running and communicating with their website, which was once again live. The data loss at this point seemed minimal, and any data breach appeared to only be a potential threat and not a realized one.

By 6:30 p.m., he was exhausted but oddly exhilarated. Despite the fact he had quite possibly thrown his career away, for the first time in over a month he had put himself to task on a critical imperative that required the deepest levels of his expertise. He confronted what seemed to be an insurmountable challenge and resolved it.

He may lose his job, but he felt like he accomplished something significant that no one else had been able to do. He had proven his worth when, for a long time, he had done nothing but doubt himself.

That, if nothing else, earned him a drink.

"Journeyman," Pauline said upon his arrival.

"Well, hello! How were your days off?"

"Just productive enough to satisfy the brain," she said, "and just indulgent enough to nourish the soul."

The restaurant looked busy, but at this point the bar was sparse. Pauline stacked glasses against the back wall. Walt talked with a couple at the couch.

"Excellent! Let's celebrate. How about one of those Change of Seasons?"

She stepped back from the glasses with a thin smile. "I will prepare that for you."

He blinked, squinted to the stoic reply and smiled. "Okay, then."

She muddled the peas and added the rum, simple syrup, lime and tarragon to the shaker.

As she began to shake the mixture over her head, she looked at him. "Word has it you left a nice surprise for our crew last night." Her warm smile immediately made him go cold.

"Oh, shit."

"Fortunately, not shit. But still."

Somehow, amid his intense dive into fixing the migration issues, he had completely forgotten about last night. Even now, being reminded of it in such a flagrant way, the incident seemed more like a story he heard about someone else. He had a hard time taking ownership of it.

"I—I'm so sorry about that. I don't know, I think I came down with something. Food just wasn't sitting right. I'm totally embarrassed."

She nodded and shook her drink shaker.

"I had hoped my tip would somehow make up for it."

She nodded and shook.

"I really had tried to clean it up. I was so embarrassed, but so sick—"

She nodded and shook.

"Right." He had nothing more to say.

She poured the mix into a glass and dropped in the pomegranate, beet juice and allspice dram ice cubes. The glass made loud contact with the bar top as she put the cocktail before him. "Drink up."

He looked at the glass, the foamy green head aloft on a crimson body. Raising his eyes, he saw her daring him to take a sip, as if he were about to steal candy from a child or kick a puppy.

"Listen," he said. "Should I just go?"

Her dark brow line rose and softened the glare of her judgement. "But, I went through all that trouble to make it."

His hand teased contact with the glass. "Well, again," he said, fingers slowly moving up and down the drink, "I'm really sorry. No excuse."

"Appreciated, but not the appropriate audience. If you see Kenny, make sure you let him know. He discovered your remains of the day. Walt said our young teammate looked rather green as he emerged from your purge."

He looked up and her eyes flared. He couldn't help it. A laugh bubbled up from his gut. Pauline smiled, then barked laughter, which made him laugh harder, his eyes tearing up. He winced and held his aching gut muscles that hadn't recovered from his retching.

"'Emerged from your purge?' Oh, ouch. Pauline, you are one of a kind."

She laughed again. "I am kind of one, for certain."

She crossed the bar and checked on an older gentleman. He waved and nodded to indicate he was fine and she came back to Jason's side.

Jason wiped his eyes, eased back and studied her. "So. There is an apology I owe you."

She pulled out three limes, a small knife and cutting board. "Is there?"

"You shared a very personal story and I was—"

"An asshole?" She smiled as she sliced the sour citrus fruit.

He mulled that over and nodded. "Yeah. An asshole."

She chuckled as she sliced. "Mr. Jason. You have no idea what I have to deal with stationed behind this bar. Honestly, you were fine."

"I wasn't, and I apologize. But also, thank you."

She slowed her cutting and cocked her head in his direction. "For what?"

"For sharing such a personal story. I get it, and I appreciate it."

She gave him a broad smile below either sad or thoughtful eyes. "You are welcome."

"But, you need to answer something for me. You are a recovering alcoholic, and you work at a bar?"

She gave a smug grin.

"I don't get it."

"It wasn't exactly planned, but I needed a job, one where I could have most of the daytimes free. And, there wasn't a high demand for librarians, so I took it. I figured, 'Pauline, here's a great way to steel your resilience, and maybe even help a couple people in the process facing the same dark hole you were facing.'"

She lingered on him with those deep, dark eyes. Unlike two nights ago, he accepted being one of those people tonight. He wouldn't dwell on it.

"So, you never saw that guy again? The one you talked about?"

Pauline opened the door to the cooler below the counter and grabbed a clear container. She started loading it with lime slices. "Oh, I saw him again." She gave a devilish grin. "But that, I'm afraid, is another story."

"Fair enough." He looked at his drink, reached for it, but left his hand on the counter. "What about your parents? Didn't you say you were estranged from them?"

"For a time, yes. But I started speaking with my mother and we slowly grew close again. My father—well, we remained distant for many years until my mother died two years ago. That's what actually brought me to Springfield, to take care of him."

"I'm sorry about your mother." Florence slipped into his mind with her carefully prepared face and styled hair. Her casual, detached demeanor. He tried to distance himself from those memories.

"Thank you," Pauline said. "It was hard, but I think she'd be very happy to know that it brought me home and reunited me with my father." She put the lid on the container and stored it back in the cooler. A waitress approached with a drink order and Pauline went to work mixing up what looked to be a Manhattan.

"What about you?" she asked. "Parents?"

"None living." His fingers flitted about the sweating glass of crimson cocktail.

"Sorry to hear that," she said as she finished the drink and put it on the rubber mat of the server area.

A waiter followed with another order. Walt came back around the bar and grabbed two tumblers and a martini glass.

Pauline stepped back toward Jason. "Recent?"

"A while ago. My father died back in 2008. Cancer."

"That's rough."

He nodded. "I—didn't handle it very well. Wasn't there for him the way I should have been. I blamed my mother, actually. I thought she had underplayed his condition. But it was really me that had done that. His illness had been—inconvenient."

He drew the drink closer to him, spun the glass and stared into it. "My mother was not one to exist on her own. After my father died, she called me a lot. We didn't really have much of a mother-son relationship. She wasn't terribly affectionate. Neither of my parents were. My older brother died when he was four, you see. I think they never really got over that. Well, suddenly she's calling me all the time. The woman had buried both a son and a husband, but she's talking about all this trivial crap. Crap I'm sure she would have otherwise unloaded on my dad. About her hairstylist, about her neighbor's overseas vacation, her car mechanic. Meanwhile, I'm working sixty or more hours a week, right? I'm fighting rush hour traffic to get home before seven o'clock so I can get a couple hours of peace and quiet before I have to run the rat race all over again tomorrow at 5am. And she's talking to me about the shade of lipstick she can't fucking find anymore. You know?

"So, finally, I just—one day, I cracked. I say, 'For Chrissake, Mom. I'm exhausted. Don't you have friends or something? Why do I want to hear about this shit? Why do you think I care?'"

He reached for the glass and his hand trembled. He grabbed it, set it down, then picked the glass up again and took a long drink. Pauline just stared at him.

"It was two days later, I got a call from the Wausau police department." He tried to say the next words but they wouldn't come out. His throat tightened and his face twisted up. He took another drink.

Pauline reached out a hand and laid it over his arm.

"She drove her car off the Snake Bridge. Killed herself."

Pauline looked at him with strained eyes. His breath hitched and sputtered. His face was malfunctioning. He coughed out a laugh, choked on a sob and his mouth contorted into a grimacing wince of a smile. He covered his face with a clawing hand.

Pauline rested a warm hand lightly on his arm and he breathed deep. He took another drink and wiped fiercely at his eyes that felt swollen and burned with tears. Where did all that come from? He had not wanted those memories to resurface, had kept them stashed away like a dirty little secret stuffed in the middle of the pages of his life—a life that had recently been shook from its binding.

Not even Jen knew about his last conversation with his mother. She knew how annoyed he had been by his mother's constant calls, but he never confessed those last words to Jen or to anyone. At the funeral, he had wept, but that grief was as much for the part of him he wanted to die, to bury deep down inside him. The part of him that tainted his very soul.

He buried those memories, just as he avoided thinking about his father's death. Yet, they had always been just below the surface, his own cancerous growth, that horrible shitty part of him he didn't want to face. No matter how much success he gained in his life, how much he achieved at his job, how good a husband or father he could try to be, it was all a costume worn over the scarred face of a horrible son.

"You have demons," Pauline said finally. "Demons are thirsty. I know. Believe me."

She leaned down and got into his face. He wanted to look away.

"Hey. Jason. Look at me. Don't give in to them. Send them to the desert. Let them die of thirst. You hear me?"

He tried to look at her but felt his emotional dam fracturing again.

She grabbed his face and forced it up to hers. "Call your fucking wife. Okay? Talk to her about this. I'm guessing you've been leaving her in the dark."

He remembered Jen's last message to him. *Call me if you want. I'm here. I love you.*

He nodded to Pauline. She let go of him and his gaze fell to the bar top.

"I know what it's like to hate yourself," Pauline said. "The problem is, you end up taking it out on all the ones around you. The ones you love. Hating yourself is just about the most selfish thing you can do. Stop it. Don't worry about loving or hating yourself. Let the ones around you do that for you."

He fought back an emotional swell of remembrance, regret and remorse. Pauline reached over the counter and hugged him, and he hugged her back tightly, desperately.

He thought, *So this is rock bottom.*

Part 2

CHAPTER EIGHTEEN
Tuesday, December 24, 2019 - Christmas Eve

Snow blew past the frosted living room window beside the glitter and glow of the Christmas tree while Bing Crosby caroled through the eve of joyous Noël. Jen nestled up against Jason on the couch while firelight flickered and Nicholas built his new Lego Star Wars battlecruiser.

They had opened presents when darkness fell, as was the tradition when he was a child. Nicholas tore through his with a fury, each time offering a quiet, understated exuberance that translated to a bouncing body and long, concentrated stare at the video game, puzzle, Lego set or coloring book. He opened the present from Zeke and Dee, a plastic air gun that shot ping pong balls.

He showed extra enthusiasm with the new sport toboggan sled Jason had picked out, its sleek orange plastic featuring molded seat and backrest. Jason's favorite moment came when he brought out the new bicycle with big red bow on it. A real bike, not the kiddy toy Nicky had been riding. His boy's smile ran across his entire face and Jason hadn't felt that elated by anything in a long time.

He and Jen had stopped getting presents for each other years ago. Getting Nicky's presents took up most of their time, and there wasn't much either of them needed or wanted, so they tended to get themselves new furniture or appliances, and two years ago a Florida vacation. They hadn't decided what their present would be this year, but Jason surprised Jen with a ruby heart necklace entwined in gold and silver and surrounded by diamonds. She, of course, scolded him for spending so much while her eyes lit up to the dazzle and shimmer of precious metals and jewels.

They sipped eggnog as they sat and enjoyed the peace of their holiday evening together. As he held his wife and watched his son, Jason counted his blessings that he could be in this moment instead of alone in a hotel, perhaps without a job or future. He had done almost everything possible to make that happen.

Pauline was partially to thank for that not happening. She was a strange, attractive force, called forth by serendipity.

After he broke down to her that night, he spent the last two days at the conference attending sessions while he caught up on work in his hotel room in the early mornings and late afternoons. In those remaining evenings, he would grab a sandwich from the sub shop across the street, bring it back to his room, and spend the rest of each night on the phone with Jen, just as Pauline had suggested.

They discussed everything. Not just his sudden and quick lapse into drinking, but his work, Pauline, and the deep scars of regret he had over his parents. They spoke a lot about Nicholas, but he hadn't been ready to talk about his violent reaction on the Saturday before he left, other than to say he was sorry over and over. He appreciated that Jen hadn't pushed the subject, as much as he figured she may have wanted. She shared that Leslie reported progress and they shouldn't be concerned.

Those two nights talking to Jen brought them closer than they had been for a long time. Jason hadn't realized how much their marriage had become habitual, routine, and lacked any depth of conversation. Their complacency with life and each other had made them—him?—averse to anything that could disrupt the smooth idle of their status quo. That was the problem with being cozily content. It was its own addiction. To maintain it, one often became oblivious to or discounted the voracity of threats—even at the expense of others—until it became too late.

Friday night, he had returned to the bar. Pauline, Walt and Kenny were wrapping up what looked like a busy night. He apologized to Kenny for the bathroom incident. Kenny received it cooly with little response other than the bob of his top knot. Jason didn't worry about it. He hadn't come for that reason anyway.

He said goodbye to Pauline. It wasn't a dramatic goodbye, it wasn't an emotional goodbye. It was a period at the end of a chapter that exhibited its share of dramatic punctuation, of exclamation points and question marks. There was nothing memorable about the goodbye, but he would likely never forget everything that had led up to it. There were certain people in life you could know for years, but whom were of little consequence. Meanwhile, there were the Paulines—rare individuals who, in a brief fragment of time, could make a significant and unforgettable impression on your life.

He knew, of course, that he was likely not one of those rare people for her, and he was fine with that.

His return home on Saturday after two weeks living in his alternate reality of hotel rooms was like being told a terminal condition had miraculously reversed. Reconnecting with Jen and Nicky involved slow, gingerly steps forward, but they both seemed as invested as he was in healing the wounds of the past two months.

Snowfall covered the dead land and provided a magical blanket that changed the landscape and, by extension, the setting of their drama. What had been a brown and dying backdrop to their disfunction was now a beautiful canvas of white. Immersing themselves in the holiday for the past two weeks was an analgesic to their strained and inflamed family unit.

Today represented the culmination of the last two weeks, of the concerted effort to return to some kind of normalcy. They had a long journey ahead of them, but he felt certain they would endure that journey together.

Christmas morning. Racing down the small hill of their front lawn in the fresh powder of the Christmas Eve snowfall. Jason in back and Nicky between his legs in front. Jason spent an hour piling up snow into a huge mound at the top of the hill that they used as a launch. It was a comfortable midwestern winter temperature of twenty-five degrees with a light breeze under gray skies. They zipped down the hill faster and farther with each run as they packed down the snow to a smooth, slick sheen.

Jen joined them after five or six runs and he let her take the back seat while he got out the snow blower and cleared the driveway of the seven inches of snow that fell last night.

A peaceful stillness had fallen upon Fairview Lane as it rested under the most significant snowfall of the year so far. Snow was nature's shroud laid over the corpse of the season, and Christmas, for Jason, was a memorial service—a celebration of life—before the long, cold desolation of winter mourning until spring.

His father was as Catholic as he was Irish—meaning to say, his heritage labeled him as such, but neither defined him. Holidays had been mostly secular for Jason, other than the obligatory Christmas and Easter church attendance. His mother, an uninterested Methodist, saw mass as a wonderful excuse to dress up, get her hair done and present herself lavishly to the public.

But none of that meant spirituality was completely wrung out of the Christmas holiday for Jason. He had a soulful reverence for the season, much like he had at a wake—an indefinable awe to the mystery of life and the respect for intangible yet powerful sentiments of compassion and good will from others, all against the bleak darkness of death. Beyond that, only Christmas could ignite a spark of hope in one's heart that such an absurd concept as peace on Earth could possibly be achieved, even for just a day.

As he guided the snowblower up and down his driveway, a high, wide arc of snow thrown to either side, he caught glimpses of both his immediate neighbors' yards. Some of that lofty wonder and spirit of the holiday fell to earth.

To the right of their home were Fred and Vivian Greeley's yard signs blaring their candidates and slogans—about making the country great again. On the other side, Thomas and Erika Johnson's yard signs shouting their candidates' names and a promise to build back better. It had been an ongoing escalation between them ever since Fred first put his yard signs out. Most recently, the Johnsons added their "Black Lives Matter" sign and the Greeleys had countered with "Blue Lives Matter."

Jason knew little about either of them. Fred and Vivian were both retired. Fred sold his successful roofing business many years ago and built their 4,200 square foot house on Fairview as a pitstop for their constant travels. Jason was congenial to Fred's aggressive personality but had little chance to build a comfortable relationship, let alone any reasonable pretense, to judge his character.

Thomas and Erika Johnson were a younger couple with no kids. He was a university professor and she worked at a non-profit, but Jason wasn't clear on either because they were rarely visible in the neighborhood. They had a nice house, but did little around it and seemed deep in their careers. Jason waved to them the few times he saw them coming and going. They seemed friendly enough, but he had no idea of their personalities or characters.

He hated those signs, though. It felt like a disruption to the Fairview Lane neighborhood. It reminded him of what he had seen at the Lincoln Museum. Political signs were springing up all over Fortune Falls like 150-year-old weeds that, no matter how many times they were ripped from the ground, their deep, wide roots kept them coming back.

He finished clearing his driveway and paused to watch Jen and Nicky laugh and cry out as they made another pass down the hill and slide into the cul-de-sac. Jen looked over to him with a smile and he waved and gave her a thumbs-up. He pointed to the snowblower and then to Glen's driveway and she nodded.

He had started blowing Glen's driveway last year after he watched Glen struggle with a shovel during a particularly heavy snowfall. Glen was the only one in the neighborhood without a snowblower. He had a small one once, but it gave up on him two years ago and he never replaced it.

Jason propelled his snowblower down the street and to Glen's driveway, where he made quick work at clearing it out. Since it took little time, he skipped over to Travis and Dawn's driveway and plowed Glen's tenants as well. What the hell. Merry Christmas.

Glen wasn't home. He drove to Minnesota to spend the holidays with his daughter and her family, then flew to his younger son's place in Maine for a New Year's Eve out east, where Glen and Maude were originally from.

As Jason swung the snowblower around to head back home, he noticed Suzie had pulled in across the street to Agnes's house and was getting out of the car. Jason put the blower in its highest gear and motored it across the street.

He shut the blower off as he reached the edge of the driveway. Suzie stood by her car and waited for his approach.

"Merry Christmas," he said as he reached her. She had a black stocking cap snug over her head with a graying ponytail sprouting out from under it. Her long, well-worn quilted jacket looked as tired as she did.

She waved a mittened hand. "Merry Christmas."

"Need a snow blow? I figured, long as I was right here and have it—"

"Oh, you don't need to do that."

"My pleasure."

"Well, thanks, then."

He tilted his head toward the house. "How's it going in there?"

Her face lost its composure. "It's a disaster. He tore the place apart. And it wasn't in great shape to begin with. It's going to be weeks of work to get it ready for showing."

He could see how overwhelmed she was by the task ahead of her. He wanted to ask if she had anyone to help her and realized he didn't even know if she was married or had a family. Seeing that she was on her own on Christmas day told him she was likely alone. Alone, just like her mother had been.

"I'm so sorry."

"Meanwhile, I'm trying to sort through all her assets and debt to figure out what, if anything, will be left ."

Sorting through the remains of his mother's life had not been a favorite moment of his. After Jason turned down the Lahey Hardware torch his father tried to pass him, Ed Lahey managed to establish a buy/sell agreement with the owner of two ACE Hardware stores in the surrounding area. When his father died, the business continued under new ownership and Florence gained a nice retirement nest egg. A year later when she died and he dove heavily into her finances, he discovered she managed to spend much of that money on overseas trips, fine dining, high-end clothing and other frivolous expenditures. She lived her last year lavishly, as if she had planned her final drive over the bridge. After all her remaining debts, he and Jen were left with a seed of a college fund for Nicky and a modest down payment on their Fairview Lane house.

Despite the challenge of settling his mother's estate, it likely bore no comparison to what Suzie was going through.

She paused, her fatigue turning to strained but steely eyes and lips pursed in both fury and fear. "Has he been back here at all?"

"No. Not that I'm aware of. I was gone for a couple weeks, but Glen didn't mention anything and he certainly would have."

She nodded without much assertion. "He found my phone number somehow. He's been threatening me. Ever since I put the house up for sale. Telling me he deserves half of whatever it goes for. Bullshit. That ain't going to happen."

There was so much he didn't know. Was she local? Was he local? He hoped to hell that bastard was half the world away from them.

"Are you here in town?"

She shook her head. "I'm over in Medford. About an hour away."

"And where is he?"

"No idea. Last I heard, he was somewhere around the Eau Claire area, but I don't know. Don't care. Just as long as he can't find me."

Less than two hours away. Close enough to be a threat. His

worry for her increased. He recalled his encounter with Greg. He couldn't remember the last time he felt so intimidated.

"What about the police? They called me, you know. I told them what I could."

Her expression soured and she looked at her feet. "The police have a warrant out for him. I doubt they're spending any time looking for him though. Fat lot of good that will do me."

"Well listen. You have my number if you need anything. In the meantime, how about you pull your car out into the street and I'll get this driveway plowed for you."

She looked him right in the eyes. She was only five or so years older than him, but she looked fifteen years older. He didn't think those eyes had seen a lot of generosity from others. "Thanks," she said. "I appreciate it."

He started up the snow blower as she got in her car and pulled it out onto the road. He ran the snowblower up and down the driveway and hurled snow in either direction as he cleared away the remains of the winter storm from the Polnzy driveway. All the while, he wished he could do more to help her clear the bigger messes that wouldn't simply blow away.

CHAPTER NINETEEN
Wednesday, December 31, 2019 - New Year's Eve

He and Jen spent the cusp of the new year in each other's arms, having just made love before midnight struck and the calendar turned. His consciousness bobbed and swayed from a ferocity of lovemaking unlike anything they shared before.

It was their first time being intimate since long before his return from Springfield. It felt as right to do it now as it hadn't felt right until now. They entered into it with the caution of pumping hearts and ended with the intensity of lightning-filled muscles striking against each other like a building storm. They clawed and grasped and clutched in a silent passion of sadness, anger, blame, apology and forgiveness. He finally collapsed on top of her like a heavy downpour until, after a time, they broke away from each other, the parting of two fronts, where they laid next to each other with breaths heavy and deep. Time passed like a soft breeze, and their bodies entwined as he fell into a euphoric semi-consciousness.

In this singular moment, teetering on the edge of an old decade that overlooked the misty and vast unknown of the next, he was ready to put the past behind him.

Jason never felt more eager and excited for the fresh start this new decade offered. Until living through the smoldering embers that were the final months of this year, he hadn't realized how much the last decade had burned through him. The axial spin and orbital path to age forty had strengthened the gravitational pull of those last ten years.

Three years ago, he and Jen had taken a short holiday southeast. Seth and Rachel offered to take a then four-year-old Nicholas for the six days they'd be gone (an offer they didn't make again: "There were some—challenges," Rachel told them with exhaustion). Jason and Jen had gone as far as Indianapolis and spent the day downtown. When they came upon Monument Circle, they were both speechless. There, in the center of downtown, rose a 300-foot monument on a massive base. Standing vigil all around the towering stone spire were statues of sailors and soldiers from the American Revolution, Civil War, Mexican-American War, and the War of 1812, among others. After they visited the small museum at the base, they walked the steps to the top observation area. The stairwell was completely enclosed concrete and baking hot. Up and up and round and round they went as the stairwell slowly closed in on them, tighter and narrower. Jason had no concept of how high or far they were going—he just trudged forward, step by step by step. They laughed and commented during the start of their endeavor to the top, but stopped talking midway up and slogged upward through the final flights.

When they reached the top, sweat-covered and exhausted, to the small glass-walled room that overlooked Indianapolis, he only then realized how far they had climbed from the ground floor.

That's how it felt as the clock switched over to 12:01 a.m., January 1, 2020. He had reached the observation deck of the new year and could only now see the length of the journey where the climb up the previous decade had brought him.

In those ten years of lumbering ascent, his father died from cancer, his mother drove herself off a bridge, his son was born and diagnosed as autistic, his estranged in-laws tried to work their way into their lives, and he and Jen had slowly, imperceptibly, stopped communicating and drew apart from each other.

And he had simply climbed each step, one by one, without giving thought or attention to anything other than each foot planted on the next stair up. In some strange way, Agnes's death had flung open a window to reveal the vista of years they trudged up.

New year, new Jason, and new path for the Laheys. He couldn't help but notice he had glided into the year 2020 at a point when he felt, for the first time in a long time, his vision—both nearsighted and farsighted—was focused and acute. Forgiving himself of his past failings, especially those of his parents, would likely never happen. That regret would always be interwoven with his psyche. But at least now he could acknowledge and accept it as a part of himself. He would use that regret to become a better husband, a better father, a better friend and a better person. Somehow, he had managed to take his quality of character for granted over this latter course of his life and assumed himself a good person.

In this new decade, he would earn that status.

Chapter Twenty
Thursday, January 9, 2020

Morning in the dead of winter. The alarm went off at five a.m. It was still pitch dark outside. Jason's eyes felt glued shut and he had to force them open. He had been getting to work by six almost every day since his Springfield trip to catch up on projects and deadlines he had fallen behind on. As much as he enjoyed the time off, the holidays only increased his backlog of work. He often stayed at Boswell until six-thirty or even seven at night. Jen wasn't happy about it, but she was still treating him like a volatile chemical and tried not to make a big deal out of it.

To his mind, he kept his job—or at least his position as director of information technologies—by resolving the issues he himself had largely created while he presented a sob story to the CIO about his family life and the current struggles they were facing. Although Boswell Software could be cutthroat with its expectations of senior staff, it was family-focused, so it supported his predicament as long as he sought help, which he did in the form of a workplace counselor. After three visits, he felt the woman's primary training was based on hugging and sympathizing, but whatever he had to do to keep his seat at work was fine with him, especially when he could do it over lunch once a week.

Nicholas continued his return to his old self. He spoke more and was more responsive and less prone to outbursts. They recently met again with Leslie and she explained she had just started to engage Nicky on the "bad day." That's how Leslie identified it with Nicky. She reported strong progress and felt she would be able to break down the traumatic experience into processable moments so she could neutralize those elements that were causing him harm.

Blah blah blah. Fine. Whatever. Just give him his boy back. He missed his Nix.

While Jen slept, he brushed his teeth, showered, and got ready for work while the soothing drone of early morning hosts reported the news on the radio. He heated up milk and had a quick bowl of shredded wheat with some sugar just like his mother used to make, then poured coffee into his travel mug. Jen awoke as he got ready to head out, gave him a tired kiss on her way to the coffee, and he got in his car and drove off. The neighborhood was completely quiet, dark and still.

Until he got to the Polnzy residence.

There, amid the snow and freezing cold, he saw the beat-up black truck back in the driveway being loaded up with more furniture and items. Greg was beside the truck bed, tossing in a recliner with the help of his associate. They both froze as Jason's car approached. Without any thought—completely reactionary—Jason rolled down his window with the flick of a button and called out, "I'm calling the cops!"

Greg stared right at him, not moving.

Jason took two seconds to lock on to the license plate, then hit the gas and sped away with a torrent of emotions coursing through him, veins pumping a cocktail of chemicals—the testosterone of rage mixed with the adrenaline of flight. He voice-activated his phone and told it to dial the police department. He reported the incident and supplied the license plate as best he could remember. Hopefully it would seal the fate of that son of a bitch so Suzie—and Jason—could be done with him. By the time Jason arrived at work, he was almost giddy with the excitement and exhilaration of the moment.

A little after noon, his phone rang. He looked at the display, then got up quickly and shut his office door. He sat down and sucked in a deep breath.

"Hi, Zeke. How's Dee doing?"

"Hey. Jason. Yeah. Dee's doing okay. Treatments are going well. One more and they think she'll be cancer-free."

"That's great to hear, Zeke. By the way, thanks again for Nicky's Christmas present. He loved it."

A pause on the other end. "Yeah. Speaking of Nicholas. Seth filled us in on a few things. How is Nicholas doing?"

Oh, shit. The last thing he wanted them to know about. Fucking Seth.

"Fine, Zeke. He's absolutely fine. Nothing to worry about."

Heavy breath through the other line. "Kid sees the dead body of an old woman who offed herself and you say he's fine?"

"Yup. That's exactly what I'm saying, Zeke."

"And what about you, Jason? You going to tell me you're fine as well?"

The implication hit him like a jab to the gut. He was getting a pretty good idea what was happening, and he didn't like it at all.

"If you have a point, Zeke, I'd get to it pretty quick. I have work to do."

Zeke coughed out a dry laugh. "Seth told us about your drinking. Your behavior. Your separation from Jenny—"

"Not separated from Jen, Zeke," Jason spat out. "We're tighter than ever." Tasting the bitterness of the attack, he couldn't resist adding, "Unlike you, I know how to apologize and recognize when I'm wrong."

"Cute." Zeke got quiet. Jason relished the moment. He kept in contact with them out of his own generosity and this was his thanks. Completely bullshit accusations.

"Zeke, I don't know what game you're playing, but considering I'm one of your only advocates with Jen, I don't get your logic in coming after me."

"Not sure how much you are 'advocating' for us, Jason." Zeke's tone shifted dramatically. His words came in bitterly hot and heavy. Jason wasn't familiar with this level of hostility. It was a Zeke Jen had talked about, but one Jason had never experienced. "You sit there and you listen to me beg and plead and you do nothing but silently judge and ignore. I'm not even sure you're talking to Jenny at all about us. In fact, maybe you aren't sharing anything with her. Turning her against us."

"For Christ sake, Zeke, how can you—"

"How? I don't know. Seth tells us you basically kicked them out after he tried to talk to Jenny about seeing us."

Jason was almost speechless. "He—what?"

"We're sick of this, Jason. For the better part of seven years, we've been begging for a chance to talk to Jenny, see her, see our grandchild, and all we get is you telling us to back off and be patient. No more. I'm telling you right now, either Jenny tells us to our face that she doesn't want to see us anymore, or you're going to find us on your doorstep demanding to be seen and heard."

The line went dead.

Jason stared at his cell phone for many seconds, unable to fully comprehend what had just taken place. He had experienced levels of frustration from Zeke before, had heard Zeke get a little hot under the collar, but this was new. And why was Seth stoking this fire? Was this revenge for Thanksgiving? It seemed so completely petty and infantile, yet he couldn't put it past Seth.

What the hell was he going to tell Jen? This was not at all what she wanted, and the absolute last thing he needed while he tried to mend their family. All the blame would be put onto him, and he didn't know how to quell this coming storm.

An urge to step out of the office nudged him, to find a bar and have a drink. He buried that impulse quickly and degraded himself for even thinking it. He wouldn't fall down that hole again. There was no reason to react yet. He'd allow himself time to cool off, be reasonable, and figure out the best course of action.

Heading home, he was no closer to a good solution to the problem of Jen's parents. He knew the one thing he needed to do. Tell Jen. Secrets wouldn't save him from this. They would handle it together. That's what a family was all about. That's what will make them stronger.

Stepping inside and taking off his shoes, he walked into the kitchen where Jen sat at her desk off the mudroom. She kept her head down, staring at the desktop.

"Hey," she said in a flat, direct tone.

Something was wrong. Had her parents already called her? Would they dare? Did they get her number from Seth? That would be the worst mistake they could ever make. They had to be smarter than that.

"Everything alright?" He leaned in a bit to take a look at what she was staring at. On the desk sat the day's mail: bank notices, a direct mailer from a shoe store, an EOB from their healthcare provider. On top of all that was a rough, crumpled piece of paper with severe, scratchy writing, each letter gone over and over with black pen in bold, jarring handwriting.

"I don't think so, Jason." She looked up at him and handed him the paper. "This was in our mailbox. What the hell is it? Are we in some kind of danger?"

"What?" He grabbed the paper and read it.

MIND YOUR OWN
FUCKING BUSINESS
OR I'LL BE
ALL OVER YOURS

"What the hell is that, Jason?"

He stared at it. Tried to make sense of it.

"What have you gotten us into?"

He shook his head and crumpled the paper in his hand.

"What have you done, Jason?"

His panicked mind started to think about every window, every door, every access point into their house. Had he been naïve? Had he actually thought some glass and wood could keep out someone who wanted to do them harm? Jesus Christ, just how vulnerable were they?

"What kind of danger are we in, Jason?"

Security cameras. Motion detectors. He could set the whole place up so anyone who tried to get in would immediately trigger sensors and bring police. Flood lights. He could put those up in every corner of their property—light the place up so no one could come here without being exposed.

"Goddamn it what the hell is going on?"

He looked at Jen, her face torn apart with fear and anger and confusion, and he shook his head. "I'm so sorry."

CHAPTER TWENTY-ONE
Friday, January 10, 2020

In August of 2016, just before noon, the storm sirens went off all over Fortune Falls. On the radio, the loud, grating alerts of the National Weather Service interrupted normal broadcasting to issue a tornado warning in their area. He had been at Boswell, and remembered darkness soaking into his office. Out his large office window, the jaundiced sky churned and the trees buckled to the sudden fury of wind.

The torrent of rain came next, immediate, the great sky faucet cranked to full. He felt the air pressure change, and those sirens kept blaring, coming in a wave of volume, shifting into the distance, then swinging back Pend blaring with that steady tritone of terror.

Panic had overwhelmed him. A three-year-old Nicky was in daycare. Jen was just finishing up her half-day at Grand Avenue Publishing. They were out there as a tornado twisted through their community with one-hundred-plus mile-an-hour winds, and he could do nothing. He couldn't get to them, couldn't protect them.

They ended up being fine, of course, but he recalled the tense panic in his chest. The frenetic energy that made him pace his office with nowhere to go.

That's how he felt now. He had sirens blaring in his head, the trepidation of a storm coming.

It took a while to settle Jen down. She jumped up from the desk and circled the island repeatedly with brisk steps, asking him what he had been thinking, why he had gotten them involved in another family's shit. He let her expel the hostility and fear, then calmly explained the situation to her. He tried to reason with her. Suzie was all alone and he couldn't let Greg get away with what he was doing. It seemed like Jen understood and agreed, but it took her longer to accept.

He called the police to report the incident. An officer showed up forty minutes later. It was the same woman who had questioned him the day he found Agnes. She asked how his boy was and then got to business, getting every detail from him. She jotted down everything he said in her notebook, then took the threatening note as evidence. The officer told them to keep in contact with any new information and to call 911 should any potential emergency arise.

On Friday morning, he lingered in the house before he headed to work. He didn't want to leave Jen and Nicky alone. He hovered around and about them, kept them in sight, secret service to his family. Once Jen got in her Subaru and headed safely down the street on her way to drop Nicky off at school, he got in his car and headed to Boswell. Jen would be at work all day, and after that she would pick up Nicky and bring him to therapy. Jason planned to be home by four that afternoon so they wouldn't be alone.

Shortly after 8:00 a.m., he called Suzie.

"Hi. Jason?" She sounded tired and he feared he woke her.

"Sorry, is this too early?"

"No, I've been up for a few minutes."

"Sorry for not calling you sooner about this. Greg came back to the house yesterday morning."

"Son of a bitch." Fury and nervousness honed those words to an edge.

"He had a truckload of furniture and things."

"Oh, shit."

He paused with hopeful desperation. "Have you heard anything from the police? I called them as soon as I saw him there. I was hoping they might have grabbed him already?"

"No, nothing."

He expected that. Why had he felt the need to shout out at Greg? If he would have kept his mouth shut, none of this would be happening.

"He's threatened my family, Suzie."

"What? Why?"

When he had shouted at Greg that morning, he thrummed with bold aggression and defiance. Now, he felt too much like an idiot to let her know he did that. "He saw me drive by. I'm guessing he figured I'd be calling the cops."

"Oh, no. Oh, Jason." The hopelessness of her voice over the phone caused his stomach to fall. He kept looking for something to suggest the situation wasn't as bad as he presumed, but instead he received continual confirmation of its severity.

"I told the police. They have his license plate and truck description. I'm sure they'll find him."

"Get yourself a gun."

That took Jason completely by surprise. Her statement had come so fast and so direct that it took a moment for him to understand what she was saying. Was she serious?

"Sure, right, I—I wouldn't even know—"

"I'm not kidding, Jason. I'm never without mine."

"Seriously?"

Her voice remained low and steady and severe. "That bastard ever comes anywhere near me, I will shoot him. I suggest you do the same."

It was unworldly. He couldn't believe what he was hearing, what kind of skewed reality he was living, yet he knew she was completely serious and the threat was real.

"I need to get back to work, Suzie. I'll let you know if there's anything new."

"Same here. Be safe."

His next call was to HomeGuard Security Systems. He spoke to a representative for a half hour and detailed his home's doors, ground floor windows, egress windows, patio door and surrounding property. Jason made it clear he wanted a full package—total security on his property. The salesperson said he could be out that afternoon to survey the premises and property. Jason imagined the guy getting off the phone with him and immediately calling his wife to tell her she could order that new Jeep Grand Cherokee she'd been pining over.

He honestly didn't know why he hadn't installed a security system at their home before now. The cul-de-sac in the small division on the outskirts of town had lured him into a false sense of security. The fact was, even if Greg wasn't threatening his family, they were still at risk considering their house was one of the biggest on the block outside of Fred and Vivian's. Certainly the Greeley's house had the latest and greatest security system.

The world was dangerous, filled with unscrupulous, even malevolent people out to inflict harm on others. He had a responsibility to make sure his family was as insulated from those threats as possible. There would be no storm warning, no sirens blaring, when a cyclone of malicious intent struck.

He emailed Jen and told her about the HomeGuard salesperson coming in the afternoon. Her reply was, "How much will that cost?" He told her not to worry about it.

Over lunch, he headed to the west side of town to carry out his final errand of the day. He pulled into the ratty strip mall that stretched out along old highway 16 where the adult video store, hookah lounge and coin-op laundromat was, and Jason stepped into Freedom Arms and Ammo.

Chapter Twenty-Two
Monday, January 13, 2020

He returned home on a frigid, snow-covered evening a little later than he had planned. He had stopped to pick something up. It sat now on the passenger seat.

He pulled into the garage and grabbed his briefcase along with a smaller, black hard case secured by two hefty latches on each side, one of them padlocked. Inside the injection-molded case was a Beretta M9 and clip with fifteen hollow-point bullets.

"The perfect, all-purpose gun for home protection and recreation," the burly guy with mutton chops, mustache and camo cap told him last Friday over lunch. "Semi-automatic. Features a fixed-barrel design for increased accuracy and handling, has a manageable recoil and is totally reliable."

Jason had looked up at the sales guy. "Wait a second. Isn't that the gun Riggs uses in *Lethal Weapon*?"

The guy cracked a grin. "Bet your ass."

In his hand, he had no other way to explain it other than

it felt good. Balanced. Molded to his grip. He felt like a knight wielding a sword. Even without clip, with safety on and aimed at nothing on the opposite wall, he felt powerful. He thought of Mel Gibson as Martin Riggs as he emptied out the clip at bad guy Joshua's helicopter as it flew away. He had an almost irresistible temptation to reenact the scene. Every ounce of him wanted to fake recoils while making explosive "bang bang bang" sounds and firing on an invisible helicopter.

"I'll take it," he said, and dropped close to a grand on the gun after adding bullets and case.

Three days later, he got the call that his background check had cleared and he could pick it up. The Beretta nine-millimeter was his. More importantly, he could keep the threats at bay. He could defend his family.

Inside the house, he was met with the smell of roast beef and garlic. Jen was cleaning up in the kitchen while she nestled in the nostalgia of her youth listening as nineties hip-hop pop played through the house.

"Hi, hon," he said as he kicked off his shoes and set down his briefcase and the gun case on the back entryway bench. He stepped into the kitchen.

"Hey, darling." She wiped off the counter by the oven while mashed potatoes sat in a pot alongside simmering carrots on the stove top. "How was your day?"

"Okay."

Nicholas trotted up to him holding a piece of paper out. "Dad, look!" He waved the paper before him, a drawing of some kind.

Jason was taken aback. He hadn't seen Nicholas this full of energy and calling for attention since Halloween. Nicky hadn't even referred to him as Dad in as long a time. He was stunned, overwhelmed with emotion to see his son looking so eager and interested in Jason's arrival. In some ways, this was seeing him for the first time in almost three months.

But he remained cautious. He wouldn't ruin this moment by overreacting to it.

"Hey, buddy! Wow, let me see!" He took the page. On it were the colored marker scratchings of Nicky on his new bike, with what Jason guessed was himself behind it, pushing the bike up into the air where it flew amid sun and moon and big five-point celestial stars. Jason's eyes blurred and he had to blink away tears. "Nix, this is amazing. It's so awesome. You did this all yourself?"

He nodded, eyes on the paper. "Leslie asked me to draw something happy that happened on the bad day."

Jason knelt down to Nicholas's level and looked him in the eyes that wouldn't quite look back at him, but were bright and wide. "Do you know, this was one of my most best and happy days, too? I was so proud of you, buddy."

Nicky gave a laugh, let go of the picture and skipped off. "I can't wait to ride my new bike!"

Jason watched his son dance away. "Me too, Nix." He turned to Jen, flabbergasted. "Wow?"

It seemed that Jen had watched the interaction. Warm satisfaction softened her face and brought a youth back to her that he hadn't noticed in a while. "Nice, huh? Just like old times?"

Jason stood up and went to the refrigerator. He grabbed a Disneyworld magnet and hung the picture up on the front of the appliance next to Jason's birthday card Nicky had made for him so many months ago. "Yeah. I—I almost forgot what it was like."

"Leslie had a lot of good things to say today. But she warned there's still work to do. He's opening up to her, though."

"Good," Jason said and approached Jen. "Let's hope we can put all this behind us." He wrapped his arms around her. "You two are the most important part of my life. Whatever needs to happen to keep us happy and safe."

They enjoyed an exceptional dinner of roast beef, garlic mashed potatoes and honey-glazed carrots. Nicholas managed to clear off a respectable portion of his plate, even if his servings were small. Jason and Jen asked Nicky about school and he spoke about his favorite teacher, Mrs. Abernathy, who had Mr. Peepers the bunny in the classroom. The teacher let them pet the bunny at the end of the day if the class was good. Mr. Peepers liked carrots, and Nicky liked that carrots were also one of his favorite foods. He even got to feed Mr. Peepers a part of a carrot over lunchtime.

Jen talked about running into Sam and Delilah Peterson at the store and that they asked about Polnzy's place and what was going on with Suzie. They just had Liver the hound dog in at the vet to remove a tumor from his back. Jason wondered when they would stop running that LED light display every night. "Christmas is three weeks gone, for God's sake. Pull the plug. It's over."

After dinner, Nicky wanted to go out to sled on their little front yard hill, so Jen bundled him up in a warm snow suit, scarf, hat, gloves and boots, and sent him out. Jason joined, too nervous to leave his son outside unguarded. He kept an eye on Nicky as he watched the road for any potential trouble entering their cul-de-sac.

After a half hour, Jason was cold and tired and told Nicky to pack it up and head back in. A bit of that temperamental Nicky showed himself and the boy slid down the packed-down run one more time in defiance of Jason's calls to stop. Jason held his temper and focused on getting Nicholas back into the house. With some gentle encouragement—and a bribe of hot chocolate—he succeeded.

As the night grew late, they put Nicky to bed and retired to the living room. Jen reached for the television remote but Jason halted her. "Can I show you something quick?"

She set the remote down. "Sure."

He went to the mud room, retrieved the gun case, and returned to the living room with a bit of trepidation. What seemed like the smartest and best idea now made him nervous. She was going to hate the idea of a gun.

He sat down on the couch next to her and set the case on the coffee table in front of them.

"Listen. I'm guessing the cops will grab Greg Polnzy at any time, but, just in case." He opened the case and the nine-milli-meter Beretta took command of the room. The black steel alloy blared like a silent trumpet when revealed, and Jen gasped when he opened the case.

"Just a precaution, but it will protect us in a worst-case sce-nario."

Jen stared with big, straining eyes. Those eyes looked like they couldn't comprehend—either what they were seeing, or the reason it was there.

"*It?* Did you say *it* will protect us?"

"*I* can. *We* can use it to protect us." He looked at her, trying to exude a confidence he found harder to feel, let alone convey.

"Have you even fired this thing?" She reached out to touch it, but pulled away, as if it were a snake ready to strike.

"No. Not yet. I thought we'd hit a firing range somewhere to get the feel of it."

She stared at it. "Get the feel of it—"

"Right. Could be fun. Target practice."

Jen started to shake her head.

"Hold on, now," Jason said. "Don't kill this before you give it a chance. I know you're upset at me getting involved with the whole Polnzy thing, but damn it, Suzie is all alone and she needs help. As long as Greg is out there, we all may be at risk. And even if it isn't Greg, there's always something, right? Especially lately? I think we need to have something—"

Jen had been slowly shaking her head during his entire speech. "No, Jason. Not that, we don't." She pointed at the gun, face pinched with distaste. "That isn't us. I don't even know what *that* is."

He wasn't an idiot. He expected resistance, but he thought he could turn her around. He could see how frightened she was over Nicky's safety, and to a lesser degree for herself and for him. If she had met Greg—if she had seen Suzie's face as Suzie shared what exactly Greg was—she would be twice as scared as she already was. It would be a week or more before the security system was installed. They were completely vulnerable until then. That gun was an equalizer.

"That is our way to balance the odds if danger comes to our doorstep."

Jen looked at him, incredulous. "Are you serious? That only brings danger into this house. You really want to bring a gun into our home with a seven-year-old? A seven-year-old autistic boy recently traumatized?"

"Jen—" She was getting melodramatic now.

"No. Absolutely not. I do not want that in my home."

She was being obstinate and he was losing ground with her. "Look. It can be locked. And we'll keep it high up and out of his reach. There's no way he can get to it or get in the case."

She put out her hands in glaring refute of his point. "Hold on. So you're telling me that, when someone breaks in here to kill us, you expect one of us to run to a closet, climb a step ladder to grab the case, find the key, unlock it, and load the gun in time to defend ourselves? Really?"

"Jen, you're—"

She put the barrier of a stiff palm up between him and her. "No. Sorry. Not the answer. Get that out of this house and off our property. That is not us, Jason." She got up and walked out of the room, leaving him alone with the Beretta.

He closed the case, locked the gun away, and with it, a little bit of his fantasy to be some kind of human lethal weapon that could protect his home and family. He would not, however, be getting rid of it.

CHAPTER TWENTY-THREE
Monday, January 20, 2020

Over the last week, Clan Lahey had gone through several levels of fortification. Jason kept the gun in his car. He didn't share that with Jen. She didn't understand. Besides, he had the privilege of being a white man in a small northern Wisconsin suburban town, so he felt perfectly safe, and had already applied for his conceal carry permit.

Meanwhile, HomeGuard Security installed a premium security system in the home. Motion detectors were placed throughout the house to detect any movement other than the hallway off their bedrooms at night. Door and window sensors, including window break sensors, would immediately sound an alarm to any forced entry. Motion-sensor flood lights were installed on all four exterior walls of the home. Anyone who moved about on their property would get 160 watts of light thrown on them no matter which side they approached. If they were bold enough to make it to the house and try to get in, alarms would immediately go off and the police would be called within twenty seconds unless cancelled by a call to the security company and stating the Lahey's special password, "Trick-or-treat."

His castle now had a moat, drawbridge, guard tower and turrets. Greg Polnzy could not get to them without alerting the neighborhood and the Fortune Falls police force.

Come and get us, you son of a bitch.

Jen had mixed emotions about all the changes. She admitted to sleeping easier, but she also felt as imprisoned by the fear of Greg as they were liberated from the threat of Greg. She was resistant to learning the security system and frustrated by its restrictions and burdens. The alarm had already mistakenly gone off twice and they had to call the security company.

Whatever inconvenience or annoyance the system may cause, it was worth it. The security system was the best defense against both the unknown and the known.

As Jason got ready for work on Monday morning, he held to the peace and satisfaction of their quiet weekend at home. Jen had eased on her tensions over Greg Polnzy, Jason felt safe and secure from Greg, and both of them enjoyed time with a Nicholas who seemed more stable, more happy, and more himself. He clicked on the radio, stepped into the shower, and gradually woke up in the steamy heat.

As he shut the water off and stepped out, the news on public radio wrapped up a story about Prince Harry leaving the royal family. He brushed his teeth as he half-listened.

"…And Harry, of course, saying he wants a more peaceful life here. Any sense, briefly, what he means by that?" asked Morning Edition Reporter David Greene.

"Yeah," answered London Correspondent Frank Langfitt. "I

think that he wants to get away from the tabloids. He feels—he and his wife feel totally victimized by the British tabloids here."

Jason spit out a mouthful of toothpaste as the next story started.

"A new virus appeared in the Chinese city of Wuhan last month. Health authorities say in the last couple of days, they've identified dozens more people who've been infected, and that includes new cases in Beijing and Shenzhen. There are now more than two hundred cases in this outbreak. NPR's global health and development correspondent Nurith Aizenman is with me in studio. Thanks for ..."

Jason shut off the radio and got dressed for work.

When he got home that night, he pulled into the garage and left the garage door open. Garbage pickup tomorrow morning, so he tilted back the garbage container and wheeled it to the curb under cold, dark, clear skies. Down the street, headlights came toward him. He tensed, stood frozen, watching and waiting to see who it was and where they were going.

The vehicle veered to his left and the Johnsons' garage door opened. Red Cherokee. Erika. He waved as she drove up their driveway and he went back for the recycle bin. As he hauled it to the curb, Erika walked down her driveway alongside him. Her short legs motored quickly and she overtook him heading for her mailbox. He reached the end of his driveway as she grabbed her mail and closed the mailbox door.

"Howdy, neighbor," he said and dropped the recycling next to the garbage can. A month ago, it would have been filled with beer bottles and rum bottles. Now, a few light beer cans were overwhelmed by iced tea bottles and cans of seltzer and diet cola.

She looked up from the mail, round face colored by dark lipstick and eyeliner, black hair curled and parted at center to show a prominent forehead over black-framed glasses. "Oh, hi. It's John, right? Oh, no, it's James—Jason!"

He grinned. "You got it."

She winced and groaned. "Goodness, I knew it was a Jay-name! I'm so sorry." She waved her mail at him, long manicured nails painted burgundy.

"Don't worry about it. It's been a while since we introduced ourselves."

More than half a year ago, actually. He and Jen watched the slow progress of the house being built after ground broke in the early spring of 2019. Once the house was framed and sided, they caught the new owners surveying their property a couple months before the young couple moved in and he and Jen stepped over to say hi and welcome them. They had hoped for a family with a child around Nicky's age, but Tom and Erika, a decade younger, had no children. Since then, it has only been the occasional hand-waves with the rare greeting shouted out in passing.

"I know! We feel horrible that we haven't had a chance to get to know the neighborhood more. We always seem to have something going on between Tom's classes and my work."

"Well, I hope we can remedy that at some point. We'd love to have you over some time."

Erika gave a big, broad smile. "That would be fabulous. It's hard to believe we've been here over six months now."

"Time flies, huh?"

"Faster every year. It's a nice neighborhood." She pointed to Glen's place across her yard. "Wonderful having a neighbor like Glen. Just had a chance to talk with him the other day. He's a sweetheart."

"Yes he is." He turned his gaze to the north. "Meanwhile,

seems like you and the Greeleys are having a friendly little rivalry."

Erika's smile stiffened and she appeared to choose her words carefully. "You—you could say that. It appears we have a difference of opinion on certain subjects affecting our nation right now."

Jason shifted his weight. He probably shouldn't have brought it up, but they were the ones blaring their opinions to the whole neighborhood, so why should he feel so restrained by discretion? "Well, it's a complicated time, for sure. Fred and Vivian are decent folk, though. Just have their own ideas about things. Like you said. It's a nice neighborhood. We're all friendly around here, regardless of opinions."

She nodded, though without significant conviction. "Well, it's cold." She motioned back to the house.

"Yeah. Good to catch up. Hope we can get together soon."

"You bet."

It was safe to assume his neighbors on his left and right would not be enjoying any backyard cookouts together this summer. And honestly? He didn't care. As long as they didn't ruin his.

The following night, for the first time in a long time, Glen dropped by, his fingers hooked around the cardboard handle of a Sprecher Root Beer four-pack. "Never come empty-handed." He smiled and held it out to Jason.

"Get in here before you freeze that old butt of yours off." Jason took the root beer, let him in and closed the door to the dark, cold night.

Glen peeled off his orange parka and sat down on the entryway bench to take his snow-covered shoes off. "Wasn't sure if I needed a password or something to get clearance into

Fort Knox here."

"Whatever. Asshole."

Glen had walked over while the HomeGuard van sat in their driveway and the technicians installed the security system. As he watched them mount cameras and lights and detectors, he asked them questions that transitioned from curiosity, to shock, to amusement in reaction to the level of security being installed. Jason got the impression Glen didn't take Greg as seriously as Jason did. Of course, Glen apparently had never faced Greg Polnzy up close and personal.

Glen stood up, looked around and eyed the motion detectors mounted in the corners and the control panel by the door. "How's it working? Any troubles?"

"Just human error. We're adjusting."

Glen flashed a smart-ass grin. "Is she?" His head gestured into the direction of the living room where Jen sat watching television.

Jason swung away from him. "Shut up. Come on downstairs."

Glen had been making his occasional evening visits ever since Maude's death. Before then, Jason and Jen most often stopped by their place during an evening stroll through the new division, first with Nicky in a stroller, then later with him pedaling furiously on his trike. In the winter months, Glen and Maude sometimes invited them over for dinner. Maude broke out her pickled root veggies and offered a hefty serving of baked cobbler made from her canned strawberries and rhubarb. Just like her vegetables, those moments were canned and preserved in his memory.

It's only been recently, though, that Jason dwelled on Maude's death. More specifically, on Maude's absence, of her no longer existing in Glen's life. It made him imagine Jen being taken suddenly from his world. What would he be like if that happened? Would he become an inconsolable wreck? The ruination of a man? Or would he move beyond it?

Is that what Glen did? Had he moved beyond the loss of Maude? Or was his composure and good nature a pretense for a much darker post-Maude existence? At night, did he sit alone in that dark living room, a broken man before an empty rocker draped by the afghans knit by the love he lost?

Jason already had a taste of what it would be like to lose Jen, to be alone. It had driven him to the brink. His mother had her dramatic, flamboyant response to being left alone—right over that brink. Agnes Polnzy, he supposed, faced something similar. Each of us responded in a different way to the ominous, encroaching figure waiting at the other end of the alley or edge of the forest.

If Jason waded in the mire of these thoughts too long, they would suck him down like the spongy bottom of a bog and he wouldn't be able to pull himself out. It was those times, stuck in that mulling quagmire, that he honestly wondered how society held itself together amid the looming shadow that death cast over every single person.

"Something on your mind, Jase?"

At the bar, Jason realized he was holding the root beer bottle in hand, bottle opener frozen at the ready. He shook his head clear and popped the bottle cap off.

"Too much lately. Sorry."

"Nope. I get it. I've been a little more lost in thought myself, of late."

Jason slid the bottle across the bar to Glen, who sat on a bar stool. Jason opened another for himself. "Yeah? What about?"

Glen took a drink and ran an open hand against the bar top, as if doubting the flat surface. "Oh. Well, been thinking back to that road trip of ours." He raised his eyes to Jason. "Remember that?"

Jason did. Vividly. Yet none of that experience had entered

his mind for months until Glen mentioned it. "Sure I do. Embarrassed as hell about it all."

"Don't be. Still. Not clear what it was all about, but it's been bothering me more of late."

"How so?"

"You mean besides a mysterious disappearing detour leading you down a road to nowhere?"

"Yeah. Besides that."

Glen straightened, back arched and shoulders rolled back. "Okay. You said something's coming. You told me you could feel it."

"Oh, shit." Jason's own words echoed in his head from that day, but he had no way to substantiate them.

Glen nodded. "Yeah. Well. What the hell did you mean by that?"

Jason could only be honest at this point. "I have no idea."

Glen scrutinized him with a severe brow. "What did you see that night? You said that thing, that slot machine, told you something."

"Forget about it."

Glen leaned in. "You said you thought Polnzy saw it, too."

"I didn't know what I was saying."

Glen slapped a hand down hard on the bar counter and Jason jumped. "Now damn it, give me a straight answer. You said you saw something that night. You said something's coming. Ever since then, everything's felt—off. You know? From here in our neighborhood to the world around us. Now, we got this—virus—"

"What?"

"You haven't heard? Some damn virus infecting hundreds of people in China. They just reported the first case here in the US."

Jason laughed, if only to try and diffuse the situation. This wasn't like Glen. He seemed truly agitated, and Jason feared he was the cause of it. "Oh, Glen. Serious?"

"Well, the media's sure taking it serious."

"Just like they scared us about Ebola, Bird flu—"

"Those were real threats, Jason."

"Maybe. But not, I would argue, to the degree the news media wanted us to think."

Glen stared into him hard and unwavering. "I'm asking you, as a friend. What did you see? What did it tell you?"

There was no way out of this conversation other than to tell him, and Jason absolutely hated the idea of telling Glen. He couldn't clearly understand his revulsion to sharing it, but it stuck in his throat like a lie or a dirty secret.

"Okay, fine. I don't like thinking about it, alright? But— okay. I walked up to this antique slot machine thing. You follow? It had this crank on the side. I turned the crank, and these three dials spun. When they stopped, they read—" He took a deep, slow breath. "They read, 'You are. Going to. Die.'" The words fell from his mouth like a confession.

Glen looked at him. "That's it?"

"That's enough, for fuck's sake."

Glen's arms crossed over his chest. "And you say Polnzy saw the same thing?"

"No. She—Hold on."

He went upstairs to the den and grabbed the page he tore from the photo album. In his hands, it felt too rigid. Too heavy. Too real. And yet, there was a fragility to it, like a dead sea scroll or sheet of Egyptian papyrus. An ancient message brought forth to the present.

Until this interrogation from Glen, he had wiped everything related to that experience, including this page, from his head. He hadn't thought about any of this in longer than he could remember. Now, he faced it all over again.

Back downstairs, he showed Glen the page.

"What's this?"

"That was in a photo album of Agnes's. She wrote it. Over and over. I think just before she killed herself."

Glen stared at the page, head slowly shaking in confusion or disbelief or incongruity. "I don't understand."

Jason pointed at the trisected words. "See? She spaced out the words. Just like the three cylinders that showed my message. 'You are. Going to. Die.' 'All are. Meant to. Suffer.' You get it?"

Glen's squint and frown were dubious. He looked up with questioning eyes.

"Hey." He held up his hands. "I didn't want to bring any of this up. I had put it behind me."

Glen stared and drilled his concentration into the page. Finally, he pushed it away with frustration.

"I get nothing from any of this. These—statements—aren't meaningful. They aren't predictions. They're just points of fact. They aren't anything."

Jason shrugged.

Glen got off the stool and paced along the bar, hand to chin.

"Glen." Jason was frustrated. This wasn't how he had wanted to spend a night with a friend. He was done dwelling on the absurdity of that slot machine. "Glen, I'm over this. Why is it suddenly bothering you?"

Glen stopped pacing and looked at him with a painful desperation Jason hadn't seen on Glen's face since talking with him about Maude's final days. "If it doesn't mean anything, why am I getting that same feeling you were? That something is coming? Huh? Goddamn it, Jase. I just can't shake it."

CHAPTER TWENTY-FOUR
Thursday, January 30, 2020

It's the dead time. The vacant time. Deep into the winter stagnancy, when the season dragged on through days that still have more darkness than light. Each morning rising to the lingering night and each evening returning home to the dark end of day. Winter came to December cool and crisp and fresh, but now its frigid touch burned skin and strangled breath.

Jason sipped a light beer as he sat in the sunroom that over-looked their back property, now obliterated by snow. He tried to enjoy the resolve of the day in the quiet of the evening before bed, but he couldn't help but feel the gloom of being deep in the midwestern, northwoods winter.

He watched it weigh down Jen even more. Winter lost its charm for her a while ago. It had become a personal affront. She spent more time at the television watching "reality shows"—a genre that required quotes to encapsulate it. She also spent a lot more time on social media, which concerned him. She mumbled about politics and people in ways he tended to stay quiet about. Her demeanor was turning as dark and chill as the late January Wisconsin winter.

Nicholas was more lethargic, but managed to stay occupied with his video games and toys. Jason's boy was much more like his old self now. Not even the icy shroud of winter impeded Nicky's progress. It was much easier to be welcomed into Nicky's world, or at least more tolerated. Jason made sure not to force himself into Nicky's bubble. He let Nicky be in charge of the activity and Jason either participated directly or was a sideline cheerleader, depending on Nicky's comfort level.

Nicholas continued to have occasional nightmares, but they were less frequent and disrupted his sleep less often. As far as that goes, Jason's nightmares were coming weekly, so all things considered, Nicky seemed to be doing better than Jason.

Jason's nightmare two nights ago featured new horrors mixed with old favorites. As with many dreams, there wasn't a lot of sense or cohesion to it. From the little Jason remembered, his latest nightmare had him walking down Fairview toward the Polnzy house. He was overcome with anxiety as he reached Agnes's driveway and saw the Petersons' Frankenstein's monster staring at him with dead rubbery eyes from their porch.

Then, he suddenly found himself in the colorless, dark and gloomy maze of Agnes's house, doing everything he could to avoid the living room and what he knew was in there. He went down a long flight of stairs to a vast expanse of dark basement, just concrete floor and cinderblock walls. He weaved around discarded piles of garbage, going from empty room to empty room, deeper and deeper into the subterranean labyrinth. The unease in the pit of his stomach expanded with every step. Ahead, the shadowy shape of the slot machine, its click and whir of spinning cylinders like the chitter of a cat about to pounce. He rounded a corner—

—and Greg Polnzy jumped out and threw a plastic bag over his head.

He woke up sucking in gulps of air.

Boswell required him to meet one more time with his counselor. Emily? No, Amy. Or Angie. He should probably tell her about these dreams. But what was the point? He hadn't told her about Agnes, or about Agnes's son threatening him and his family, or about the slot machine, or about his mother's suicide.

He understood that he should tell someone about all of that, but not her. Jason didn't think Boswell's overly-sensitive, hug-loving counselor would be able to handle the complexities of his situation, his psychology, or his delusions.

When he returned home from his Springfield exile, he sincerely believed he was on some kind of redemptive path. He still believed it, but hadn't realized how dark and deep into the pathological woods that path would lead him as he tried to reach the other end.

But honestly, how much of his dread and foreboding had anything to do with some mental crisis, and how much simply involved the circumstances he faced? After all, he was being menaced by a dangerous man. His wife's estranged parents were threatening to force their way back into her life, and his boy was still coming to terms with seeing the graphic suicide of an old woman. On top of that, Glen—and now Jen—was fixating on news of some Chinese virus the CDC apparently just declared as a global health emergency.

So much for starting off the new year fresh and positive.

He woke up to the thump-thump-thump-thump of country music. It was muffled and distant, but loud enough to get him out of a sleep where he had somehow ended up miles in the air on some insane overpass with no railings as Nicholas walked against the extreme edge with Jen beside him. Nicky started to tumble over the side and Jen followed as she tried to catch him. Jason reached for them, but he was too slow, too late, and watched them both go over the edge and fall into the abyss.

He got up from bed, the digital clock glowing 2:43 in the morning. Heading down the hall, the music grew louder and he realized it was coming from outside.

At the end of the hallway, the living room bay window came into view. Through it, his driveway and the dark, snow-covered cul-de-sac below. In that circular dead-end of Fairview Lane, in front of his driveway, an old, black F-150 pick-up truck with tinted windows idled. A flannelled elbow poked out from the open driver-side window as a bouncy honky-tonk bass vibrated the living room glass.

Jason's panic seized his breath and wrang his gut like a rag. He experienced true paralytic helplessness in those long and jagged minutes the truck sat there and faced his home.

A blue and white can—looked like a beer can—flew out the window of the black truck and the F-150 sped away to the deep growl of its V-8 engine, a cloud of noxious oily smoke left behind over the end of his driveway.

He wasn't able to sleep for the rest of the night. He draped an arm around Jen, fingers clutching her shoulder, a perpetual grasp of reassurance that she was there and safe. He thought of the gun in his car. He thought of that gun in his hand, aimed at Greg.

At 4:59 a.m., he shut off the alarm clock before it went off and got up. As he headed to the bathroom to get ready for work, he thought about doing many things: calling the police, telling Jen, phoning Suzie.

He did none of those things.

Greg would win if he succumbed to fear. None of those

things would keep Greg Polnzy away, but they would disrupt his family, upset Suzie, and make life more miserable for all of them—exactly what Greg wanted to achieve.

Greg didn't care about the police, or himself, or anything. He was a disrupter. He was a chaos-generator. His destructive compulsions drove him without regard to repercussions. So many dangerous people were like this. They did not act. They reacted. Their reactions were based on apathy, anger, and loathing—for themselves, and for every part of the world that made them miserable.

No alarm system would keep Greg at bay. No motion sensor would turn him away. Jason had simply become one more thing in Greg Polnzy's life that found its way under his skin.

It was very clear to Jason. He had become an itch that Greg Polnzy needed to scratch.

Chapter Twenty-five
Monday, February 3, 2020

He stared at the black silhouette of a male figure through the sights of the Beretta. He aimed for the chest—center mass. How many cop shows had he heard that mentioned? You aim there because it's the largest target on the human body and your best chance of hitting something. A bullseye would probably be lethal, though if the target was moving, that level of accuracy wouldn't be likely.

He applied slow, even pressure to the trigger as he kept the iron sight right where the sternum would be. Jason's mind flashed back to fifth grade, when a police officer came to his school to talk to the students. A classmate asked if a police officer aimed for the leg or arm to just wound the bad guys. Jason never forgot the officer's solemn, direct reply to the room of ten-year-olds. "Firing our gun is an absolute last resort. But, if we shoot, we shoot to kill."

Jason pulled the trigger.

The recoil caught him off-guard. The explosive volume, even with ear protection, shocked him. The sheer magnitude of power from the gun was staggering. He wasn't prepared for the level of violence inherent in the action of discharging a firearm. He stood there, stunned, as the Beretta's eruptive force still rang in his ears and transmitted through his arms and into his shoulders. It took several seconds for him to realize he hadn't taken a breath since before he pulled the trigger. With an unsteady hand, he carefully set the gun down on the metal shelf beside him and pushed the button that brought the paper target closer to him on its track.

He scanned the large sheet of brown craft paper. The man-sized silhouette was unblemished. Unsullied. Wound-free. A small bullet-sized hole sat two inches off the right shoulder.

A stationary target ten feet away and he had completely missed. Jesus.

He pressed the button to send the target back, took the gun into his hand, braced it with the other, aimed, inhaled, and pulled the trigger.

Again.

And again.

And again.

An hour at the shooting range, emptying 120 rounds into targets, and one thing was clear.

He was not a natural.

But by the end, he consistently hit the target from twenty feet away, and he grew accustomed to the feel and power of the gun. To say he was comfortable with firing the weapon—any weapon—was an overstatement, but he was now acclimated.

His thoughts and emotions were mixed as he drove home

from the gun range with his 9mm Beretta on the passenger seat, his defense against hostile threats.

Until a few weeks ago, he had never felt the true threat of danger or harm. His worries were either conventional, an act of God or, as a juvenile, blissfully ignorant. Never had he felt such a visceral, poignant and ever-present fear of malicious intent like the direct threat he faced from Greg. The gun was a tangible reminder that a real, viable, imminent threat to him and his family existed. He pined for those days, not long ago, when he had little and no one to fear.

But that nostalgia of safety and comfort now seemed to be the height of naivete. That gun was a rite of passage to a manhood he had never fully embraced or experienced. This wasn't some childhood game of cops and robbers or a glorified, stylized Hollywood movie. He was taking responsibility to be the last line of defense for his family. He would not cower. He would not buckle to Greg's intimidation.

That gun drew a line back to the wilderness—the wildness—of pioneer days. The severity and leanness of colonial days. The dark days of defending feudal lands. Modern times had become the fantasy bedtime stories of happily-ever-afters, but the vast span of human history has been far more like a Grimm's fairy tale narrative. Ages of blood and violence and cruelty based on the simplest concepts of either, "You have what I want," or, "You are what I don't like." Much of that had transformed itself into the political and social capitalism of brand wars, corporate takeovers and market domination, where the serfdom of consumerism represented both the spoils and the victims of modern conflict.

Now, with a contentious election and intense polarization, plus talk of a looming pandemic? Make no mistake. Real aggression, violence and conflict still existed everywhere, and it would only get worse, just as it did over one hundred fifty years ago.

That gun was there because, no matter how hard he worked, obeyed the rules and played society's game, there would always be someone out there who wanted to take it away from him. Right now, life presented him with the ultimate question: Are you hunter, or prey?

Jen was extra-quiet through dinner that night. Not standoff-ish, but one of few words, her attention tending to linger in no particular place. It put Jason's guard up, but he fought against his normal instincts to try and excavate her silence and uncover the shards of her mood. Instead, he ate. He commented on how tasty the teriyaki chicken was. He cheered and gave Nicky a high-five when his son told them about his home run in kickball during gym class. That entire time, Jen gave distracted attention, smiled or nodded, and replied with few words.

He helped Jen clear the table and they stood at the sink as she rinsed off dishes and handed them to Jason to load the dishwasher.

Despite his full intention to be completely honest with her and not withhold anything, circumstances worked against the truth. The threatening note from Greg circumvented his opportunity to tell her about the phone call from Zeke. He intended to tell her about Greg's subtle threat of a visit at three in the morning, but worried it would cause additional fear without any productive outcome. Did she find out about one of these events and the knowledge was stewing over the heat of her anger until it boiled over?

She gave a plate a quick spray of water and handed it to him. "My father called me today."

So that's it. Damn it.

He loaded the plate in the dishwasher, was slow to rise and

used the open appliance like a hole in the ground to hide his head. He opened his mouth to say something, not even sure what that something would be, but she interrupted him.

"Fucking Seth has been telling them *everything*. He gave them my phone number. He told them our marriage was falling apart, that Nicky is all messed up and seeing a shrink, that you're a drunk, and that we kicked them out at Thanksgiving because he brought my parents up. Can you fucking believe that?"

He slowly uprighted himself and stared at Jen. His mouth remained open but there were no words. He couldn't believe Zeke would call Jen and risk the meager chance of reconciliation. But even that seemed more believable than Zeke not mentioning his phone conversation with Jason. Did he realize somewhere deep down in that crotchety obstinacy that Jason was better to him as an ally than an enemy? Meanwhile, he continued to be shocked by Seth and the level of his retribution—something he felt more responsible for than anything Jen had done. Seth was making it more likely that Jen would talk to her parents again before she ever saw or spoke to her brother again.

Jen reacted to Jason's mute response with a bitter chuckle and nodded. "Yeah. Insane, right?"

"I—I can't believe it." And he couldn't in more ways than Jen could know. "Did—did you talk to him, then?"

She grabbed a bowl and resumed her rinsing. "I was going to hang up on him, but when he started throwing out all the outlandish accusations, I just had to set him straight."

It should have been a momentous moment—the first time in sixteen years father and daughter communicated. Instead, it had been antagonistic and hostile.

"Well, what happened?" he asked. "What did you say? What did he say?"

She handed him the bowl. "You know what he didn't say? Sorry. That's what he didn't say, and what neither of them will ever say. And that's why I told him to go to hell and never call me again."

She snatched a pot from beside the sink, rinsed it out and put it in front of Jason. Her movements weren't aggressive or severe, but deliberate and resolute. She gave every impression that Zeke cleansed her of any residual thoughts she may have had on reconciling.

You just fucked yourself, Zeke. Why didn't you listen to me?

He placed the sauce pan in the dishwasher and squirted detergent in the soap trap. He closed the door and looked right at Jen.

"Just what exactly happened, Jen?"

"Nothing. He said all that bullshit and I told him how wrong he was and told him to go to hell."

"No. Not the call. What happened that made you hate them so much?"

She huffed as she turned to the sink and started to scrub it with a scouring pad. "You know that. I told you all the things they did."

"Yeah. I know about the drinking. Not letting you go anywhere or do anything. The verbal abuse. But—there's something else. Isn't there."

"Why does there need to be anything else? Why is that not enough? Jesus!" She slammed the faucet off and threw the sponge in the sink.

He put his hands on her shoulders and gently turned her toward him. She didn't fight him. "Jen. I am one-hundred percent ready to tell Zeke and Dee to go to hell forever. Seth too, quite honestly. But be straight with me. Something happened, right? Something that was the final straw?"

Jen made a weak effort to pull away. "Nothing that makes any difference."

"Please."

Whatever resistance remained in her drained down and out her feet. It was clear she wasn't angry, not mad at him, but just sad and tired—maybe sixteen-years-tired of carrying whatever she was holding.

"You don't need to know this. It serves no purpose."

Jason's gut wrung. "So there is something. Christ, did he—"

Her eyes widened. "No. God. No. I would've killed the son of a bitch if that had happened."

Jason exhaled heavy relief. "Thank God for that." He took a moment to let that sink in and calm himself. "So, what was it, then?"

Jen pulled away and he let her go. She moved over to the kitchen table and sat down. "Just remember, this was a little over twenty years ago. I was seventeen."

Jason nodded, walked over and joined her at the table. He reached out and took her hand in his.

"I barely had any social life in school. You know all about how they never let me go anywhere—afraid of what I might do, what I could get into. But I could get away every once in a while—lie to them about having to stay after school for a social studies project, or to do extra credit for my geometry class. That was the only way I could get any time with friends—we'd hang out at the Burger King, or in the alley by the school smoking cigarettes. That's how Steven and I first got together."

"Steven?"

That took a direction Jason hadn't expected. The sad smirk she gave him made him realize the look of surprise he obviously wore. "Despite my sheltered upbringing, my dear, I was still able to sneak a boyfriend now and again."

"Oh, sure. Sure." Jason squeezed her hand and smiled.

"Steven was special. He was my first true love. Curly blond hair, blue eyes, and this cute little peach fuzz goatee. We had homeroom together, and science class, plus a study hour in the library. He wanted to be a writer." Her attention drifted out of the present, aloft on a thought carried by the current of a memory. "He wrote me poetry, about how our love was eternal."

She held on to those words. He watched her seeing him again, reliving moments with Steven. It made him remember Helen Osteen, his high school love, and how it seemed they were destined to be together. Every love song he heard was about them, as if written for them. Teenage love was an opioid, a compulsive and overwhelming addiction. It drove you crazy when you didn't have it, and made you senseless when you indulged in it. The rush of its high squirmed around in memory like a craving.

"When we became serious, just toward the end of senior year, he insisted on meeting my parents. He knew what they were like, but he wanted to play the gentleman and ask their permission to date me." She shook her head. "I think he liked the idea of being in some Jane Austen novel."

That meant nothing to Jason, but he smiled.

"I had warned him, told him we should just get out of town after graduation. He wouldn't listen. He thought they might ease up on me if they saw what a polite and decent boy he was." She gave Jason a knowing look and he caught the connection to himself right away.

"We confronted my parents together after school." Her voice trailed as her eyes wilted.

"I'm guessing it didn't go well," Jason said.

Jen shook her head. "That's putting it mildly." She withdrew her hand and sat stiff and upright. "My mother told him I was a whore and that he was just a horny little pervert trying to get laid."

"Oh. Oh my—my God."

"My father said he would beat the shit out of Steven and—and cut off his—his—well, you get the point—if he ever laid a hand on me."

"Unbelievable." Zeke's voice, from countless conversations, played in his head, now twisted into the rant of those words.

Jen's eyes reddened and teared. "It was never the same between Steven and me after that. After a while, we stopped speaking. In the end, he barely even looked at me when we passed in the hall."

"That's fucking crappy, Jen."

Jen shrugged. "I really couldn't blame him. He saw what a shitty life I had. Horrible, drunken parents in a dirty little house. That stink carries over, you know? Steven thought so, at least. Who would want to get involved in that?"

All those years, Jen told him how her parents had been too young, her father a hot-blooded, angry young man and mother a bitter, harsh young woman. They verbally abused her and kept her from having any kind of life. Maybe they believed they were keeping her from making the same mistakes they had made, making sure she didn't turn out like them. And maybe they had succeeded, but at the expense of any future relationship with their daughter.

This was certainly the most graphic and painfully detailed Jen had ever been with him. All of it too painful for her to want to revisit, so she kept it buried. He could certainly relate to that.

He should have accepted all along that it was Jen's decision, not his, to decide what and where her parents would be in their life, but he hadn't. He had been so enamored with the idea of reunion and reconciliation, of having a second chance with parents, that he hadn't bothered to realize how he was continually irritating an already festering wound.

He got up and walked behind her, wrapped arms around her and held her tight. "I should have listened to you better. I should have realized how bad it was."

She patted his hands and rubbed them. "Your intentions

were good."

"No, they weren't. They were selfish. I've been an asshole, and I'm sorry."

She looked up at him. "I know."

He gave her a quizzical look. "About me being sorry, or me being an asshole?"

"Eh." A wan smile.

He kissed her on the forehead. "Nice. Still, I'll admit, I'm a little surprised that in all these years you never shared that story."

Jen shifted in her seat, turned and laid a hand on his cheek. "I suppose I just never wanted you thinking you were my second choice."

He grinned and kissed her forehead. He could live with that answer.

CHAPTER TWENTY-SIX
Sunday, February 9, 2020

Afor-sale sign stood on the front lawn of the Polnzy house. Suzie had been at the home off and on for the last month to clean up the place and make repairs. Ollie came over several times and helped fix the front door, replace the lock and do some minor patchwork inside. The Petersons stopped by to check on her, offered some baked chocolate chip cookies, and helped with general clean-up. Glen spent a fair amount of time over there giving her car a tune up and doing some minor electrical work. Jason kept the driveway cleared of snow and helped move the few pieces of remaining furniture. He hooked the trailer to Jen's Crosstrek and drove a load to the dump

The neighborhood was stepping up to show their support, and it seemed to be bringing neighbors closer together as well.

By now, everyone knew about the danger Greg posed to Suzie, as well as the threat he made to the Laheys. Jason appreciated everyone's willingness to step up and come together as a community.

With that for-sale sign, it appeared Suzie had been given rightful ownership of the house and land. From what Jason understood, after remaining debts were paid and if the sale went well, Suzie could possibly come away with a nice little nest egg. Good for her.

Somehow, over the course of time, the ugly tragedy of Agnes's death might transform itself into the possibility of new beginnings. Had Agnes known this would happen? Was this part of her plan? Or was all this just a random outcome from the violent and self-absorbed end of an old woman's life?

Jason couldn't help but remember Pauline's statement: "Hating yourself is just about the most selfish thing you can do." At the time, he had only applied that to himself, but now he saw how it carried over to Agnes as well. It certainly seemed like her suicide had been a selfish endeavor. But maybe even an act like that could, through circumstance, translate to a positive outcome, intended or not. Jason liked the idea of something good coming from Agnes's death.

Unfortunately, someone bad had come into their neighborhood as a result of her death as well. It was a curious thought. Was Greg's hostility and lawlessness a result of his own self-loathing?

It didn't matter. He was making conscious decisions to hurt others. Greg willingly brought disruption, fear and malice wherever he went.

Last night, three inches of snow had fallen, so Jason started up the snowblower and cleared his driveway, taking long runs up and down the slope of blacktop. The late morning was tolerable, temperature in the upper teens, the wind light, gray overcast sky holding in what little warmth the obscured sun brought to the day.

As he finished up his driveway, Fred came out in his parka

and deluxe snowblower with full enclosure, headlight, and 29-inch front scoop. Jason waved and Fred raised a hand in return as he blew snow a full twenty yards down his property in a lofty frozen arc. As they crossed paths, Fred stopped his blower and kept it in low idle. He tilted his head forward as a beckoning, so Jason stopped his blower and stepped to the edge of his driveway and closer to Fred.

"Seems our neighborhood's been seeing a bit of activity these last few months," Fred shouted over the thin strip of snow-covered yard between their driveways.

"Interesting times, huh?"

"Saw you got a fancy new security system. Something in particular bring you to getting that?"

Whenever Jason talked with Fred, his neighbor only seemed to ask leading questions. He tended to dig for more information, as if everything involved either ulterior motives or a curious or sensitive backstory.

"Just taking precautions, Fred. Seems sensible nowadays."

"Hell yes. You got that right." He gestured beyond Jason to the Johnsons' place. "Especially with where this country is headed."

The conversation was quickly turning uncomfortable. "A lot of conflicting beliefs, that's for sure," was all Jason could think to say.

"Then, you take everything going down at that Polnzy residence down the street. Never did feel right about any of them."

Jason turned back to his blower. He needed this conversation to end. "Speaking of, I have to get over there and snow-blow that driveway. Trying to do what I can to help Suzie out. You know, it's the neighborly thing to do." He locked eyes with Fred.

Fred looked like he just tasted something sour. "Yeah. Sure. Well, see you around." Fred wandered back to his blower.

Jason did the same and finished his driveway with a couple

more passes. He swung the blower around and guided it down his driveway to head for Agnes's place—well, officially Suzie's place now.

As he made contact with the road, his stomach lurched as he saw the black Ford F-150 approach and begin to turn into Suzie's driveway. Jason killed the engine and abandoned the snowblower, legs pumping as he dashed to his garage and the Lexus.

Driver-side door yanked open, he pulled the gun case out from under the seat, dug for his keys and unlocked the case. Gun in hand, he slapped the clip into place and drew back the slide to cock it, safety engaged. His brain was on autopilot and his body shifted to overdrive, blood and adrenaline coursing through his veins in equal measure.

He started toward Suzie's place, holding the gun behind his back, finger straight against the trigger guard. Greg stepped out of the truck, his friend joining from the passenger side. Jason was halfway there as they started toward the front door. Jason picked up his pace to a trot.

He reached curbside of the driveway just as Greg and his compatriot approached the front door.

"Hey!" Jason's voice was too high and too shaky, too thin in the cold, still winter air. He had gone for commanding, but it came out instead like a weak question.

Greg turned to Jason, looking as if he was holding back a laugh. He walked back down the stairs as Jason moved up the driveway.

"Look'it here, Darryl. It's the Welcome Wagon. You can just leave your goodies where you stand and move along, Welcome Wagon."

Jason stopped midway up the driveway. Electricity was triggering every muscle in his body. "You need to leave Suzie—all of us—alone."

"Do I? Is that what you think?"

Greg kept approaching and Darryl followed behind. Both men had arms rigid and ready at their sides.

"That's what I know." Jason kept the gun at his back, gripping it firmly, reassured by the weight and cold steel of the grip.

"Do you, now?" Greg stepped onto the snow-covered driveway. "None of this is your fucking business, so why don't you do yourself, your wife and kid a favor and get the fuck out of here?"

Greg approached at a steady and resolute pace. He was fifteen feet from Jason and closing.

Jason brought the Beretta around and pointed it at Greg. His hand vibrated with intensity. Drawn, the gun gained density and heft. The grip suddenly felt fat and awkward in his hand. "Get out of here. Both of you."

Greg laughed loud as he continued his approach. "Whoa! Careful, son. Don't hurt yourself with that thing."

"Stop. Swear to God—"

"Or what?" Greg moved closer. Less than six feet away now.

Jason's chest could barely contain his beating heart. He flicked off the safety as his finger wrapped around the trigger.

Jesus fucking Christ are you going to shoot this man? Center mass. Center mass.

"You better do something right now," Greg said and he reached out and smacked the gun hard with a blinding-fast swing. Jason almost lost the gun, tried to bring it back in front of him as Greg threw a solid punch to Jason's face. White light and a reverberating thump like a bell ringing in his skull as his face blazed with a fiery flash of pain before going fat and numb with shock.

The punch to his solar plexus stunned and disabled him. He no longer had any control of the gun, didn't know if he held it anymore. Jason crumbled.

Hard, intense kicks hammered his head, his ribs, his kidneys. He curled into a ball of pain as what felt like a crowd of limbs pummeled him. He covered his head to blunt the bashing, tucked in his elbows to fend off the pelting steel-toed boots to kidneys and ribs. He couldn't think anymore, couldn't orient himself. He simply counted blows and measured pain as his consciousness clouded.

A deafening eruption paused the anguish of punishment. Another loud crack of thunder, feet kicking and stepping on and over him, a splash of something warm across his face and a cry of shock or pain.

"Die you bastard!" A woman's voice. "Die you piece of fucking shit! Die die die!"

More explosions, more shouts and cries, as Jason succumbed to fear and pain and darkness.

He came to as sirens wailed and voices clamored. He couldn't locate or distinguish pain. Pain was existence now. Around him, a commotion of steps and voices.

"I've got no pulse!"

"This one's breathing!"

He felt hands all about him, breath over him. He groaned as parts of his insides grated and shifted.

"He's alive!" Shouted directly over him.

He choked and coughed as hands groped about his neck, stomach and chest. He was rolled onto his back.

"What—?" All he could get out.

"Take it easy. You're going to be okay."

"Is that his blood?"

"I don't think so."

"Jason!" A familiar female voice. Jen.

"Let them take care of him." Another voice, older and male. Glen. "He'll be okay."

Jason fought to open his eyes.

Two paramedics over him. A backboard slid under him—head, chest and legs strapped to the board. He looked to his one side and saw Jen, her face twisted with worry as Glen held her, his eyes strained and mouth frowning. He turned to his other side and saw two bodies lying on the ground, snow dark red around them. One was Greg. As an EMT pumped his chest, Greg's lifeless gaze seemed to aim right at—right through—Jason. Even vacant, those eyes emitted malice.

Red, blue and white lights flashed. Two officers passed him, their hands on Suzie's shoulders, her expression flat other than a slight curl of satisfaction on her lips. They led her away, hands cuffed behind her.

He was picked up and carried to an ambulance. Jen came up to him. "Jason! You'll be okay! I love you! I'm right here. I'm not leaving you."

Looking to the street, he saw a repeat of the scene from the beginning of November. His neighborhood audience of spectators gathered in the street around Polnzy's house—Petersons, Mickelssens, Greeleys and Johnsons, and Glen. They all gawked at the cinema of chaos occurring once again on a Sunday afternoon on Fairview Lane.

CHAPTER TWENTY-SEVEN
Saturday, March 14, 2020

It was out there. He was certain of it. Beyond the ravine, through the barbed wire, and across the barren field. He sensed it, standing solidary in the snow, facing east, in the direction of Fairview Lane.

Watching.

What a ridiculous thought. As ridiculous as him driving out here and parking on the side of the mysterious, unmarked road to stare at nothing. But he was certain the something that should not be there, something he still couldn't rationalize, was indeed there.

On the news, they talked about the World Health Organization declaring what was now being called COVID 19 a global pandemic. What a dire phrase, and yet he couldn't scale it, couldn't acclimate to the repercussions of that statement, any more than he could put perspective to the more than four thousand dead and over one-hundred-thousand confirmed cases from this virus. He sat. He stared out across the unsullied expanse of white that ran into the horizon, where the spindly pines stood tall against the gray late-morning sky, where an old and mysterious thing that didn't belong stood in defiance, an ancient harbinger of doom.

Just over a month had passed since the attack, and his fractured ribs still shot sharp pain whenever he moved. His eye was no longer swollen from the orbital fracture but was still tender to the touch. Headaches from the concussion remained, but were no longer severe. His lacerated liver was the most lingering injury. A steady, deep ache radiated from his side and abdomen.

Between the pain meds, antibiotics, and decongestants prescribed for the eye injury, he was popping pills like a seventy-year-old. Hell, between his liver and his ribs, he felt like a seventy-year-old. But he appreciated being mobile again after forty-eight hours in the hospital followed by weeks of bedrest.

The events of the last month played over and over in his mind. He was still troubled by so much of it, how to feel about it, what to do with what he knew—what he didn't want to know.

Greg Polnzy was gone. Jason had stared into his dead eyes and Greg's stared back. He couldn't stop seeing those eyes, the threat in that dead gaze, as if, even in death, Greg's look had said, "Just you wait."

In the span of six months, he had seen the dead bodies of two Polnzy's. That other guy, Darryl, survived. He had been shot in the stomach, chest and throat. He was in rough shape, apparently still in the hospital under police custody and awaiting trial for multiple crimes past and present.

Glen filled him in on much of what happened when he visited Jason in the hospital. Glen called the police as soon as he saw Greg's truck pull up, something Jason should have done. Glen had just stepped outside when Suzie opened fire on Greg and Darryl. Glen turned ashen as he described it to Jason. "I've never seen anything like it. She just walked out that door, all calm and cool, gun raised, and started unloading it into them. Jason, I don't think one bullet went astray." His head shook. "Then she just sat down on the stoop, set the gun down in front of her, and looked off down the street, like she was waiting for the police."

When Glen explained the scene, Jason recalled—and still couldn't stop recalling—pointing his gun at Greg. How terrifying and simple an action, to move a finger and take a life. He had walked over with nothing in his mind other than shooting Greg and felt a perverse testosterone-filled excitement at the possibility. When he aimed that gun, everything twisted and distorted. He had felt sick and horrified, weak and pathetic, and so, so very human.

The police questioned him the next day while he laid on the hospital bed enveloped in pain. He told them everything. His Beretta, though never fired, had been confiscated as evidence. In the end, it appeared he would not be charged. He didn't care if that Beretta was ever returned to him. He didn't think he could ever touch a gun again.

And yet, sitting in the car now, he felt glad—or at least deeply relieved—that Greg was dead. What a strange duality of thought and emotion, to know he would have let himself die before killing Greg, and yet feel such satisfaction that Suzie Polnzy had taken that action herself.

That put him upon dark paths of thought to navigate, and he wasn't sure he had the moral breadcrumbs to find his way back.

Suzie was arraigned the following Tuesday and officially charged with second-degree murder. She pled not guilty. Based on the testimony of some neighbors who shared Suzie's exclamatory statements as she fired her gun as being suggestive of her intent to kill, the judge set a ten-thousand-dollar bail. The trial was scheduled to begin at the end of May.

Much of the neighborhood pooled their resources and did collections through church and social groups to raise the money and get her out of jail after a week. Jason and Jen had put up five thousand of those dollars.

Jason remembered how different she appeared when she came by the house shortly after she was released, both to thank him and Jen for the money, and also to see how Jason was doing. She looked ten years younger. All that dread and anxiety she experienced over her brother, all those years wearing the emotional scars inflicted by him, appeared to be gone. Despite facing a second-degree murder charge and what could be a long trial down the road, Suzie Polnzy almost glowed.

Jen introduced herself, then hugged Suzie and thanked her over and over for saving Jason. They talked together for a while. Jen filled Suzie in on Jason's injuries and recovery, how it could have been so much worse for Jason had Suzie not acted. How Suzie had been so brave and strong to do what she did. After a time, Jen excused herself to check on Nicky.

"I need to thank you, you know," Suzie said, looking down at him in his bed as his ribs ached, head throbbed and side was jabbed with pain.

"Oh, please," Jason strained to reply through pain and false modesty. "I didn't do anything. Just tried to help, but that didn't go so well."

She gave a wide smile. "Oh, but you did help. More than you realize. It would have been first-degree murder."

He had stared, confused. "Wh—?"

"Then you showed up. My hero. When they fell on you, it was perfect. Self-defense. I can't begin to thank you enough."

As he stared in shocked silence, she bent down and kissed him gently on his cheek. "I saved your life, and you gave me mine back. And that bastard can never hurt any of us again."

With a warm, loving smile, she touched his cheek and held

his gaze in hers. Then, she walked away.

It was the first time Jason recognized how much sister and brother looked alike.

She had baited her brother. Somehow lured him to the house with a promise or concession. She must have decided she couldn't live any longer with her brother back in her life, a constant threat looming over her. Agnes's death had drawn him back into Suzie's orbit despite her every attempt to hide from him. That house had become an unwanted beacon, and she decided she would also make it a trap.

Premeditated murder, plain and simple. First degree. He couldn't prove it, but he believed it without any doubt.

Jason sat and looked over the field. He imagined turning the crank on that antique machine, waiting to see what answer it might reveal, because he didn't have one. He had no idea what to do.

When he returned home, Jen met him at the door. "Well, they're closing down the schools." Her arms flapped to her sides in flustered exasperation.

"What?"

"This shit is getting pretty serious, Jason. I think we need to start preparing for the worst."

His arm crossed his aching ribs, hand over the dull throb of his liver, and all he could think was, *And this, with* everything *else going on, isn't already the worst?*

Chapter Twenty-eight
Wednesday, March 25, 2020

The world had turned inside out. Moments dragged through the sandy mire of time while, amid the thinning streets and empty restaurants, a collective breath held.

It was day one of a complete lockdown. Amid the caesura pause in Fortune Falls and across the state, the country, and the world, people found themselves with toes hanging over the edge of a societal cliff. A general breakdown of common sense and decency was happening all around, while the final threads of unity were fraying and snapping. The crumbling of modern society spread out from the personal pulpits of social media and the video screens and radio speakers of news programs and talk shows. If the pandemic didn't scare the hell out of you, then your government should, or this ideology, or that foreign country, or those foreign people. Fear and paranoia laid across the land like dry brush in an old forest, and now this global pandemic struck like lightning on a hot, dry day.

Into this world, Jason took his wife and child shopping.

He suggested he should go alone, but Jen was going stir crazy and wanted to get out, so the three of them headed into this new, unfamiliar world where a silent threat hung invisibly in the air and on whatever they might touch.

Compared to the news coverage that saturated the airways and internet, Fortune Falls still had a relatively normal appearance, other than empty parking lots at restaurants and most businesses. Traffic was lighter, but many people still walked their dogs and rode their bikes. Snow lingered on the ground, but temperatures were rising. The greening grass peeked out from the pale and peeling skin of winter, and sidewalks were clear.

The grocery store was a hub of activity.

There was barely an open spot in the Shop n' Save parking lot. Stepping inside, Jason squeezed antibacterial sanitizer onto his hands as he entered. Jen did the same and took extra to wipe on Nicky's hands, who whined and balked as she did it. Jason grabbed a cart, wiped it down with an antibacterial wipe, and they stepped inside.

Signs called out to them asking to maintain social distancing—six feet apart. Jason saw a fair number of people in surgical or cloth masks. A few people even wore latex gloves as they picked out their produce. Jen held Nicholas's hand and kept him close to her as they entered the produce area. He kept reminding himself of the CDC's warning: don't touch your face. There were no words to describe how bizarre life had become when you were terrified to itch your own eye or scratch your nose.

They grabbed some fruits and green vegetables, but mostly stocked up on russet and sweet potatoes and sturdy root vegetables. Like so many here, they were after more long-term items to hopefully carry them through the viral storm.

A spattering of cans cluttered the soup aisle, the variety decimated. They grabbed what remained of styles they could tolerate: cheesy broccoli, beef vegetable, chicken and wild rice. They loaded up two dozen cans and moved on to grab from whatever pasta and rice remained. Thank God there were still boxes of mac and cheese or Nicky might have starved. They loaded those into the cart, then moved on to boxes of cereal and powdered milk.

Jen had her essential list of items to make sure she could make some decent meals: seasonings and bouillon, jars of sauces, grains, oils and vinegars. After that, they dove into the heavy and frenetic crowds of the frozen foods area. Vegetables, fish, meats, fruit. The shelves grew sparse as people filled their carts, so they didn't waste time with much discretion. Once they were done in that area, their cart overflowed.

They scrabbled for what beef, chicken and pork they could get their hands on. Again, so much was already gone. Jason realized how, in his lifetime, he had come to expect that whatever he desired would—and should—be immediately, accessibly, and cheaply available to him, as if it were a right.

They grabbed blocks of cheese and bags of Cheetos for Nicky's snacks, plus soda, seltzer water and juice. Little remained in the bottled water aisle—some gallons of distilled and a few of the big shrink-wrapped multipacks of bottled water. They loaded up two 24-pack bottles and headed to the cleaning and toiletry aisle.

He stopped and stared. It was unbelievable.

He faced an almost empty aisle. People climbed on the shelves to get at remaining items far in the back. A big yellow sign glared at them:

Due to supply issues, we ask that customers take no more than two (2) of each cleaning and toiletry item. Thank you.

They grabbed what they could: paper towels, toilet paper,

Pine Sol. Pushing a cart heaped with groceries, Jason headed to checkout, Jen and Nicky following with even more items in their hands.

Big circles on the floor told them where to stand and wait in line to keep a safe distance from other shoppers. They were almost back to the aisles as they spread out to wait in line with their overflowing cart. Ahead of them, some stood patiently, some showed frustration, and a few expressed outright hostility, but most merely wore a weary look of worry.

Back home, they left the bags of groceries in the garage. Jason and Jen made Nicky wash his hands while they also washed theirs. Jason's red knuckles burned, skin chapped and cracked from so much washing.

For the next half hour, they walked between garage and kitchen bringing in handfuls of produce to dump into a sink of soapy water and wash. They removed bags from cereal boxes and threw the boxes out. They wiped down what they could of remaining packaging with antibacterial wipes and wrapped meat in butcher paper to put in the freezer drawer. They washed their hands three more times during that process.

Done, Jason and Jen left Nicky to play his Nintendo while they stepped into the sunroom and sat down. Jason stared out their backyard, his eyes sticking to whatever his listless gaze randomly fell upon. The space around him seemed to have more weight to it. The light, the air, the silence of the room—all had mass and pushed up against him. He turned to Jen and she seemed to experience the same thing—a fatigue of existing. The struggle of moving through each moment. That was how it felt in this pandemic.

His ultimate security system suddenly seemed absurd when the greatest threat to him and his family came in the form of a microscopic virus, devoid of anger or malice, but with one singular purpose. He looked around at his overly-secure home, which now would be more than simply home—it would encap-sulate their existence. Somehow, within these walls, they would need to not only live, but work, be productive, and find enter-tainment and fulfillment, all while they educated and raised their son.

This, likely, would be their life for at least the next couple of months.

"It's fine. We're all fine," Jason said to the squares of faces on his screen as he met with his department via Microsoft Teams—their new virtual office for the foreseeable future.

Scott, one of his programmers, barked a bitter laugh chopped by an intermittent connection. "Sure, we're fine. But ninety percent of our clients won't be if they aren't deemed essential. Then what?"

Alex, Jason's number one software developer, scrunched up her face and tossed her hair back. "No way this lasts more than a month or two. They can't shut the world down, for God sake."

Troy cut in. "I wouldn't be too sure about that. Have you been watching what's happening in New York? They already have like twenty thousand cases."

Bob, one of his newer network analysts, scoffed. "Give me a break. They're calling every cold and sniffle COVID. Typical overhyping and overreporting of a non-issue."

"Okay, people," Jason said. "Let's not get off track here. Reality is, like it or not, this is how we're going to operate for a while. And for us, that means a lot more work as all our clients, including Boswell, move to remote work. We have thirty of our own team alone who need support to get their remote sys-tems working, and we have a queue of over twenty businesses so far with a list of employees who need tech support. Because of this, I need all hands on deck. I don't care if you're web, database or network support. We're all customer service right now, you hear me?"

Everyone's video box lit up as collective moans and grumbles sounded over the speaker.

"For the next week, I need all of us, me included, getting into the CRM, running through our active tickets and taking care of them. By next week Wednesday, I want all but the most serious tickets closed. Questions?"

There were. Lots of them. After an hour sitting in his home office dealing with each one, he cut it off. "Okay, time's short and we have a lot to do. If anyone has any other serious questions or issues, reach out to me or Troy directly. Otherwise, you know what to do. You're a fantastic team. I know this is a rough time, but this is also your time to really shine. I know you have it in you, so let's get it done, okay?"

His team left the video conference appearing to be in a better mood than when it started, so Jason felt as good as he could. In reality, though, a lot of their concerns were real. And imminent. With many area businesses facing shutdown if they weren't declared an essential business, Boswell could lose a huge share of its revenue—not to mention whether or not they were deemed essential.

But that fear wasn't realistic. Several of their clients included medical clinics, not to mention the county health department. If anything, this pandemic would add to their work load, even as a huge section of workforce suddenly found themselves without a job.

He looked around the home office that sat off the main entrance hallway. When they were first shown the house, he had felt it a funny little room, something that maybe a lawyer or consultant might find useful, or someone who ran their own business and needed to receive clients at home but didn't want them walking through their house. Now, it was his official office, his workplace—an extension of Boswell Software.

Meanwhile, Jen took residence in one of the upstairs spare bedrooms she had planned to use as a crafting room but never had the time to take advantage of it. She had been preparing it since late last year when she kept Nicholas home from school after the incident.

He tried to be thankful. They had a beautiful home, one that could comfortably accommodate their new work-from-home reality. They resided in a small, secluded neighborhood with friendly, helpful and caring neighbors. They lived in Fortune Falls, Wisconsin, a small but well-developed city that was not New York or L.A. or Seattle, so the threat from the pandemic must surely be less. The phrase, "All the comforts of home," took on so much more significance and certainly a reason to be grateful.

Yet he found himself once again with that pressure against his chest, that tense anxiety of being prey to some lurking beast, somewhere out there, in the shadows.

CHAPTER TWENTY-NINE
Saturday, April 4, 2020

The northern Wisconsin winter knew its time was up, but it clung like a child to the pant leg of the burgeoning spring. Snowbanks sat stubborn at the ends of driveways and cowered in the shadows against the north-facing sides of homes. The hint of warming weather was beat back by the last gasping breaths of a cool wind. Fat-breasted robins bounced along the open areas of grass, their cheeps and chirps edged with irritation at the cold, hard ground and the chill air while the sun shone and insisted the season was turning.

Jason took a stroll down the street to join the weekend morning Fairview Lane coffee klatch. The neighborhood folk started to do regular streetside meet and greets, keeping to their personal force shield bubbles of space. Winter's relaxing grip usually led to neighbors peeking their heads out and starting to socialize with each other, but with the advent of the pandemic and being relatively sheltered for over a week, everyone felt a more desperate need for human interaction.

Ten long days had passed since lockdown—twice that long since Nicholas had been home from school and without therapy. They'd spoken with Leslie and they were going to try therapy via video conference next week. The talk was, it would be another month before things started to open up again, if they could "flatten the curve," the latest catchphrase that buzzed about everyone's conversation like a cloud of gnats. Jason doubted any steamroller of public unity would flatten out the curve anytime soon. He couldn't deny that some people were making points that caused him to question what was fact—about the severity of the virus, how it spread, and how it could be controlled.

But, if a few weeks staying at home might prevent a lot of people from getting sick and dying, he wasn't going to fight it.

He walked by Ollie and Lynn's place and waved to them as they stepped out from their garage. Just past their place, he glanced uneasily at Suzie's house. The dour property sat quiet. Suzie hadn't been back since she visited Jason. Jason wasn't sure how he would act or feel around her, but for the time being, he was glad he hadn't had to face her. He told no one about what she confessed to him. What did that make him? An accomplice? But she hadn't actually told him anything. Legally, there was no reason to be worried. Ethically? He was compromised.

His motivation had always only been self-defense, the gun a last resort. Suzie planned to kill Greg, he felt certain of that, which made it murder. Could he really allow a murderer to get away with it?

On the reverse side of his coin of conscience, could he actually turn in someone who removed from this earth a person who had tortured his own parents and sister, abused and raped Suzie at sixteen, physically beat his mother, threatened Jason's family and tried to beat Jason to death? God knows what else Greg had done between those times, or what future crimes he would have committed.

The ethical complications smothered his ability to come upon any rational conclusion. Every time he thought about it, he ducked and ran from the moral onslaught.

On the other side of the street, he saw Glen through the picture window of his living room as he moved toward his front door. Jason stood in the middle of the street while Ollie and Lynn took a position at the end of their driveway.

"Morning, Jason," Ollie called out, those tufts of hair on either side of his head fluttering like wings in the breeze. He wore a plush royal blue fleece robe and slippers, a cup of steaming coffee in hand. "How's it going? All healed up?"

"Good. Mostly healed. No permanent damage."

Lynn's silver hair stayed comically in place, apparently cemented by hair spray. She pulled her pink frilly jacket tight around her while she stood in fluffy slippers. "Can't believe it's been two months! You had us so scared, Jason. What an awful scene that was. All the police and emergency vehicles, and all the blood! Goodness gracious Lord in Heaven, I don't know if I have ever seen so much blood! I can't believe that one fellow survived. I don't really know if he didn't maybe deserve to die, what with everything they did to you and to poor Suzie. And now you just have to wonder what he's telling the police to make them change what they're charging her for. What in the world—"

"Wait, what?" Jason had heard nothing about any change in Suzie's situation, but since that day, he stayed away from social media and news. Seeing stories about the incident, stories that included him and Fairview Lane, ignited flashes of unwanted memories. Every time he saw a picture of Greg Polnzy or Darryl Eckles, his heart raced and he felt like throwing up.

Lynn gawked. "Why, it was just in the paper this morning! Didn't you see?"

"He obviously hasn't, Lynn," Ollie said as he stuffed his

hands deep into his pajama bottoms. "They're now charging her with first degree murder based on what the paper is calling, 'new evidence.'"

Sam and Delilah Peterson joined the group during Lynn's monologue. Sam held Liver's leash and they kept their social distance. The old dog wanted to get at everyone's knees to sniff, but after being tugged back several times, the dog plopped down hard on its butt and sat.

Sam interjected. "Now, I've been lurking in some of the local social media groups, and someone claims to know someone else who is a nurse at the hospital who said that this Eckles guy is saying Suzie called her brother and invited them over."

Lynn looked disgusted. "Well, I just cannot believe that, not for one second. No sir. Why would she do that, for goodness sake?" Lynn suddenly waved enthusiastically and shouted, "Hi, Glen!"

Jason turned and waved to Glen who stood at the edge of his driveway. He raised a hand and nodded.

"Glen, did you see the paper this morning?" Lynn shouted. "About Suzie?"

Glen nodded and moved out into the street, his position the final point in the Fairview COVID Quadrangle. "Yup. Can't imagine what that's all about."

Jason grew more perplexed and uneasy by the news. "But, can they really alter the charges after the arraignment?"

"I sure think they can," Delilah said as she drew her robe tighter around her. "If they got more evidence, they sure as heck can."

"Yeah, hey," Ollie said. "Can't believe it'll stick though."

"No," Jason said with tapered tone. "I wouldn't think—"

"She's got just about the whole neighborhood as witnesses," Glen said. "If that don't sway a jury—"

Jason's composure deteriorated. "Do you think they'll call

any of us as witnesses?"

"I would suspect," Glen said. "Especially you, all things considered."

His neighbors continued to chat about Suzie's house, how much work it needed and what they guessed it would sell for, then moved on to the weather and spring projects. Jason couldn't focus and barely paid attention.

Was it perjury if he withheld information from the witness stand? Did he have an obligation to disclose any pertinent information? As far as he knew, he only needed to answer their questions. After all, he didn't know if she called Greg. He only suspected.

"I'm absolutely chilled to the bone, Ollie," Lynn said and shivered dramatically. "I need to get inside."

"Right," Ollie said. "We need to get some breakfast in us anyway. Good seeing all of you. Glad you're healing up, Jason!"

"Yup," Sam said, arms wrapped across his chest. "Sorry all. Not the best morning to be out. Heading in!"

"Talk to you all later," Glen said.

Jason waved goodbye, distracted by additional complications brought by Lynn and Ollie's news about Suzie. His thoughts paced back and forth in his mind, creating well-tread tracks of worry.

"You doing okay there, Jase?"

He gave a smile to Glen. "Yeah, fine. Lots of things going on to distract me lately. How are you holding up, by the way? Stocked up on supplies?"

"Doing okay. No worries."

"Even toilet paper?"

"Even that. Could probably sell each roll for ten bucks if I wanted. What the hell is up with that, anyway? Didn't know the shits were one of the symptoms."

"The world has gone a little crazy, my friend."

Glen aimed his nod down the street toward the cul-de-sac. "Speaking of, it seems like you're in the middle of a little political showdown."

Jason didn't need to turn around to know what Glen referred to. The Johnsons had upped the ante by adding a black sign with multi-colored lettering that read, "In This House, We Believe: Black Lives Matter, No Human Is Illegal, Love is Love, Women's Rights Are Human Rights, and Science is Real." The Greeleys countered with a large blue and red banner across their front porch that displayed their enthusiasm for their presidential candidate, which more and more appeared to be the primary way for some Americans to profess faith, ideology, and morality.

He grimaced and answered, "Aren't we all?"

Jason needed to pick up his last refill of antibiotics. He put on his jacket and grabbed his keys.

"I'll come with you," Jen said. "We need to stock up on some other things anyway, and I just have to get out of this house."

They told Nicky to get his shoes and coat on, grabbed the new cloth masks they bought online, and headed out.

The city was more dead than ever. So many restaurant signs that either said "Closed" or "Curbside Pickup Only." They passed one of their favorite restaurants, a steak and seafood place where they celebrated every birthday and anniversary.

"Oh, Jason," Jen said. "I hope they make it through this."

"I know. We'll need to order some takeout to support them."

"So sad we won't be able to go there for a while."

"Things will get better. They have to." What a stupid statement. He immediately felt like a fool to say it, yet it made him feel better to hear those words from his mouth, even if he absolutely could not back them up.

When they arrived at the drug store, Jason parked the car, slipped on his black cotton cloth mask and pinched the bridge of his nose to get a tight fit. He felt foolish, but the CDC recommended it, and more and more people were wearing them. The evidence suggested that airborne transmission through particles accelerated the spread of the virus, and masking helped reduce that spread.

He looked at himself in the rearview mirror. "If no one else is wearing one of these in there, I'm taking it off."

Jen tucked the straps around her ears and looked at him. "Don't be a baby." She grabbed the smaller mask, got out of the car and opened the back driver-side door. "Come on, Nicky. We need to get your mask on you."

She reached out and started to cover his face, but Nicky turned his head away. "No." It was a flat, obstinate statement.

"Nicky. Come on." She tried again and managed to get it over his mouth and nose, but he cried out and slapped at Jen's hand, writhing away from the mask before she could secure it.

"Nicky! We have to do this."

"Come on, pal." Jason watched the entire scene through the rear-view mirror. "Don't be that way. It's no big deal."

Jen tried one more time, and as soon as she covered his mouth and nose, he screamed and kicked and cried, a body of wild kinetic energy. It had been a long time since one of Nicholas's tantrums. Was this still related to the bad day?

Whatever. It obviously made Nicky miserable.

"Jen. Enough. Let him go. Let's not torture the poor guy." Jason got out of the car and snuck around Jen to put a hand on Nicky. "Hey. Sorry, buddy. We'll work with Leslie on this, huh? Don't worry about it now."

Nicky stared at him with wide eyes. Jason had no idea how he looked to Nicky with the mask on, but all this had to be freaking his poor son out.

"Should I stay here with him?" Jen asked.

"No. It'll be fine. Don't worry about it. If he's still upset when we go inside, you can bring him out."

They stepped inside the store, but not before they saw the sign that said the store would be drive-through only starting tomorrow. The store itself teemed with customers, and more than three-quarters of the patrons wore masks, including all the employees. The mask already seemed to constrict his breathing and thin his oxygen. The very presence of the mask on his face made the entire surreal situation feel even more dire. His head thrummed with the word, "Pandemic."

The shelves were emptying fast in the drug store as well. No toilet paper, and basic medications like aspirin, Tylenol and ibuprofen were in short supply. Cold medicine was nowhere to be found. They grabbed what medications were still on the shelves and went to the prescription window to get his refill.

While they stood in line at the pharmacist station, Jason noticed the older woman in the flowery mask ahead of them staring at Nicholas with scornful eyes. Jason smiled at her, then realized she couldn't see him smiling.

Good God, no more smiles in this pandemic world.

Not able to transmit his good will, he instead gave a nod and said, "Hi."

"That little boy should be masked. There's a lot of elderly here and they're at higher risk."

"I'm—sorry. This is all new to him, and he was very upset when we tried to put a mask on him."

She very deliberately turned her head away. He looked at Jen and Jen looked back, but he had no idea what she felt or thought under her mask, and she probably had no more clue about his shock and annoyance.

This pandemic, without a doubt, would require a serious period of adjustment.

Chapter Thirty
Sunday, April 12, 2020 - Easter

It was the Thanksgiving of springtime for Jason and the Laheys. Easter was not the kind of holiday that overwhelmed their lives and surroundings with decorations or music. Few Easter movies played on their television screen other than a couple animated classics for Nicky like *It's the Easter Beagle, Charlie Brown* and the Rankin and Bass stop-motion *Easter Bunny is Coming to Town*. Jen did make Jason suffer through the 1973 hippy-dippy *Jesus Christ Superstar* musical, but that's about as spiritual as their holiday got.

Like Christmas, Jason recognized the deeper, mystical story that instilled the true meaning of the holiday into so many. His childhood had included Easter mass, the only time other than Christmas that his parents took him to church. He had little clear memory of the service. As a child, he was bored and eager to get home and dive into his easter basket and toys. By his teenage years, church became all but a memory as his parents fell out of the habit, or maybe decided they had fulfilled their obligatory duty. Whatever skin of belief he wore as a child had molted and been shed by his early teens, the same as his beliefs in ghosts and monsters under the bed.

Jason had no faith in the resurrection. He certainly couldn't deny the power of the passion story, of the three-year mission of Christ that began at age thirty and ended on a cross. In the end, despite how that narrative carried through the centuries to become one of the dominant belief systems of the western world, for him Christ's passion story was just a nice—albeit somewhat dark and troubling—story that lent flavor to the celebration in the same way Jesus's birth added a touch of heartfelt fantasy and wonder to Christmas.

Jason and Jen still recognized Easter as a significant holiday—one that, like Thanksgiving, celebrated a change of season that culminated with a fancy dinner, only with a porcine entrée instead of fowl.

The holiday tried so hard to emulate its big brother Christmas. After all, Christmas and Easter were the bookends of Christian faith. Like Christmas, Easter had its gift-delivering fantastical mascot in the form of the Easter Bunny. Nicholas got his basket of jelly beans, foil-wrapped chocolate eggs and hollow chocolate bunny that gawked with wide eyes as it nestled in a bed of vibrant green fake grass.

The toys Nicky received exuded the fresh magic of spring: the balsa glider and the Gayla Baby Bat Kite with the huge bloodshot eyes just like Jason used to get as a kid, springtime coloring books with pastel markers, and a stuffed bunny rabbit. They dyed eggs the day before, which was a complete waste of food since Nicky hated eggs. After Nicholas went to bed, Jen and Jason hid pink and blue and yellow and green and violet plastic eggs around the house and outside. They would be filled with coins, Easter candies and little toys for him to find Easter morning.

Seth, Rachel and the boys often spent Easter day at their place, the egg hunt a much bigger and more elaborate event for Nicky and his two cousins. Not this year, though. They didn't need a global pandemic as an excuse to avoid each other, but it certainly created a convenient one.

Easter morning arrived with blue skies and a warm breeze. It was the first truly spring day they'd seen that year, and they spent the latter part of that morning watching Nicky find his Easter eggs hidden behind trees, under rocks and all around their property. They gave hints to guide him along his hunt until he had a heaping basketful. No doubt Jason and Jen forgot the location of a few and would stumble upon one or two come midsummer.

Nicky wanted to fly his kite, so Jason brought him out to the cul-de-sac where they could take advantage of the open space and have more room to run. A gentle, persistent breeze blew, enough that they should be able to get the kite off the ground with a little work. With enough elevation, that baby bat kite would catch a thermal and soar.

At first, Nicky tried running while he held the kite behind him to get the it off the ground. Even with those long legs of his, the seven-year-old couldn't move fast enough to give it any lift. The kite just spun and dive-bombed nose-first to the ground. He swung his arms with frustration and yanked at the string to try and bring the dead kite to life.

"Hey, Nix. You hold on to the kite, okay? I'll move back and give it some lead. When I tell you to, toss it up in the air and we'll get this baby flying, okay?"

Jason positioned Nicky at the edge of their driveway and put a wing in each little hand. Jason backed up, unspooling as he went, until he had about twenty feet of line between them.

"You ready?" he called out.

"Yeah," Nicky replied tamely.

"Toss it!" Jason yelled and pulled on the string just as Nicky let go. Jason ran backward, pulling as he went, and the black bat kite fluttered with fury and shot up into the air. It spun and dipped and Jason yanked and ran to send it back up and higher. A nice breeze lifted the kite and Jason fed it some line, spool spinning. He stepped forward as it reached fifty feet. Seventy-five feet.

"Nicky! Come here!" He kept feeding it line and the kite took it like an eager dog on a long leash. The baby black bat found a current of wind above them and Jason tugged lightly to keep it reined in and aloft.

Nicky came over and stood next to him. His eyes followed the string up and up to the ruffling black bat that danced and soared on the air.

Jason stood between the Polnzy house and Glen's duplex. He looked over at Glen's place. He hadn't seen Glen for several days now. This was an extra-special day for Glen, one that would have been celebrated in earnest with Maude, and always with at least one if not all three of their kids and families. But COVID killed any chance of celebrating it with his sons or daughter. Glen was alone for the holiday and Jason hadn't realized that until now. He hated the idea of Glen being alone today. The coronavirus kept them from having a more intimate gathering, but Glen could still come out and enjoy the kite flying and sit outside while they socialized at a distance and shared some Easter ham.

Nicholas looked up at him. "It's flying high, Dad!"

"You bet it is." Jason held out the spool. "You want it?"

"Yeah." Measured excitement tempered Nicky's voice as he reached out for the spool of string.

"Okay, but just make sure you don't feed it too much line too quick. If it dips, give it a good tug to send it back up, okay?"

"Okay."

Jason passed the spool to Nicky. His boy took it with trepidation, but also with wide, excited eyes. Holding it tightly with both hands, he released a few feet of string, then tugged and moved the spool to get a feel for and adjust the kite flight.

"You got it. There you go. Great job, buddy."

Jason put a hand on Nicky's shoulder.

"You're doing great. I'm going to head over to Glen's place super-quick. You going to be okay for a couple minutes?"

All attention dedicated to the kite, Nicky nodded intently as he kept the baby bat in the sky.

"Be right back, pal." He jogged up Glen's driveway to the front door and knocked.

He should have thought of this earlier. Why hadn't he planned it? He felt bad leaving Glen alone on Easter Sunday. He couldn't go to mass or be with his family. That was no way for Glen to spend such an important holiday.

After twenty seconds with no answer, he rang the doorbell and gave a few more solid wraps with his fist. He looked over at Nicky. His son had total control of the kite. He remembered when Nicky learned to ride his bike on that cold November afternoon, the pride he felt seeing his son take a big step forward. Nicky was almost eight now, his birthday a little more than a month away, and Jason's chest swelled to watch his boy growing up.

Still no answer from Glen. There's no place he would be— no church during the pandemic, no place to go unless maybe another neighbor had a similar idea and invited him over.

Jason rang the bell three times and knocked hard on the door.

He barely heard the muffled crash of something inside, like furniture toppling over or someone falling.

"Glen?" He called out, little more than normal volume.

No answer.

"Hey! Glen!" Much louder through the door.

Some kind of sound, maybe Glen's voice, but too weak, too quiet. Jason tried the door. It wasn't locked. It flashed in his mind that he didn't have his mask, but that wasn't going to stop him at this point. He threw open the door and moved inside.

"Glen! Jesus!"

He dashed over to his friend tangled in Maude's afghan on the floor next to the couch. All around him, a tissue box, wads of used tissues, boxes of decongestants and bottles of aspirin and cough suppressant scattered about an overturned TV table. Glen's eyes were open but distant, his forehead beaded with sweat. One hand grasped the couch seat cushion above him, as if he was trying to get up, but had only the will and not the way.

As Jason approached and knelt down to Glen, he could hear his thin, tight breaths.

"Jason—"

Jason put his hand to Glen's forehead. "Oh Christ, you're burning up."

"Funny, 'cause I'm not feelin' that hot." Glen's voice was barely a hoarse whisper. He exhaled in some weak attempt at a chuckle.

Jason got up. "Hang tight. I'm getting my car and taking you to the hospital."

Jason ran out of the house, down the driveway and scooped Nicholas up in his arms. Nicky cried out, reaching for the spool of kite string as it fell out of his hands and skipped against the tarmac. "My bat!"

"Hold on, buddy." Jason looked up just long enough to see Nicky's kite swooping free and easy, having been released from its tether, rising higher into the fluffy white clouds of Easter morning and sailing off into that great blue yonder.

He sat in his car in the driveway of his home, the last hour a slurry of panicked action. His muscles were rubbery with anxious fatigue and his emotions were twisted and rung out. He stared at the garage door, lost and uncertain what to do now.

He had just taken one of his closest friends to the emergency room with what he desperately hoped was not the coronavirus—but feared it must be. Glen had barely been able to walk, and Jason half-carried the tall, lean body that still filled out one hundred eighty pounds of muscle to the car. Jason had his mask on by then, the one he kept in the glove box. Glen didn't speak much in the car, but managed to tell Jason that he had felt a little under the weather for the past few days, but nothing serious—sore throat, congestion and a slight cough. It hit him hard last night. His lungs tightened up, his coughing became deep and hard, and his fever shot to a hundred and three.

"Just can't catch my breath," he said through short gasps.

Jason sped the entire way to Mother of Mercy Hospital. He pulled up to the emergency room doors and turned on his hazards. He worried the hospital would be a scene of chaos, of nurses and orderlies frantically tending to the sick and dying in waiting rooms and hallways as their beds filled up. That's what New York looked like on the news.

But no. Here in Fortune Falls, Marathon County, Wisconsin, the hospital was a haunt. Barely a car in the parking lot, and no one in the emergency waiting room. It sat quiet and still, an abandoned institution, all elective surgeries cancelled and only emergency visits admitted. Somehow the empty parking lot and quiet building unsettled Jason more than if it had been overrun with the dead and dying. Nothing felt right or normal.

"My friend needs help immediately. He's very sick."

It took only seconds for the hospital staff to come alive. The woman behind the counter asked him a couple of questions as an RN and two orderlies rushed out in full personal protection gear and rolled a wheelchair to the car. They spoke briefly to Glen, helped him into the chair and wheeled him through the automatic glass doors and between the heavy admittance doors.

Jason stayed for a few more minutes to provide what information he could to the nurse at the desk and left his name and phone number. His drive back was slow and sluggish.

Parked now in his driveway, he wondered what he would do. He likely experienced significant exposure to COVID-19. If he was ever going to get it, this was it. He couldn't bring that home to his family. But where could he go? A hotel? He heard stories of individuals sequestering themselves from the rest of their family at home, either staying in a room or in their basement. Would that be safe? Would that be appropriate?

He sat in his car, mere feet from his home and family, uncertain what to do next. He thought about Glen, ashen with a sheen of sweat, his breathing thin. Then he thought of Jen, of Nicky, and fear wrenched his insides. He kept telling himself that only a small percentage of people were contracting COVID. An even smaller percentage of the population were dying from it, with most of those fatalities having compromised health. The threat was more on the societal level, not as much on the individual level.

And yet, it may have just hit his very own neighborhood in north-central Wisconsin, two doors down from his home.

He grabbed his phone, speed-dialed Jen and put it on speaker. He tore his mask off when he realized he was still wearing it.

"God, I've been waiting to hear from you. How's Glen?"

"I got him to emergency. He's been admitted."

"So, is it COVID?"

"Don't know. I'm guessing so."

"What are they doing for him? What's the prognosis?"

"Jen." He breathed. "No idea. They just admitted him."

"Well, where are you?"

"I'm parked in the driveway."

"What?"

He watched Jen step in front of the living room bay windows and look down at him, phone to her ear.

"What are you doing?" she asked.

"Trying to figure out what I do next."

"What do you mean?"

"Jen. I just spent the better part of an hour with someone who probably has a severe case of COVID. Fifteen minutes of that time in the closed quarters of a car. I can't get anywhere near you and Nicky. Even the little bit of time I spent with Nicky when I brought him home has me freaking out."

A few seconds of silence. "But—serious?"

"Of course I'm serious."

A few more beats of quiet. "Was he really sick?"

An image of Glen on the floor, twisted in the afghan and too weak to get up. Strong, tough Glen, barely able to talk or breathe. "Yeah. Bad."

"Oh, Jason. What are we going to do? What can we do?"

"I don't know. Do I stay in the basement? Is that safe enough? I have no idea."

"I don't know either."

The more he thought about that, the more risks came into his head. "How do you keep Nicky from coming downstairs? How do we know airborne particles won't float upstairs? Jesus, I don't fucking know anything."

Jen's voice dripped from the phone. "Neither do I."

"I just know I couldn't live with myself if either of you ended up like how I saw Glen."

"God. This can't be happening."

Jason couldn't ignore the nagging persistence of the only obvious answer. "I think I have to get away from you both.

Maybe isolate in a hotel. For what, twelve days? Longer if I get it. What else can I do?"

"Oh, God." Jen's voice was weak. He wasn't used to hearing her sound like this.

He watched her put her hand against the glass, reaching out to him and unable to make contact. Her voice lost all its inflection and became a monotone of exhausted despondency. "Oh no. I—we can't go through this. I don't want to be alone again. Not after everything that's happened. I can't do it."

"I know." The two weeks he spent away from them had felt like months, and the last four months back have only felt like weeks. He couldn't fathom leaving them again, not for how long he would need to. But any compromised solution put them at risk.

Silence. Jen wasn't saying anything and Jason didn't know what to say. He wanted to deny any risk, any danger. He honestly didn't want to accept this pandemic reality.

A click on the phone. "Jen?" He looked at the screen. Flashing text said the call ended.

Jen wasn't at the living room window anymore. He stared at his phone screen, bewildered. Was she angry with him? What could she possibly expect him to do?

Out the front door, Jen moved with swift feet down the walk and to the driveway. Before he could react, the driver-side door flung open and Jen moved in, grabbed the back of his head and drew him to her as she leaned down and kissed him hard.

With force, he yanked his head back. "What the hell are you doing? Stop!"

She pulled him forward again, kissing him harder. Her cheeks were damp with tears.

He pulled away again. "For Christ's sake—!"

His head was in her hands, her face close to his, and she stared deep into his eyes. "I need us to be together. More than ever right now. Do you understand? We need to be a family. That's how we survive this."

He writhed in his seat. Every part of this seemed wrong, dangerous. He felt dirty, covered with infection and disease. He wanted to be as far away from her as possible, and yet he didn't want to leave her for a moment.

He got out of the car, eyes blurring and burning, and he grabbed her hard and hugged her. "Oh, shit, Jen. What did you do? Oh, Goddamn it. What did you do?"

Into his ear, she whispered, "What I had to. For us."

Chapter Thirty-one
Saturday, April 18, 2020

A week since he and Jen got tested for COVID. Jason did not know anything could go that far up his nostril without doing brain damage. Both tests had been negative and neither of them showed symptoms. Jason and Jen thought long and hard about getting Nicholas tested but decided not to unless he showed any symptoms. The test would likely be too traumatic for him.

They plummeted through the remainder of the next week in a freefall of suspended time, waiting for the ground of reality to meet them hard. Jason attempted to work, but he became easily distracted, unable to focus. He stepped away from his computer regularly and paced about inside. Eventually, he would wander upstairs and find Jen just as inattentive to her work as he was, so they often took breaks and stepped out of the house for a walk around the block.

The urge to escape triggered every muscle and joint in the

body—to run from the moment, flee this pandemic that felt like a monstrous creature on a rampage they were running in circles from to avoid being trampled underfoot.

Glen's daughter Betty had called Jason the Tuesday after Easter with an update. Glen had COVID. An acute case. His condition hadn't worsened, but hadn't improved either. As soon as the hospital notified her, she drove over from the Twin Cities to be with her father, only to find out the hospital wouldn't let her see him. Apparently, they weren't allowing any visits to COVID patients due to the risk of further spreading the virus. The best she could do was look at him through a pane of glass as he lay in bed feverish and fighting for air.

It killed Jason to know he wouldn't be able to visit Glen. He desperately wanted to see him, and his concern grew exponentially each day. Having little other way to be there for his friend, Jason and Jen sent flowers daily.

When Jason talked to Betty on Thursday, she said Glen's oxygen levels had dropped so low they put him on a ventilator. Because of that, the hospital was keeping him on lorazepam, and since that time, he had barely been conscious. She said they were trying some experimental treatment that had shown some promise in New York. Jason could hear hope withering in the tone of her voice.

Much like the hope of that curve flattening enough so life could return to normal had dried up like a Russian thistle and tumbled away with the wind. The governor extended his stay-at-home order to May 26. Protests were taking place in Milwaukee, Madison, Eau Claire and other communities. People waved signs with bold letters that called out, "FREEDOM NOT FEAR" and "REOPEN WISCONSIN" and "FIGHT SAFETY NAZIS". They wanted life to get back to normal.

Apparently, their neighbors weren't in the hospital fighting for their lives on a respirator.

The Lahey family larders were getting lean, so Jen started ordering groceries online and having them delivered. Their internet orders at other major suppliers more than doubled. Amazon boxes, Walmart orders and Target shipments piled up up at their front door daily. FedEx, UPS and USPS became the modern-day ice cream trucks for adults, bringing their goodies daily to offset the fear and isolation of a global shutdown.

Yet, so many things were no longer available. Cleaning products, canned and dry food items. Every time they went online to find something, half the screen populated with products listed as "Out of Stock" or "Unavailable." The weak links in the supply chain had snapped.

Social media's claws dug deep into Jen's psyche. She was on constantly, though no longer scrolling through her Autism support groups. Instead, she battled anti-maskers and pandemic doubters. "They don't get it. It's not about *them*, it's about the people *next* to them. Their neighbors. Their community. It's not a risk to them individually, it's a risk to our society! What the hell is wrong with these people?"

She continually called out opinion pieces in the paper, or comments on a Twitter feed, or a meme shared by someone on Facebook. She seethed with disgust that, because people were the way they were, we couldn't flatten the curve, and now it would just get worse.

Jason didn't know, didn't understand, and he didn't really care. It frustrated him to some extent, but the situation seemed beyond masks and sheltering in place. All the rhetoric and opinion and contradicting facts overwhelmed him, both from the uneducated public, and the conflicting messages of health departments, healthcare professionals, the government and the CDC. He started to wonder if they were all hiding from the inevitable, unable to accept the vulnerabilities of humankind. Life had gotten too easy. Anything desired was available and accessible with a click of the mouse or pick from a shelf. The greatest generation had faced hardship and sacrifice. This generation abhorred those conditions as unAmerican. Instead, we expected to clack some computer keys and have our convenience delivered in perfect condition, cheaply and timely to our doors.

There was only one absolute and irrefutable truth: as a society, we were in no way ready to deal with a pandemic.

On Friday, April 24, Betty called, barely able to control herself. Glen Overby, age 67, husband of Maude, father of Michael, Betty, and Christian, narrator of Fairview Lane, died at 7:43 p.m. from complications due to the coronavirus.

Jason threw his phone against the wall and sobbed.

Chapter Thirty-two
Monday, May 28, 2020

Minneapolis was burning.

For the second night, demonstrations took place over several blocks in the left ventricle of Minnesota's heart that was the Twin Cities. Jason had fond memories of their six years living there. They loved walking the Nicolet Mall pedestrian thoroughfare, visiting Brit's Pub, the Brazilian steakhouse, and seeing shows at the Dakota Jazz Club.

The uprisings were the reaction to the death of a man three days ago who had been selling cigarettes on a street corner of east 38th and Chicago Avenue and found himself unable to breathe when three police officers tried to restrain him.

When it happened, many cried, "Police brutality."

Many others rebuked, "Resisting arrest."

Demonstrators declared their presence a peaceful protest.

Others decried it as a violent riot.

Some wore face masks with words that said, "I can't breathe."

Others refused to wear face masks because they claimed they couldn't breathe.

Misinformation. Confusion. Suspicion. Conspiracies. Intolerance. Violence.

Two universes were crashing together and forming a thunderhead of chaos and division. No other phrase better encapsulated the torrent of political, social and ideological divide amid a global pandemic during a political campaign:

It was a perfect storm.

And now, on a late-spring, mid-morning Thursday, he stood at his bay window and watched as his neighbor, Tom Johnson, yanked up a campaign sign from his front yard—a sign blaring the name of the incumbent candidate that seemed to have replaced Tom's suddenly missing sign that had endorsed the opposing candidate. Tom stormed across Jason's driveway and onto the Greeleys' property.

With a dramatic flourish, Tom tore that sign in two and threw it on the Greeleys' yard, uprooted the Greeleys' sign that endorsed their candidate, tore that in two, and tossed the pieces on the Greeley's front lawn. Tom finished by kicking the "Blue Lives Matter" sign over and, with a flourish of fuck finger thrust in the direction of the Greeley home, he stomped back to his property, yanked open his front door and slammed it shut behind him.

Jason had just watched a national passion play take place right outside his window. He sipped his one-hundred-percent Arabica Colombian coffee and shook his head.

"We are so fucked."

He stepped away to start his day.

Over lunch, he and Jen took their stroll through the neighborhood and surrounding areas while Nicky rode on his new bike beside them. The weather had switched from the mere seven days of full-on spring they had briefly enjoyed to early summer heat. Eighty degrees, sunny and dry. Jen basked in the warmth of the day. Jason pined over the refreshing Spring breezes that disappeared under the beating heat of the sun.

Let's add the fear of climate change to a growing pandemic on top of social and political unrest.

As they walked past Glen's house, a pulse of grief shot through him, a deep ache that momentarily overtook him. He wasn't dealing with Glen's death very well. There was no closure. He hadn't been able to see him, to say goodbye, to tell him any of the things he should have said that now would be left unsaid. He tried to recall that miserable Thanksgiving night. Had he told Glen what a good friend he was? He had a vague recollection, but he honestly couldn't get through his fog of drunkenness that night to remember.

He missed his neighbor, his friend. Fairview Lane was diminished without him. It wasn't fair. None of this was fair.

They walked to the end of their street and turned onto Prairie Dale Road. They had walked the road many times over the years, originally pushing Nicky in a stroller and now with him on his bike. It wasn't a busy road, but usually saw regular traffic pass by, either coming from or heading to Old Mill Road, the most direct route into town. Today, it was an abandoned stretch of road. No cars at all.

Surreal.

That word had burrowed its head into his lexicon like a tick. A little over six months ago, one little detour diverged him onto an alternate course. From that day forward, his life had been on some wayward journey, some dreamlike tangent he kept trying to get control of while it, in turn, seemed intent upon grinding him into the ground.

"Hey, Nix, don't get too far ahead, okay?"

Nicky competently swung his bike around from about a hundred feet ahead and pedaled back to them.

"Riding like a pro there, pal." Jason gave him a thumbs-up as he passed.

Jen's phone buzzed and she lifted it out of her back pocket to look at the screen.

"Oh, shit."

"What?" Jason asked.

Through a wince, she said, "Rachel."

"Oh, shit."

Jen looked at him, nodded, and put the phone to her ear. "Hi."

They slowed their pace and Nicky hopped off his bike as Jen kept the phone to her ear.

"Oh, no," she said.

After a few more moments, "Oh, God."

Jason gave her an intense, questioning look. Jen nodded and put up a finger.

"Sorry, Rachel. Do you mind if I put you on speaker? Jason is with me."

Jen poked at her phone and held it in front of her. "Okay."

Rachel's voice carried over the phone speaker. "So, we're not at the point of taking him to the hospital, but he's in pretty rough shape, so I just wanted to let you know. Just in case?"

Jason widened his eyes as he looked at Jen, still uncertain what had happened.

"I appreciate it, Rachel. Really. How are you doing? You okay? You need anything?"

"I'm a little freaked out, to be honest. But he's a strong S.O.B. He'll shake this off."

"So, any idea how he might have caught it?"

"Oh, yeah. I told him not to go, but he wanted to see this

country band playing at Chester's Bar just outside of town. No mask. No common sense. You know your brother."

"I sure do." Jen shot a glance at Jason and shook her head. "So, is he in too rough of shape to talk?"

"Yeah, probably. Sorry."

"Well, tell him I'm thinking about him and hoping for a speedy recovery."

Jason piped in. "Both of us! Tell him we want to see both of you at our Fourth of July cookout!"

"Will do. You two hanging in there?"

"Best we can."

Jason thought about mentioning Glen, since they had shared Thanksgiving dinner together, but he realized that telling Rachel about his death would only throw gloom on Seth's condition.

"You do the same," Jason called out. "We miss you both."

A pause. "It's been a hell of a time, huh? Makes you re-evaluate what's important, you know?"

"For sure," Jen said.

"Listen, Seth feels horrible over everything with your parents. I told him he was being stupid talking to them like that. He was just angry. He regretted it almost immediately. He didn't know how to say he was sorry."

Jen chuckled. "Yeah. That runs in our family."

Jason spoke up. "I'm sorry too, Rachel. I can't begin to excuse what I was like at Thanksgiving, but I'm sorry for it. Bad time, but things are different now."

"Appreciate that, Jason," Rachel said over the phone. "You both mean a lot to us. It's been hard not having you in our lives more. Hope that can change."

"It will," Jason said. "You can count on it."

CHAPTER THIRTY-THREE
Monday, June 2, 2020

106,028 dead in the U.S.

At least 379,000 dead and 6.3 million cases worldwide.

And Nicholas Lahey turned eight years old.

They made a special dinner—all his favorites. Macaroni and cheese, buttery yam with brown sugar, and steamed carrots. For dessert, Jen baked a carrot cake with orange-dyed cream cheese frosting. On it, eight candles burned which he blew out after he made a wish. Jason didn't presume to guess what his son's wish was, but Jason knew what his would be.

After dinner and cake, they retired to the living room. Jason had set up their Zoom account to run on the large smart TV for Nicholas's therapy sessions with Leslie.

He gave Jen a cynical look. "You sure you're ready for this?" He wasn't sure if *he* was ready.

"Link up. Let's get this over with."

He nodded, almost hoping she'd have reconsidered, but

proud of her that she hadn't.

He clicked on the Zoom link and the window opened, showing him and Jen peering into the camera. Nicky showed up behind them on the couch, legs swinging as he sat with nervous energy.

After several long, drawn-out moments, a second window popped up on the screen.

"Hey, Zeke. Hey, Dee," he said, waving.

"Hi, Jason," Zeke said. Then, Zeke and Dee's heads came together as they sang, "Happy birthday, Nicky!" Dee looked good with her short crop of silvery hair and steel-blue eyes, sharp, small nose and thin lips. Jason couldn't help but see an older, rougher Jen. The buzz cut Zeke once sported had gone mostly grey and grown shaggy, but also thinning a bit. His straight Greek nose angled over his long-toothed, broad smile.

Jen moved forward with cautious steps. "Hi, Mom. Dad."

"Oh, sweetheart," her mom said. "It's so good to see you. All of you."

"Been a long time," Jen said. She showed no emotion, her voice without inflection.

"Too long," Zeke said. "And that's on us. We're sorry, honey. We're so sorry for everything, and we can't tell you how much this means to us."

Jen nodded, wiped her eyes and turned away.

Jason moved over to Nicky on the couch. "Hey, Nix. These are your grandparents. Grandpa Zeke and Grandma Dee. They're the ones who sent you those cool toys for your birthday and for Christmas. Remember? Say, 'Hi,' huh?"

Nicky waved, eyes not quite making contact as hands fluttered.

Jason looked at Zeke and Dee through the camera. "It'll take time."

Jen nodded and turned away from the screen. "Yeah. It will." She stepped out of the room.

Memorial Day weighed heavier on him this year than any previous one. Certainly, its intention was to honor our military dead who served and gave their lives to protect our freedoms. This year, amid everything that had happened and continued to happen, Jason couldn't help but extend the meaning and purpose.

He stood before the simple, dignified headstone:

GLEN OVERBY
Sept 7, 1952 – Apr 24, 2020

MAUDE OVERBY
Feb 11, 1955 – Dec 2, 2017

The field of headstones and monuments spread out as a forest of forgotten lives. Generations born, living and growing and working and loving and dying. They struggled through hardships, wars, atrocities, plagues and disasters. Every one of them would likely have begged for one more day and not taken back a single moment on earth.

"I miss you, you ol' son of a bitch."

He broke into a short sob, a blubber of infantile denial and resentment, of wishing Glen back and on their porch, legs up, telling stories of the neighborhood. He finished with a deep breath of reconciliation and acceptance.

"Say hi to that tough ol' broad of yours. I miss her, too."

He stood a moment longer, took in all that surrounded him and tried to resurrect, in some fashion, all the names and dates around him, but knew it was impossible. The past kept the dead buried.

He walked deeper into the cemetery, up a small hill and

beside a crop of tall arborvitae. He hadn't been there in seven years, and honestly never thought he'd be back.

The marbled pillar stood shoulder high with LAHEY chiseled in bold letters. Cropping up around it were several smaller, ornate marble headstones. He looked at the one to the left.

"Hello, Dad. Mom."

On that stone, their names and dates:

EDWARD ALEXANDER LAHEY SR.
June 18, 1949 – July 17, 2008

FLORENCE ELIZABETH LAHEY
March 4, 1952 – August 21, 2009

He turned to the stone at immediate right of the pillar.
"Hey, brother."
A marbled tombstone bore the name,

EDWARD ALEXANDER LAHEY JR
May 25, 1977- Oct 3, 1981

And next to Alex's stone, his own:

JASON ROBERT LAHEY
1979 -

There was room for Jen's name below.

The large monument was not originally part of the Lahey plots. After Florence died, Jason ordered the monument and had it added. He had approved the stone and etching by email. This was his first time seeing it in person.

He reached out and laid a hand on it. Felt the hard, cold marble.

For the better part of forty years, Jason envisioned death as the lurking killer, the monster in the shadows. Now, the mask was off, and underneath was the parent, the brother, the neighbor and friend—all those who have passed before him—the perpetual reminder of inevitability.

He looked more intently upon his own headstone. He thought of Ebenezer Scrooge falling in terror and grief upon the tombstone emblazoned with the old moneylender's name. Jason always understood Scrooge's reaction to be one of abject horror seeing his final resting place and his inability to accept his own mortality. As he looked at his own stone, he realized how foolish he was, how young and naïve his interpretation had been. Scrooge hadn't been terrified of death. He had been overcome with facing his own unresolved regrets and the possibility of an unrepented life.

He headed down the hill and back on the path toward his car, passing tombstones as recent as last year and as ancient as two hundred years ago. Every tombstone represented chapters of a continuing story of humanity carved into granite and marble and spanning centuries.

Yet, whether a hundred years or a day ago, each stone also had its own story, a unique narrative with a beginning and an end. He realized his story had moved far beyond its exposition, expatiated its rising action, and now ruminated on the crest of its climax.

He was ready for his story arc's falling action and resolution, be it for good or ill, while he desperately strove to one day deserve a peaceful denouement upon a bed of forgiveness and atonement.

EPILOGUE
Thursday, October 29, 2020

219,374 dead in the United States and over 1.6 million deaths worldwide from COVID.

The coronavirus continues to rage. A vaccine is still months away. Isolation remains the name of this game. And Jason Lahey is about to turn forty-one years old.

The expanse of the past year has been overwhelming in many respects—death, inner turmoil, personal crisis, family struggles, violent threats, murder, global pandemic, societal and political struggle, and painful loss.

It has been a series of events that insisted upon personal growth. In all honesty, Jason didn't think he could claim that as much as he'd like. Midway through life, he is still stubborn to inevitability and reluctant to face finality. But his eyes are more open and his perspective more nuanced.

Under the smoldering glow of ochre skies, he drives away from their home with Jen and Nicholas. There is a "SOLD" plaque perched atop the realtor's sign in the Polnzy yard. Earlier today, he watched a contractor walk the property, study the siding and climb up to survey the roof. That sad old ranch home would see some significant updates—likely new siding, new roof, updated windows and doors. When it is finally reskinned, will his heart no longer beat faster when passing that place? Will the dreams finally stop?

He is glad nothing more came of Susan Polnzy's trial. In the end, Jason wasn't even subpoenaed. The defense had an entire community—including the judge—on Suzie's side, and the prosecution had no motivation to pursue the case. As morally conflicted as Jason continues to be about the situation, he gladly stepped aside to let the judicious arm of law make the decision for him. He isn't sure he could ever be comfortable around Susan again, yet he is still unable to resent her solution.

A "For Sale" sign stands in Glen's front yard. A memory flashes of Maude in their front yard, picking weeds from the landscaping, wearing her bulky yellow gardening gloves and her flowery shorts while Glen walked a lawn mower back and forth over plush green lawn. Such a contrast of emotion as those two properties face each other, throwing off opposing emanations, of lives and of deaths, buffeting against him like a swirling gale over a bridge.

He drives with his family on a path he drove with Glen almost a year ago. Back then, he had been uncertain how to navigate that trip. He felt lost and confused and hadn't known which way to turn. Now, he drives with certainty and confidence. He knows the way.

He thinks about his mother and his father. His father had known where he was going, but didn't seem to know how to get there. His mother had simply been along for the ride with no interest in a destination. He still wears their emotional distance like a scar on his skin, but maybe he understands them better and can sympathize with them both. He has certainly shared his father's misguided pursuits for happiness and his mother's attraction to the frivolous. As such, though he is unable to forgive himself, he has come to accept his own coldness and detachment toward them and his past. Because of this, he has discovered little moments to cherish.

West now on the darkening Old Mill Road, he has no trouble finding the unmarked stretch of blacktop that heads south on an undulating road through barren fields.

"You need to come with me," Jason had told Jen.

"Where?" she had asked.

"Trust me."

"I do."

Jen is quiet beside him. Nicky sleepy in the back seat. They are together on this journey.

Jason had almost lost his family. He is disgusted by his wintery memories of November and December, but he will not bury them. That part of his past, too, is an ugly scar to remind of both pain and healing.

He pulls the car over on the side of the road and kills the engine. He leaves the vehicle and his family joins him. He leads them across the ravine and through barbed wire.

On this autumnal evening, within an hour of his birth forty-one years ago, he walks with his wife down a barren field as he holds his eight-year-old son tight against his shoulder. They close in on an old, mysterious machine standing like a mystical pylon before them. The sun has almost set in the horizon, the sky blazing orange with wisps of purple clouds.

They step across the dirt field and no one speaks. Nicholas squirms at one point and Jason sets him down on the muddy ground. Nicholas walks the rest of the way with his hand in Jason's.

All of them have their eyes fixed on the archaic slot machine ahead of them. They do not ask questions. They do not comment. They approach with silent reverence.

When they reach it, they stop. They stand and stare. They take in each element of the slot machine. Its cast iron flourish of scrolls accentuating the corners, the bursting colors of wood finish that make up the radiating dial decorating the front panel. It is ageless. It is a horror and an enigma. It terrifies as much as it intrigues. It is a grotesque mystery that looms before them, compelling and repelling them.

It suggests answers, and it confounds with questions.

Jen looks at Jason with hesitant but absolute trust. He looks back with a singular acknowledgement.

Slowly, reverently, he reaches for the crank on the side. As he does, he takes Jen's hand. Jen holds onto Nicky's hand. They stand together—a family, a unit.

Jason looks at his wife, his child. He tries to give a reassuring smile.

He says, "Here we go," and he turns the crank.

it's a bottomless cup
we carry

where even walking alone
is never really alone,
whether walking toward

or away from,
there's still *walking*
for company,

and pity and mind
here in the amiable dark
where we live now

> ~ from "Here in the Amiable Dark"
> by Max Garland

ACKNOWLEDGEMENTS

First and foremost, my best friend, my strongest support, and the love of my life, **Melanie Peters**, who not only endured multiple readings, but my constant ramblings and neurotic outbursts.

Second, **my brother Bob Peters**, who believes in me more than I ever will, and who eagerly dove heavily into discussions of scenes and characters and motivation and provided great ideas.

To **my brother Dan Peters**, who seemed the least likely to be my biggest fan, and of whom that designation means more to me than he will ever know.

To **Ann Noser**, whose literary attention to detail helped me shake out all the passivity of the narrative and helped rid me of some of those pesky gerunds.

And to **my cousin, Mary Sheetz**, whose early enthusiasm for this work kept me going when I had serious doubts about its potential.

I also owe a huge thank you to **Erin Swanson**, who has done more to promote me than anyone I know, and through her book club has provided me with the most rewarding experiences of my life.

Thanks to **my nephew Ryan Peters** for the deep dives you have taken in my past works, for the discussions we've had about them, and for being the kind of reader every writer hopes for.

Thanks to **Cup and Quill Founder and Editor Linda Tucker** for taking genuine interest in Fortune Falls, and to **Dr. Joe Dornich** for the suggestions, analysis and encouragement he provided.

Thanks to **Max Garland** for the allowing me to use excerpts of his wonderful poem.

A long-overdue thank you to several people who had guided me forward on the path of writing. To **my college creative writing professor, Bruce Taylor**, who opened up a new world to me on the power and meaning of the written word, and who got me into an advanced fiction class where I was able to lock on to the kind of writer I wanted to be. And thanks also to **Dean Bakoupolus**, whose help with my previous novel was a stepping stone to completing Fortune Falls.

Special thanks to all my early readers who suffered through early drafts and provided invaluable encouragement and feedback. They include: **Roxanne Aehl, Joe Becker, Bonnie Best, Jan Brenner, Kevin Brylski, Colleen Chmelik, Travis Christopherson, Debra Cook, Jasmine Elizabeth, Maxine Farmer, Kelly Fischer, Kari Fisher, Tim Fulford, Elisia Gonsowski, Deb Hoover, Jennifer Kane, Laura Kaufman, Bill Konkoly, Renee Larson, Frank Lontz, Lisa Lontz, Stephanie Marie, Amber Matson, Jennifer Meese Becker, Teri Melcher, Laurie Mohlman, Abby Nesheim, Ann Noser, Dan Peters, Melanie Peters, Robert Peters, Ryan Peters, Sarah Peters, Carissa Saffert, Carol Schimmel-Strehlow, Mary Sheetz, Abigail Sheetz, George Stone, Erin Swanson, Chris Tabor, Erin Trowbridge, Bonnie Feltz, and Nikki Yankton.**

Thanks to **all family and friends who have shown support** and been an encouragement.

Thanks also to **Amy Glaser** for her proofreading and editing skills which helped to make this a tighter narrative.

Last (but certainly not least), thanks to **you, dear reader**, for bothering to pick up one of my books and give it a chance, and huge thank you to anyone who bothered to share that experience through reviews, or a social media share, or just with me. You are what makes all the endless hours and hard work worthwhile. (It sure ain't for the money!!!)

ABOUT THE AUTHOR

A lifelong Wisconsinite and lover of writing, James began his career in television production and moved on to all forms of marketing and advertising, always with a writing and creative focus. When not writing professionally or creatively, he invested significant time and money along with bandmates pursuing music.

At the end of 2003, he and his wife Melanie left their careers, sold their home, and joined James's best friend and fellow musician on a multi-year musical focus performing live across Wisconsin (for the first time in their lives in their 30s). It was during that time James wrote his first two novels, Shrugging and Turntable (the latter very loosely inspired by their musical adventures).

Having shook the music bug out of their systems, they transitioned back to careers. It wasn't until the pandemic and doing a small run of his first two novels that he discovered people seemed to enjoy his writing, and he dove back into his one true, life-long passion.

He lives with his wife in the beautiful Chippewa Valley of Wisconsin where he writes fiction, designs board games, and also occasionally does things to earn money.